OLYMPUS S

# WRATH OF LOVE

VANESSA STOCK

Copyright © 2024 by Author Vanessa Stock

All rights reserved. No part of this book may be reproduced, distributed, or transmitted in any form or by any means, including photocopying, recording, or other electronic or mechanical methods, without the prior written permission of the publisher, except in the case of brief quotations embodied in critical reviews and certain other noncommercial uses permitted by copyright law.

Development Editor: E & A Editing
Alpha & Line Editor: Michele Potts
Second Editor: "Reacher" a.k.a. Jessica Colafranceschi
Blurb Writing: Memos in the Margins
Cover Designer: Disturbed Valkyrie Design
Formatter: Disturbed Valkyrie Design
Map Designer: Ink & Velvet Designs
Character Art: Bell.Arttt

This is a work of fiction. Names, characters, places, and incidents are either the product of the author's imagination or are used fictitiously. Any resemblance to actual events, locales, or persons, living or dead, is entirely coincidental.

ASIN: B0CW1KVGCL
ISBN: 978-1-9990116-3-5
First Edition, 2024

*To anyone who thought Ares was just a misunderstood bad boy,*
*this is for you.*

# CHARACTER LIST

Aetos Family
1. Aphrodite
2. Gaia
3. Ouranos
4. Titan

Olympus Leaders
1. Hades Olympios
2. Zeus Olympios

Zeus Children
1. Hephaestus
2. Ares
3. Apollo
4. Artemis (Artie)
5. Athena

Secondary Characters
- Hermes – Zeus's secret son
- Atlas – Friend of Ouranos and foe of Zeus
- Eos – Had a fling with Ares
- Poseidon – Zeus & Hades' Brother
- Chaos Olympios – Ares Grandfather
- Hera –Zues's wife

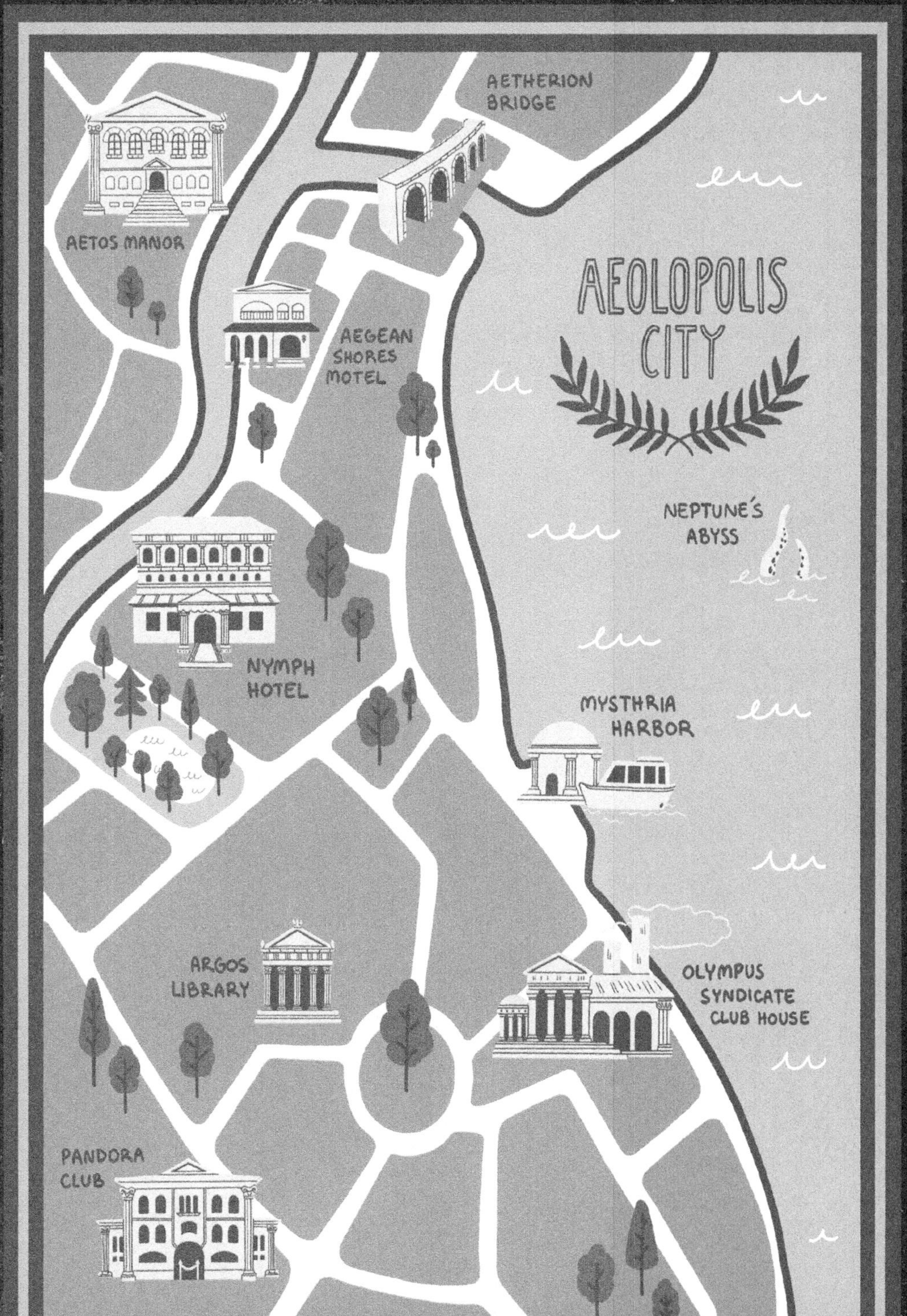

AEOLOPOLIS CITY

AETHERION BRIDGE

AETOS MANOR

AEGEAN SHORES MOTEL

NEPTUNE'S ABYSS

NYMPH HOTEL

MYSTHRIA HARBOR

ARGOS LIBRARY

OLYMPUS SYNDICATE CLUB HOUSE

PANDORA CLUB

# PLAYLIST

Toxic by 2WEI
Survivor by 2WEI
Hit the Road Jack by 2WEI, Bri Bryant
Gangsta Paradise by 2WEI
Faded (Odesza Remix) by ZHU, Odesza
Young and Beautiful by Lana Del Rey
Blue Jeans by Lana Del Rey
White Mustang by Lana Del Rey
Fucked My Way Up To The Top by Lana Del Rey
What Kind of Man by Florence + The Machine
Take What You Want by Post Malone, Ozzy Osborne, Travis Scott
Hey Now (Arty Remix) by London Grammar
Be More by Stephan Sanchez
Into Dust by Mazzy Star
Dead Man by David Kushner
Skin and Bones by David Kushner
Maneater by Nelly Furtado
You Don't Own Me by Lesley Gore
GFY by Dennis Lloyd

# PLAYLIST

Small town Boy by Sanders Bohlke
Work Song by Hozier
Deep In Your Love by Alok, Bebe Rexha
Love and War by Fleurie
Duality by Slipknot
Midnight Ride by Orville Peck, Kylie Minogue, Diplo
Feels like Summer by Sander van Doorm

# A MESSAGE FROM THE AUTHOR

Step into Aeolopolis City, where the echoes of Greek mythology intertwine with the gritty underworld of organized crime. In this city, ancient legends come alive in a modern world where the line between myth and reality is blurred. Here, gods of old walk among mortals, and the thunderous roar of motorcycles reverberates through the streets. It's a place where timeless myths and contemporary crime collide, giving rise to new, powerful narratives.

Through extensive research and creative adaptation, I reshaped these mythical elements to fit the fictional world I envisioned. What began as a mythological love story between Ares and Aphrodite has evolved into a contemporary romance, blending the old with the new.

When I brought these reimagined characters, places, and storylines together, Aeolopolis City came to life before my eyes, breathing life into a realm where the boundaries between myth and reality converge.

**Please note: This story is re-imagined and not a retelling.**

All of this originated from a creative mind. Below are subjects I've discussed that may be sensitive to others.

1. Assault
2. Forced proximity
3. Mention of weapons
4. Execution
5. References drugs and alcohol
6. Gang violence
7. Death

VI
BELL ART
THE LOVERS

# CHAPTER ONE

## APHRODITE

The tempest howled across the sky as it grew enraged. Lightning cracked in the darkness with vengeance as thunder sent a shockwave rumbling through my house. The electricity flickered as I stared at myself in the mirror. Something awakened inside me; its presence became known.

The French doors of my Juliet balcony flung open with a gust of wind, causing the gauzy drapes to dance in the cool night air. The wind had brought with it a touch of dampness and a faint, salty taste reminiscent of the ocean.

My parents were hosting their yearly Halloween gala. My father used this charity event to conceal his list of wrongdoings, specifically his interactions with the Aeolopolis City authorities. It was his way to pay off the government without getting in trouble for his heinous crimes.

Nothing like giving back dirty money.

I applied the final touches of my blood-red lipstick and positioned my delicate gold leaf tiara atop my head. I suppose tonight was a coming out of sorts. My father had deemed it was time for me to find a husband. I was to be presented to eligible suitors at the party this evening. It was a fate my parents insisted upon, one which tore away the last pieces of my freedom.

Rising from my vanity, the maroon fabric of my gown enveloped my silhouette. The plunging neckline cascaded down to my waist, perfectly showcasing my diamond necklace. I peeked out at the October night sky, watching the mesmerizing glow of the lightning while I downed the remainder of the champagne the staff had brought by. The fizzy liquid filled me with delight, temporarily quelling my anxiety.

Watching the dark forest and witnessing the winds dance, I felt a sense of heavy oppression. At twenty-one, my father had declared that I must find a suitor. Tonight, I would be auctioned off to the highest bidder, a decision that shattered me to the core. All my life, my parents had prepared me for this exact moment. Yet, I despised the idea of conforming for their benefit. I had always dreamed of going to school, or traveling abroad, but my family had other plans for me.

I fought the tears as they threatened to consume me.

Deep within, I sensed that something significant would unfold tonight. An unsettling wave coursed through my veins, burdening my soul. I took a deep breath and shut the doors of my balcony.

Standing there, as I gazed out my window, I examined the marble fountain in the courtyard composed of two carved figures. A woman on her knees, pleading to her god, while the other stood as the Almighty, with his hands pointing to the heavens. Our father deliberately selected this display as a reminder of his aspirations. My father, Ouranos, governed the underbelly of Aeolopolis with an iron fist. He mirrored the statue's yearning for eternal life. He believed he was a deity among the less privileged. He was a strict defender of our Aetos Mafia family and swore that nothing would disintegrate the lines that he helped build.

My ruthless father.

*You're a foolish girl, Aphrodite.*

My father often reminded me that I existed as a pawn on his

chessboard, waiting to be exploited for his advantage. That's how it unfolded for my mother. She experienced what it was like to go against Ouranos.

At thirteen, I discovered a photograph of a mysterious woman hidden inside my father's dresser. I bore an uncanny resemblance to the woman in the photo. I had her chestnut curls and her deep red lips. The freckles on her cheeks and her hazel eyes mirrored my own. My father's skin was pale ivory, but her dark olive skin was identical to mine. The only trait I possessed of his was the ability to be ruthless.

Ouranos was the type of man who found satisfaction in being unfaithful in his marriages. Contrary to my stepmother's beliefs, he strayed from his marriages frequently. Gaia, my stepmother, was no exception. Early on in their marriage she discovered that he was disloyal, and he had sworn to her that my mother had seduced him and tricked him into getting her pregnant.

Gaia had always painted a vivid picture of my mother's insatiable desire for my father's wealth and would often tell me that my mother was a nasty, promiscuous, and greedy woman. She claimed my mother only had me to take my father away from her, but when she got pregnant, despite father's instructions to get rid of the baby, she refused. She wanted me.

So, my father separated us. I don't know how, but I knew that one day she vanished without a trace. I was naive not to see the truth, because I knew what my father's specialty was—making people disappear. The memory of my worthlessness continued to haunt me.

The only protector I had throughout my life was my brother.

Titan was the only child of Gaia and Ouranos. Thankfully, he did not inherit a drop of either of their personalities. He was older than me by nine years. He helped raise me along with my nannies, and that made Gaia look down on him. She would try everything to pull him away from me, but Titan always came back running. The nights that I cried, he would sneak into my room and cradle me in his arms until I fell asleep.

Titan tried his best to carry the weight of the Aetos name, wanting to hide me away from the family business, but significant news has its way of getting back to me. Just last week there were whispers of a shooting that occurred at a cafe. The rumors were that it had ties to my father and the mafia.

*There was no proof though.*

*There never is.*

Information was slowly seeping through the cracks of the walls we'd built around me, and I felt the teeth of the transpiring crimes surrounding me sink into my very being.

Titan was no longer able to disguise my reality.

My bedroom door swung open, revealing Gaia in the doorway. She wore a black tulle gown, her blonde hair slicked back in a chic bun. The Botox made her look like she lacked emotion, but father liked them looking young, so she tried to exude a vibrant and youthful appearance.

"Good, you're ready." She inspected me. "You look a little fat—no dinner for you."

She turned and left.

As the daughter of Ouranos, I remained under his control, with no freedom of my own. As his extension, Gaia also took pleasure in exerting control over me. He had granted her the power to dictate every aspect of my life, from what I could eat to what I could wear. Most days, it felt as though I were imprisoned.

I was on a constant diet to try and keep my body approved by her. "*Curvy bodies are not attractive,*" or "*Men do not value when you talk back,*" and "*Men like virgins.*"

*Too bad I lost my virginity at a young age,* I thought.

Gaia's statements were ingrained in my head. I let out a defeated breath as I clutched my necklace, rubbing the diamond as if the stone would give me strength.

*You will never be beautiful. You're just the daughter of a whore.*

The words echoed in my mind as I made my way down the hallway toward the grand staircase. Mahogany walls, adorned with wainscoting, were lined with portraits of family members whose haunting eyes seemed to follow your every move. The curved black steps led down to the checkered floors of our grand foyer.

A conversation echoed from my father's office as I eased toward the doorway to hear more clearly. A fire illuminated the dim chamber through the parted door.

"Why do you always assume I'm incapable of handling it on my own? I want this to happen," Titan thundered. I watched him pace. Across from him, Ouranos cradled a glass of his expensive scotch as his eyes darkened with anger.

Father possessed a warrior's spirit; he was a haunting figure at over six foot tall with dark, menacing eyes. He had a thick, silver beard, and his hair was white as lightning, features he knew women found attractive about him.

He threw the glass into the fire, causing the flames to burst. "That's enough! You're done, do you understand me?" His emotions were explosive. I hastily turned away from the door and continued walking. The last thing I needed was to be caught in the crossfire between them.

A moment later, father's steps echoed through the foyer. He looked at me once before moving toward the front doors. Titan walked out of the room after him, his fingers squeezing the bridge of his nose. His golden waves rested on the shoulders of his all-black suit.

I reached for him and asked, "What was that about?"

My father's blood boiled with anger toward Titan no matter what he did. On Titan's thirtieth birthday, he brought in guests who should never mingle with the likes of our family. The staff claimed he'd invited a gang of bikers, but I didn't think it was true. The day after, he had a busted lip and a black eye from my father. I hadn't been able to bring myself to go to the event, consumed by an overwhelming sense of anxiety about father's reaction.

"It's fine, Aphrodite." He pushed my arm away. "Just stop." Father had hammered into Titan the belief that to survive in the Aetos Mafia, he had to be an alpha—a relentless force commanding respect through fear. But Titan wanted no part of this legacy. The more his father pushed, the more he longed to break free, to carve out a life where he wasn't just another extension of his father's brutal influence.

"I'm sorry." I said apologetically.

He nodded, his eyes brightening as they caught mine.

"Let's go to this party."

The Argos library was renowned for its opulence. It held the most expensive and exclusive first editions from a variety of authors, which were inaccessible to the average person. It was part of the city's university, a place that only caters to the invited. Like most parts of this city, if you had money and power, you could control everything.

Photographers cascaded down the steps with flashing cameras as our limousine pulled up. My parents walked out first, father waving like he was some god being inducted into the heavens by his followers. He absorbed their energy and channeled it through his monstrous ego. He never cared for anyone but himself.

As for me, I've spent my life doing everything I could to remain in the shadows, trying my best to stay hidden and unnoticed. I knew that when I was brought out into society, I would only be seen as Ouranos's pawn in a twisted game of power and control. I was nothing but a bargaining chip, a mere object to be traded with and manipulated at will by those around me.

The buzzing sounds of security surrounded us as we passed under the marble arch that led into the library's grand entrance. The curves on the beams above us reminded me of gothic tales from my childhood. I stared at the ceiling in awe.

"You're doing it again," Titan whispered as he waved at guests.

"This is one of my favorite places." I broke my gaze, and he flashed me a smile.

Growing up, Sundays always meant our nanny would bring us here for reading studies. As we grew older, Titan would venture off on mysterious escapades, while I found comfort in the cozy nook by the expansive windows, losing myself in the pages of a book. During those moments, I could escape from my identity and imagine a different version of myself. I craved the adventures I read about—sailing the seas or discovering lost treasures. It was a time when I allowed myself to forget what I faced at home.

"Are you prepared to be bombarded by beautiful ladies all wanting your attention?" I teased, leaning my head on his shoulder. Even in heels, my brother towered over me.

"I don't want any of them," Titan whispered, flashing a fake smile to onlookers as we walked toward the grand staircase. Above us, a domed glass ceiling framed a glittering crystal chandelier. Titan held my hand as we descended the steps, our parents in front of us, greeting the guests below. The crowd erupted in cheers and waves, but I couldn't shake the feeling that I was entering a realm of nightmares.

I braced myself for the impending torment.

We made our way toward my stepmother and her circle of friends, offering the obligatory polite greetings.

"Gaia, darling, you look absolutely radiant," they cooed, their voices dripping with insincerity.

I leaned in close to Titan, whispering, "I'll be back in a bit," hoping to slip away unnoticed. Just as I turned to leave, Titan's hand lightly brushed my forearm, halting me in my tracks.

"Don't go too far," Titan said, giving me a stern glare.

"Really? With the amount of father's henchmen here, I'm not going anywhere."

The grandeur of the great hall was imposing, with decor that was dark and rich. The walls were adorned with tapestries in deep shades of burgundy and forest green, their intricate designs illuminated by candlelight. The tables were draped with luxurious velvet cloths of gold and copper, while centerpieces of crimson roses added a vibrant touch to the opulent setting. As I walked through the crowd, I could feel eyes locked onto my every move. I tried my best not to falter under their gazes.

A voice called out from behind me. "Well, well, did mommy dearest play dress-up with you tonight?" I turned to find Paris, her slender fingers elegantly wrapped around a champagne flute as she took a sip, a sly smile playing on her lips.

I couldn't help but think that Gaia had chosen my outfit to make me look like a dessert in the eyes of these men. "My future husband must think I look like a real treat."

Paris swayed with the music, her crimson gown clinging to her body. A gold crystal mask covered half of her face, and she wore enough diamond jewelry to buy a yacht.

Paris and I had first connected in the cold isolation of boarding school, where I had been little more than a ghost—until she noticed me. She reached out with a warmth that pulled me from my solitude, becoming my sole refuge from my father's suffocating control.

Outside those walls, Paris was the only light in my darkness, offering solace when the weight of his dominance became unbearable. Besides my brother, she was the only one I truly trusted with my deepest fears.

"You can say that again," Paris shot back her champagne. "How old are you going for? Eighty plus? At least he'll be dead in a few years, and you'll get an inheritance," she teased, as macabre as ever.

"I don't want any of them," I whispered.

"Let's walk." She linked her arm with mine, and we walked along the edge of the dance floor. I saw Titan chatting with a group of ladies. Something felt off about him.

"Why doesn't my brother need to find a wife?" I groaned.

"Because your father gains more to sell you to the highest bidder than your brother. We are women, and in their eyes, we are a resource to gain power," Paris said.

"I have a plan," I replied.

I confided in Paris about my decision to leave this life behind for good and that I had turned to Titan for help. As my brother, Titan had always been there for me, deeply understanding the burden I carried. But when I asked him to assist me in finding a way out, I saw the worry etched in his eyes. He knew the danger involved and was torn between his instinct to protect me and his fear that this plan might not work.

Titan's hesitation spoke volumes, but I knew he would do everything in his power to help me escape, even if the path forward was uncertain.

"I pray you can break free from your father's grip, though I fear he's already taken hold of your entire life." Paris said, her voice tinged with desperation. Before other guests could interrupt us, we ended our conversation. Paris understood me in ways no one else did, offering acceptance and support when I needed it most. She wasn't just a friend; she was my anchor, helping me find strength during some of the darkest times in my life.

Her words pierced my heart, a harsh reminder that every choice I'd made was never truly mine. It was as if I was perpetually teetering on a tightrope stretched over a pit of fire, with every misstep threatening to send me plummeting into the abyss.

As I stood amidst the crowd, my anxiety surged, amplified by the sinister whispers about my father, the embodiment of malevolence. The weight of their words pressed upon me like a suffocating blanket. I felt overwhelmed, a sense of urgency arising within me as I looked around for a way to escape.

Sensing my distress, Paris flashed me a look of worry. I squeezed her hand tightly, a silent plea for understanding and support in my desperate need to get away. All I wanted at that moment was solace.

I mouthed an excuse from the group as Paris nodded her approval in my direction.

I navigated my way back through the crowd. The men all seemed like monsters lurking in the shadows, trying to lure me into a world that was of no value to me. Finally, I reached the library terrace and opened the door, feeling a wave of freedom wash over me. No one else was present, and I experienced liberation under the radiant full moon. The rain had stopped, but the humidity clung to my skin.

My ears perked up as I heard a stir of activity coming from the gardens. Adrenaline surged through my veins. The moonlight pierced through the branches, casting an eerie glow on their mysterious faces. Shadows danced ominously around the figures, concealing their identities.

I inched closer, my breath held captive in my lungs. The scent of damp earth mingled with the scent of danger, filling the air with a palpable tension. Every rustle of leaves sent shivers down my spine, as if the forest itself was warning me of impending doom. I caught sight of my brother. He was barely visible, as if the darkness attempted to hide him.

"You can't be serious?" an anger-filled voice said, its face concealed by a hoodie. "You were supposed to do what I asked." I could only get a glimpse of the man's back, yet his voice flowed through me like molten lava, leaving behind a trail of warmth in my body.

"He will listen. Don't worry. I have it under control." My brother's response was straightforward as he pressed his hands against his waist.

Suddenly, a wave of urgency washed over me, and I felt an overwhelming need to protect my brother. Before they could speak, I walked out from the bushes. Titan's gaze widened, "Aphrodite, go back to the party!"

I had never seen my brother so angry.

"What is going on?" My dress dragged behind me through the wet grass. The moonlight illuminated the area, and I saw the face of the man standing in front of him. We caught each other's eye, and it felt as though he was investigating the depths of my soul with his intense stare. His jawline was dusted with facial hair, and he was taller than my brother. His jacket hugged his physique which accentuated the muscle underneath. It seemed contrite to say, but I was intrigued by his presence.

"Aphrodite! Go now!" Titan hissed, pointing to the stairs. I blinked twice before nodding to acknowledge what he demanded of me. I looked at the strange man one last time before he turned away to face my brother.

A WHILE LATER, I WAS LEANING OVER THE RAILING OF THE TERRACE TO TRY and see where Titan went when I felt a hand touch my upper arm. "There you are!" Paris rolled her eyes and crossed her arms. "I had to listen to some old man talk about utter nonsense for like, the past hour."

I couldn't help but snicker. "I'm sorry I left you. I couldn't stand listening to people giving praise to my father." My gaze weakened as I felt the walls closing in on me again. Everyone around us lurked like ghouls, waiting to get a moment alone with me.

"Okay, well, you got your fresh air—now let's go inside! They are starting the music." She shimmied her shoulders, then pulled my hand. I faked a smile and followed her lead.

As we danced, I monitored the doorway to the terrace from the corner of my eye. Despite Paris's attempt to keep me swaying and moving to the sound of the music, I remained focused on the return of my brother. More than an hour passed, and something felt wrong. He was missing the entire party.

Worry and panic surged through me as I thought about what to do. Finally, I approached my father. His eyebrows pulled together as his lips tightened from my appearance. I saw his jaw twitch with annoyance at my intrusion.

"What is it, Aphrodite?" he whispered, his voice brimming with barely repressed anger.

"I apologize for interrupting, but do you know where Titan is? He's missing the entire party." A wave of doubt crashed over me, and my gaze fixed on his expression, searching for any signs of danger.

Father adjusted his posture and let out a deep breath, his nostrils flaring. He scanned the room. "I will deal with it," he affirmed, making a quick beeline. I walked away from the guests he had been speaking to with a polite smile as I quickly followed my father.

His eyes widened in sheer terror just before a deafening explosion ripped through the library, the force of it so violent that the windows shattered in an instant, sending shards of glass slicing through the air.

The roar of the blast consumed everything, drowning out all other sound. The ground shook beneath me, and in the next heartbeat, darkness swallowed the world whole.

# CHAPTER TWO
## APHRODITE

Blinking my eyes open, the sound of an ear-splitting screech drowned out all other noise. Acidic smoke permeated the room. The impact of the explosion had forced me to the ground. I coughed as the odor heightened my anxiety and cost me my breath.

For a moment, I lay there, utterly paralyzed, stunned beyond comprehension. Blood trickled down my face from shards of broken glass that had cut my forehead. I lifted myself using my upper body and a dull ache spread down to my legs.

Rolling onto my side, I pressed my hands against the cool porcelain tiles, slowly pushing myself up, my body aching with every movement. My shoes had flown off during the explosion, and I struggled to steady myself on the debris-strewn floor. I scanned the room, desperately searching for familiar faces amidst the chaos. Everyone was rushing to escape, and the library was filled with the sounds of panicked footsteps and screams.

I located Titan immediately. My head throbbed, and I couldn't hear what he was saying as he hurried over to me.

"Oh my God!" Titan pressed his hands to my face. "Aphrodite, are you okay?" He pushed my curls aside.

"I'll be fine." I breathed. "What happened?" I whimpered, feeling hot tears suddenly begin streaming down my cheeks. "What is going on?" I asked.

"You need to get out of here! Look, if something happens to me, look under the floorboard in my room." Titan said, his voice frantic and laced with an undeniable urgency.

Despite the disarray caused by the explosion, I still nodded. "Are you in danger?" My tears clouded my vision as I trembled from shock.

"I love you, sister, always will. Run before they capture you!" His strong arms pulled me up and he pushed me away from him.

"Wait, no—what are you talking about? Who is coming? I'm not leaving you!" I reached for him, but he pulled away.

"Go!" he screamed. The library echoed with the sound of bullets. Masked men rushed through the terrace. Chaos erupted in the grand hall.

My heart pounded as I sprinted up the grand staircase, the guests' panicked cries ringing throughout the library. I stopped on the landing when I caught a glimpse of Paris stuck underneath a fallen bookcase. While people rushed and jostled around me, I stood frozen in place. I couldn't desert her. I descended the stairs against the crowd and rushed to her side. She was unmoving.

I shook her with all my might, my voice breaking into a mournful cry. "Paris!" I stared in horror at the lifeless body of the only friend I had in this world, helpless to do anything. My heart clenched with desperation—I had to save her. She was all I had, the one person who truly understood me, who stood by me through everything. I couldn't lose her, not now, not ever.

Tears streamed down my face. "Paris!" I tried pushing the book-case off her. Bullets started flying everywhere as I ducked beneath the object that lay on top of my friend. I pushed as hard as I could to move the heavy furniture.

"AH!" I screamed at the top of my lungs as my feet slid along the cool porcelain floors. With another push, the heavy piece moved from Paris's legs. The slight movement was enough for me to pull her out from under it.

A glass shard jutted from her hip. I would have to carry her out, even if it meant I had to drag her. Only armed men remained in the empty room, and they were picking off father's henchman one by one, like flies being swatted down. I struggled to contain my fears. It was clear that if I didn't rescue Paris and manage to escape, we would both fall into the hands of these killers.

Lying next to her, I whispered, "We are getting out of here." My adrenaline surged as I glanced over the bookcase, trying to stay concealed from the view of the men. I didn't know what they wanted, and I wasn't going to find out. I had nothing to protect us with, but I noticed a small opening through the shattered window that led onto the terrace. Closing my eyes tight, I tried to take a deep breath to calm my nerves.

I had started to drag Paris toward the window when a commotion caught my attention.

"What do you want? Who sent this hit?" Titan's voice resonated throughout the hall. I hid behind the scattered furniture; Paris lay in my arms as I tried to shake her to wake up. Her breathing was slow, almost like her life was slipping through my hands.

Turning my head to peek over the fallen bookshelf, I watched as my brother was being held upright by two men. He must have suffered a severe beating based on the blood dripping from his head.

"Listen, Titan." The man in front had a skull mask covering his face and he wore all black. "This isn't personal." He pointed a gun at Titan's temple.

He pulled the trigger.

I covered my mouth, stifling the scream that threatened to escape. My teeth clenched so tightly it hurt, but it was nothing compared to the agony tearing through my chest. The fear of them finding us was suffocating, choking me from the inside out. Desperately, I clung to Paris, praying with every fiber of my being that they wouldn't discover us. All I could do was hold on and hope the darkness wouldn't swallow us whole.

"Police! Drop your weapons!"

The SWAT team descended the grand staircase, ready to take down the perpetrators, but the men who had done this had already fled.

I raised my hands to the sky and shouted, "Please help me!" I felt like I had barely escaped from the depths of hell. My hands trembled, and my body grew feeble, tears eroding my strength, while I stood before the men. One officer pointed his gun at me, then lowered it.

"Please! My friend! My friend got injured! Please!" I begged.

The officer rushed towards us with urgency as he kneeled in front of me. "Are you hurt?" he asked, grounding me for a moment.

I blinked, my heart was racing, unable to focus, "I—I don't know," I looked down at Paris, "I can't—everything happened so fast! My friend needs help! Please!" I managed to stammer out, my voice trembling.

"I will take care of her," He mouthed as he reached for his walkie-talkie, "We need a medic, we have one female with a low pulse." I listened to him for a couple more seconds before reality set in. I couldn't stay here any longer. I needed to see my brother.

I mustered every ounce of strength left within me and rushed toward my brother's lifeless body with desperate immediacy. Titan's soul had vanished. I dropped to my knees and cradled his head in my lap. His blood soaked my dress. I shook from adrenaline, and I couldn't control myself as my body was wracked with sobs.

I locked eyes with his ghostly gaze, my fingers trembling as I closed his eyelids. My heart hammered against my ribs, pounding with terror. Screams clawed their way from the depth of my soul, draining all my strength. The blood-curdling cries that tore from me couldn't match the excruciating pain squeezing the life out of my heart.

As I walked out of the library, my heart pounded, and a cold sweat trickled down my back. I was conscious of the watchful eyes of the crowd as my bare feet touched the unforgiving concrete. Covered in my brother's blood, I walked away from the scene, leaving the onlookers in stunned disbelief. Some people were crying, unsure of what had happened. Hell had descended upon what was once a beautiful and vibrant library, a sanctuary of wonders was now marred by an execution that stained its hallowed halls.

Women clutched their chests, their mouths agape from my appearance while men screamed at the police over what had taken place. The explosion had been a clear indicator that it was meant for my family. The guests became unwitting casualties of a ruthless attack of violence.

My father, consumed by an overwhelming sense of anger, paced alongside the police chief. Gaia emitted a deep, animalistic howl upon hearing the news of Titan from the detective. A raindrop landed on my hand, as though even the gods were weeping.

A middle-aged paramedic with piercing blue eyes approached me.

"Where are you hurt?" His gaze seemed detached from the chaos that surrounded the building. With lights blaring and police roping off the entrance, I felt utterly closed in by the chaos around me.

Locking eyes with him, I reached up instinctively to brush my hair from my face. My fingers were wet, slickness coated my skin. I pulled my hand back in front of my face to see blood dripping down my fingers. Reality crashed into me; my head must have been cut open in the explosion.

"Come with me. Let me fix the cut on your face." He reached for my hand, and I couldn't stop shaking. As he guided me toward the ambulance, I looked over and saw Gaia whip her head toward me.

She was enraged, and her nostrils flared outward. She looked as if she was ready to kill, and I felt like I was the target.

As we kept walking, I spotted my father talking to some detectives huddled near the ambulance. My father had no business with the police, but somehow, he embedded himself in the situation like he was in command. The paramedic cleaned my wounds, and I observed my father conversing with a man on the steps. Ouranos sought blood.

One of my father's goliath-sized bodyguards showed up at the ambulance. "Ms. Aetos, it's time to leave. We have word that your father wants you at the manor for protection."

I thought about Paris, and I pleaded with the paramedic, "Please, update me on my friend's condition." Fear took over as I said, "I can't lose another person." When I rushed to my brother's side, I had momentarily forgotten my best friend. I knew that it was terrible of me to leave her behind, but I was consumed by the fact that my brother was dead. I felt like I was being pulled in every direction.

"Listen to me, Aphrodite. Ouranos wants me to return you to the manor. He was very clear that you must leave here for your safety." The bodyguard gripped my arm tightly, and I pulled as hard as I could, attempting to break his hold. I battled with all my might, but my lack of strength hindered me.

"Please!" His hand felt like shackles. I screamed out, and that was when I sensed my father's presence.

"Stop making a mockery of this family," he took hold of my chin as he spat the words. "Your brother's dead. I don't need any more bodies to handle. Do as you are told!" Anger filled his eyes, and I saw him as the devil himself, inches from my face. His fingernails dug into my jawline as I swallowed with fear. I nodded once before he ripped his grip off me.

I exhaled as I followed the bodyguard to the SUV nearby. I stood there, paralyzed with shock, unable to comprehend what I had just witnessed. It made little sense. Why had there been a hit on Titan?

My lips trembled as I watched them carry him down the library steps in a body bag. I wiped the tears away that blinded my vision. This was all my father. His underworld had finally slipped to the surface. Ouranos' empire teetered on the brink of collapse, and we were all collateral.

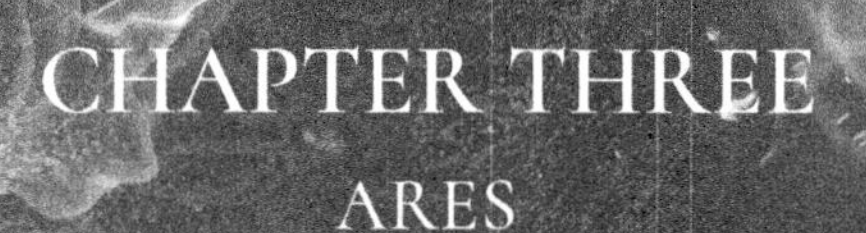

# CHAPTER THREE
## ARES

*THE SAME NIGHT.*

As I waited on my motorcycle across the street from the Argos library, the cacophony of traffic faded, granting me a moment of solitude with my thoughts. It had been a foolish assumption, on my part, to think that meeting with Titan would be a good idea. Yet, I couldn't escape the realization that my presence had exposed my betrayal of the club.

I turned off my engine and observed the vehicles approaching the library. Onlookers crowded along the edges despite the barricades blocking them, as esteemed guests exited their vehicles. The elite embraced this as the biggest night of the year.

They masqueraded as compassionate philanthropists, loudly proclaiming their dedication to give back to the city of Aeolopolis; however, only the naive would believe their generosity. It was merely a facade, a strategic move to garner favor and mask their true motives.

The Aetos family had an insatiable thirst for dominance with their ruthless tactics and mafia dealings. Everything in this part of the city embodied the Aetos family, marked by their tainted money and powerful influence over people.

Aeolopolis City once had pristine parks and gardens, where citizens sought solace and found respite. Now, the city has been transformed into a barren wasteland that killers and drug lords use as their battlefield.

In certain parts of the city, walking without protection is a death sentence. People disappear without a trace, their faces eventually plastered on missing persons posters or flashed across the news. But everyone knows the truth—once you're gone, you're not coming back.

The once lush and vibrant landscape was replaced with desolation, scarred by the Aetos family's destructive path. Ouranos, the city's untouchable crime lord, reigned supreme while the citizens suffered in his wake. People paid for Ouranos' protection, but those who didn't, paid a much steeper price. These conditions only emphasized the stark division among the people: those in power and those barely surviving.

The Olympus Syndicate ruled these streets, ready to exact revenge on anyone who dared challenge them outside the elite's protection. The people of Aeolopolis were known for their influence and affluence, often with deep ties to the Aetos family, but they would never set foot near the squalid, crime-ridden area of Mythsia. That part of the city was a world away, avoided by the elite who preferred to keep their distance from its harsh realities.

The anger and thirst for vengeance that my father, Zeus, had harbored toward Ouranos was unparalleled. Ouranos held power over most of Aeolopolis, except for Mysthria, where our club held dominion.

We had always known he would leverage his power to try and gain control over our turf and displace us, but he underestimated the resilience and solidarity among us. The people of our part of the city would never submit to the Aetos family, not if they stood with us.

My grandfather, Chaos, was tortured and forced to cede control when Ouranos's father was running the show. Amid the mafia's torment, Chaos struggled to survive. Yet he didn't run away. No—he fought back. He created the Olympus Syndicate to lead and fight for innocent men overtaken by the elite.

After Chaos died, my father, Zeus, assumed control of the gang, but following my mother's death, an all-consuming darkness began to seep into the very core of his being. He was gradually eroded by a chilling, relentless void, which devoured every remnant of goodness within his heart.

Zeus was not just the man with dark tendencies, but a true monster. His eyes, that once were filled with warmth, now mirrored ruthlessness. Every word he spoke carried a threat, and his actions left a trail of despair. The fear he instilled wasn't just in his enemies; it seeped through the clubhouse. He became a monster, and under his guidance, my brothers and I were transformed into the very demons that haunted the nightmares of others.

As much as I fought it, I embodied my father's brutal nature to create wars. I was molded to be his punisher. I found a thrill when I became the villain that everyone was terrified of; the last person people saw before their souls left their bodies.

When someone crossed the Olympus Syndicate, I became blinded by rage. I had blood on my hands, and the screams of my victims still paid me a visit when I slept. So, I tried not to sleep.

Leaning on the handlebars of my bike, I watched as Ouranos's limo pulled up. The crowd cheered. How unaware could you be to idolize someone who found pleasure in killing his own kind?

The burner phone in my pocket vibrated. I slipped it out and looked at the screen.

TITAN

Meet me in the back in twenty.

My jaw twitched as I stared at the message. Titan was walking a tightrope. He came to me about a year ago with the idea of opening a bar near our clubhouse. The clubhouse compound was around

Mysthria Harbor, which was near the shipping yards, and it was a haven for pleasure. Strip joints and casinos, infused with the latest designer drugs. It was a place you didn't go unless you had a reason to do so.

When Titan said, "I wanna set up a business on your side of the city. It's going to be called, *Pandora*." I had to admit I was surprised. He explained that to make this work, he needed to ensure he wouldn't gain a reputation as the owner. Titan and I were determined to break away from our families and build a better future for this city. We didn't want to keep repeating the same old cycle of generational trauma that had already done so much damage. We saw what could be, and we weren't about to let the past destroy what we could create together.

As the frontman of the business, my reputation as a ruthless killer and formidable warrior preceded me. This notoriety ensured that no one dared to ask questions, as everyone was aware that crossing paths with me could be lethal.

I wasn't sure what to think at first, but it was clear that Titan was desperate to break free from his father's control. Pandora offered him a way out, a place where he could carve his own path, away from his family's notorious reputation. I never fully understood his need to escape. We had countless talks about his reasons for opening the bar, but he always sidestepped my questions with vague answers. Still, despite the risks, I decided to take him up on his offer. Deep down, I realized we shared the same desire—we both wanted freedom from the grip our fathers had on us.

My father depended on me for everything, and I did my best to conceal the pain it caused. As Zeus's chosen weapon, he thrust me into the heart of every perilous situation, wielding me as his warrior. He commanded me to eliminate rival gangs with ruthless fury.

I was engulfed in the darkness of my actions, my hands stained with the blood of countless victims, each one dragging my soul deeper into the abyss. Every inch of my body was covered in tattoos that marked the wars I had faced. The bullets, stabbings, and attacks on the Olympus Syndicate were etched into my skin, a permanent reminder of the hell I could never escape.

My other phone rang in the inner pocket of my jacket. I pulled it out seeing my brother's name, Apollo, on the screen. My family could wait, whatever my brother had to say was certainly less important than the situation at hand.

Ignoring the call, I threw the phone back into my pocket. I needed to meet Titan.

Apollo was the youngest of the boys and a twin to my sister, Artemis. Hephaestus was the eldest, and I held the position of being the second youngest. Our sister, Athena, was two years younger than Hephaestus; yet she always appeared to have control over everything. It was clear that she constantly tried to stay in our father's good graces, and as a result, she received special treatment.

STANDING IN THE GARDENS OF THE LIBRARY, I FELT VULNERABLE—THIS wasn't my territory. As I stood beneath the tree, I watched Titan rushing down the steps of the terrace. I had suggested meeting at our usual spot on a dead-end street, but for some reason, he needed to talk to me sooner.

"What am I doing here, Titan?" I asked, annoyance creeping into my voice as I crossed my arms over my chest.

"Ares, I'm working on getting the cash, but I've hit some obstacles," Titan pleaded. "We need to talk about the future of Pandora."

Despite my efforts to maintain a calm and collected demeanor, frustration bubbled within me. Titan's pacing and agitation only added fuel to the fire. It had been months since he had contributed to our shared financial responsibilities for Pandora. I found myself shouldering the burden of forking over the money to keep the club afloat. It was heavy, and I couldn't help but feel the resentment build within me toward Titan. I promised him a grace period to gather the funds, but now it was time to settle the payment.

"Titan, I can't keep this up for you." I stood there with my hands in my pockets, keeping my demeanor cool while watching him have a meltdown. He was a grown man who had never experienced the real world. At thirty years old, Titan still depended on his daddy for support.

"I know," he hissed as he looked back at the terrace of the library, then back to me as he continued, "I know you wanted me to ask Hermes, but I had a better idea. I asked my father." The mention of Hermes's name caused my fingernails to dig into my palm. He was my half-brother. My father had slept with Hermes' mom when he and my mother were fighting, and he wound up getting her pregnant. That had not been a fun conversation. Zeus never claimed or acknowledged Hermes as his own, or so he told us.

The main reason I wanted to reach out to Hermes in the first place was because he had control of some high-end hotels nearby that were doing well. An investment from him would give us the opportunity to keep up with our club. I acknowledged the risk of aligning with him, but his support would prove beneficial. The last thing I thought Titan would do was ask his father to invest instead.

"You can't be serious." I felt my blood boil as the rage surfaced. I flared my nostrils, inhaling as fire clutched my throat. "You were supposed to do what I asked."

"Father wants to help. He insists on being part of this. Don't worry, I've got it under control." He pressed his hands together like a prayer, his eyes wide with fear. Titan must be in deeper trouble than I thought—he'd never ask his father for help unless he was desperate. Getting in bed with Ouranos would be the final nail in my coffin. If the Olympus Syndicate caught even a whiff of that, I'd be excommunicated, no questions asked.

Suddenly, a woman appeared to step out from the bushes. We froze.

The moonlight shone on her porcelain skin and gave her an ethereal glow. My lips parted, enamored at her grace as she walked toward us. Cascading curls framed her radiant face, and her plump lips were an irresistible temptation. The fabric of her dress clung to her body, hinting at the softness beneath. With each step, her hips swayed, accentuating her curves. She was a celestial vision with a goddess's likeness.

As she approached us, I could almost feel the warmth of her energy encompass me, as if electricity surged between us. The scent of her perfume wafted toward me, a heady mix of floral notes and something elemental; it ignited a fire within me. My fingers itched with the desire to trace every inch of her delicate silhouette, to feel the softness of her brown curls as they slipped through my fingers. The thought of grasping her neck, my hands exerting a gentle pressure, sent shivers down my spine. I wanted to soak up all her alluring beauty as my primal soul devoured hers.

"Aphrodite, go back to the party," Titan snapped as he pointed toward the building. I wanted to break his hand for yelling at her, but I kept my cool. My eyes drifted towards a diamond necklace that dipped between the curve of her breasts, and I pictured her naked, wearing only that. A growl left my lips.

"What is going on?" Aphrodite demanded, dragging her dress through the wet grass. Something inside my soul was pulling me toward her. I have never felt such a burning passion to be near someone. I clenched my fists, forcing myself to stay grounded as the fire within me surged, threatening to consume every shred of control I had left. The moonlight glinted off the diamonds nestled against her skin, and I wanted nothing more than to tear away the distance between us.

"Go, Aphrodite. Now!" Titan blocked her view. She gave a dainty nod before turning to head back inside.

I had to break these feelings because I knew it would drive me to do something reckless. But even as I turned away, the image of her, draped in diamonds and moonlight, was burned into my mind.

Aphrodite managed to enrapture me within minutes. I felt screwed. There was no chance of escaping her.

I shook my head, attempting to get back to the focus of this visit.

"Titan, figure your shit out. We have until Friday before we get some heat about this." My eyes narrowed in his direction. We needed the money to keep the business afloat. Pandora has been killing it this past year, but in the last couple of months, money has been draining faster than we can make a profit.

I wouldn't ask my family for help; my goal was to avoid being associated with dirty money. It would attract unwanted attention from the police, and I didn't need that heat on me as well. I wanted Pandora to remain separate from OS.

"Fine." Titan ran his hands down his face as he released a deep breath.

I had to leave before someone caught sight of me.

# CHAPTER FOUR
## ARES

Pandora was the hottest spot in Aeolopolis City, and I took pride in that. Zeus had already started talking about using it to launder money for the gang, but I had to remind him—Pandora and OS business don't mix. This was my nightclub, and I'd sworn that no gang dealings would ever happen under my roof.

Earlier this year, we pulled off a job smuggling a truckload of guns and drugs. It ended in a crossfire with another gang, and that was my breaking point. I knew I couldn't keep risking my life like that. So, I took my cut from the job and poured it into Pandora. In hindsight, it felt like the dumbest thing I could have done—because now Zeus wants to sink his claws into it.

Zeus has a way of wanting a piece of anything that promises even a flicker of revenue. I remember talking to some of the other club members about it, and they gave me hell for even thinking about a side project. Everyone except my uncle Hades. He's always been good at reminding me that death is part and parcel of our world. He was the first to support me in opening the nightclub, but he also recognized how Zeus took advantage of me. He knew I wanted out, to break free from the family's grip, and he understood that I needed to make decisions that would give me that chance.

I shook hands with the guards as I walked into the club. Music blasted through the speakers as strobe lights scattered through the dark space like lightning. My mind kept drifting back to Aphrodite, the woman who stood beneath the moonlight, her beautiful body stirring a deep longing within me. No one had ever made me feel this way—I desired her so intensely that I could hardly control myself.

*I didn't even know her, yet I craved her.*

I nodded to a group of ladies and saw Eos standing by the bar in a fitted black dress, but all I could think about was the woman who interrupted my conversation with Titan. She was the girl I'd been seeing, no big deal. She was an attractive woman who had the power to weaken men with just her words, but I knew her desires. She wanted me. I didn't feel the same way. She was a siren, and I knew how it would end—she'd either break me or leave me. I wasn't going to let her sink her claws into my heart.

I'd seen enough to know where this was heading. Girls like her always leave a trail of wreckage, and I wasn't about to be the next victim. I couldn't shake the feeling that sooner or later, she'd either tear me apart or disappear, leaving nothing but chaos in her wake.

"Well, if it isn't Ares Olympios." Eos pouted as she leaned against the bar, baring her cleavage at me as she flashed me with a seductive glance.

Her strawberry-blonde hair fell in loose waves, contrasting with her fair, almost ethereal skin. She was a siren; her gaze held a magnetic pull, silently promising secrets and desires.

"Not right now, Eos." I rubbed my chin, then waved at the bartender for a drink.

"Why so uptight? How about I help you relax?" Eos wrapped her fingers around my shoulders and placed her lips on my neck. I grabbed her wrist and pushed her away.

"Don't," I snapped.

Eos brought her lips closer to mine. "You know you want this."

She pressed her body against my chest. She caressed my neck, and I felt her lips glide down my jugular. I licked my bottom lip, I couldn't fight the urge for long. "Come on, Ares. Don't you want to have fun in the office again?"

"Stop." I fought back, but I recognized the familiar urge I was craving. "This needs to stop." Releasing her hands was the biggest mistake I could have made, because she reached down and grabbed my shaft. Before she could attempt to make something of it, I pushed her hand away. "That's enough!"

"What the fuck, Ares? You weren't like this last night," She narrowed her glance. "Stop messing with me. What are we doing?"

"You are just a chick that I fuck. Nothing more. Get that into your pretty head." I lashed out at her, knowing she wouldn't like it. "Go fuck Hephaestus instead."

Eos would do anything to join this family, including fucking my brother. I grabbed my drink and headed toward where I could see my uncle sitting. He was in the spot that was designated to Olympus Syndicate members. Eos was bitching to her friends as I walked away, but I couldn't hear her over the sounds of music and people.

At the table sat Hades, Apollo, and our prospect, Prometheus. He seemed to get along with everyone except Athena.

Hades smirked, his voice teasing as he asked, "How's the siren?" He had that same presence that always drew attention, with thick blond hair that fell in easy waves and a matching beard that made him look rugged yet confident. His deep blue eyes, sharp and intense, were a total contrast to my dark brown eyes and hair, standing out against his tanned skin. He was built like someone who'd seen his share of fights—broad shoulders, solid muscles, and a face that looked like it was carved from stone. He had that undeniable air about him, probably because he was Zeus's brother and my uncle, carrying that family charisma effortlessly. Standing next to him, I couldn't help but notice how different we were—my dark features and olive skin clearly showed I took after my mom, while Hades looked every bit the part of his side of the family.

"Don't fucking start." I shook my head. "Happy Halloween," I teased as I slipped into my seat. Apollo couldn't take his eyes off his phone. "What's wrong?" I asked, curious about his expression.

"Fuck." Apollo mouthed before widening his gaze at me.

"Speak." Hades rested his arms on the table, cradling his drink as he turned to face Apollo.

"Zeus messaged me. Someone attacked the Aetos Family."

"What do you mean 'attacked'?" Hades furrowed his brow.

My mind raced back to the library. Had there been something I was missing? Apollo lifted his eyes to us, with a stern glance, "They were attacked at the Argos library. He wants us to get to the compound now." Apollo looked up from his phone as his eyes scanned all of us.

"Let's leave," Hades barked, slamming his hands on the table. We dove out of the booth and ran outside.

As we started our engines, Apollo received one last message. "Titan is dead."

Rushing through the streets, sirens were all around us, and I knew something was not right. I couldn't believe it. I needed proof. If Titan was dead, it would change everything for us.

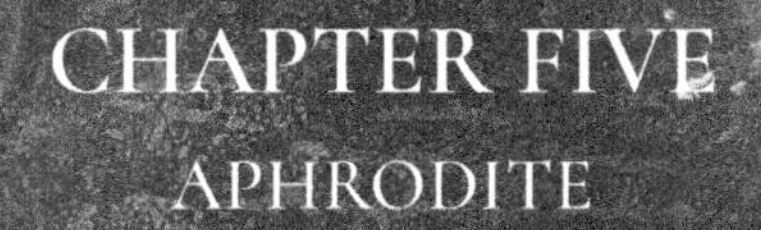

# CHAPTER FIVE
## APHRODITE

*ONE WEEK LATER...*

I woke up in a cold sweat, my heart pounding, realizing today was the day I would bury my brother. I had tried to convince myself that I could go on without him, but the loneliness I now carried with me was heavier than I ever imagined.

Gaia avoided the manor at all costs. Father maintained his mafia responsibilities. I wondered if he would show any emotions about his son's death, but there was nothing behind his haunted eyes. Meanwhile, I felt like a ghost—completely unseen.

Other than going to the funeral home, father had forbidden me from leaving the house. He also eliminated all electronics to prevent hacking or interference within the manor. Ouranos used the manor for his meetings, but not anymore—it had become a prison. Anyone who harmed a member of the Aetos family would face consequences. Guards surrounded the property as if we were preparing for a lingering war.

*I felt like a prisoner, waiting for my day of reckoning.*

To make matters worse, I had barely heard anything about Paris or her condition. One of my father's guards let it slip that she's been in a coma since the attack. I couldn't shake the feeling that what happened to her was my fault, and I wished more than anything that she could be with me today.

The maid's insistent knocks on my door jolted me out of my thoughts. "Morning Aphrodite, I've ironed your dress for the funeral." She entered the room as she placed the dress inside my closet, then nodded before closing the door behind her. I gently brushed away the tears and stifled my cries.

I got out of bed and headed toward the balcony. The sun lingered behind the clouds, rays of golden light breaking through as if the heavens were making their plea. My brother was somewhere up there, watching over me. I had to stay strong for him as I said my goodbyes.

As I dressed, my consciousness lapsed briefly, leaving me feeling disconnected from reality. A profound sense of numbness filled me as I made my way down the staircase. I could hear the echoes of laughter my brother and I had through these halls; running around, chasing each other as we played. He'd read me stories in the library, and we'd tried to find constellations through his telescope.

I closed my eyes and could hear his voice. *"Where's my strong sister?"*

Titan hated funerals. He always tried to avoid attending them, but since he was next in line to take over the family business, Ouranos would force him to make himself present.

"Hurry!" Father shouted.

Gaia had to be carried out to the car. As much as I despised her, I couldn't help but feel a pang of pity for her loss. Titan had been her world and losing him had shattered her completely. This week, Father brought in a doctor to prescribe her antidepressants. She screamed so violently that they had to sedate her. Now, she's barely functioning, relying on a cocktail of pills just to get through the day. She couldn't even walk without Father's firm grip on her arm, her once unyielding spirit now reduced to a hollow shell.

I stepped outside, November's bitter cold weather sent shivers through my body. I wasn't ready to say goodbye to my brother. I struggled to articulate my thoughts. How does one manage to live without loved ones? I desperately wanted to vanish.

Sitting in the limousine, father checked his phone. Gaia's body seemed weak, as if she had no soul left inside. I watched through the window as the dull light of dawn lingered, foreshadowing the long day ahead.

"Even after your son's death, you're still obsessed with business," Gaia spat, her voice dripping with venom.

I couldn't help but agree with her. Titan had been the future of the Aetos mafia—the heir to everything my father had built. But me? I was just the bastard. My father never saw me as anything more than a pawn, certainly not as a potential leader. It wasn't just tradition that held him back; it was his inability to fathom a woman at the helm of his empire. The idea of me taking over was laughable to him.

And yet, deep down, I envied Titan. He had the freedom to live as he pleased, indulging every whim without consequence. Meanwhile, I—along with the other women trapped in the mafia's grip—lived a life of confinement.

We were nothing more than objects—controlled, manipulated, and stripped of our autonomy. We were trapped in gilded cages, our every move dictated by the men who wielded power over us. The freedom Titan had enjoyed was something I could only dream of, while I remained bound by chains I could never break.

A DESIGNATED MAUSOLEUM FOR THE AETOS FAMILY PROMINENTLY showcased the deceased members along the wall. Titan was placed alongside my grandfather. The casket had a sheen over the black stained wood where, in the middle, the Aetos family crest was embellished in gold. The men carefully placed him into the crypt, a resting place that seem almost too fitting for the prince of Aetos. It was as if the cold stone embraced the darkness that surrounded him his whole life.

While the rest of the mourners patiently waited outside the ornate golden gates that enclosed the building, we found ourselves as the sole occupants inside. A cool breeze wafted through the room, and the pungent smell of decay created an unsettling ambiance around us.

Gaia was pressed against the cold, hard wall, her hands shaking as they covered her face, eyes darting around the room.

A single tear trailed down my cheek, knowing my brother would be forever sealed inside these walls. I would never hear his voice again, never feel his comforting embrace during my darkest moments, and he would never be able to save me from the torment that consumed my life.

A marble plaque with a short inscription about Titan sealed the wall of our ancestral resting place. Seeing his name engraved gave me a sickening sense of finality. Father took a deep breath and walked out of the mausoleum. Gaia stumbled behind him. The pallbearers proceeded while I stared at my brother's grave.

I walked up to the plaque, touched my fingers to my lips and placed a kiss on the cold metal where his picture was hung.

"Titan, I will find the person responsible for this." My voice cracked, and I gasped for breath. I took a step back.

"I love you." I whispered; my voice barely audible as a tear traced down my cheek.

Outside the family crypt, Ouranos tenderly embraced the people who expressed their condolences. He played the part of a sad father, but he wasn't fooling me. As I scanned the crowd, I noticed someone standing way off in the distance, behind the willow trees and marked graves.

"Excuse me for a minute," I patted one of the mourner's arms as I sidestepped the guests. The crowds surrounded the gates of the tomb as I slipped through the sea of people lurking about. There were ten rows of headstones that separated the mausoleum from the man who stood by the tree. My heels sank into the fresh, wet grass, frustratingly slowing me down as I struggled to reach him.

His back was turned as I approached him, but I called out, “Hey! Stop!” I hurried in his direction. The man was walking toward a motorcycle, not acknowledging me. “Stop!” He pivoted to face me.

My eyes widened in disbelief. It was the man from the party, the one Titan was talking to. His gaze shifted, and suddenly his brown eyes were on me, holding me captive. I felt a jolt, like an electric current running through my veins. The sadness that had weighed me down moments before seemed to evaporate under the heat of his stare. I swallowed hard, feeling an inexplicable pull toward him, as if the very air around us had changed.

I felt my chest tighten with desire. His leather jacket hugged his body like fitted armor, and he had a hood pulled low over his head.

“Aphrodite.” His voice was a symphonic temptation as he growled my name. It made my body weaken in ways I’d never felt before.

“You—” I tried to compose myself. “I recognize you. You were with my brother at the library.”

“You don’t know what you’re talking about.” He bit back as his jaw twitched.

I straightened. “Why are you here?”

“This was a mistake.” He turned away and headed toward his bike. I rushed toward him and tugged at his arm, feeling his muscles flex as my fingers grasped hold of him. I was not giving him a chance to run. I needed to know what his connection was to my brother. He whipped his head around in my direction, and our faces were inches apart.

“Titan was a friend.” His furrowed brows and expressive eyes held onto my gaze for a minute before his full lips parted. I noticed he had a little scar on the side of his upper cheek. “My name is Ares.”

He said, as he licked his bottom lip, his eyes igniting with a burning intensity.

I dropped my hand, and he turned away from me once more. I watched him get on his motorcycle, the engine growling to life beneath him. He pulled on his helmet, then tugged his face mask over his lips, the last piece of the puzzle clicking into place.

It hit me then, like a punch to the gut.

"Olympus Syndicate."

The name carried a weight of fear and power. Ares was infamous for his ruthless brutality, an enforcer against anyone who decided to go against his gang. Whispers of his reputation had reached even my ears—he was the embodiment of a warrior spirit, the kind that made his enemies tremble.

He glanced back at me one last time, his expression hidden behind his dark Ray-Bans. Then, without another word, he roared away, leaving nothing but the sound of the engine echoing in the air and the unsettling realization of who he truly was.

I ran my hand through my hair, trying to make sense of what I had just seen.

*What was Titan doing with Ares?*

Our families have been fighting for decades, a bitter feud with no end in sight. There was no room for peace, no chance for reconciliation—only death and destruction on both sides.

The thought of my brother being associated with him hit me like a cold, hard slap. It was unthinkable. It felt as if the ground beneath me had suddenly shifted, leaving me reeling and questioning everything I thought I knew.

Gaia was hosting a celebration of life after the funeral. Back at Aetos manor, the staff helped her freshen up, and then led her down the stairs. She wore a black gown which draped dramatically behind her as she swayed, unsteady on her feet. Her face was covered with a birdcage veil fastened atop her head. The drugs must have kicked in because she seemed desperate for a party.

Walking through the halls of the manor, there were whispers all around me. The only thought that was on everyone's mind was who the successor of the family would be now that Titan was dead. I knew in my heart and soul my father would never give that title to me.

The party was being held in the glass atrium of the manor, which overlooked the surrounding forest. It felt like a cage, enclosed by black metal arches. A massive black crystal chandelier dripped down, with black velvet drapes cascading from the ceiling, creating a gothic, enchanting atmosphere. The full moon dancing amongst the clouds above us cast shadows throughout as conversations filled the room. I stood there, frozen, and alone.

Tables and chairs filled the room for guests to be seated.

I looked around, unsure where to go. The only person I had left that I considered family was not here. Paris remained in a coma. Her injuries had left her unresponsive, and without her, I felt completely adrift. I constantly asked the manor staff for updates, desperate to know any details about her condition, but all I could do was wait.

I was consumed by a relentless need to escape. Each passing moment stretched into an eternity, pulling me deeper into suffocating despair. I headed to the grand staircase, each step heavier than the last. I needed the sanctuary of my room, a place where I could temporarily escape the overwhelming tension. As I climbed the stairs, the low murmur of men's voices floated from my father's office, making me pause for a moment.

I headed toward the doorway. I needed to know what was going on in there. I would not be kept in the dark about my brother's death. I crept toward the door and pressed my ear against it, trying to hear the conversation.

"You truly think they would have done this?" My father's muffled voice sounded angry.

"It's hard to say for certain," replied another voice, steady and calculating. "Considering their long-standing grudge against us, it's a possibility we can't ignore. But what if we turned this into our advantage? Consider this: an alliance could be a way to keep them closer, monitor their movements, and perhaps even infiltrate their ranks. Keep your friends close, but your enemies closer."

There was a pause, a tense silence as the suggestion hung in the air. "An alliance with Olympus Syndicate could be a strategic move," the voice continued, unflinching. "They could be more beneficial to us than we realize."

My father's anger flared like a raging fire. "Are you out of your mind?" he roared, his voice booming and echoing. "You know the devastation they've caused this family! To even think of aligning ourselves with them would be an affront to everything we stand for. That would be beneath us, Atlas."

*My father's best friend,* I thought.

The room fell silent again, the weight of his words settling heavily as the intensity of his anger hung thick in the air.

"I hate Zeus as much as you do. But, if we ally with Olympus, it opens the floodgates to Mysthria, which you've always wanted control over. We could use the alliance to gather intelligence and weaken them from within."

"I don't want to give a single cent to Zeus. What do we have besides money that would be beneficial to them?"

"You have Aphrodite."

My vision warped as the sound of my name sent pure terror coursing through my body. The sudden realization hit me; I was going to be used as a bargaining tool for my father's relentless pursuit of domination. The air ripped from my lungs, and I leaned my head against the door, clutching my chest, feeling his control wrap around me like anchor, dropping into the deepest part of the ocean.

I couldn't let this happen. The thought of being sold off, used and abused by the Olympios family, ignited a fierce resolve within me. I had to fight against becoming a pawn in my father's ruthless schemes. I would not be their victim.

"You're right. I will talk with Zeus."

The finality in my father's voice sent a chill down my spine. I would rather be in the crypt with my brother.

*My brother.* His voice echoed in my head, the memory rushing back to me. The night of his murder when he'd said, "Check the floorboard." I couldn't believe I'd forgotten. I turned and raced to his room in search of what he had left for me.

We used to hide letters and secret messages underneath his floorboard. I swung the door open and was instantly hit with the sorrow of his absence. Taking a steady breath, I moved through the room, my eyes scanning for the familiar loose board. When I finally located it, I pried it up with trembling hands, my heart pounding as I prepared to uncover whatever remained of his hidden words.

Inside was a black duffle bag. Confused, I pulled it out and unzipped it. Inside was ten thousand dollars, a gun, and a letter from Titan.

*You'll know what to do. Remember what I taught you. Protect yourself, sister. Demons are all around us.*

# CHAPTER SIX

## ARES

A loud thud broke the silence, jolting me awake. Eos was still asleep on my chest, her breathing steady. Last night, I'd drowned myself in alcohol, trying to escape the gnawing desperation that haunted me. As I rubbed the sleep from my eyes, memories of Titan's funeral resurfaced. I'd gone against my better judgment, but I owed it to him—he was a friend, even if he never fully grasped the dangers around him. Despite everything, he had tried to break free from his father's shadow, a struggle we both shared.

The tempestuous storm in my mind was playing tricks on me. I couldn't stop thinking about Aphrodite, and the horrors she must have endured that night. I couldn't fully explain it, but something inside me wanted to protect her. I was nothing to her, a stranger who associated with her brother. Yet, something deep within me drew me to her, an unexplainable force pulling me closer, as if our fates were somehow intertwined.

The gray skies on the day of the funeral only emphasized her beauty. Her entrancing hazel eyes had lingered in my mind. When she reached out to me, I experienced a fire in my heart as though she launched an arrow through it and manipulated it with delight. I couldn't tear my focus away from her.

I desperately wished for that sensation to vanish, fully aware that getting involved with Ouranos Aetos' daughter could only lead to chaos. I knew better than to let my emotions lead me down a path that would inevitably drag me into a world of trouble, yet the pull was undeniable, like a dark temptation I couldn't shake.

Eos's scent filled the air, but I imagined the softness of Aphrodite's touch. The desire I felt for her was forbidden, a craving I had no right to entertain. Yet, the more I tried to push it away, the stronger it grew, threatening to spiral out of control. If I didn't rein it in soon, I'd find myself caught in a dangerous web I couldn't escape.

"Hey, wake up! It's fucking three in the afternoon. We gotta go." Hades kicked my bedpost. He had casually strolled into the room, but I was too lost in thought to notice.

"What the hell?" I croaked as I brushed my hand across my face, leaning over to my phone to realize how late it was. I rubbed my eyes, exhaustion weighing me down. I hadn't gone to bed until five in the morning—or maybe it was even later? I couldn't quite remember.

"Zeus wants us out front, now. You've got five," Hades growled, leaning against the doorframe. "Eos, grab your shit and move it."

"Fuck off, Hades!" She muffled her cries against my chest. I withdrew from beneath her.

"I'll be ready in five," I sat on the edge of the bed only semi-covering my naked body and cradled my head in my hands.

Hades didn't respond before closing the door. I stood and headed toward the bathroom. "Want me to join you?" Eos teased from where she lay naked on my bed.

"You heard Hades. Get your shit and go." I spoke. I closed the door behind me and rushed through a shower. I was aware that this would be related to Titan's death. Every person in Aeolopolis City was wondering what was to happen next.

Eos had vanished by the time I emerged, wearing only a towel. I attempted to dry my hair before leaving the room.

As I made my way down the stairs, the clubhouse was empty, which I thought was odd. There would often be girls hanging around the bar, while guys on their second round of shots.

The clubhouse was a three-story haven that we'd transformed from an abandoned mill. My grandfather's vision was evident in every detail—the exposed red brick, the metal beams, and the rich scent of dark leather furniture. He'd wanted this place to be more than just a retreat; it was his mission to create a sanctuary, a place that stood in stark contrast to the ruins it once was. His touch was everywhere, turning what had been a rundown shell into something exceptional.

As I descended the metal stairs, I spotted my oldest brother, Hephaestus, emerging from his room. Hephaestus, the vice president of the Olympus Syndicate, oversaw the sale and distribution of all weapons. His influence extended over all of us, a power he frequently leveraged to his advantage.

"Hurry up," Hephaestus snapped, already in a foul mood.

I rolled my eyes, my frustration bubbling up. He was already getting on my nerves.

We had always clashed, even as kids. Despite him being only four years older, he always treated me as if I were a child. You would assume that someone like him would have a different outlook on life.

When we were younger, he survived a life-threatening car accident that left him with a limp and a deep scar across his face. He was never the same after that. He became an unstable, heartless bastard, a change Zeus welcomed. It was as if the accident had carved out his compassion, leaving only the ruthless side that my father valued.

"Good afternoon to you too," I said as I put my leather cut on over my zip-up sweater.

The clubhouse door swung open, revealing the group already mounting their motorcycles under the November skies. The midday light was dim, muted by the lingering clouds from a recent rain shower. Zeus watched us get ready for whatever he had planned. Apollo and Prometheus smoked while Hephaestus put on his helmet.

"Where's Athena?" Hades asked, leaning on his handlebars. I also wondered where she was. Athena always had to know every detail of what our father was up to.

"I have plans for her today." Zeus said and then paused as he rubbed his chin. "Now that Titan is dead, things will change for both our families." He paused, letting us adjust. "Ouranos has an offer for us. We will listen to what he has to say."

"Does he think we attacked them?" Apollo narrowed his eyes. "We have proof we were nowhere near that party."

Zeus threw his hands up. "If he thought we had any part in the attack, he wouldn't be asking for protection. He probably messed up a drug deal and now his son's dead, people are beginning to doubt his abilities. Either way, we need his partnership as much as he does ours."

"Why? We don't associate with that part of the city." Apollo chimed in.

"It's not like we need their influence. We've been doing just fine on our own," I stated matter-of-factly.

The boundaries of Aeolopolis City were drawn by our grandfathers, forged in blood and power. We stand as guardians over the forsaken, the casualties of Ouranos' brutal reign. Anyone he deemed unworthy to march alongside his elite, he cast into the shadows. We swore an oath to protect those outcasts, to be their shield against the wrath of the powerful.

Ouranos was relentless, always looking for ways to expand his control. He had a knack for turning any situation to his advantage, and if we were to get in bed with him, it wouldn't be long before he tried to dominate us too. He'd find a way to edge us out, bit by bit, until we were just another steppingstone in his climb to the top. Aligning with him would be risky, and it wouldn't take much for him to decide we were more useful gone than as allies.

Hades ran his hand over his face. "This should be discussed in a brotherhood meeting, not out here on our fucking bikes!"

"We made a deal with him already. We didn't need anyone else's approval," Hephaestus snapped. My brother puffed out his chest as if he was going to attack Hades.

"Did you have a say in this?" I asked my brother, who seemed to be all too eager.

Listen, Ares—you're always bringing chaos and bad luck wherever you go," Hephaestus snarled, pointing at me. "And don't even get me started on your whorehouse of a club. It's clear that's all you care about and not the OS."

"I bring the bad luck? Are you fucking kidding me?" I snapped back. Who did he think he was talking to? He was a fucking prick, always knowing how to get under my skin.

"Cut the crap, both of you. We've got to meet them now. Move it." Zeus barked, straddling his motorcycle and firing up the engine. Hephaestus followed suit while Hades and Apollo shook their heads in disbelief. This was all wrong.

You don't fuck with Ouranos and live to talk about it.

THE SOUND OF OUR ENGINES ECHOED DOWN THE LENGTHY DRIVEWAY LEADING to Aetos Manor. Ouranos chose to hide away in the mountains, seeking refuge from unseen threats. The Gothic mansion radiated a chilling, eerie energy, like stepping into the heart of a nightmare. As we pulled up to the concrete columns that marked the porte-cochere, Ouranos stood looming at the doorway, flanked by two men.

I removed my helmet and mask, letting the cool air hit my face. A tingling sensation crept up my spine, the unmistakable feeling of being watched. My eyes instinctively flicked toward the tall arched windows above, shadows playing tricks in the dim light. I was the last to park, the growl of my bike fading as I swung my leg over and dismounted, the weight of unseen eyes still pressing on me.

"Welcome," Ouranos' voice boomed as he extended his hand to Zeus.

"Thank you for having us," Zeus nodded as they released their handshake and made their way inside.

"You won't mind if my men search you?" Ouranos said, though it was more of a demand than a request.

"Not a problem," Zeus nodded, spreading his arms to let the henchmen frisk him. They quickly found his gun and confiscated it. Meanwhile, the rest of us stood still as the other henchmen moved in, patting us down with rough, practiced hands. Each of us tensed as they searched, their fingers lingering a bit too long, making it clear they weren't just checking for weapons but asserting their dominance. We exchanged glances, silently sizing up the situation as the henchmen went about their business with an air of arrogance.

With a slight nod from his lead man, Ouranos flashed a devilish smile, signaling for us to come inside.

Zeus pressed a firm hand on Apollo's shoulder. "Wait here."

Apollo narrowed his eyes, glancing between Hephaestus and me, as Zeus added, "And Prometheus too. Keep an eye out."

The air was thick with tension, and we knew the odds weren't in our favor if this turned into an ambush. Zeus had subtly suggested that leaving them by the bikes could shift the balance—if things went south, they could make a quick escape to call for reinforcements.

We stood in the entryway. The home was massive, and a grand chandelier hung above us, its crystal pendants catching the dim light and casting eerie shadows on the walls. The overall design screamed of a devil's playpen, with dark, Gothic elements woven into every detail.

Gaia descended the steps, draped in a fitted red dress with her golden waves cascading to her shoulders. Titan had spoken often about his mother and sister. He'd confided in me about his mother's relentless attempts to insert herself into his life, though all he ever wanted was to sever ties with the family. His sister, however, was different. Titan watched over her like she was a fragile bird taking its first flight. He had an unwavering devotion to her, a fierce need to protect her at all costs. That's why he made me promise to look after her if anything ever happened to him—because she was his everything.

I watched my father's eyes roam up and down Gaia's body like a piece of meat. He had no shame in sizing up someone else's wife.

"Zeus, it's a pleasure to meet you." Gaia gave a venomous glance but couldn't stop herself from staring at him.

Zeus approached the head of the mafia's wife, he flashed a charming smile and said, "Now, I see why he's so hard to negotiate with—he's got everything worth fighting for right here at home."

Gaia gave him a sly smile, "Flattery won't get you everything Zeus, but it's a good start."

"Let's go to the study," Ouranos said, flashing a tight smile and pointing toward the library, clearly annoyed by the exchange.

As we followed them in, Hades leaned in close and whispered in my ear, "You think he's gonna snap, or is that devilish grin just for show?" Hades smirked as he walked ahead of me.

I licked my bottom lip, rubbing my chin with a cocky smirk. But as I glanced back to make sure no one was following, I froze. There, at the top of the stairs, stood Aphrodite. My confidence wavered, and for a moment, I couldn't move, caught off guard by the sight of her.

My heart quickened, feeling the undeniable pull to climb those stairs and wrap my fingers around her neck, feeling her pulse race beneath my touch. I wanted to taste her, to feel her tremble as I claimed every part of her, consumed by the darkness and lust that only she could ignite in me.

The air between us crackled with tension, a magnetic pull that threatened to shatter my control. Every instinct screamed to close the distance, to give in to the raw desire surging through my veins. But I knew the danger all too well—one wrong move, one slip, and I'd be plunging headfirst into a chaos I might never crawl out of. The thought of being caught with the mafia king's daughter sent a cold shiver down my spine, but the temptation was nearly unbearable.

I continued inside the room, ignoring my desires.

Zeus took a seat on the leather couch while Hades scanned the bookshelves, looking disinterested. Hephaestus sat in the chair across from our father. I stood with my arms across my chest, already feeling uncomfortable with this deal before even learning the details.

"Zeus, I know we are quite different." Ouranos began, his hands cupped behind his back as he walked toward the fireplace. He exuded calmness and composure.

"That's an understatement," Hades said as he pulled a book off the shelf. I let out a snicker and rubbed my jaw, but my brother tensed.

Ouranos' eyes flashed with anger toward Hades, barely holding back; his frustration was written all over his face. His voice was strained as he took a deep breath, trying to steady himself.

"I know this seems desperate, but you must understand the gravity of the situation. My position is more precarious than ever. The death of my son has shaken the very foundation of my power. I need your help, and I need it now. An alliance with you could turn the tide and secure my place. This isn't just about survival; it's about maintaining control and crushing any doubts about my strength."

"What would this alliance entail exactly?" Zeus sat on the edge of the couch and rested his elbows on his knees. Hades approached me, shaking his head while I caught his narrowed glance.

Ouranos approached his whiskey decanter and poured it into the tumblers neatly displayed on the bar cart.

"You possess Mysthria Harbor." he said as he walked toward Zeus with a glass, his eyes glinting in the firelight. "What I'm proposing is that you help me find my son's killer and grant us access to your territories. In return, I will offer you my daughter and exclusive access to my private channels. This isn't just a negotiation; it's a chance to forge a powerful alliance that could shift the balance of power in our favor." He settled into the leather sofa across from Zeus.

The way they used Aphrodite as a bargaining tool had me seething with rage.

*She's mine,* I thought the possessiveness burning like fire in my chest.

Zeus shifted his gaze to Hephaestus, a steely resolve in his eyes. "My son, as the vice president of our MC, it's time you take a wife."

*For fuck's sake,* I thought.

Hephaestus would destroy everything good about her. Aphrodite had a rare quality, something delicate, like a flower just beginning to bloom. I could already see how she'd wither under my brother's influence. He had a way of twisting people, breaking them down bit by bit until there was nothing left but dust.

"She's not some ugly broad who can't find a man, right?" Hephaestus chuckled and reclined in his chair. I felt an urge to walk across the room and punch him square in the jaw, but I squeezed my fingernails into my skin, resisting the thought.

"Gaia, call Aphrodite," Ouranos barked the order at his wife, his gaze fixed on his glass of whiskey. "My daughter holds value that you may not realize. Her worth could tip the balance of power in ways you can't fathom."

I leaned into Hades's ear, "I don't like this."

Hades mumbled, "Me either."

"When will the wedding be? If we are going to do this tradeoff, it has got to be soon. We can help you find the killer. Hephaestus is the best tracker we have."

"We can make it official by next month." Ouranos nodded as he took a sip of his drink.

"We will take her with us tonight," Hephaestus demanded, his gaze intense.

"Here she is." Gaia walked back into the room, and I turned to see

Aphrodite standing in the doorframe. Her lips parted and her eyes caught mine. Her long curls were pulled away from her face, and she wore a fitted black dress. She was a sight to behold, and that familiar energy pulsed between us. She walked further into the room; her hazel eyes darkened by the firelight. She smelled euphoric as she walked past me. I wanted nothing more than to take hold of her and stake my claim. I wanted her all to myself. She was my ultimate obsession.

"Hello." Her voice was a whisper as she stood in the middle of our group.

"Hello, Aphrodite. I'm Zeus—"

"I know who you are," she said, standing up taller. Hephaestus watched her, his eyes focused on her every move with a predatory gaze.

Zeus let out a cocky chuckle as he rubbed his chin. "You are going to marry my son."

Aphrodite tilted her head to the side, glancing in my direction before returning her attention to Zeus.

"Which one?" Aphrodite looked nervously between the two of us.

"Me." Hephaestus stood. "And I'll make damn sure my future old lady knows better than to even think about bailing on this deal," he growled, a dangerous glint in his eyes.

"Then it's settled." Ouranos stood up and reached for Zeus. "We have an agreement?"

"Welcome to Olympus Syndicate." Zeus shook his hand, sealing our fate. I felt a deep sense of dread rattle throughout my body as it shattered my inner soul.

Ouranos glanced down at his daughter.

"Aphrodite, you have preparations to make," Ouranos demanded as I watched her, seemingly stunned by everything that had unfolded. I felt my fists clench, nails digging into my palms as anger surged within me.

*How could a father just give her up like that?*

Aphrodite lifted her chin, her expression unyielding as she

calmly said, "As you wish." She turned on her heel and walked out of the library, her stride steady, betraying no sign of the turmoil within. I felt a surge of desperation to go after her, to pull her from the fate that awaited, but my feet stayed rooted to the floor, held back by the weight of what I couldn’t change.

# CHAPTER SEVEN
## APHRODITE

*All eyes locked on me.*

A suffocating darkness wrapped around me as my world began to collapse. Ouranos's deal with the Olympus Syndicate had stripped me of any sense of worth, reducing me to nothing more than a mere bargaining chip in my father's ruthless game.

The realization hit me with the force of a sledgehammer, igniting a searing rage that made it nearly impossible to keep my emotions in check. My heart hammered violently in my chest, and my fists clenched so tightly that my knuckles turned white. Each breath felt like a struggle against the oppressive weight of my own helplessness.

I was determined to conceal any hint of vulnerability, to mask the turmoil roiling inside me from my father's cold, calculating gaze. Every ounce of anger I felt was an attempt to shield myself against the crushing reality that I was nothing more than a pawn in his ruthless scheme. Before exiting the meeting, I plastered on a fake smile and nodded in agreement, but inside, rage consumed me. My footsteps echoed as I stormed toward my bedroom, seeking a moment of solace before the sudden upheaval of my life. The air was so heavy and stifling in the manor that it made it difficult to breathe.

The terrifying stories of Olympus Syndicate, the feared motorcycle family, were spoken in whispers and instilled fear in those who listened. Their reputation of being the most dangerous gang in Aeolopolis City was earned.

I pressed my trembling hands against my forehead, feeling a shiver run down my spine.

*I needed to run.*

My pulse thumped loudly in my ears as I grabbed a bag from my closet, adrenaline sending tremors through my body. Tears flowed down my face as I clutched onto the crumpled bills and gun my brother gave me.

Without another thought, I threw on a tracksuit and shoes, then quickly zipped up the bag. I snatched a hat off my shelf, attempting to tame my unruly curls as I hurried to the Juliet balcony. Swinging the doors open, I felt the cool breeze brush against my face. I tossed the bag to the ground and quickly swung my leg over the railing. I wasn't going to wait to see what they had in store for me.

"What is taking her so long? Go and get Aphrodite, bring her down here!" Ouranos demanded, he spoke with an animalistic growl, the urgency in his voice growing with each passing second as it echoed from the hallway.

A wave of nervousness washed over me. My hands became clammy, and my breath caught in my throat. I climbed down the thick ivy covering the brick wall, my fingers stinging as they dug into the rough vines. It was a long drop from the second floor, but I managed to make my way down. It wasn't my first time using this as an escape route and I knew the ivy gave me enough to grip onto keep me from falling. Picking up the bag, I sprinted toward the forest, my heart pounding as the deafening thud of my footsteps reverberated in my ears.

Within the forests dense foliage, concealed paths unveiled a route that led straight to the beach. If I managed to get there, I could find a hiding spot until it was safe. Flashlights illuminated the area, casting shadows as the faint sound of men shuffling around echoed in the distance. Retreating was not an option.

I raced through the pitch-dark forest, pushing branches out of my way. The sky was a dark abyss looming above me. I slid down the dirt banks and crawled under a fallen tree. Fear overwhelmed me as I leaned against the cold, wet surface. With a quick glimpse over the log, I saw the flicker of flashlights weaving through the thick underbrush.

"Aphrodite!" people called from various directions. The haunting echoes reverberated throughout the forest, intensifying my sense of internal doom.

Before the lights could get closer, I pushed off the muddy ground and continued my descent down the hill. I sprinted, heart pounding, knowing my life was on the line. Every nerve was on edge, my senses sharpened as I scanned the shadows for danger. I sprinted, my life hanging in the balance, constantly on alert for any sign of the henchmen following me.

Fear surged through me, shoving me to go faster, desperate to escape. In an instant, I lost my footing, and I slipped and tumbled down the rugged dirt hill, frantically grasping for anything to hold onto. My mind went blank as a surge of fear took over, and with a sickening thud, my back crashed into a jagged rock. Pain thundered through my body, but I fought the urge to give up.

My head spun, and I pressed my hands against my forehead, desperate to block out the terror that loomed ahead. Gasping for air, the pain tightened its grip on me, the metallic taste of blood lingering on my lips. Covered in mud, I forced myself to rise, pushing through the throbbing pain in my ankle.

A bright light landed on my face.

The clouds emitted a thunderous crack as the rain began and a frigid wind brushed against my face. I collapsed to the ground, aware that escape was impossible. The light drew near, so I shielded my eyes with my hand to protect them from its intensity.

"Just kill me now! I will never be his wife!" I screamed with all my might, hoping my voice would reach the heavens. I blinked to adjust my vision, the beam of light unmoving as I saw who my captor would be.

*Ares.*

He dropped to one knee, pushing his hoodie back, the flashlight casting sharp shadows across his face. His dark eyes burned with an intensity that pinned me in place, igniting a confusing, undeniable pull within me. My breath hitched, a sudden rush of heat flooding through me, unable to tear my gaze away from him, even as I struggled to understand why I felt this way. With a gentle touch, he brushed my swollen lip, and a soft gasp escaped me. "I need to bring you back."

"No! Just say you couldn't find me," I violently shake my head as I pleaded for my life.

"No one's going to lay a finger on you, not while I'm around." His eyes locked onto mine, while his jaw twitched with tension.

He was an enigma that made my heart go wild. My throat tightened as the heat of his fingers slipped away from my skin.

My lips trembled and tears escaped my eyes despite my efforts to remain stoic. Defeated, he hoisted me into his arms. As he carried me through the forest, I rested my head on his chest. He smelled like leather and warm, rich amber. An undertone of tobacco clung to his jacket. I clutched onto him, feeling the strength of his arms bound me to his comforting warmth.

"Why are you protecting me?" I implored, placing my hand on his firm chest, capturing the beat of his heart.

"Your brother was a friend of mine." His voice trembled as he whispered, "He told me to protect you if anything happened to him. This, moving forward with our father's plan, is the only way to keep you safe." His eyes darted around the forest as if he expected danger to arise from the shadows. Ares's voice carried the weight of his sadness, leaving a lingering sense of sorrow in its wake.

*He was the friend—the person Titan mentioned.*

Dread washed over me.

I nodded, then pressed my head against his chest again. I could feel the rapid thumping of his heartbeat against my cheek. The manor's imposing silhouette grew smaller as we disappeared into the distance.

"How did you know about this street?" I inquired, scanning the surroundings. I noticed we were on the road I was running toward.

"I used to meet your brother here. Nobody ever uses this route. I figured this is where you'd run off to." Ares's voice sounded rough and raspy. I struggled to discern his facial expressions in the darkness with beads of water dripping down his face.

"I was easy to p-predict," I stammered, embarrassment made my cheeks burn.

He licked his bottom lip, with a smirk, "Maybe, but that's what makes me reliable. I know what you'll do before you even do it."

As we reached the forests edge, I noticed a man straddling a motorcycle, parked next to his own. Ares set me down, the rain still drenching me. I trailed behind him, observing the man in the helmet. The name embroidered on his leather vest identified him as *Hades*.

Ares handed me his helmet, and I took it from him. My heart thrummed in my chest as I imagined the dangers that awaited us on the road. "Hop on," he urged, "before the night swallows us." I grabbed his damp hand and swung onto the bike.

Ares pulled me close, my heart pounding with a mix of unease and excitement. My fingers brushed against the hard lines of his well-defined muscles, his broad shoulders bearing the emblem of the Olympus Syndicate. I wrapped my arms tightly around his waist, feeling the rumble of the motorcycle beneath us, every inch of him radiating power and control.

Ares shouted over his shoulder, "Hold on!" as he pulled his mask over the lower half of his face. He started the engine and trailed down the slick road at a decent speed while Hades trailed behind. I laid my head on his back, closed my eyes, and felt a sharp pain in my chest.

The roar of his engine reverberated through the stillness of the night, as the flicker of streetlamps flashed above us. Time felt like it was being stretched and rushed all at the same time. Ares turned his head ever so slightly, his brown eyes deepening to a captivating shade that sent a shiver down my spine.

As we entered the Olympus Syndicate compound, I was stunned by the bustling city hidden within its walls. I had always assumed they lived in some rough part of town. The rumors painted them as the cockroaches of the city, but this was nothing like I'd imagined.

A tall building towered in the center, casting shadows over the people below, while smaller buildings clustered around it. The clubhouse flickered with light as muffled music seeped through the closed doors.

The rest of the group had already parked, their laughter echoing in the distance as we pulled into an empty spot. Though the rain had ceased, my body still trembled from the bone-chilling ride, as if the storm's fury continued to haunt me.

With the engine silenced, Ares swung his leg off the bike. He extended his hand, and I placed my trembling one in his, letting him guide me into the clubhouse. My cheeks burned, and I shook from the cold and fear that permeated my body. As we entered, I was embraced by the sudden warmth of the clubhouse.

"You found the princess!" Zeus shouted, propping himself up on the bar. Ares quickly dropped my hand as he moved past me without a glance. His indifference was a blade, cutting deep and leaving me hollow as he moved toward a blonde, rendering me nothing more than a shadow in his wake.

Maybe the electric charge I felt between us had been nothing but a figment of my imagination. Perhaps the heat in his eyes was merely a trick of the light, a desperate projection of my own desires. Yet, as I watched him walk away without a second glance, doubt crawled at me, sharp and relentless, gnawing away at my certainty. The ache in my chest twisted painfully, as if the connection I thought we had was nothing more than a cruel illusion.

*Of course, he had a girlfriend.* The thought hit me harder than I expected, a strange pang of something I couldn't quite name twisting in my chest. It shouldn't have mattered—I wasn't marrying him; I was marrying his brother. But the knot in my stomach told a different story.

"Are you capable of having a conversation? Or are you a mute?" Zeus sneered as he approached me, his tone dripping with contempt. Ares had no resemblance to his father. Zeus stood at the same height as him but had lighter features. His icy blue glare made me feel weak.

"I can speak," I responded.

Zeus's gaze slithered over me, a predator sizing up its prey. I felt the weight of his scrutiny, making me feel exposed.

"My son finds you quite intriguing," he said, his smirk carrying an undercurrent of menace. "You might believe you have value here, but don't deceive yourself. We all have our roles to play."

I swallowed hard, trying to steady my breathing as he continued. The room's oppressive atmosphere seemed to close in on me, heightening my sense of dread.

My eyes fell upon Hephaestus, standing just behind Zeus. His face had a scar that ran along his temple to his jawline. From the whispers that I've heard over the years, I knew that Hephaestus was in a terrible motorcycle accident that caused him to become deformed.

You could tell he had once been an attractive man. His well-defined jawline, accentuated by a neatly groomed black beard, gave him a distinguished look. His icy-blue eyes, striking and unmistakable, mirrored those of his father. Yet, I couldn't help but feel a disturbing presence about him. Something inside me felt off, a sense of unease settled in the pit of my stomach.

Hephaestus approached me with a noticeable limp in his stride, yet he still radiated dominance. His fitted black t-shirt clung to his muscular frame, highlighting his powerful presence despite the slight hitch in his step.

He was the epitome of a bad boy, with tattoos adorning every visible inch of his skin. "You're soaked," he remarked, noticing the water dripping off my clothes. "Come on, let me take you to my room so you can dry off."

"Your room?" I gulped, realization hitting me that this was the man who was going to be my husband. I wasn't ready to share a space yet, nor was I prepared to be some woman that he could do whatever he pleased with. Despite everything, I refused to let the fear of being mistreated again consume my heart. I stiffened, and my gaze locked onto Zeus with wide, terrified eyes, frozen in anticipation. "I demand to have my own room until we're married."

The laughter was malicious as it pierced through my ears, fueling my rage. I clenched my fists, ready to confront those mocking me.

"Demand?" Zeus's laughter filled the air, each mocking chuckle a stab through my heart as tears welled up in my eyes. The hairs on the back of my neck stood on end as I stared into his cold, calculating eyes. Hephaestus's eyes narrowed; his stare filled with a fury that made me want to squirm.

I would not let them intimidate me.

"Is that a problem?" I retorted. They expected me to submit to them, but I would fight with everything I had before allowing anyone to lay a hand on me.

Zeus's nostrils flared, but I held my gaze steady. The thought of being confined to Hephaestus's room sent chills down my spine, imagining what he might impose upon me.

"Fine," he snarled through clenched teeth.

"What the fuck?" Hephaestus growled. His face turned red, and his fists clenched tightly into fists as his voice seethed with venom. "She's mine."

His statement made me shudder, and I scanned the room, looking for a way to escape.

*You won't have me,* I thought.

Zeus's expression darkened, his eyes narrowing with a cold fury. He stepped forward, towering over Hephaestus. "Hephaestus, you don't make demands here," Zeus's voice was a low, dangerous growl. "I'm the president of this MC. You forget your place, and you forget who controls this empire."

Hephaestus recoiled, his anger momentarily quelled by the sheer force of Zeus's authority. Zeus's gaze was unrelenting, a chilling reminder that even the most powerful within the Syndicate were subject to his rule. I could see the power struggle unfold, and for now, I was spared the immediate threat—but the danger was far from over.

"You can stay with my daughter, Artemis." Zeus exhaled deeply as he looked toward a woman at the bar. The one Ares was talking to.

*His sister.*

"Thank you, I appreciate the—"

"I need a fucking drink! Where are the girls?" Zeus turned his attention elsewhere. Music filled the air, the thud of the bass sending reverberations up my body. Hephaestus gave me one last glare before stomping off behind his dad like a grumpy child. Artemis came around the bar, and Ares glanced over at me before heading elsewhere.

"Hey, Aphrodite, I'm Artemis, but you can call me Artie." Artie's sun-kissed waves cascaded down her shoulders. It added to her radiant beauty. Her petite height accentuated her curvaceous silhouette in all the right places. Her eyes were a mesmerizing blend of green, yellow, and brown, swirling together like a vibrant mosaic. Her warm olive skin radiated a glow, reminiscent of a life spent under the sun.

"It's nice to meet you," I shook her hand, feeling immediately comfortable in her presence. She had a sense of certainty about her.

"Let's get you changed. You're all wet!" She looked me up and down and said, "You can use the shower and get settled in at my place." She paused and turned over her shoulder, "Watch the bar!"

she shouted. I observed the girl now sitting with Ares. I gulped, that hollow feeling growing within as I tried to concentrate on Artie.

We left the clubhouse and headed toward the neighboring building. As I took in my surroundings, awe washed over me, making it feel like I had stepped onto a different planet. Everything was so unfamiliar, so far from what I expected.

On the side of the building's exterior, emergency steps led to the second floor. Artie walked towards them. We ascended the steps toward a sturdy, metal door. Artie turned the key in the lock and swung the door open, revealing a warm and inviting interior.

Her loft had massive windows that afforded a picturesque view of Neptune's Abyss. The place had a small white kitchen with a spacious island. The living room had a massive sectional and a grand fireplace, the crackling warmth called to me. Art dominated the walls, and one piece caught my eye. It was a painting which depicted a skeleton wearing an opulent velvet cape on a large canvas. The flowers surrounding it seemed to transform into wings.

Artie leaned in and whispered, "Ares painted that. He's an incredible artist." I was mesmerized by the piece, as I saw the beauty within the pure darkness it had conveyed.

"Your brother's talented," I mumbled, my voice barely audible, afraid that my thoughts about Ares would betray me. From the corner of my eye, I saw her nod.

An ache settled in my chest, and I thought about Titan. I yearned for my brother, and my heart longed for his protection.

"Let me show you the bedroom," she said. With a heavy sigh, she opened the door to a small, cluttered bedroom that smelled of faded perfume. A queen-size bed loomed against the massive window; casting shadows that made the room feel suffocating.

"This room is yours. Make it your own. I gotta get back to work. The guys are useless managing the bar," Artie laughed, but her eyes lingered on me, studying my reaction as I surveyed the room. The space, though a temporary refuge, felt like a prison—a stark reminder of my new reality. The harsh truth of my forced accommodation settled over me, a reminder of the life I was trapped in.

"Thank you," I mumbled, sinking onto the bed. I felt tears blur my vision, and her gaze remained fixed on me.

She sat on the bed as she spoke to me. "Take it one day at a time. We will make things work, okay?" She wiped the tear on my cheek. "Get some sleep," she added. "Tomorrow will bring a fresh new day."

"Okay." I nodded, grateful for her comforting words.

Artie smiled at me before leaving the bedroom.

It felt as if I had traded one cage for another, each more suffocating than the last.

# CHAPTER EIGHT
## APHRODITE

After Artie left, I showered, washing away every trace of mud and blood that clung to my skin. As the droplets of water trickled down my body, I closed my eyes, allowing the memories of the past week to consume me. Life had lost all value.

The night of the explosions haunted my dreams. Whenever I tried to sleep, the screams and violence replayed in my mind in a nightmarish loop, dragging me back to those moments of chaos and despair.

*All I did was switch from one monster to another.*

Hours slipped by, my anxiety gnawing at me, keeping sleep just out of reach.

A cold sweat drenched my body, and I felt the tingling sensation down to my bones. I turned to face the window, tracing lines in the condensation, feeling trapped once more. I had a view of another building which looked like this one.

As I gazed down at the people below, my attention was drawn to a couple stumbling through the compound. I quickly realized it was

Ares, pulling a woman close as they made their way to his apartment.

My heart sank as I watched him kiss her, feeling a flush of jealousy spread across my cheeks. Despite my efforts to look away, I couldn't tear my gaze from the way he touched her. It felt crushing to realize that what I had sensed between us might have been an illusion. I struggled to understand why his behavior had shifted so suddenly and why the connection I thought we had now seemed so empty.

I couldn't help but wonder—was Ares just as wicked, if not worse, than the rest of his family?

Doubt crept into my thoughts, wrapping around my mind like a vice. I was just a pawn in the twisted game his family was playing. Confusion weighed heavily on me as I questioned my place in their schemes. Was I merely a tool, a piece in their strategy for power? The uncertainty gnawed at me, leaving me to wonder how deeply I'd been ensnared in their web.

*How could I have trusted him?*

A dull ache spread throughout my chest. Ares had lied to me. Tricked me and brought me here, claiming it was the only way to keep me safe. Deep down, I was convinced that Ares and his family had a hand in Titan's demise, even if I had no concrete evidence to prove it.

Despite my suspicions, I couldn't ignore the magnetic pull he had over me. The allure of danger and the forbidden ignited something within me, a confusing blend of desire and fear that made me question my own judgment and instincts. An intense, inexplicable longing for him twisted through me like a serpent, making it impossible to reconcile my feelings with the reality of his potential involvement in Titan's death.

THE MORNING SUNSHINE AROSE FROM BEHIND GRAY CLOUDS, AND I FELT THE warm beam of light against my face as I glanced out the window. I had barely slept, and when I did manage to sleep, I dreamed of Titan; the sight of him lying on the ground, his lifeless eyes staring up at the ceiling.

My thoughts were interrupted by the sight of Ares getting ready to leave his apartment. He didn't seem to own curtains, so I had a vast view into his apartment. A knock on the door of my room broke my curiosity. I turned just as Artie eased open the door.

"Good morning." Artie smiled, opening the door fully. She crossed her arms as she leaned against the doorframe.

"Morning," I muttered, barely awake and trying to drag myself out of bed.

"I heard you crying last night." She pushed a strand of blonde hair away from her face.

"Oh." I felt instantly embarrassed, and my heart lodged in my throat. "I'm sorry."

"Why are you sorry?" She sat on the edge of the bed. "I know what it feels like to lose a loved one." Artie looked down at her hands. "When our mom died, I had a hard time coming to terms." Artie looked up at me. "Your brother's death is still fresh. Allow yourself time to mourn."

Her words weighed heavily on my heart. I fought to bury the pain deep within, determined not to reveal any sign of weakness. Vulnerability wasn't an option.

"Thank you," I replied, my voice steady despite my uncertainty. I couldn't be sure if she was a friend or foe. I was an outsider here, and I had to figure out if she was working against me. "Well, breakfast is being cooked in the main clubhouse, whenever you want to come down." Artie got up from the bed and headed out of the room.

As the door clicked shut, I began to prepare for the day, my mind still clouded with uncertainty. The overwhelming feeling of being an outsider weighed heavily on me; trust was a rare commodity here, and I was grappling with the same mistrust. The more I reflected on my situation, the more I felt like a stranger, adrift and out of place.

I walked into the clubhouse, my attention immediately landing on Artie who was behind the bar with Hades. They seemed to be engrossed in a deep conversation. The rest of the family was nowhere to be seen.

The bar decor consisted of motorcycle statues, trophies, and photos of their history scattered across the walls. String lights were draped above me, and metal bridges connected one side of the second floor to the other. The space, although it was quite large, felt cramped.

As I approached the bar, a movement caught my eye. Hephaestus descended the steel-framed stairs, each step echoing through the space, drawing the attention of Artie and Hades, who both turned to look at him. "Well, look who's here, my precious fiancé." Hephaestus charged toward me, his limp evident in his stride. He stood in front of me, his eyes narrowing with an intensity that sent a shiver down my spine; they resembled the darkest depths of the ocean. He placed a kiss on my cheek, and I felt his rough beard brush against my face as he pulled away from me.

"What? You don't like it?" I must have instinctively recoiled from his touch.

I stared at him, my stomach churning with unease. I grappled with the challenge of expressing my desire to keep my distance, knowing that any confrontation would only heighten my fear. The terror that gripped me was paralyzing, leaving me searching for the courage to articulate my discomfort. I put on a fake smile. "I do."

Making this complicated would only lead to chaos. That was the last thing I needed. I hesitantly took a deep breath and said, "I want to get to know you better, since we're getting married soon." Smiling, I reached up to trace his jaw, feeling the way the scar from his accident marred his skin under his beard.

Hephaestus chuckled and scratched his chin, taking a step back from me. "Of course. I gotta take care of some things today, but I'll see you tonight."

My instincts were on high alert, like walking a tightrope over a chasm—every subtle movement raised my anxiety, but the exact nature of the danger remained unclear. Despite this, I needed to gain his trust.

"Okay, I'll be waiting for you." I flashed him a flirty smile, playing the part of the woman he wanted—the one who would submit to his control.

"Hephaestus, let's go!" Zeus's booming voice caught me off guard as he walked toward us.

Hephaestus turned to face him and then focused his attention back on me. "Duty calls." He gave me a wink and a gentle stroke on my cheek before walking toward his father.

I was frozen in place, my throat tightening as my emotions surged through my body, my chest heaving with effort to hold them back. My hands trembled slightly, and I drew a deep breath, mentally preparing for the storm I was getting myself into.

THE NIGHT SKY DRAPED ITSELF OVER THE OLYMPUS COMPOUND, A DARK blanket that seemed to muffle the world outside. During the day, I stayed confined to my room, my eyes constantly drifting to the windows as I watched the compound's members move under Zeus's direction.

My heart ached with an inexplicable pull towards Ares, a constant, gnawing obsession that I couldn't shake. I found myself yearning to catch a glimpse of him, though I couldn't fathom why he had such a hold on me.

The little city that Olympus Syndicate had built inside its walls was unlike anything I had ever seen before. It had shops, apartments, and entertainment. A bar called The Odyssey operated next to the clubhouse. According to Artie, it was a legitimate way to contribute money to the MC without the authorities snooping around. She managed the Odyssey for her dad because he never wanted her to become a full-fledged member of the MC, but she was determined to contribute somehow.

Artie laid out some clothes on my bed while I finished applying the makeup she lent me. Eventually, I'd have to find a way to repay her. The only bag that had money I managed to pack was still left in the forest.

"Why aren't you a member if your sister is?" Intrigued by the rumors surrounding this family, I paid close attention to the gossip at every party I attended. The people I surrounded myself with despised the Olympus Syndicate, painting them as a blight on the city, a gang that would stop at nothing to spread bloodshed.

Stories circulated about the havoc they wreaked, with one particularly chilling tale sticking in my mind: a news report showing a body hanging from a bridge, strung up like a grim warning in some violent act of retaliation. The whispers all pointed to one name—Olympus.

"Dad always says I'm just like my mother. I see the goodness in others, which he deems as a weakness. He never wanted me part of his--," She paused before responding, "work."

Artie was being vague when she spoke, but I didn't blame her. I would be the same if the tables were turned.

"What are your thoughts about me bartending for you?" I asked as I applied some lipstick. In order to find out what the others knew about my brother's killer, I would need to try to socialize with them. Working at the bar would allow me to get them drunk and then ask for whatever information they might have.

"Sounds good," she agreed, admiring her reflection and touching up her red lipstick. "I can ask my dad, but I think he'd be cool with it. You're gorgeous and would make bank in tips."

I shook my head. "Not as hot as you." I looked at her reflection in the mirror.

"I left you an outfit on the bed." She looked down at it and flashed me a teasing look. "It may be outside of your boho style." She winked. My clothing preferences typically lie in simplicity and elegance. I loved wearing dresses in pastel shades, and anything floral.

I got up and walked over to my bed. A sleek black leather dress was waiting for me.

"I...I—" Looking over my shoulder in confusion. "I...can't wear that."

"Why not? It's not like you'll stand out around here if you do, you're more likely to if you don't." She shrugged and left the room.

I looked closer at the dress. It looked like a sausage casing. I wasn't sure how I was going to squeeze into it.

I moved to close the drapes but stopped as the sound of bass coming from across the way caught my attention. As I gazed out the window, I saw Ares in his apartment. He was listening to music, and it echoed towards my room.

In the daylight, the apartments were closer than I expected. He stepped out of the bathroom, a towel slung low around his waist, and made his way through the living room toward his bedroom.

*Does this guy not have any curtains?*

I watched him discreetly as he gathered some garments from a drawer. I couldn't take my eyes off the tattoo that stretched across his back. Watching him made me feel hot all over. Suddenly, he froze. Ares turned to face me, and our eyes met. With a hitch, I pulled the curtains closed. *Aphrodite, you're such an idiot!* My inner voice screamed while I closed my eyes tight.

"Let's get into that fucking sausage casing of a dress," I said in defeat.

Artie and I arrived at The Odyssey just as the party was ramping up. "Icky Thump" by The White Stripes echoed through the wall, the dim lighting cast shadows on the demons lurking within. The floors were made of rough cobblestones, with dark wood beams supporting the exposed roof. Edgy and dark artwork adorned every wall, some of it reminiscent of the piece hanging in Artie's loft. Women clad in leather were scattered all around. The brotherhood of the Olympus Syndicate gathered in the rear section, beneath a glowing red neon sign that displayed their logo.

The overpowering scent of alcohol mingled with the thick fog of smoke, making it difficult to tell who was nearby as I walked behind Artie. Eyes scrutinized me like a new toy. I brushed my curly hair out of my face and took a seat at the bar while Artie elbowed Apollo out of the way so she could pour our drinks.

"Hey, Aphrodite." Apollo glanced my way as he gave a settled nod.

He tossed a beer cap into the garbage as he walked past me. I nodded, still feeling out of place. Apollo and Artie were twins, and Apollo bore a striking resemblance to his sister, with golden hair and a strong jawline. His full lips and short beard added to his rugged charm, while his well-defined muscles pressed against his tight shirt and jeans. His warm hazel eyes offered a sense of comfort, setting him apart from the others, who seemed much more abrasive.

"What do you want to drink?" Artie leaned on the bar as I rested on my elbows.

"You wouldn't happen to have prosecco in this fine establishment, would you?" I teased her, and she rolled her eyes, letting out a laugh.

"Sweetheart, we have hard liquor and beer. Would you like me to mix you a cocktail?" She poured a bunch of stuff into a glass.

"Sure."

"I'll mix you up something sweet. Oh wait—" She turned around, grabbed the tequila, and poured it into a shot glass. "You'll need this to deal with my brother." She slid the golden liquor over to me. I knew I would regret it, but she was right. I held the shot in my hand.

"Bottoms up." I shot it back, instantly regretting the taste. It burned my throat and made me gag. "Ugh!" I covered my mouth. "That's gross." I scrambled for a lemon to ease the intense flavor of the alcohol.

"I know." She bit her bottom lip with a grin. "But it'll get you to relax. You're so tense."

I reached for the cocktail she made for me because I could still taste the medicine-like notes of the tequila lingering in my throat. I chugged the drink to mask the taste before heading over to where Hephaestus was sitting.

The sudden rush of alcohol coursed through my veins, igniting a fire within me. I needed that edge, a bit of liquid courage, before facing my fiancé. I had to present an image he could trust, a façade that would keep him from seeing just how emotional and unstable I was. I needed information, and I couldn't afford to let him see my vulnerability.

There must be a deeper reason for the deal the club made with my father. No one just decides to suddenly jump into bed with the Aetos family. Why did my father turn to this gang for help when he could have chosen anyone else? To uncover the truth, I had to blend in, playing the part and navigating the dangerous currents of the club. I needed to convince them that I was one of their own.

A group of women surrounded Hephaestus as I approached him. Their hands all over his muscular body. I stood in front of him, trying to maintain a composed exterior. Inside, my heart pounded with frustration at their shameless display. A bitter mix of anger and wounded pride simmered within me. This was going to be my future husband, and his desperate need for these girls' attention showed a blatant lack of respect.

As I fought to keep my emotions in check, one woman suddenly charged toward him. She wore an Olympus Syndicate leather cut, the name "Athena" emblazoned across the front. The sight of her only intensified my fury. My eyes widened. The notorious maneater ravaged her victims in search of the truth. Athena resembled her brother Ares as well with her chocolate hair and eyes. Tall, strong, and exuding the aura of a fierce warrior, she briefly glanced in my direction before locking her gaze back on him.

“Hephaestus, your future wife is standing right here, and you’re fucking around with these sluts?” Her voice was a harsh, seething rasp, leaving me with no doubt that her disdain was genuine. She turned to walk away but I grabbed her wrist to stop her.

“Thank you,” I said.

“Don’t thank me. I wasn’t doing it for you; I was doing it because these sheep are driving me up the wall.” She shoved past me and dropped onto the leather bench beside Hades.

“Sheep?” I asked, trying to understand her choice of words.

“Yeah,” Hades said, taking a long sip from his beer. “Sheep are just girls who fuck guys in the gang, hoping to score a spot as an old lady.”

Hephaestus started removing himself from beneath their touch.

“Sorry, ladies, fun’s over. My future old lady is here.” He shrugged and withdrew his arms, observing me with the same predatory gaze he had given me earlier that morning. The women glared at me with snake-like eyes while I tried to maintain my composure.

I sat in the chair directly in front of him and placed my drink on the table, aware of his menacing stare.

Apollo raised his beer, his tone dripping with sarcasm, “Welcome to the family. We clearly need another woman around here.”

His comment earned him an annoyed look from Athena.

Prometheus skillfully whittled at some wood with his pocketknife while Hades reclined in his chair. Hades had a comforting presence about him, even though we barely knew each other.

"Where's Ares?" Hephaestus's voice rumbled, and I instinctively glanced over my shoulder.

"He's just finishing up." Hades sighed. A silence fell upon the group, leaving no sound between them. I knew the reason was because of me. I was still a stranger who invaded their personal space.

"Maybe I should go hang out with Artie," I suggested to Hephaestus who held a beer in his hand.

"You should," he said, then, getting closer to my ear, he whispered, "I need to chat with the group. We don't discuss club business in front of significant others."

"I thought we were going to get to know each other tonight." I had to avoid making him angry, so I tried flirting with him again. Leaning closer, I swept my hair away from my bare shoulders.

"We have all the time in the world to learn about each other. But right now, I need you to go. I have to talk to them." He nodded toward the rest of the MC members sitting around the table. "Wait for me there at the bar?" he said with a wink.

His arrogance was insufferable. I kept my cool, determined not to let his words get under my skin. I wasn't about to give him the satisfaction of seeing me falter. Just as Ouranos had taught me, I was skilled at concealing my genuine emotions behind a mask of indifference.

I faced him, tenderly touching his cheek as I uttered, "Very well." I walked away and made my way outside, craving the fresh air to help ease the weight on my chest.

I NEEDED TO GET THE HELL OUT OF THAT BAR. THE ATMOSPHERE WAS stifling, and it felt like the walls were closing in on me. Every pair of eyes seemed to bore into me with hostility, fueled by the gossip that I was the daughter of Ouranos. The noise, the crowd, the suffocating tension—it was all too much for me.

I quickly exited the main doors of the building. The chilly November air on my skin chilled the sweat from inside and sent shivers down my spine. Arms crossed, I made my way to the porch's edge and settled on the cement steps.

Ares rounded the corner, appearing out of nowhere. My lips parted, and he gazed at me, evoking the same lingering feeling I experienced in my room while observing him. I heated at the sight of him in the cool night.

He stood mere inches away. In a hushed tone, I whispered, "Ares."

His face was unshaven, and his bare arms revealed the sleeve of artwork adorning his skin. I longed to feel his arms around me again, protecting me from the darkness that lurked nearby.

*Stop thinking that way—he's the enemy.*

"Aphrodite," he whispered, leaning in. His voice resonated deep within me as his eyes locked onto mine. Every subtle shift of his body, every smoldering glance, intensified the heat in my core. His presence ignited something within me, a fire that grew hotter with each passing second. The way he moved effortlessly drew my attention, making my pulse quicken and catch my breath. My self-control slipped as the temptation became almost impossible to resist.

"I think I found some details about your brother," Ares said. But his words barely registered. His deep, smooth voice was like a melody that wrapped around me, scattering my thoughts. I struggled to focus, trying to remember what mattered most.

My brother

Titan.

*That was what I needed to prioritize, not this overwhelming attraction*

Blinking a couple of times to try to focus, I struggled to clear my mind. "You did?" I asked, shooting Ares a confused look, trying to break away from the intensity of his gaze. "What is it?"

"Come to Pandora on Friday. Hades should be there for this discussion—I'll make sure he brings you," he said, his voice urgent.

"Okay," I replied, fighting to keep my voice steady. There was something in the way he commanded that made it hard to resist.

Ares ascended the steps, each one bringing him closer until he was standing right beside me. His presence was overwhelming, the air between us charged with an intensity that made my knees weaken. I could feel the heat radiating from him, the unspoken connection drawing me in, making it hard to breathe. Every instinct told me to resist, but I found myself surrendering, letting the sensation wash over me as he stood so close, dominating my senses.

"If you let me watch after you, I'll make sure you won't regret it," he murmured, his voice a dark, seductive whisper, our lips just a breath apart. His words weren't just a request—they were a promise, laced with a dangerous allure that sent a shiver down my spine. The world around us faded into oblivion, leaving only the electric tension between us, a pull so intense it felt like it might devour us both.

# CHAPTER NINE

## ARES

Aphrodite's eyes haunted my dreams, lingering in the shadows of my mind long after I woke. I lay awake, staring out the window, the ache for just one more glimpse of her gnawing at me.

It was foolish, I knew, but the longing devoured every rational thought, leaving me restless, yearning, and on the edge of obsession. I couldn't shake the urge to see her again, even if just for a fleeting moment. The need to be near her was overwhelming, driving me to the brink of madness.

When I saw her at The Odyssey last week, the desire for her presence struck me like an insatiable hunger. I tried to resist, to pull away from her intoxicating allure, but the craving only grew stronger. I wanted to taste her, to feel her beneath my touch, to see how she would react in my grasp. The thought of her caught between desire and resistance only fueled the fire. She was beyond my reach, yet the need to claim her, to make her mine, was almost unbearable.

My hands twitched with a desperate need to touch her, as if she held the key to everything I was missing. Hephaestus could never be enough for a woman like her—no one could.

*Not even me.*

Darkness consumed me, no matter how hard I tried, the blood on my hands wouldn't wash away, staining every part of me with an inescapable shadow. Redemption was a distant dream, one I knew I didn't deserve.

If I ever dared to touch Aphrodite, I'd only drag her into the abyss that I couldn't escape. She was like a delicate flower, meant to bloom in the safety of a sunlit meadow, far from the shadows that clung to me. My very presence threatened to smother her light, to destroy the beauty she brought into this world. The more I longed for her, the more I knew that touching her would only bring ruin.

I threw myself into every job my father assigned, desperate to keep my mind off her. The road became my escape. That week, I rode my motorcycle along the desolate coast, letting the sound of crashing waves blend with the roar of the engine, trying to drown out the painful memories of the man I used to be.

After Titan's death, my main goal was to enhance security at Pandora. Trust was scarce when it came to money and power. Something significant was unfolding. I sensed it deep within me, and I wouldn't be caught unprepared.

I decided to assign Hades as head of security at Pandora. Losing my business partner changed everything, and I didn't want to feel vulnerable. Hades despised being involved, but he knew I trusted no one else. His imposing presence ensured that no one dared to challenge him without cause.

To unravel the mystery surrounding Titan's murder, Hades became my unwavering pillar of support and guidance. Each night, he would summon his soldiers as if from thin air and trained dogs would scour the club, sniffing for the slightest hint of explosives.

It didn't really make sense that someone would want to hurt Titan. He was the family's playboy, loved by everyone, always living it up with his money. Sure, he could be a target because of his wealth, but most people seemed to like him, so the thought of anyone wanting to harm him just didn't add up.

I knew Titan could be reckless with his questionable choices, and it was my mistake to think he could manage our investment wisely.

When I suggested involving Hermes in the club, I had my reservations. I was aware of Hermes's disdain for me, but with Titan's connection to him and Hermes's track record of success, there was a chance we could make something valuable out of it.

Hermes hated everything about Olympus Syndicate. He even claimed he wasn't my father's son, despite looking just like him. For a moment, I entertained the hope that Hermes might align himself with me and my business. However, that possibility quickly faded, and it became clear that things wouldn't unfold as I had hoped.

I needed to uncover the truth before it was too late. Aphrodite wanted every detail, so I invited her to visit Pandora on Friday. I hadn't mentioned that we'd be meeting with Hermes, but I was certain he wouldn't harm her.

Hermes was Atlas's son, and with Atlas being a close friend of Ouranos, Hermes would be cautious of any repercussions should any harm come to Aphrodite. It pained me to use her as leverage, but it was the only way to get the information we needed.

Friday nights at Pandora's were where the money was made. In the brisk November air, people waited in line for a chance to enter the nightclub.

As I sped down the road and took in everything ahead, a fire ignited in my heart, assuring me it was all worth it. Zeus despised everything about this business, but I had seized it as a chance to go legit. After countless close calls with arrest and brushes with death, I couldn't afford to take any more risks.

The street shimmered with vibrant blue lights as I entered my establishment, the glow hinting at the lavish experience inside. Warm golden tones illuminated the grandeur of the space, with walls adorned in intricate carvings that whispered of luxury and mystery. Designed to captivate, this place was a realm where opulence and exclusivity reigned supreme.

Enticing fragrances filled the air, skillfully masking the undertone of people and alcohol, creating an atmosphere that was sophisticated and alluring.

This wasn't just a club; it was a sanctuary for those cast aside by the elite and Ouranos. Nestled in Mysthria Harbour, Pandora became their haven, where they could indulge in the luxuries and pleasures often denied to them.

Here, amidst the opulent decor and enticing ambiance, the discarded found their escape, reveling in a world that celebrated what they'd been denied.

Everything was going well with the nightclub until we hit a snag after Titan's funds had dried up. He informed me that his father had restricted access to his accounts. His excessive spending was causing problems, he couldn't afford it. Meeting with Hermes became crucial to keeping the club afloat after Titan's loss.

"Hey, boss." Hades leaned against the polished railing, his all-black suit exuding sophistication. He cleared his throat, and the sound echoed in the spacious room, commanding attention. With his hair slicked back, he appeared groomed for the occasion.

I could tell he was uneasy when I mentioned the need to dress up. This isn't the clubhouse, and formal dress was required. Hades hated wearing suits— he always grumbled about feeling like a total idiot in them. Just mentioning it made him tense up, and I could practically hear him complaining about how ridiculous he thinks he looks in one right now. Hades nodded toward the person I dreaded facing, and a jolt of anxiety surged through me.

"She's here," he said, his tone heavy with the weight of the moment.

I scratched my chin, keeping my eyes on Hades.

"Good," I murmured, just as I felt a vibration in my pocket. Pulling out my phone, I glanced down to see Hermes's name flash across the screen. "Hermes," I told Hades, my voice low. "I'll meet him upstairs. Bring him up to the office, and I'll go get Aphrodite."

Hades looked at me, the strobe lights casting an enticing glow on his skin. "Yes master," he teased, a mischievous smirk playing at his lips. Unfazed, I simply shook my head and brushed past him, my mind already on what was next.

As I navigated through the crowd, I saw Aphrodite leaning against the bar, her eyes fixed on me. Her red dress hugged her curves, radiating an irresistible allure. My pulse quickened, desire flaring as I approached her. She was a temptation I was eager to surrender to, like a sweet addiction I craved more than anything.

I couldn't shake the feeling—she was luring me in.

She was a force I couldn't resist. My fingers lightly grazed her lower back, the warmth of her skin seeping into me like a forbidden flame. The heat between us was undeniable, a tantalizing promise of what lay beyond the boundaries I had just crossed.

"You've been hiding from me," I growled. Sexual tension surged through me, sending a rush of blood south and warmth flooding my veins. Control slipped further away with each passing second. Our eyes locked, and I couldn't tear my gaze from her lips, imagining the heat of her kiss. What would she do if I grabbed her waist, pulled her in, and let myself indulge in the taste of her delicate skin?

"No, I haven't," She cleared her throat.

"Whatever you say."

Our faces were so close, I could feel the warmth of her breath. As I slowly slid my fingers along her cheek, the softness of her skin sent a spark through me, igniting a fire deep inside. She was a goddess of passion and beauty, the embodiment of every desire I had tried to bury. My thoughts were consumed by her, by the way she drew me in without even trying, making me want her with a need that was almost impossible to resist.

Aphrodite gently pulled her face away from my fingers, creating a tantalizing distance that only made me crave her touch even more.

"Let's go," I said, my voice steady despite the tension between us. "Hermes is waiting for us in my office." I reached for her hand, and when she placed her palm in mine, a surge of warmth spread through me once more. If this was the only way I was going to touch her, I would savor it.

I led her through the crowd and up the stairs. As I released her hand, a hollow ache settled in my chest, intensifying with each step toward my office. I paused before entering the room and turned to her. Aphrodite seemed anxious, her breaths quick and shallow.

"What's wrong?" I asked, my voice laced with concern.

She ran a hand through her curly hair, her fingers trembling slightly. "I'm scared," she admitted, her voice tinged with vulnerability. "I know it sounds childish, but there's this heavy feeling in my chest that I can't shake."

I stepped closer, my gaze steady. "Titan always said you stayed out of this mess. But if you choose to dig into the truth, you're walking straight into hell—and I'll be right there with you." I brushed my fingers over her arm, feeling the warmth of her soft skin as she managed a small, determined smile.

Her eyes hardened with resolve. "I'm tired of being kept in the dark. I'm not naive. I know exactly what my father does and what my family represents. I need to know who killed my brother." I studied her, sensing the shift in her demeanor.

"And if you find out? What then?"

"I want—" She averted her gaze. I don't think she ever considered the outcome of finding out the truth. Aphrodite stared at me and said, "Justice. I want them to pay for what they have done. My brother died right in front of me. He's always had my back. This time..." She took a deep breath. "I'm going to have his."

I nodded but didn't say anything. I opened the door to my office, holding the door open and allowing her to enter first. The room was locked down, soundproofed, and equipped with monitors showing every nook and cranny of the nightclub.

A curved sofa lined one wall, while near the door, a formal desk stood, cluttered with the gaudy decorations Titan had insisted on.

While I was out working the floor, Titan would be holed up in this office, his presence lingering in the air. I hated this place. I'd rather be out in the club, feeling the energy, than stuck in here like he was. Titan loved it, though—usually with some girl in tow, looking for a little extra fun. This office felt like a cage compared to the life pulsing through the rest of the club.

Hermes lounged on the sofa, a drink already in hand, as we entered the room. The moment he saw Aphrodite, he rose to greet her, his movements oozing with that practiced charm I had always found infuriating. He took her hand with a smoothness that made my blood boil, then pressed a kiss to her knuckles. It wasn't just a polite gesture; it was a sleazy come-on, and I could see right through it. My chest tightened, a surge of anger flaring hotter than simple envy. It was a burning jealousy, a primal, uncontrollable need to claim what should be mine.

Hades stood by with his arms crossed, an unimpressed look on his face as I moved toward the lone chair beside him. Hermes lounged on the sofa with an easy smirk, looking far too comfortable for my liking. Aphrodite settled next to me, her presence grounding me.

"Thank you for coming," I said, adjusting myself and giving Hermes a hard look. He couldn't tear his eyes away from her, staring at her like she was a treat he longed to savor. He was the spitting image of our father, from his facial features down to his mannerisms.

Hermes stretched his arms across the back of the sofa, a smirk playing on his lips. "I guess Titan was supposed to come, but it seems you can't get a signal where he's at." He flashed a devilish grin, clearly thinking his joke was the perfect icebreaker.

*What an absolute fucking asshole.*

I noticed Aphrodite digging her fingers into the chair, her tension evident

Realizing his mistake, Hermes added, "I'm sorry, that was insensitive of me."

But Aphrodite wasn't having it. Her voice was firm as she demanded, "Tell me what you know about my brother's death."

Hermes raised an eyebrow, then took a sip of his drink before setting the glass down. "I guess we'll skip the foreplay," he said, clearing his throat. "I heard Titan was in financial trouble and used some of your father's enterprises as collateral."

Aphrodite's eyes widened in shock. "Titan didn't have control over those enterprises. He wasn't authorized to make any significant financial decisions," she said, her frustration edging into disbelief.

"Are you fucking kidding me? How the hell did that happen?" I spat, shaking my head in rage. My disbelief was raw and intense. I didn't trust a word coming from Hermes's smug mouth.

Hermes shrugged. "Atlas mentioned that Ouranos handed Titan a few businesses to play with last year." He paused, taking a slow sip of his drink before continuing, "But honestly, I can't believe Ouranos would give him that kind of responsibility. Titan was all talk when it came to business—guy was a fucking mess with money. And if that wasn't enough, he was sinking cash into another club here in Mysthria, thinking he could play the big shot like his old man. What a joke."

Aphrodite frowned, her voice tinged with confusion and disbelief. "My brother wasn't like Ouranos. He wouldn't have made a move like that without clearing it with our father first." Titan had potential—he could have achieved so much within the Aetos family. None of this added up.

I leaned in, frustration evident in my voice. "Titan made it clear he wasn't interested in any other ventures. This club was his sole focus—he didn't want distractions or side projects. His only goal was to make this place successful." I glared at Hermes, my impatience boiling over. "Don't play games, Hermes. Tell us the truth."

"I've heard that's the truth, straight from Atlas himself. He's tight with Ouranos, so I'd say he's got the inside scoop—unless, of course, someone's playing us for fools," Hermes said, his tone casually dismissive. He glanced at Aphrodite and added, "You know your father always leans on Atlas for advice. Maybe there's more going on that my old man doesn't want me in on." He shrugged, rubbing his chin thoughtfully, as if trying to piece together a puzzle he wasn't fully privy to.

Aphrodite's gaze darted between Hermes and me, confusion clouding her expression. "This just doesn't make sense. Why would Titan take such a risk?"

Hermes leaned back, his tone nonchalant. "All I can say is, maybe you didn't truly know your brother."

I snarled, "We don't even know if that's the truth."

Aphrodite's irritation was clear, her patience wearing thin with his dismissive attitude. The frustration etched on her face spoke volumes.

"Hermes, cut the bullshit and give us the real answers," Hades growled, his voice icy with anger. "Stop acting like a little prick. I know what you've been up to behind your father's back. You're no better than Titan was, and if you don't start talking, I'll make sure you regret every fucking second you've wasted." His eyes were dark and unforgiving.

*What was going on between Hermes and his father?* I thought.

Hermes conceded, the weight of the situation sinking in. He knew it would end badly for him if he didn't cooperate. "I can ask around," he said.

Aphrodite nodded. "Please do."

Hermes rose from the sofa, smoothing out his jacket. "I gotta bounce," he said. "You know if anyone catches me here," he smirked, throwing a wink our way, "People are gonna start talking." With that, he sauntered out, Hades following close behind. The door slammed shut behind them. I leaned back in the chair, watching as Aphrodite buried her face in her hands, the weight of everything settling in.

"It just doesn't add up," she murmured, her voice tinged with confusion. "Titan understood the risks of crossing Ouranos. He knew the consequences of meddling with things he wasn't supposed to. Ouranos knew Titan's habits; it's hard to believe he'd ever trust him with anything."

"Why?" I asked, my curiosity growing. Ouranos was a man who

kept everything close to the chest, and Titan's demeanor always shifted to something cold and distant whenever he spoke of his father.

"Ouranos is obsessed with control. He wouldn't just hand over his assets to Titan. Sure, he tried to involve Titan more in the business, but he wouldn't simply relinquish anything. You need to understand, I was never clued in on these details," she explained.

"I get it, Aphrodite," I said, my voice low as I rubbed my chin, trying to process everything. It was clear she was in the dark about much of this, and I was at a loss for how to ease her confusion. "Don't let Hermes get to you. He's a master at twisting the truth," I added. "I promised Titan I'd keep you safe, and I intend to follow through."

She looked up at me, her eyes rimmed with red and full of unspoken pain. I knelt before her, feeling the weight of her sadness in the silence between us.

"Thank you," she whispered, her voice barely audible but filled with gratitude.

I reached out, brushing away a solitary tear from her cheek. The electricity between us was palpable, the warmth of her skin beneath my fingers sending a jolt through me. My hand lingered, tracing down her jawline, every fiber of my being yearning for more.

I took a knee in front of her, caught in the pull of her gaze. The air between us was thick, every breath she took, every slight movement, pulling me deeper into the whirlpool of emotions I'd been trying to bury. Her lips parted slightly as if she was about to speak, but no words came—only silence, heavy and charged.

Aphrodite's hands trembled in her lap, and I couldn't stop myself from reaching out, my fingers grazing over her skin. The softness of her touch sent a shockwave through me, every nerve ending coming alive. She looked down at our hands, then back up at me, something unspoken passing between us—something neither of us was ready to acknowledge, but both of us felt.

"Why do you do this to me?" she whispered, her voice barely audible, but I heard it as clearly as a shout. The vulnerability in her tone cut through me, and I knew she felt it too—the magnetic pull that drew us together despite everything that should keep us apart.

"I can't help it," I admitted, my voice hoarse with restraint. "You're everything I shouldn't want, but the only thing I need."

She sucked in a sharp breath, her eyes fluttering shut for a moment as if to steel herself against the words. When she opened them again, the conflict was there, warring with the desire that simmered beneath the surface. My hand slid up her arm, fingers tracing the curve of her shoulder, and I felt her shiver under my touch.

"Ares..." she began, but the way she said my name, it wasn't a plea to stop. It was an invitation, a challenge. The tension between us was unbearable, coiling tighter with every passing second until it was ready to snap.

I leaned closer, my face inches from hers. My hand cupped her cheek, thumb brushing over her lower lip. The softness of her mouth beneath my touch was intoxicating, and I knew there was no going back.

She leaned into me, her eyes half-lidded, lips daring me to close the distance. And I did. With a surge of pent-up desire, I closed the gap, my lips crashing against hers with a hunger that had been building for far too long.

The moment our mouths met, everything else faded away—the confusion, the uncertainty, the promises we couldn't keep. All that mattered was the taste of her lips against mine, the way she melted into me, her hands clutching at my shoulders as if she needed me just as much as I needed her.

Our kiss deepened, the urgency in our movements intensifying as we gave in to everything we'd been holding back. Her fingers threaded through my hair, pulling me closer, and I groaned against her mouth, the sound vibrating between us. I was lost in her, in the way she moved, in the way her body pressed against mine, leaving no space between us.

When we finally broke apart, both of us were breathless, our foreheads resting against each other's. Her eyes were dark with desire, her lips swollen from the kiss, and I knew I was in deep—too deep to ever get out.

A knock sounded at the door, shattering the moment and bringing us back to reality. We quickly separated, the intensity of what had just happened still lingering in the air. "Come in," I commanded. Hades strolled back into the office, his presence a stark reminder of the world outside our bubble. "Hades will take you back to the compound," I said, my voice more composed than I felt.

I stole a quick glance at her, memories of our heated kiss still fresh in my mind. I wanted to reach out, to offer her some semblance of reassurance in the chaos that surrounded us.

"I have something for you," I said, picking up a burner phone from the table and placing it in her hand. "Keep it. Mine and Hades' numbers are saved. If you need anything, anything at all, just call."

Her eyes lingered on the phone, a mix of emotions flickering across her face. For a brief moment, I thought she might refuse it, but then she took it from my hand. "Thank you," she whispered again, her voice soft but sincere, yet tinged with the weight of everything we'd been through tonight.

As they left the office, the door closing behind them, the reality of the situation crashed down on me. The kiss, the anger, the confusion—it all boiled inside, threatening to tear me apart. I cradled my head in my hands, trying to stave off the overwhelming frustration that gnawed at my insides.

"Fuck!" I let out a thunderous growl, the sound echoing through the room as I hurled a tumbler with all my might. The glass shattered against the wall, the noise reverberating in the silence that followed. "What the fuck did you do, Titan?" I muttered, the words laced with a mix of anger and helplessness, the unanswered questions still burning in my mind.

The memory of Aphrodite's touch, the way she'd looked at me with those eyes full of unspoken words, only added to the torment. How had we ended up here, tangled in a web of lies and betrayal, with no clear path forward?

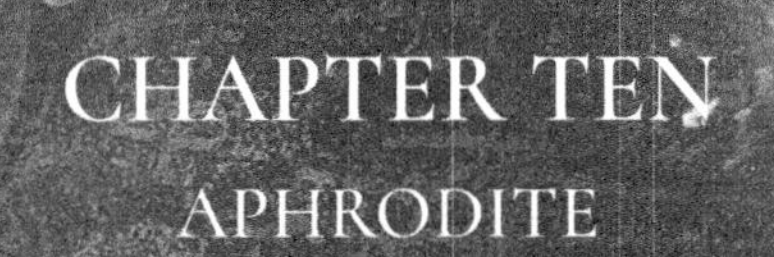

# CHAPTER TEN
## APHRODITE

"Where the hell have you been?" Hephaestus didn't bother to hide his irritation.

When Hades and I walked into the clubhouse, Hephaestus was lounging in a leather chair, puffing on a cigarette while Zeus and Apollo sat across from him.

The kiss with Ares had left my world spinning, the taste of him still lingering on my lips, a memory I couldn't shake. My thoughts were tangled in the heat of that moment, but as I stood before Hephaestus, I forced myself to bury it deep, acting as if nothing had changed.

Hades whispered, "Lie," then casually made his way toward the men in the sitting area. I kept my posture confident, determined to mask the turmoil brewing inside me. There was no way I was going to reveal where I'd really been.

"Hades helped me grab some personal items from the store," I replied smoothly, stepping closer to Hephaestus, slipping seamlessly into the role of his future wife

Hephaestus eyed me up and down, his scrutiny making me swallow hard. "You went to the store looking like a hooker?"

I met his gaze head-on, pushing down the rising fear. "I dressed like this for you. You don't like it?" My voice was steady, even as I felt the fury simmering beneath his menacing stare. Just then, Ouranos stepped forward from the shadows, his presence revealed.

He'd been there the whole time, silently observing. He made his way toward us, settling in front of me and grasping my chin with an aggressive touch, forcing me to meet his gaze. "You look pale," he remarked, his voice devoid of concern.

My blood boiled at his touch, rage bubbling up from the depths of my being. Ouranos filled me with such deep-seated hatred, it was a constant reminder of the pain he caused me. His mere presence felt like a weight on my soul, making me long to break free from the chains he represented.

*The wrong man died that night*, I thought.

He released his grip on me, but the sensation of his fingers lingered on my skin. He stalked back across the room and took a seat.

Hephaestus's eyes raked over me possessively. "I think she's perfectly fine," he declared, the edge in his voice unmistakable. As I tried to move toward another seat, his hand shot out, gripping my waist and yanking me onto his lap. His grip was unyielding, his fingers digging into my hip like he had no intention of ever letting go.

I turned to meet his piercing gaze, my heart pounding with a mix of anger and uncertainty, bracing myself for whatever twisted game he might be playing.

Ouranos watched from across the room, his presence a cold, silent force among the others. "Any progress catching the bastard responsible for my son's murder?" he asked.

"We have some insiders working on it," Zeus supplied.

Ouranos usually had an impressive poker face, always appearing detached, but tonight was different. Sweat beaded on his forehead, and his skin looked ghostly. Was Titan's death finally getting to him?

"Goddamn it!" He slammed his hand on the chair's armrest. "Your reputation is the best in this damn city. Zeus, you're usually fast as fucking lightning when shit hits the fan. How the hell do you not know who did this by now?"

Zeus fixed his gaze on the beer in his hand, his jaw tight as he cleared his throat.

"Ouranos, we formed an alliance that most people in our positions wouldn't ever consider. I'm tearing apart everything in my path to get to the truth, but that kind of shit doesn't happen overnight." He paused, taking a deliberate sip, the silence heavy between them. "I'm putting my entire empire on the line for you. So, before you fucking think about disrespecting me, you better take a long, hard look at what you're about to say next."

Fear was clear in Ouranos's expression.

Something wasn't right.

Ouranos leaned back in his chair, a calculated smirk playing on his lips. He looked around the room, his gaze icy and unyielding. "Let's discuss the wedding," he said, his voice cutting through the tension with deliberate, almost disdainful calm.

The abrupt change in topic was jarring, as if he were purposefully shifting the focus away from the heat of the earlier confrontation. The way he said it, with a tone that masked an undercurrent of control, made it clear he was ready to exert his influence in a new arena. The room seemed to tense in response, the air thickening with the weight of unspoken implications and the shift in power dynamics.

"So soon?" I blurted out, unable to keep my thoughts in check. The words were out before I could stop them, and instant regret shot through me as Hephaestus's grip on my hip tightened.

Hephaestus leaned in closer, his breath warm against my ear as he growled, "What, don't you want to marry me?" His voice was rough, tinged with both irritation and a challenge that sent a shiver down my spine.

Desperation gnawed at me. I needed to find a way to stall or derail this wedding, to give myself more time to figure out a solution. My gaze darted towards Hades, silently pleading for any sign of help or intervention. His expression was unreadable, but I could see the tension in his jaw and the flicker of concern in his eyes.

"Gaia wants her only remaining child with her," Ouranos said, a hint of finality in his voice. "So, you can go back home."

His words felt like a punch to the gut. Gaia had never shown any real concern for me before. Why this sudden change? I couldn't help but feel it was just another way to control me.

I looked at Hades, my heart heavy with the thought of going back to the manor. While this place was far from perfect, at least it offered some semblance of freedom compared to the stifling control I'd faced under my father's rule. Going back now felt like stepping into a cage, with Ouranos and Gaia pulling the strings from behind the bars.

Hephaestus snapped, "She's not leaving."

The command was sharp, his grip on my waist tightening possessively. I could feel the tension in the room escalate, like a brewing storm. My father's voice, however, was steady, calculated.

"You'll have plenty of time with her, but our time as a family is running out. I want my daughter with us leading up to the wedding," Ouranos insisted, his tone attempting to mask the underlying threat. "Plus, it's considered bad luck for the happy couple to share a bed before the wedding night."

My father, being protective? *What a joke.*

But I knew better. It wasn't about tradition or bad luck. It was about control. The manor was a different kind of prison, one I'd escaped only to find myself in another.

"She stays with my daughter," Zeus supplied, his voice final.

It was odd that my father had requested my presence at the manor. It was also out of character for Gaia to show interest in having me join them there. Thoughts raced through my mind. Was he aware of more than he let on? Was it risky for me to stay here? I couldn't ask him outright. He wouldn't tell me anyway.

My gut urged me not to rely on him, or any of these men for that matter. "I want to stay here so I can get to know my fiancé," I said, forcing a smile that barely masked the tension coiling inside me. I knew I had to play the part, to keep myself safe and in control.

Hephaestus's hand was like a vice on my waist, unrelenting, as if daring me to resist. I turned to meet his gaze, tightening my grip on his shoulder, willing myself to relax against his body. Beneath me, he felt solid, powerful, and I could feel the dark heat of his desire as his body responded to mine.

"See? She's fine with us," Hephaestus said, his voice laced with smug satisfaction as he held me close, as if I were a prize he'd won.

But he was delusional if he thought this game would lead to anything more. The tension between us crackled, charged with a mix of defiance and resentment. The darkness in his gaze only fueled my determination to keep him at bay. He might have thought he had control, but he couldn't have been more wrong.

I wasn't about to let him break me. This charade was all he would get, and if he expected anything more, he was going to be sorely disappointed. The grip he had on my body meant nothing; he would never touch my soul.

Ouranos rose from his seat, his expression hardening as he took in the unwelcome looks directed his way. "Fine," he said, his voice cold and clipped. "Keep me informed, Zeus." He straightened, holding his chin high, and then his gaze flicked toward me.

The bitterness twisted in my chest as I realized the cruel irony—now, of all times, he chose to be indifferent. The sting of his apathy cut deeper than any blade, a painful reminder of the father I'd never truly had. I'd always longed for a protector, someone who would shield me from the brutal reality of our world. But Ouranos had never been that man. Instead, he'd made it clear that I was nothing more than a pawn, a disposable piece in his twisted game.

I was meant to return to the Olympus compound, where I would be under Zeus's watchful eye. And despite the circumstances, I preferred the compound over the suffocating restraints of the manor. At least there, I could breathe, even if the air was heavy with expectations.

Hephaestus and I remained after everyone else had cleared the room. His grip prevented me from moving. All I wanted was to stand up and leave, but he wouldn't allow me to move.

"Tell me," Hephaestus's eyes locked onto me, his intense stare triggering a simmering anger deep within me, "why are you scared?"

I studied his face, anxiously chewing the inside of my cheek. "What do you mean? There's no reason for me to be afraid." I tried to sound convincing.

"It seems like you are." he whispered, his breath hot against my ear.

Hephaestus twirled a single strand of my curly hair around his finger, his touch deceptively gentle. "You have no reason to fear me," he murmured, his voice smooth but laced with an underlying threat. "I'd never harm you." As he released my hair, his hand slid to my neck, the possessiveness in his gaze sending a cold shiver through me. It felt like I was treading on thin ice, every step threatening to crack beneath me. His fingers tightened around my neck.

"You're lying to me," he hissed, his voice low and venomous.

"About what?" I forced out, trying to keep my voice steady.

He leaned in closer, the air between us charged with tension. "I can feel your heart racing," he said, his hand still tight around my neck. His thumb brushed against the pulse at my throat, a dark smile playing on his lips. "You're scared."

"I'm not," I whispered, though my voice wavered, betraying the fear I struggled to hide. His lips lingered near mine, his thumb tracing the curve of my neck. Without warning, he kissed me forcefully, his mouth overpowering mine with a dominance I couldn't escape. His tongue was assertive, demanding, but as I closed my eyes, my mind drifted to someone else—someone I truly wanted.

I imagined Ares, his lips crashing against mine with fierce intensity, the playful bite of his teeth sending a shiver down my spine. I longed for the way he made my heart race, the heat of his breath mingling with mine back in his office. The memory of his kiss consumed me, igniting a fire deep within that refused to be extinguished.

Hephaestus retreated and his eyes grew darker. He inhaled, and I could feel his body tensing. "Come to my room tonight?" Hephaestus's voice was a dark command, his eyes narrowing with expectation.

"Let's wait until after the wedding," I replied, forcing the words out as calmly as I could, even though the thought of being alone with him made my skin crawl. I knew I had to play the role of the future OS wife, pretending to be smitten with this man, when all I truly wanted was to uncover the truth about my brother.

His lips curled into a smirk. "You better be worth it."

*You unimaginable bastard.*

The thought burned in my mind, but I swallowed it down, knowing better than to let it slip.

"Wait and see," I spat through clenched teeth, barely restraining the fury simmering within me. My nails dug into my palms, a futile attempt to keep control when all I wanted was to scratch his eyes out. I straightened, meeting his gaze with a defiance I hoped masked the revulsion twisting in my gut.

Artie walked in. "Hey, Artie," I called out, rising from Hephaestus's grasp before he could restrain me again, thanking that Gods for this welcome interruption.

"Oh hey, I have some news." Artie went and stood by the bar, motioning for me to join her. Out of the corner of my eye, I noticed that Hephaestus didn't follow me. Instead, he got up and left the clubhouse.

I reached behind the bar, my fingers brushing the cool glass as I pulled out a shot of tequila. Artie's eyebrows shot up in curiosity, clearly wondering what that was all about.

Ignoring her questioning gaze, I tossed the shot back, savoring the burn as it scorched away the lingering taste of Hephaestus. I forced a smile, composed myself, and turned back to Artie as if nothing had happened.

"What's the news?" I asked, my smile still in place, though my thoughts were miles away.

"Zeus gave me the go-ahead for you to work with me at the Odyssey!" Artie nodded her head excitedly, her enthusiasm cutting through the tension I'd been holding onto.

"That's amazing! Thank you for this," I said, pulling her into a warm hug, which she eagerly returned.

This was exactly what I needed—a way in, a chance to gather the information I was after. If I was going to find the truth, I'd need all the help I could get.

LIGHTNING SHATTERED THE DARKNESS OF THE SKY, THE THUNDER JOLTING ME awake and out of my nightmare. It was the same dream every night, a flashback of the night of Titan's murder, his death on repeat. I groaned, covering my face in frustration.

Shadows danced on the walls as I fumbled for the lamp. Outside my window, movement caught my eye. I saw Ares entering his apartment, his silhouette framed by the rain-soaked night. I glanced at the clock—*three in the morning.*

I had left the drapes open, hoping to catch a glimpse of him, and now that I had, a tangled web of thoughts raced through my mind. I reached for the burner phone, hesitating as I considered calling him.

The kiss that had sparked between Hephaestus and me still burned vividly on my lips. Ares might already know about it, but I needed to hear his voice, to bridge the chasm of silence and tension that had built between us. The need to connect was overwhelming. I wanted to hear his voice, not just for the reassurance it might offer, but to feel that familiar warmth.

Instead, I reached for my phone and dialed Paris. Her number was a comfort, a familiar voice that could provide some solace. When her phone went straight to voicemail, I felt a pang of unease. I desperately wanted to know what was happening to her. The uncertainty gnawed at me, and the lack of information about her situation only deepened my helplessness.

*I was stuck.*

Just as I was about to put the phone down, my finger hovered over Ares's number. I hesitated, feeling the weight of the decision press heavily on my chest. My breath caught, and I bit hard on my bottom lip, torn between the intense longing to hear his voice and the fear of what giving in might mean.

I pressed the call button, the sound of the dial tone echoing in the quiet of my room. It rang twice, and I could already feel the heat rising in my cheeks, the anticipation mingling with the lingering confusion from earlier events.

"Aphrodite?" Ares voice was raspier than usual. I glanced through my window and observed him standing in his apartment.

"Ares... I had a nightmare," I began, my voice barely more than a whisper. "And I'm sure he's already boasted about it, but I thought I should tell you—Hephaestus kissed me... aggressively."

The confession hung in the air, heavy with the weight of unspoken desires and unresolved tension. I could almost hear his reaction, feel the intensity of his response even through the phone. The silence that followed was charged, a stark reminder of the electric connection that existed between us, lingering and undeniable.

He sat on his couch. "Tough night."

"I couldn't stand it, Ares." My voice weakened, guilt gnawing at me over kissing Hephaestus. But Ares wasn't mine, and I wasn't his. Our connection was nothing more than a fleeting, dangerous spark in a world where we were kept apart by more than just our feelings. Despite the kiss and the electric tension between us, we remained two separate entities, bound by circumstances and the harsh reality of our situations.

"Hephaestus becomes downright obsessive when he wants something," Ares said, his voice a dark rumble. "He turns into a relentless predator, a crazed stalker who will destroy anyone and anything in his path to get what he wants. He won't hesitate to tear apart anyone who stands in his way."

His statement left a tainted feeling in my heart.

I tried to change the subject. "My father was here, wanting an update."

"Did Ouranos say anything?" Ares asked.

I sighed, recalling the conversation. "He wanted me back, which was strange. He never really cared about me before, so it was surprising to hear him suddenly worried. And then, out of nowhere, he asked if there was any news," I explained, my tone reflecting the confusion and frustration I felt.

I got out of bed and walked over to the window, staring out as I tried to make sense of it all. My instincts told me to trust him, but it didn't make the situation any less perplexing.

"Him and Zeus had a tense conversation," I continued, turning back to Ares. "Ouranos mentioned that Gaia has made some new demands. She wants me to move back to the manor before the wedding."

Ares's expression darkened, and his voice grew cold. "Gaia's demands? That's not good. It means Ouranos is under pressure, and it's likely causing more instability. What does she want you for?"

I took a deep breath, trying to keep my composure. "She's insisting on more involvement from me in their family matters. It's strange, and I have this feeling there's more to it. But Ouranos wasn't very forthcoming with the details."

Ares's frustration was evident. "This is exactly what we didn't need—more complications. If Gaia's getting involved, it could mean she's planning something we don't know about. Be careful. They are using you as a pawn in their own games."

"I understand," I said, feeling a surge of anxiety. "I'll stay vigilant. But for now, all I want is to navigate through this with my sanity intact."

Ares's tone softened. "We'll figure this out together. Just keep your head up and stay focused."

"I will," I promised, determined to face the challenges ahead with whatever strength I could muster.

"Tell me about your dream," he asked, his voice low and sincere.

My heart ached, a deep, relentless pain that refused to let go. Ever since the explosion on Halloween, my dreams had been the same, night after night. I relived the horror of my brother being executed right in front of me. "I still see him, Ares. I see him being killed," I whispered, my voice trembling as my lips quivered. My lungs constricted, the memory suffocating me as if Hephaestus's hands were around my throat.

"I'm on my way," Ares said, his voice steady, before he hung up. I watched through tear-blurred eyes as he stood and headed for his door.

I dropped my phone on the nightstand and crawled back into bed, curling up as the immobilizing fear washed over me. I had never felt so paralyzed, so utterly lost. Time seemed to stretch unbearably, each second filled with the crushing weight of my anxiety. It felt like an eternity before he arrived. Then, I felt hands grasp mine—Ares, my lifeline amidst the chaos, grounding me when everything else was crumbling.

When he finally sat on the bed beside me, he pulled me close, wrapping me in his arms. Tears streamed down my face as I clung to his neck, my heart hammering against my chest. His hold on me tightened, and for the first time in what felt like ages, I felt safe—like he was a shield around me, protecting me from the darkness. Tremors coursed through my body, but Ares was there, his touch tender as he held my face and looked into my eyes. His gaze was raw, filled with a quiet strength that I desperately needed, and in that moment, I knew I wasn't alone.

"I will protect you, Aphrodite." he whispered, his voice barely audible over my sobs.

Ares licked his bottom lip, and a cold shiver ran through me at the mere thought of being bound to someone like him.

"I'm scared, Ares. I can't trust your family—or you," I admitted, feeling as if I were surrendering all my power to him. Ares's face remained a mask of stoic resolve, but his eyes were soft, carrying a depth of emotion that made my heart ache. "I understand where you're coming from, but you need to know that you don't have to face this darkness alone. I swear you can trust me. I promised your brother I'd protect you, and I will keep that promise."

"But why?" I asked, my voice trembling with uncertainty. "You have no obligation to me. I'm nothing to you."

His expression softened, and he reached out, his hand brushing against my cheek with a tenderness that made me shiver. "Stop," he said gently, his voice a soothing murmur. His thumb swept away a tear that had slipped down my face, and his touch was warm and comforting. In that moment, I felt a rare and profound sense of safety, as if his presence was a shield against all the chaos and fear that had been consuming me.

"Stay with me?" I asked, my voice barely more than a whisper. My fingers brushed against his cheek, feeling the roughness of his unshaven skin. I traced the line of his jaw, seeking solace in the closeness that now enveloped us.

"It's too risky." Ares's finger traced the slope from my neck to my shoulder before his face inched closer to mine. His breath brushed against my skin, sending shivers through me and leaving me feeling exposed and vulnerable in his embrace. I gently ran my fingers through his hair, relishing the silky softness and the intoxicating scent of his cologne that seemed to envelop me.

"I have to go before anyone notices," the urgency in his voice barely masked his reluctance.

"Okay," I replied softly. I leaned in and pressed a tender kiss to his cheek, savoring the taste of his skin, the warmth that lingered there.

Ares lifted me gently and placed me on the bed, his movements careful and deliberate, making sure I was settled comfortably beneath the blanket. Before he left, he bent down and placed a soft, lingering kiss on my forehead.

I didn't have any more nightmares after that.

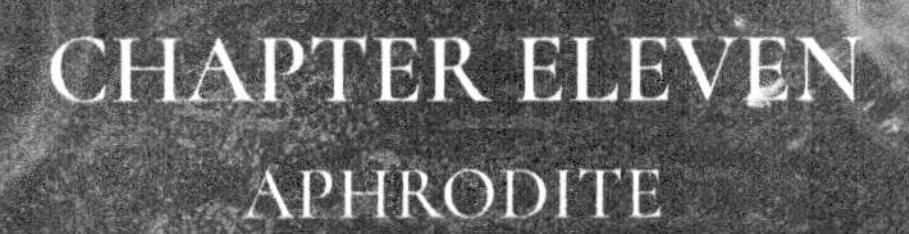

# CHAPTER ELEVEN
## APHRODITE

It was late afternoon, and Ares had been absent the entire day. I couldn't question his whereabouts without raising suspicion. Hephaestus was missing too. I had a shift at the Odyssey tonight, and I intended to gather all the information I could.

For three days, I'd been working at the Odyssey, soaking up every detail and scrap of information that came my way. Dressed in my most revealing shirts, I leaned in close, listening intently to every word those drunk idiots let slip.

As I entered the back door of the club, I passed through a hallway and noticed one of the doors was slightly ajar. Peering inside, I saw Apollo deep in conversation with Prometheus. Instinctively, I jumped back out of sight but lingered close enough to catch their words.

Apollo glanced around, unaware of my presence, "The shipment's arriving at the harbor tonight. Zeus requested we be there for twelve sharp."

"Any word on the size?" Prometheus asked, his expression serious.

Apollo crossed his arm, his tone tense, "Hephaestus said it's bigger than usual—high grade stuff. We can't afford any slip-ups."

Prometheus patted Apollo's arm, but his eyes suddenly caught sight of me. Both fell silent, exchanging a glance before they turned and walked away.

Since I'd arrived at the compound, the Syndicate had kept me in the dark about their activities. I wasn't naive—I had a good idea of what they were involved in. It was clear they didn't trust me enough to share the details, and I couldn't blame them for that. But I needed to show them I wasn't like Ouranos.

*I needed to prove I could be trusted.*

Curiosity gnawed at me, pushing me to uncover the origins of the Olympus Syndicate members. From the moment I started working at the bar, I made it my mission to engage with the regulars, subtly steering conversations toward the club whenever I could. If no one was willing to openly share what I needed to know, I was determined to find out on my own.

As I quietly observed and eavesdropped, it became clear that every member played a vital role in the MC's operations. Each one moved with purpose; their actions woven into the intricate fabric of the club's inner workings.

Athena commanded unwavering authority over every aspect of the compound's operations. Her sharp mind ensured that business was handled discreetly, with no rumors slipping through the cracks. Her approach to security was strict and unyielding.

Apollo had earned a reputation as the Syndicate's peacekeeper, known for his calm demeanor and steady hand. With a surprising amount of medical knowledge, he was the first person people turned to for help with a bullet wound.

Ares was war personified—a relentless force that commanded both fear and respect. The mere thought of how many men quaked in his presence sent a shiver of dark excitement through me. He was a warrior you didn't dare cross, a living weapon honed by Zeus himself into something far beyond human. To many, Ares was no longer just a man; he was a demon in flesh, an enigma only Hades could truly understand. Together, Ares and Hades were Olympus Syndicate's harbingers of death, hellish angels who dragged their enemies straight into the inferno. To face them was to face inevitable destruction.

Prometheus, recently released from prison after serving time for orchestrating a high-profile heist that shook the underworld, was the eldest amongst them, yet still a newcomer to the MC. Despite his age and time away, he wasted no time integrating into the Syndicate's ranks. He often shadowed Apollo, the two of them inseparable, like a formidable force of nature. Their combined reputation was ironclad—no one who dared to cross them ever lived to tell the tale.

The blaring music in the bar drowned out the chatter of the guests as I wiped down the countertop. It was a surprisingly busy Monday, and the bar was packed. Regulars moved at a relaxed pace, while Artie was deep in conversation with an old man about his problems.

Suddenly, the flash of motorcycle headlights cut through the windows. I tossed the towel aside and stepped closer to get a better look. Just outside, I caught sight of Hades and Apollo hurrying toward Ares.

"Artie!" I called out, still staring through the window. "Something's up!"

Without waiting for her response, I dropped everything and rushed outside, bolting toward the men.

Unease gripped me as I watched Apollo and Hades struggle to help Ares off his bike. My heart sank with each labored step they took, and I knew I couldn't just stand by. Driven by concern, I rushed to Hades's side as they maneuvered Ares into the clubhouse. They laid him out on the pool table, and it hit me like a cold wave—the table, likely serving as a makeshift operating station, was stained with the blood of previous injuries, the green velvet marred with grim evidence of past battles.

"What happened?" I cried out as Ares unleashed a string of

curses and groans while Apollo helped Ares out of his vest with careful precision. Ares's white shirt, drenched in blood, clung to his frame. Without hesitation, Apollo ripped the fabric open, his hands working with practiced urgency, revealing the gruesome, bloodied wound beneath.

Countless scars covered Ares's chest, telling a story of previous battles fought. His tattoos adorned most of his skin, but I could still make out the raised texture of the scars underneath.

"Grab the bandages from the closet next to the mini fridge," Apollo barked, his hands pressing down on Ares's abdomen to staunch the bleeding. I darted to the closet, rummaging through the shelves until I found the bandages, along with some gauze and anything else that might help.

Hades was already at work, wiping the blood from Ares's chest, revealing the ugly wound with a bullet lodged inside.

"Get me some fucking liquor!" Ares growled, his voice tight with urgency.

Ares's command roared through the massive building, bouncing off the ceilings and walls. I quickly grabbed the tequila, hoping it would ease his suffering. Panic consumed my soul. With trembling hands, I rushed to Ares's side, desperate to give him the bottle. He devoured the golden liquid in seconds.

"This is going to hurt." Apollo readied his medical tools while utilizing a pair of pliers. I pressed my hand against Ares's face, causing him to turn toward me. His dark brown eyes were filled with agony, reflecting the pain he was trying so hard to hide.

Hades pinned Ares to the pool table, his weight pressing down as Ares's body writhed in agony beneath him. Each spasm was a testament to the excruciating pain he was enduring. Apollo, his face a mask of grim determination, started the grueling operation, his hands moving with precise, practiced motions as he fought against the bleeding and chaos.

The tension in the room was suffocating, a cacophony of grunts and commands blending into a harsh symphony of suffering. In the midst of this frantic, clinical turmoil, I felt a rising sense of helplessness.

Without fully understanding why or how, I found myself breaking the oppressive silence. My voice, trembling at first, began to cut through the clamor. I started to sing, the notes emerging softly at first, but growing stronger as the melody took hold. The sudden, unexpected sound filled the room, a haunting contrast to the brutal reality unfolding before me.

I leaned in close to his ear, the warmth of my breath mingling with the coolness of his skin. My voice dropped to a whisper as I began to sing a song that had been a source of solace in my own darkest moments. It was a lullaby, one that my nanny used to sing softly to me whenever my father inflicted his physical pain upon me. I could almost feel her gentle arms around me again.

I sang with a trembling voice, hoping to divert his attention from the excruciating moment when Apollo extracted the bullet. I attempted to ignore his pale complexion as I caressed his cheek. Ares let out a gut-wrenching roar that shattered the air, a raw, primal cry of agony. The sound of the extracted bullet clinking into a stainless-steel tray followed.

"We need to cauterize the bullet wound. Hades, grab the knife and heat it up, quickly!" Apollo shouted at Hades as he applied pressure to the wound with his hands.

"Keep looking at me," Ares begged. He trembled, his face glistening with sweat as adrenaline seized his body. He shut his eyes and clenched his teeth. I climbed onto the pool table.

"What are you doing?" Apollo snapped, blood seeping through his fingers as he struggled to contain Ares' wound.

"I am trying to keep him calm," I snarled, my attention fixed on Ares. I grasped his face. "You focus on me, you hear me?" Ares's lips quivered while he attempted to avert his gaze. "Look at me. Just me." I kept repeating as Ares tried to focus.

Hades burst back into the room, wielding a fiery red knife in one hand and clutching a towel in the other. "Here, put this in his mouth.

We need to do this now." Hades threw me the towel, and I placed it into Ares's mouth.

"Look at me," I demanded. "I've got you."

He squeezed his eyes shut, and the smell of burning flesh hit me, making my stomach churn. But I remained composed, focusing on distracting him. His arms tightened around me, muscles going stiff with pain. I could feel his heart racing beneath my touch as I held his face, desperate to ease his suffering. His grip on my waist tightened, grounding us both in the moment, as if we were clinging to each other for strength. All I wanted was to take his pain away.

His body went limp.

He had passed out.

The noise and chaos diminished, leaving behind an eerie silence.

I let out a sharp cry, panic rising as I glanced urgently at Apollo. "What happened out there?" My heart pounded as I struggled to comprehend what had just transpired.

Ares lay motionless on the pool table, and the sight of him so vulnerable sent my mind spiraling. His normally strong muscles were slack and bloodied, revealing an intimate vulnerability that tore at me. The faint trail of hair on his chest led down to his abs, each rise and fall of his chest now a fragile hope. The tattoos marking the scars he had endured only deepened my fear.

I fought to steady my breath, each one a struggle against the crushing dread. The thought of him in pain gnawed at me, making it nearly impossible to focus.

"He'll be fine—this isn't his first rodeo." Apollo wiped the sweat from his forehead with the back of his hand.

Hades looked at me with unexpected admiration, which threw me off guard. "I've never seen him so calm," he said, narrowing his eyes at me.

"That was calm?" I shot a glance at Ares, then back at him, trying to process his words.

"Yeah," Hades said, pinching the bridge of his nose. "He's usually a fucking psycho. We usually have to wrestle him down just to keep him in check. He is our God of War, afterall"

The tension in the room was palpable, but I forced myself to maintain a neutral expression, hiding the chaos brewing inside me. "I've got a knack for handling tense situations," I said, attempting to keep my tone light despite the heavy atmosphere.

"Alright," Apollo replied, grabbing his belongings. "I need to go sterilize these."

Hades sighed, then added, "I'll get the stuff to clean him up." With that, he followed Apollo, leaving me to grapple with the storm of emotions crashing inside me.

With just the two of us alone, I couldn't resist reaching out to Ares. My fingers traced the intricate wing tattoo on his left rib, where an armor crest and shield were seamlessly woven into the design. Each detail of the tattoo seemed to embody his strength and resilience. As I lingered over the design, the warmth of his skin beneath my touch stirred a deep, unspoken connection within me, igniting a mix of awe and yearning.

A voice interrupted my daze, "That one is from the time he got into a fight with this chick named Medusa. She's got a few snakes loose in the head. She attacked him with a knife and stabbed him," I didn't notice that Hades had been standing behind me, watching me touch him. I pulled my hand away, and he gave me a playful smirk.

"You don't need to hide your feelings around me," he said quietly. "It's clear there's something going on between the two of you."

"There's nothing," I shot back, but even as I said it, I knew it wasn't true. There was something between us, whether I wanted to admit it or not.

"Here," he handed me a wet cloth. "I think he would prefer if you'd wipe him down instead of his uncle."

Ares remained unconscious, and I placed the cool cloth on his chest, attempting to clean off the dried blood. Hades went to fetch more bandages, and my hands continued to trace their way from his abs to his chest. Even beaten and bruised, he was still a sight to behold.

Ares's chiseled body was a masterpiece of raw, sensual power. His abs were a tight expanse of muscle, leading to a tapered waist that exuded strength. His broad shoulders and strong arms were veined and powerful, each tattoo a dark mark of his battles.

Ares's eyes fluttered open, and with a sudden, fierce intensity, his hand shot up to cup my cheek. Our eyes locked. He pulled me closer in an instant. Our bodies pressed together, our breaths mingling in the space between us. A blush warmed my cheeks as a thrill ran down my spine, sending goosebumps scattering across my skin.

Ares's lips crashed against mine, a kiss charged with raw, unspoken anguish. The contact was electrifying, a jolt that obliterated every previous memory of intimacy. His tongue, bold and insistent, tangled with mine, igniting a shivering ecstasy that coursed through me. A soft, desperate moan slipped from my lips as his rough hand slid down to caress my lower back, igniting a fierce longing deep within me.

I longed to be intoxicated by him, consumed by his touch, and to be the only woman he desired. Our lips separated, and I rested my forehead against his, wanting more but aware of all the risks involved in this dangerous game we were playing.

"I can't stop thinking about you." The words slipped from his lips, leaving me breathless and yearning for more. I reached for him again.

"Ares." I gasped, my heart pounding as panic set in. The situation was dangerous, and the intensity of the moment left me feeling charged, every touch and glance brimming with electric tension. It was as if my senses were heightened by fear, amplifying every flicker of arousal that coursed through me.

Every brush of his skin against mine felt like a spark, igniting a fire that I was both desperate to fan and terrified to fully embrace. I was lost in a whirlwind of desire and fear, the uncertainty inside me like a storm I couldn't control. Each heartbeat was a reminder of the risk we were taking, leaving me tangled in the perilous allure of our forbidden connection.

Hades cleared his throat, and I sat up, scrambling to distance myself from Ares.

"I'm sorry to interrupt," Hades interjected, "but you need to be more discreet."

I hopped off the pool table, but Ares's hand gripped my shirt with a desperate urgency. It wasn't aggressive, but a plea, a need that spoke volumes. I glanced at him, the intensity of his gaze reflecting the deep, unspoken connection we shared.

"Hades won't say anything," Ares whispered. "He's always had my back. I know my uncle, and he would never turn on us. He's on our side, through and through." He gently caressed my hand, and I felt a heavy pull, drawing me closer to him.

*We were playing with fire,* I thought.

Hades approached Ares and helped him to sit up. Ares groaned in response but managed to sit after some difficulty. I didn't know how he was handling the pain. Clearly, he had been through much worse encounters than this.

"Here you go," Hades said, delivering the extra bandages and setting them on the table. He turned to face me, "Wrap it up with lover boy. I'll keep a lookout." He winked before heading toward the front door.

I stared at Ares for a moment, my breath hitching as his hands grazed my hips and he pulled me close. His thick thighs trapped me in between them, and I felt the warmth of his breath before his lips brushed against my neck. Temptation flooded my senses, and though I fought to resist the urge to give in.

"Who shot you?" I asked, desperate to know how he got injured but also clearly trying to divert the conversation. I picked up the bandages and started carefully wrapping his wound. As I worked, he leaned in and pressed a gentle kiss to my shoulder.

Ares fixed his hooded eyes on me, and muttered, "Someone

ambushed me." He was alarmingly calm for someone who had just narrowly escaped death.

I held his rough hand. "What do you mean ambushed? Who's after you, Ares?"

He took my hand and lifted it to his lips, planting a firm kiss on the inside of my palm. "You don't have to worry. They can't kill me, no matter how hard they try." He tried to laugh but his throat hitched, and he coughed, wincing from the pain.

"We need to be cautious with everything that we do. From digging into Titan's past to navigating this"—I gestured between us — "They could be watching our every move."

"Take a breath, Aphrodite," he paused as he squeezed my hand reassuringly, "We will not get caught, and I will do everything in my power to make damn sure you don't end up marrying Hephaestus."

My heart sank, weighed down by the false hope that seemed to linger between us. I knew this fragile optimism was nothing more than an illusion, a fleeting comfort before the storm. It would guide us straight toward our inevitable demise, the thought settling like a stone in my chest. The air between us was thick with tension, and I could almost feel the darkness closing in, threatening to engulf us both.

# CHAPTER TWELVE
## ARES

I jolted awake, heart hammering, cold sweat clinging to my skin, haunted by the memory of her lips on mine—an intoxicating vision that wouldn't let me go.

Groaning from the searing pain in my abdomen where the bullet had torn through, my thoughts still fixated on Aphrodite. Her voice, her song, the way fear had darkened her hazel eyes as she cradled my face—none of it made sense anymore. My mind was a chaotic mess.

The overwhelming magnetism that drew me to her was a force so intense it overshadowed the pain in my body. How could someone who was supposed to be off-limits, someone I was meant to protect, spark this kind of chaos within me? The way she had sung to me last night, as if she could calm the very storm that raged inside, went beyond mere care—it was intimate, dangerously so.

Her fear, the way she looked at me with those wide, hazel eyes, should have made me pull back, should have reminded me of the boundaries we couldn't cross. But instead, it only intensified the gravity between us, muddling everything I thought I knew about myself.

I swung my legs over the edge of the bed, cradling my throbbing head in my hands. A pill bottle, water, and a note with my name on it sat on the table. I reached for the note, flipping it open with trembling fingers.

*Get better, Ares. I need you.*
*-A.*

My lungs tightened as I reread that brief sentence. Nothing about this should have happened, yet I couldn't deny the visceral need to be near her, to touch her again, even if it meant unraveling everything else in the process.

The emotions raging within my heart were relentless. They consumed me, driving me to act on impulses I knew would endanger us, yet I was powerless to resist her allure.

I grabbed the pill bottle and swallowed a couple capsules to ease my pain. I needed to figure out who shot me while I was driving back from Pandora. It felt like venom was seeping into my veins, igniting a familiar, dangerous fire within me. The kind that always signals I'm on the brink of unleashing hell—the wrath that makes me the God of War. The urge to tear someone apart was overpowering, as if the poison demanded a sacrifice.

I SHOWERED AND SLIPPED INTO FRESH CLOTHES, EACH MOVEMENT A BATTLE against the sharp pain slicing through my side. But the physical agony was nothing compared to the turmoil in my mind as I headed toward the clubhouse. The events of last night played on a loop, haunting my thoughts.

I'd been on my motorcycle, tearing down the highway when I caught sight of them—what looked like the Four Horsemen, a name whispered in the shadows of the underground. We all knew who they were by now, an upstart gang hell-bent on making a name for themselves. They were nothing more than amateurs, but even amateurs could be deadly when desperate enough. Clad in black, their silhouettes blurred with the night, they were armed to the teeth as they chased me down the barely lit road. I knew someone had followed me, tracked my every move, because they'd known exactly where to intercept me on my route back to Olympus Syndicate.

As I pushed through the pain and walked into the clubhouse, I couldn't shake the sense that this wasn't just a random encounter. This was calculated—a message, and I was the intended recipient.

I burst into the meeting room, catching my father and Hephaestus deep in conversation. The moment I entered, all eyes snapped to me, their expressions a mix of shock and disbelief, as if they were seeing a ghost.

"Can someone explain what the hell happened last night? Because I could swear, I was fucking ambushed!" I slammed my hands against the table, the impact echoing throughout the room. Zeus didn't flinch, he kept his chin up, eyes narrowing with that familiar spark of anger directed right at me.

"Maybe it had to do with your little nightclub, Ares?" Zeus said, his tone cold and clipped. He leaned forward, intertwining his fingers like he had all the answers.

"It had nothing to do with Pandora, and you know it," I shot back, crossing my arms over my chest, my teeth grinding as anger boiled up inside me.

"How do you know? Maybe your partner skimmed some cash and got caught up in some drug trafficking deal gone wrong." Zeus sneered, his eyes narrowing as they flicked over to Hephaestus. "He found out Titan was messing with other crews, including the Four Horsemen. He's been running his mouth about it for weeks, stirring up shit like he always does."

My brother was already smirking, his usual shit-eating grin plastered across his face. He'd always seen me as unfit to lead, and over the years, he'd worked tirelessly to sow those seeds of doubt throughout the Syndicate. Zeus, as always, sided with him, never once trusting me to take the reins.

Hephaestus had been harboring a grudge ever since the accident. He was convinced that I was somehow responsible, even though I wasn't anywhere near it when it happened. But that didn't matter to him. He'd been gunning for me ever since, determined to drag me down at every turn. And Zeus, blinded by his own ambitions, fed into my brother's delusions, fueling the fire that now threatened to consume us all.

"No fucking way—Titan wouldn't pull that kind of shit off without me knowing about it," I growled, my whole body tensing up from the pain and frustration. Titan might've been a dumbass, but he wasn't stupid enough to cross other gangs. He knew damn well that if he crossed that line, he'd have to answer to Ouranos.

"That's your problem, Ares," Hephaestus sneered, leaning back like he'd already won. "You have no clue how things work in our world. You're always distracted with that little dance club of yours, thinking you know what's what in the underground. But you don't. You never will."

I clenched my fists, barely holding back the urge to knock that smug grin off his face. He'd been manipulating the Syndicate for years, turning them against me, and I wanted nothing more than to put an end to it, once and for all.

"Enough!" Athena's voice cut through the tension like a knife. "Stop with the pissing contest, this isn't about you, Hephaestus. Ares got shot. One of our own. We should be focused on that instead of pointing fingers right now."

Zeus exhaled sharply, running a hand through his hair. "We need to figure out who killed Titan to get Ouranos off our backs. Hephaestus thinks Hermes might have some intel, so I'm going to talk to him. We also received word that there may be some evidence left at the scene of the explosion. My contact at the station will get us the details soon."

"Let me get this straight," I snapped, unable to mask my frustration, "You have crucial information about the crime and decided not to share it with us?"

Zeus's gaze was icy. "I'm dealing with it alongside Hephaestus. We don't need to lay out every detail until we have the full picture. We're managing it."

"That's exactly the problem," I shot back, my anger flaring. "We're supposed to be a club, and decisions like this are supposed to be made together. You can't just withhold information and handle it on your own."

"That's enough, Ares!" Zeus roared with anger in his eyes. He continued, "Hades will accompany you on all your future outings." His tone leaving no room for argument.

I felt my fists clench at his words. A babysitter? Are you fucking kidding me? The irritation bubbled up inside me. I didn't need anyone riding shotgun on my runs.

I leaned back in my chair, narrowing my eyes at Zeus. "What? You don't think I can handle myself?"

Zeus didn't flinch. "This isn't about whether you can handle yourself, Ares. It's about making sure we're covered. We can't afford any more surprises like the last one.

"So now you're sending a babysitter?"

"You know damn well that's not what this is," Zeus shot back, his voice steady and controlled. "Hades knows how you operate, and he's got your back in ways others don't. We need more than just brute force; we need strategy. And if something goes south, you'll want someone who knows how to get out clean."

"Fine," I muttered, my tone grudging. "But this doesn't change how I do things."

Zeus leaned back in his chair, his tone sharp and dismissive. "Now, if you could kindly fuck off, I need to go over the plan Ouranos gave us."

Frustration clawed at me as I pinched the bridge of my nose, trying to keep my temper in check. "What plan? Did you even bother to call for a meeting, or are you just making decisions on your own now?"

Hephaestus, lounging in his chair like he owned the place, laced his fingers behind his head and watched me with that insufferable smirk of his. His eyes were locked onto mine, enjoying the show as if he couldn't wait to see me explode

"We need to get our shit together and unite this fucking club," Zeus growled, his voice low and dangerous. "All this fighting is ripping us apart from the inside. I won't stand for another fallout—not in my lifetime. You hear me?" His words were edged with a lethal determination, each one a cold promise that he would see this club survive, no matter what.

While there's plenty of history in the Olympus Syndicate, the incident Zeus referred to was a dark chapter between him and his brothers.

Zeus and Poseidon never got along, which made Hades the reluctant peacekeeper between the two of them. After my grandfather, Chaos, announced that Zeus was to be the successor of Olympus, Poseidon's rage was volcanic. He demanded that he should be the one in charge. In his fury, he broke away to make his own chapter of Olympus in the shadowy town of Neptunian. The split improved their relationship; with Poseidon ruling Neptunian, their encounters were rare, limited to major deliveries shrouded in secrecy.

Zeus continued, "I had a call with Ouranos about the future of our families and how we can benefit from each other's connections. We talked about him allowing us to use the Aetherion Bridge for when we meet with Poseidon in December. He gave us the go ahead."

The room was thick with tension, every eye locked on Zeus as the weight of his announcement hung heavily in the air. I glanced at Hades, who was clearly struggling to process what Zeus had just laid out.

"Are you fucking kidding me?" Hades slammed his hand on the

table, his voice dripping with disbelief. "We're just supposed to give him a cut? What's the fucking percentage?"

Zeus's expression was cold and unyielding. "He gets his cut. That's all you need to know."

Hades's anger flared. "And you think that's enough? We need specifics, not this bullshit."

"That doesn't matter," Zeus snapped back. "Hephaestus has already dealt with Poseidon and his crew at Neptunian. The arrangements are made. It's done."

Athena's patience snapped. "What's the fucking point of having us here if you've already made all the decisions? This is complete bullshit."

Hephaestus's frustration was clear. "I handled it. There was no need for a debate. It was under control."

Zeus's gaze turned icy as he locked eyes with Hephaestus. "Care to share the news with everyone, or should I?"

Hades's arms were crossed, his stance challenging. "What news?"

Hephaestus's voice dropped to a harsh growl. "We're moving the wedding up. Aphrodite and I are getting married in a week." His face twisted in disgust, as if he'd just tasted something foul.

Athena's laughter was bitter and sarcastic. "Why the hell are you rushing it? Did you knock her up or something?"

Zeus's face darkened with anger. "Ouranos wants it sooner. It's not up for fucking discussion."

Hades and I exchanged puzzled glances, the urgency in Zeus's words only adding to our confusion. We both understood the gravity of alliances in the world we navigated, but the rush to accelerate the wedding left us questioning why.

Zeus's voice cut through the murmur of disbelief. "This alliance with the Aetos family isn't just about formality," he began, his tone resolute and uncompromising. "It's a strategic move that will bolster our power. We're ramping this up to gain control over every single thing that moves in and out of Aeolopolis City. We're not just expanding our reach—we're tightening our grip."

He swept his gaze around the room, his intensity demanding attention. "The Aetos family brings more than just their name. They control vital trade routes and have significant influence over the local economy. This isn't merely about a marriage; it's about securing our dominance and ensuring that no one can challenge our authority."

My eyes remained locked on Hephaestus, searching for some hint of explanation or justification. His stoic expression did little to clarify why this rushed marriage was so critical.

Hades's frown deepened as he absorbed Zeus's words. "So, this is all about consolidating power and making sure we have absolute control?"

Zeus nodded, his expression hardening. "Exactly. It's about positioning ourselves as the undisputed rulers of Aeolopolis City. The sooner we solidify this alliance, the stronger our position will be."

The weight of Zeus's words settled heavily in the room, the urgency now clear but still clouded by questions about the reasons for the accelerated timeline.

THE CRISP NIGHT AIR DEVOURED THE REMNANTS OF DAYLIGHT AS I SAT ON MY motorcycle, engine rumbling, ready to roar into the darkness. I was heading back to Pandora, but as I glanced up, I saw Aphrodite emerging from her apartment building. Her loose curls tumbled down her back in a cascade of rich, dark waves, shimmering under the streetlights. She stood there, framed by the building's entrance, her gaze locked on me.

The sensual moments we shared were branded in my mind. A searing reminder of how easily she had breached the walls I'd carefully constructed around myself. Every nerve in my body seemed to remember it, and as I watched her, the haunting pull of that moment tightened its grip on me. I couldn't escape the shiver that ran through me, or the way her image seemed to burn itself into the backdrop of the night.

Aphrodite's gaze remained fixed on me, her lips so full and tempting. She mouthed a greeting, her breath visible in the cold air. I rode over to where she was standing.

"What are you doing outside? The clubhouse is closed." I scratched my neck, resisting the urge to reach for her.

"I came to see you—Wanted to see how you're feeling after everything that happened." She stepped closer and pushed a strand of hair away from her face.

"I'll be fine." I flashed her a wink, making a move to leave, but her hand settled gently on my arm.

"Ares, someone shot you."

"Scars are like trophies," I said with a smirk, running my tongue over my bottom lip. The roar of the engine masked the thudding of my heart, but I could feel its frantic rhythm. The building's dimmed exterior lights softened her gaze, yet the same dangerous allure in her eyes was unmistakable, mirroring the turmoil stirring within me.

"I saw all of the scars, Ares..." She paused, releasing my arm, which felt cold now without her touch. "Did you mean what you said to me?"

My heart twisted, torn between desire and caution. She had a way of making me feel weak, clouding my judgment. "Come with me to Pandora," I whispered, my voice a low rumble. Giving into temptation, I reached out and pulled her close.

Aphrodite's lips parted as my hand tightened around her waist, the magnetic pull between us impossible to ignore. I wanted to be alone with her.

She was hesitant, but we locked eyes, and I handed her a helmet. She took it and slipped it on, then swung a leg over my motorcycle, straddling it with graceful ease. Her arms wrapped around my waist, and I could feel the warmth of her breasts pressing against my back. My hand instinctively gripped her thigh, the undeniable pull between us growing stronger, every touch intensifying the tension that crackled in the air.

The roar of our departure made her grip tighten around me. I couldn't help but picture her naked, riding me, her skin covered in goosebumps of pleasure. Just the thought made my dick twitch, and when I stopped at the lights and she squeezed my thigh, it only made things worse. A rebellious lust consumed me, and I knew I was unable to resist its control for long.

Arriving at the rear of Pandora's parking lot, I offered my hand to assist her as she got off the motorcycle. "What are we doing here?" she asked.

I reached for her hand, my fingers lingering on hers as I whispered, "This is a place where we can be ourselves, away from prying eyes." Her captivating gaze met mine with an intensity that made my pulse quicken. The air between us crackled with an undeniable energy, and I felt a raw, almost primal urge to pull her closer, to lose myself in the depth of her presence. Her eyes, dark and mesmerizing, fueled a fierce desire within me—one that was impossible to ignore.

We entered Pandora through the back door and made our way toward the stairs leading to my office. The nightclub was in full swing, with the DJ playing loud music, setting the energetic atmosphere. The erotic energy of the dance floor pulsed all around us as we snaked our way through the crowd and up the stairs.

I closed my office door behind us while she took off her jacket and placed it on the couch. She brushed her fingers along the edge of the sofa while glancing around the room.

"Is this where you want me?" Her eyes glistened like diamonds, sharp enough to cut.

I rubbed the back of my neck, her words alone sending a surge of heat through me, my dick pulsing hard against the constraints of my jeans.

Shrugging off my jacket, I moved toward her, the need to claim her was almost overwhelming. Despite the throbbing desire coursing through me, I managed to say, "I didn't come here to have sex with you, Aphrodite." But even as the words left my mouth, I knew it was a lie—I wanted nothing more than to devour her completely.

She gasped, clearly flustered. "No, I—uh, meant is this where we can talk without being watched?" She was backpedaling, and I couldn't help but enjoy it. I sat back at my desk, relishing the sight of her squirming under my gaze. Her tight black top clung to her, her rapid heartbeat visible, and I watched as she swallowed hard, trying to regain her composure.

Without a word, I grasped her hand and drew her toward me, lifting her with ease until she was straddling my lap. Her forehead rested gently against mine, and our breaths intertwined, each exhale mingling in a shared rhythm. The tension surged between us.

"You do strange things to me, Ares. I can't explain it," she confessed. I closed my eyes and inhaled her sweet perfume. The warmth of her body was deeply comforting. "I feel the same way." I laughed. "You make me feel things I've never felt before, and that terrifies me."

Aphrodite crushed her lips against mine with such force that it pushed me back slightly. There was no time to think—only the raw, electric energy between us, igniting something primal inside me. I wanted her. Badly. The taste of her fervent kiss overwhelmed me, threatening to consume every last shred of control I had left. Our tongues tangled as she began grinding against my jeans, my cock growing stiffer with each passing second. Her movements quickened, and I gripped her thighs tightly, lifting her until we were both standing. Aphrodite wrapped her arms around my neck, pulling me closer.

In one swift motion, I spun her around and laid her down on the sofa, her breath coming in quick, shallow gasps. With another desperate kiss, I pulled her into the darkest depths of my desire. The fire inside me raged uncontrollably, consuming every rational thought and igniting an uncontrollable blaze that threatened to engulf us both.

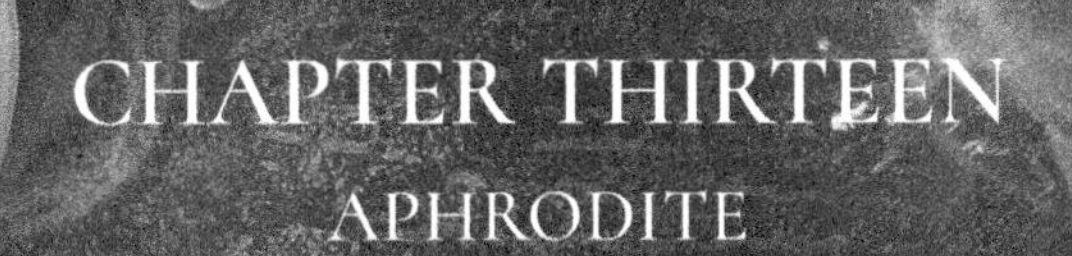

# CHAPTER THIRTEEN
## APHRODITE

Our kiss went beyond the boundaries of time and space. We couldn't deny the intense longing we felt for each other any longer. I had never seen such burning desire so clearly reflected in someone's eyes before. The intensity in his gaze, the way he looked at me as if I were the only thing he wanted, left no room for doubt. It was as if his need for me radiated from him, impossible to ignore.

I felt Ares's lips on my shoulder while I traced the waistband of his jeans. It sent a wave of pleasure through me. I tugged his shirt up, and he pulled away to take it off. The light revealed the bandage covering his wound.

He drew me in again. Ares hovered over me, looking like a Greek God, and I was overwhelmed with temptation as I felt his heat overcome me.

The hunger I saw in his eyes ignited something inside of me as his hands traced the curves of my body. He must have seen my unspoken thoughts written on my face, as his own expression changed. We withdrew from each other slightly, and Ares looked at me, forcing me to meet his eyes.

"You seem distracted, Aphrodite." he implied, hooded eyes on me. Ares rolled aside onto the couch and placed one hand behind his head while the other held me close. I leaned against him and traced his chest, feeling his heart racing.

"It's nothing," I teased with a playful smile, but his grip tightened on my hip, sending a jolt of electricity through me. I exhaled slowly, my body responding with a tingling wave of anticipation.

"You're not being honest," he murmured, his eyes dark with desire. I could feel the heat of his excitement pressing against my leg, amplifying the electric tension between us.

I was teetering on the brink, longing for nothing more than to feel him inside of me. I didn't want to hold back any longer, yet a lingering fear of the unknown held me back, keeping me on the edge. I wanted to jump.

"You make me feel like I'm dancing with fire," I confessed, swallowing my words with instant regret.

"Tell me to stop." Ares lips inched closer to mine again as his hooded eyes watched me with predatory excitement.

Our breaths mingled, a tantalizing mix of danger and desire. My heart pounded in my chest, and every nerve in my body screamed for him, for this moment.

"I can't," I whispered, my voice trembling with the weight of my longing.

A wicked smile curved his lips as he closed the distance between us, his hands cradling my face with a possessive tenderness. "Good," he murmured against my mouth, his words a sultry promise. "Because I have no intention of stopping."

Ares was about to strike a match to a fire I was not sure I was prepared to take hold of. My willpower was dwindling. I knew that if this were to happen between us, I'd be embarking on a path where I had no control, surrendering to a journey that could spiral beyond my reach.

The thought of losing myself in the unknown was both exhilarating and terrifying, a dangerous allure that promised both thrilling highs and unpredictable lows.

Ares continued, "I meant what I said, Aphrodite. I will do anything to protect you." His fingers gently brushed my cheek. "We will put a stop this wedding."

I wanted nothing to do with this wedding with Hephaestus. The way he grabbed me, pulling me close as he announced we were getting married, was aggressive, to say the least. He was rough, and the memory of that forceful encounter still haunted me. I knew that even if he wanted to, Ares couldn't step in without risking his life.

"Ares, you can't take any risks. I won't let you jeopardize your life for me." A single tear ran down my hot cheek.

"I'll go to any lengths to make sure you're safe," he murmured, his face inches from mine, "even if it means taking his life. I'll do it for you."

I saw the creases around his eyes deepen. I ran my fingers over his cheek and felt the stubble that he hadn't shaved away. His intense gaze softened for a moment, revealing a flicker of something deeper.

"What are you afraid of, Ares?" I asked, my voice gentle but insistent.

Ares took a deep breath, his fingers gently threading through my hair. "My biggest fear?" he began, his voice low and tinged with a painful honesty. "It's that the demons in my head will consume the last bit of good left in me. Zeus has molded me into his weapon, and there's blood on my hands because of him."

I looked up at him, a fierce protective instinct rising within me. "Why would Zeus do that to you?"

Ares's expression grew troubled, his eyes clouded with a mix of regret and anger. "I was his enforcer, his right hand in a world of shadows. I did his dirty work, carried out orders that I now wish I could erase. My past is riddled with decisions I can't take back—choices that have left scars on my soul. I've been used and twisted by his ambitions, and now I'm stuck dealing with the mess left behind."

He shrugged, but there was a raw edge to his demeanor. "I don't have all the answers. I don't know why he chose me or why he continues to hold me in his grasp. But you don't need to worry about it," he added, though his eyes betrayed a flicker of vulnerability.

"You will not go down that path again, Ares." I pressed my hand on his heart, "I will do anything it takes to make sure of it."

"Why would you try to protect me?" Ares narrowed his eyes, sadness lingering in his gaze. "Because something deep inside me is pulling me toward you, and I can't fight it. I won't fight it."

I closed the gap between us, and our lips met again. The forbidden attraction between us defied all logic, a powerful force that pulled us together despite the risks. Our electric connection sparked a fire deep within me, a relentless craving to intertwine with him, to merge our souls in a blaze of intensity.

I threw off my shirt in a swift motion, and Ares reached around and quickly unclasped my bra. He hovered above me again, his gaze filled with an intoxicating allure that made me gasp. We clung to each other. My body arched into him as he kissed my neck. He slowly trailed kisses down to the area between my breasts while he unbuttoned my jeans.

A moan escaped my lips as he kissed my skin gently, "Take me, Ares."

His rough hand dove under the waistband of my jeans.

"I want to taste what is mine." He tugged off my jeans and threw them on the floor, he removed my panties but instead of tossing them aside, he stuck them in his back pocket. The heat inside of me was a blazing inferno, and he was fanning the flames.

"Tell me what's yours," I said, my naked body now on display for him. He gazed down at me and spread my legs so that I was bared fully to him, a devilish smile appeared on his face.

"Every," he pressed his lips against one thigh, "inch," he repeated the action on the other side, "of your body," he whispered, moving closer to my clit, "and soul." I could feel his hot breath on me, and suddenly, his mouth.

He captured my clit in an instant, and my eyes rolled back as his tongue flickered in a tantalizing motion. I ran my hands through his hair, squeezing him between my thighs with each delicious stroke he made. Ares hungered only for me. He drove his fingers into me, and the sensation of his touch nearly sent me over the edge. My heart raced for him.

"You're my goddess, Aphrodite. I want to bow down to your pussy," he growled, making me whimper as I gave into his control. My nipples hardened while his fingers drove into me again and again without missing a beat.

My legs quivered from his fingers hitting that tender spot inside of me, as he sucked my clit with determination. His other hand reached around my waist and held me firmly in place, as he ravaged my pussy.

I squeezed my eyes shut, feeling the euphoria of the orgasm begin to take over my body. I unraveled, climaxing fiercely, my body convulsing in pleasure as he continued to pump at an unyielding pace.

"Ares!" I cried with passion as my toes curled, pulsations wracking my body as I came apart beneath him.

TIME SLIPPED THROUGH OUR FINGERS LIKE SAND IN AN HOURGLASS AS WE slept peacefully on the sofa, our bodies entangled in a comfortable embrace.

My eyes fluttered open, and I gently traced my fingers across his face, feeling the warmth of his skin beneath my touch. A heartbeat later, he stirred and opened his eyes, his gaze meeting mine with a mixture of relief and determination. He tightened his embrace around me, and in his arms, the remnants of my nightmares seemed to dissolve into the safety of his presence.

He was my warrior, my shield against the darkness and the

unknown that lurked beyond. As we talked, sharing the fragments of our pasts and our present struggles, we discovered a profound connection.

Despite the different paths we had taken, we found ourselves remarkably alike—both cast aside by the societies that should have nurtured us. We were survivors, shaped by our experiences and united by the sense of being outsiders, but in each other's company, we found a solace that felt both rare and deeply familiar.

Ares gave a low rumble and nuzzled into my shoulder. I felt his body tighten around me, and an overwhelming sense of longing surged through me—I never wanted him to let go. The desire to stay in this moment forever, to merge completely with him, was almost overpowering.

I gently ran my fingers through his hair, savoring the softness and the intimacy of our touch. As our lips met again, the world seemed to fade away, leaving only the profound connection we shared in our embrace.

He kissed me so intensely that it felt like he was attempting to inhale life itself. My heart fluttered wildly, and butterflies seemed to take over every muscle in my body. When he finally pulled away, his eyes still smoldering, he said, "We slept."

I reluctantly met his gaze, a heavy sense of dread settling over me. "We need to go," I said, struggling to shake off the reluctance that made my heart ache. The comfort of our moment was a stark contrast to the storm we were about to face.

Ares glanced at his watch, his face tightening with urgency. "Fuck—we do have to go. It's one in the morning." I scrambled to gather my clothes, and as I dressed, he pressed soft, lingering kisses along my back. The scene felt almost adolescent, like we were sneaking around to avoid being caught by parents.

But the reality was far grimmer.

The people we were avoiding weren't just disapproving—they'd kill us. Literally.

"How are we going to get inside the clubhouse without being noticed?" I asked, struggling to pull on my shirt.

"There isn't a way of not being noticed, baby," he replied, his voice heavy with unease.

HOLDING ONTO ARES, WE PULLED INTO THE COMPOUND AND PARKED HIS bike. Outside, I saw Hephaestus, Apollo, and Hades smoking cigarettes. They watched us as we rolled up, and I tightened my grip on Ares's waist.

*They've caught us.*

After we stopped, Ares reached out to help me down.

Hephaestus walked over to me with determination. He towered over me as he roared, "Where the hell have you been?" His gaze was like daggers.

I froze and couldn't find the right words to lie with, but Ares spoke up.

"Hephaestus, calm the fuck down. We took a drive." Ares's voice was deep with anger.

"You can't be whoring yourself out to other club members, Aphrodite. We're engaged." He clenched his jaw as his icy eyes darkened. He leaned closer to me, and I felt uncomfortable by his proximity. I attempted to keep it casual and walk past him.

"I'm going to head to bed," I said, but before I could take a step, Hephaestus grabbed my wrist and yanked me toward him.

"You don't have the privilege of leaving," he snapped.

Ares let out a low growl and stepped closer to Hephaestus. Apollo and Hades moved in. My heart ached as the invisible battle between these men turned into a harsh reality.

"Let her go," Ares hissed, his voice a low growl of barely contained fury.

"Stop, Hephaestus," I interjected, stepping between them. "I just wanted to go for a ride, and I'm sorry I didn't ask you first. If it helps, I'll stay with you tonight." I placed my hands gently on his chest, hoping to offer some reassurance. But Hephaestus remained rigid, his eyes locked on Ares with a scowl that seemed to seethe with unspoken tension.

I made the offer to distract him, fearing that the situation might spiral out of control if I did nothing. But despite my attempts to calm the storm, both men seemed to disregard me entirely, their focus unwavering and the air crackling with unresolved conflict.

Ares took a step closer, his presence like a storm bearing down, dangerous and unstoppable. "I said, let her go," he snarled, the warning in his voice unmistakable.

Hephaestus's grip on my wrist tightened painfully, his gaze finally dropping to meet mine, there was no softness in his eyes, "You think you can just throw yourself at me to fix this?" His voice was low, filled with a bitterness that sent a chill down my spine. "You think I'm some fool who'll just forget because you flash a smile?"

"Hephaestus, it's not like that," I pleaded, but the words felt hollow, lost in the whirlwind of tension that surrounded us. This wasn't just about a ride—it was about control, power, and a long-standing rivalry.

Ares's eyes darkened, his patience clearly worn thin. "You're making a mistake," he warned, each word sharp as a blade. "This isn't a fight you want to start."

Hephaestus's lips curled into a sneer, his grip like a vise around my wrist. "You think you can take whatever you want? Whenever you want?" His voice dripped with venom, the anger boiling over into something darker.

I could feel the situation slipping further out of control, the danger escalating with every heartbeat. "Hephaestus, please," I begged, leaning into him, trying to break through the rage that had consumed him. "This isn't worth it—just let it go."

He stood in front of Ares. A clash of the titans. They were

prepared to fight, and that was the last thing I wanted to happen. I knew it would lead to repercussions, or serious injuries.

"What? Are you worried that she would want me over you?" Ares said, flashing a cocky smile. "Why wouldn't she? You're a miserable excuse for a man—a terrible human who hurts others just to feel strong. But here's the truth: No one cares if you live or die."

Hephaestus lunged at Ares, his fist aimed squarely at his rival's jaw, but Ares was quicker. With a lightning-fast punch, he sent Hephaestus staggering back, his footing faltering.

In an instant, Ares transformed before my eyes—no longer just a man but a predator, driven by a primal rage that both mesmerized and terrified me. His intensity was like a storm, an unrelenting force of raw emotion and fury that left no room for mercy. This was the warrior Zeus had forged, a side of Ares I had never truly witnessed until now.

The two men crashed to the ground, locked in a brutal struggle, their bodies rolling as they exchanged vicious blows. I watched as Ares gained the upper hand, straddling Hephaestus and raining down punches with merciless precision. Each strike echoed with the sound of flesh meeting bone, and I could see the blood starting to stain the ground beneath them.

"Stop, Ares!" I pleaded, my voice trembling as I reached out to him, desperate to break through the storm of violence. But Ares was lost in it, consumed by a wrath so intense that it seemed unstoppable.

I pulled at Ares's arm to get him to slow down or stop, but as the other men tried to yank me out of the way, Ares thrust his fist into my ribs, and I fell backward, the impact jolting through my tailbone and knocking the breath from my lungs.

Laying on the ground, cradling my ribs, I watched as Ares finally broke free from his rage and realized what he had done. His eyes widened, and he jumped off Hephaestus, trying to rush to my side.

Hades moved swiftly, seizing Ares in a firm grip, holding him back as he fought to break free. "Aphrodite, I'm so sorry," Ares called out, his voice cracking with a mixture of anguish and regret. "I didn't mean to—I thought you were Hades!"

Apollo rushed over to me and offered his help. The pain radiating from my ribs made it hard to stand, but I leaned into Apollo, grateful for his support.

Ares struggled fiercely against Hades, his eyes locked on me with a desperate, pleading intensity. "Please, Aphrodite!" he shouted, straining against Hades's hold. "I never meant to hurt you—please, look at me!"

But I couldn't. The man I thought I knew had transformed into someone terrifying, someone capable of losing control so completely that he could mistake me for an enemy. The realization twisted my heart, leaving a cold, hollow ache in its place. I turned away, unable to look at him, the echoes of his rage ringing in my ears.

Hephaestus, still bleeding from the beating, dragged himself over to me, his expression more irritated than concerned. "Are you okay?" he asked, the annoyance clear in his tone as if my well-being was just another inconvenience.

I nodded, forcing myself to appear strong, even though everything inside me felt like it was unraveling. I could feel the intensity of Ares's gaze on me as he struggled against Hades, desperately trying to reach me.

I LET HEPHAESTUS CARRY ME TO ARTIE'S APARTMENT. "I'VE GOT YOU," HE said, planting a kiss on my forehead. It was a surprising shift from his earlier annoyance, and I wasn't sure how to react.

One minute he'd been grumbling and looking like he couldn't care less, and now he was being all sweet and caring. It was confusing as hell. I wasn't sure if I should just go with it or be suspicious of this sudden change. My mind was a mess, trying to figure out what was real and what wasn't. Artie was not at home.

Hephaestus entered my room, and I felt uneasy as he put me down. Something was not right. He went to reach for me, but I slipped away from him. I could sense the emptiness he felt in the space I left behind.

"I'm sorry, Aphrodite," he said, his voice rough with regret. "I know I've been distant, more a dark shadow than a welcoming presence. That's going to change, whether I'm ready or not." He rubbed his fingers across the bridge of his nose, a sign of his internal turmoil.

"Everything's a mess right now. I don't even know how to start being real with you. It's like I'm trapped in my own darkness, and I'm not sure how to break free."

"It's fine," I said, forcing a small smile without meeting his eyes. I was too overwhelmed by everything that had just happened, and my rib throbbed painfully from the hit. "I just need some sleep."

Hephaestus gave a nod and headed for the door, leaving me behind in the shadows of the apartment. I wanted to break down and cry. Even though I'd been terrified of Ares during the fight, all I really wanted was to hold him close. I was caught in a whirlwind of mixed feelings.

As I watched my fiancé leave, I felt completely lost.

I pressed my hands to my forehead, struggling to keep from collapsing under the crushing weight of my thoughts. It felt as though I was sinking deeper into an abyss of turmoil, unable to catch my breath or find any sliver of peace amidst the chaos.

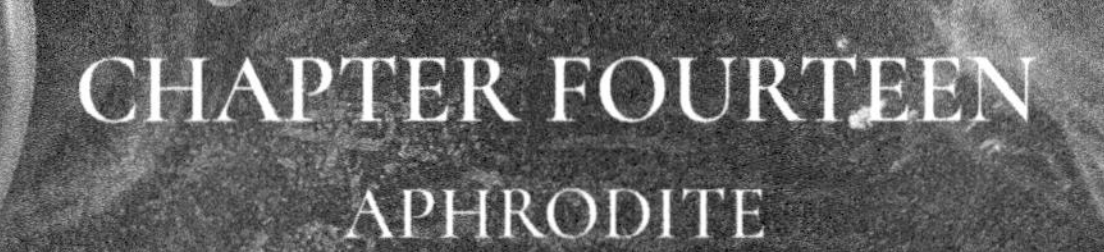

# CHAPTER FOURTEEN

## APHRODITE

"Titan!" I screamed as I abruptly sat up in bed. Two days have passed since the fight between Ares and Hephaestus, and the recurring nightmares have returned.

Since the altercation, everything seemed thrown off, like a train had been derailed from its tracks. I'd tried reaching out to Ares, but he kept his distance, leaving me with a gnawing sense of uncertainty.

I struggled to push aside my feelings for him, but my heart refused to let go.

Ares was a whirlwind of contradictions—calm yet chaotic, a source of both tranquility and turmoil. Perhaps he was keeping his distance because he needed time to sort through his own storm of emotions, or maybe he was trying to protect me from the chaos that seemed to follow him. Either way, his absence only intensified the storm brewing inside me, making it even harder to find my footing in this disarray.

His touch haunted me like a ghost that refused to fade. I closed my eyes, desperately yearning to feel the warmth of his skin against mine once more. I longed for those moments when our eyes met, sharing a silent, powerful connection as we held each other close.

But instead, I found myself alone, the bed beside me cold and empty. The absence of his touch was a void that echoed through the stillness of the room, leaving me with a deep, aching loneliness. The shadows of our shared moments lingered, amplifying the emptiness I felt.

My wedding day was quickly approaching, and all I wanted was to escape this inevitable fate. Wherever I looked, Hephaestus was there.

He was a venom that was consuming me.

It felt like he was monitoring my every move. I couldn't handle it. It felt suffocating being trapped within the compound walls. He disapproved of me working at Odyssey, but I wasn't about to stop and forfeit my plan to gather information that could potentially solve my brother's murder.

I was scheduled to have my dress fitting today to meet the demands of the rushed wedding Ouranos insisted on. Although I despised the thought of marrying Hephaestus—I, as the future bride, had to play the role. I knew that I still had to try and stop this wedding from happening, but the time to do so was slipping away from me, and fast.

I STOOD ON THE PLATFORM, STARING AT MY REFLECTION IN THE MIRROR. THE white silk dress clung to my body, but it felt more like a noose tightening around my neck—a symbol of my impending demise. A seamstress knelt at my feet, meticulously adjusting the hemline while Gaia circled me like a hawk eyeing its prey, her gaze sharp and unforgiving. She didn't miss a single flaw, pointing out every imperfection with a cold detachment.

The room buzzed with chatter, but all I could hear was the

relentless pounding of my heart, anxiety gripping me like a vise. My father's lie to Zeus about Gaia wanting to be involved in my dress fitting was apparent—Gaia didn't care about any of this. If she had her way, she'd have me eliminated without a second thought.

This was supposed to be a special moment, one I should have shared with my biological mother, but that chance was lost to me. Instead, I was trapped here with a woman who had despised me since the day I was brought to the manor as a baby. Gaia had never shown me a shred of love, and in this moment, her disdain was as palpable as the silk constricting around my throat.

Gaia looked as though she hadn't slept or taken care of herself since Titan's murder. Her skin was pale and fragile, and she wore no makeup. I couldn't help but wonder if my real mother had felt this same kind of pain when she lost me. Did she weep like Gaia, whose every breath seemed to shatter her more?

As she glanced over at me, her gaze was a haunting reflection of Titan's. For a brief, fleeting moment, I saw a shadow of him in her eyes, a resonant reminder of his presence. It was as if Titan's spirit was manifesting through her, bridging the gap between the living and the lost.

The resemblance was almost too much to bear, and I felt a sudden, overwhelming rush of his essence surrounding me. I closed my eyes, struggling to capture and hold onto that fragile, transient connection. It was a brief encounter with his memory that made the grief feel both distant and immediate, a reminder of the depth of our shared loss.

*I need to know why he was murdered.*

Salvation was what I really needed right now.

"You know you're lucky." Gaia spoke as my eyes widened from the sound of her voice. We were alone. I stared at her from the mirror as she crossed her arms tightly against her chest.

"Lucky? How so?" I questioned as I watched her slither around the room.

"You will be free from the Aetos family now that you are marrying Hephaestus."

"You think that's freedom? I was given over to him as bargaining chip." My voice deepened with anger, feeling the strain of her words. There's no such thing as freedom in this life.

Gaia let out a cold laugh, shaking her head in disdain. "You're delusional, thinking you're worth anything. You've never mattered, and you never will."

Without waiting for my response, Gaia turned on her heel and left the room, her footsteps echoing ominously as she walked away. The door clicked shut behind her, plunging me into a heavy silence that seemed to press down on me from all sides.

Anxiety surged through me like a relentless storm, its intensity making my chest feel as though it were being squeezed by an invisible vice. Each breath became labored and shallow, as if the air itself had thickened and become more difficult to draw in. The weight of her words lingered, amplifying the crushing sense of dread that filled the room.

I GAZED THROUGH THE WINDOW AS THE BLACK RANGE ROVER PULLED INTO the compound, lost in thought, before coming to an abrupt stop. I hopped out, and before I could even close the door all the way, Gaia's driver took off, peeling out of the parking lot.

My life had so little value to my family. I was nothing more than an object to be used and mistreated, something to be discarded easily, without care or appreciation.

I walked into the Odyssey and music was blaring, the bass reverberating through my feet. The song, *You Don't Own Me* by Lesley Gore was playing, which seemed fitting for my current situation. Artie was setting up for a local band that was going to be playing. She noticed me walking over as she was pulling out the tables for guests.

"Look at the blushing bride," she teased with a playful smirk.

In the short time I'd been here, Artie was the only person who seemed to genuinely care about how I felt. Her presence had a soothing effect, providing a comfort I desperately needed. Paris would have adored her. I wished she were here—or at least would respond to my calls. I'd texted her several times over the past few days, but there had been no reply.

"I guess tonight's theme is badass women in music," Artie said, heading over to her phone to select the next track. "I'm all about that energy, but don't let it fool you. I'm no badass."

"Why not?" I asked, raising an eyebrow. "You and Athena always seem to hold your own against the men around you."

"That's exactly the problem," Artie said, pointing at me. "Hephaestus can't stand that Athena is part of the gang. He believes women don't belong in his world—a world he thinks is strictly for men."

I looked at her, puzzled. "I thought you were okay with the wedding."

"You seemed fine with it."

"I'm not," she said. "Hephaestus always acts like he's better than everyone else. He's never satisfied—always wants more, always looking to crush anyone in his way. And Ares? He's his favorite target. Don't think I haven't noticed the spark between you two. I'm not blind. I can see it in the way Ares is around you. He's into you, and trust me, that's not something you see often with him."

Artie's troubled expression sliced through me, dragging my guilt to the surface. Her concern was a reminder of the tangled mess I was in. After the argument, I knew I had to distance myself from Ares to focus on what really matters—finding the killer to my brother's murder.

Avenging his death demanded my full attention, pulling me away from the intoxicating, dangerous allure of Ares. As much as the spark between us burned fiercely, the shadows of my brother's death loomed larger, and I would do anything to find the answers I so desperately needed.

"I'm trying to find the individual responsible for murdering my brother, Artie. Ares offered his help." The feelings of guilt persisted, and I found myself unable to deceive her further. Artie leaned against the bar.

Crossing her arms, she said, "I'll help, but can you promise me something?"

"Yeah, of course."

"Do not hurt my brother. He may never heal from it."

Artie had a profound affection for her brother, and I realized I had to honor and respect their bond. The same principle had applied to my relationship with Titan. Despite him being my older half-brother, I had always attempted to safeguard his heart.

I told her I would do my best not to hurt him, even though I knew I couldn't make any promises. I realized that my actions could have consequences that I wouldn't be able to shield him from, but my emotions would have to be put aside for now.

THE CROWD AT ODYSSEY WAS LOUD. THE MUSIC BLASTED FROM THE speakers, making the counters vibrate. Artie juggled serving multiple men while I struggled to make one mixed drink. Prometheus surprised us by jumping in to help and together we worked as a team.

People poured into the club, a mixture of familiar faces and strangers. Hephaestus sat in the back corner with an older man and Apollo. Although I had conflicting emotions about Ares, I had hoped to see him tonight. He was unpredictable, and I didn't know how I felt about everything that had happened two nights ago.

"Hey, do you mind bringing these over to the guys?" Artie asked while handing me a tray of miscellaneous shots. I nodded and accepted the tray.

Trying to keep the liquor balanced, I made my way around the bar and through the crowd. I noticed Ares sitting with the members of Olympus Syndicate. Hephaestus was leading the conversation, and as I approached, he stopped talking and looked up at me.

"Look, it's my beautiful future wife," he said. I placed the tray on the table, and he pulled me toward his lap. My skirt slid up, but his arms trapped me in place, stopping me from being able to adjust it. Out of nowhere, he planted a forceful kiss on me, catching me completely off guard. I tried to pull away, but he held me tighter. It felt like he was a snake wrapping around its prey, ready to crush and consume it.

"What's the matter?" His hand held the back of my neck. I looked into his eyes, struggling to come to terms with the fact that this man was going to be my husband.

"Nothing." I plastered on a fake smile as my curls draped over my face.

"So, as I was saying..." Hephaestus leaned his head away from me and continued chatting with the people at the table.

Under Ares's piercing gaze, I felt a shiver crawl up my spine. Every fiber of my being strained to look away, using every last ounce of self-control I had. I feared that any misstep or careless word from Hephaestus could ignite Ares's simmering rage, setting off a chain reaction that would spiral out of control. The weight of this anxiety pressed heavily on my chest, making it almost impossible to breathe.

"...Ouranos wants the wedding to take place at the Aetos manor. I thought it would be best to ask my future bride it she has a preference."

Everyone seemed indifferent to what he was talking about. Athena was engrossed in a conversation with Apollo, and Hades had a woman sitting on his lap. Meanwhile, another woman slid into the seat next to Ares.

With her golden hair cascading in soft waves around her sweet, angelic face, she looked stunning—almost ethereal. The fitted black dress she wore clung to her curves, the fabric hugging every contour of her body, accentuating her figure in a way that drew every eye in the room.

She leaned into him, pressing her breasts against his side, and the sight sent a sharp sting of jealousy through me. His lips moved close to her ear, whispering something that made her giggle, her eyes twinkling with mischief. I swallowed hard, trying to push down the envy burning inside me, and turned to Hephaestus.

"I would love that," I said, forcing a smile.

In a moment of weakness, driven by the need to silence the gnawing jealousy, I kissed him. I shut my eyes, desperately imagining Ares's lips tracing my skin, caressing me with the same intensity I craved. But as my eyes fluttered open, the fantasy shattered, yanking me back to the cold reality of where I was and who I was with.

The kiss with Hephaestus was empty, a poor substitute for the one I truly longed for. Hephaestus whispered into my ear, "I like kissing you," his breath caressed my skin. It didn't spark the same fire in me that Ares's breath did; instead, it left me feeling cold, a knot of unease twisting in my gut.

"I need to head back to work, Artie is a bit overwhelmed," I said, trying to change the topic, but he only clung onto me tighter.

"She can handle it." He grabbed one of the shots I had brought over for them. He threw the amber liquid back in one gulp, then emitted a low growl. His blue eyes lingered on me with determination. I pressed the palm of my hands against his chest, attempting to flirt my way out of his hold. "I'll be right back," I said with a wink, feeling his grip loosen just enough for me to slip free and stand up.

"Fine," he muttered, licking his bottom lip. I stole a quick glance at him before my gaze drifted to Ares, who was deeply engaged in conversation with the woman sitting beside him.

Desperate to get away, I headed toward the back of the club, my heart pounding with each step I took. I pushed open the door to the restroom and looked around at the cold, sterile space. It offered no comfort. I leaned against the sink, staring at my reflection, feeling the weight of my situation crushing down on me.

Foolishly, I thought I could escape. That maybe there was a way out of this nightmare. I even scanned the restroom for a window or a hidden door, something—anything—that could lead me to freedom. But there was nothing. No secret passage, no emergency exit. Just cold tile and the hum of the fluorescent lights above me.

The reality hit me like a ton of bricks—I couldn't run. The Olympus Syndicate would hunt me down, and my father would never let me go. I was trapped, with no way out, and the walls seemed to close in tighter with every breath I took.

I attempted to conceal my tears and splashed some cold water on my face to try and regain my composure. At that moment, the beautiful blonde woman who I saw with Ares entered the room. I casually reached for a paper towel to dry my face.

"You're Aphrodite, right?" The woman caught my eye in the mirror. She crossed her arms over her chest, pushing up her ample bosom as if to flaunt her curves.

"Yes?" I said as I threw out the paper towel. I could see that I annoyed her as she watched me with serpent-like eyes.

"Listen, you need to stay away from my boyfriend. I've heard rumors that you've been getting too close to Ares. He has no interest in you, got it?" She moved closer, jabbing her finger in my face. I wanted to slap her then, but causing a scene was out of the question.

"Who told you that about me and Ares?" I snapped back. *Was there talk?*

"Honey, you can't be that naive. There are eyes everywhere." She let out a devilish laugh, her glare was unsettling.

"Don't worry, I don't want him." I said, feeling small and like I wanted to be anywhere but here. Pushing the door of the women's restroom open, I headed back towards the bar focusing on my task at hand. Talk to the patrons. There was a man sitting at the bar who I managed to strike up a conversation with.

"You're Ouranos' daughter?" The elderly man was probably pushing eighty. He had a thick white beard and short silver hair. He seemed frail, but somehow, he still seemed to have life in his eyes.

"I am," I slid him his beer, giving him my full attention.

"It's sad what happened to your brother." He said to me as he took a sip.

I flashed him a small smile that didn't meet my eyes, not knowing what to say to that. "Eventually, the truth will come out," he said, his voice a dark rumble that seemed to seep into the room like a creeping shadow.

I froze, my pulse quickening as the weight of his words sank in. The way he spoke sent a chill through me, a warning that whatever he was hinting at was far more dangerous than I could imagine. "What do you mean by that?" I asked, my voice barely steady as I took a cautious step back.

His eyes locked onto mine, a sinister gleam flickering within them as a slow, wicked grin spread across his face. "Oh, darling, where's the thrill in giving everything away at once?"

His cryptic words wrapped around me like a tightening noose. I was done with the twisted games and the endless mind tricks.

I needed to speak to Hermes again. He's already given me some information about my brother's murder, and during our encounter I couldn't shake the feeling that he was holding back. If there was more to uncover, he would know.

The only other option was to speak to Atlas, who despised the Olympus Syndicate. Despite his hatred for them, he might be willing to help if it meant bringing down their power.

The problem was, talking to him could draw even more dangerous attention, and I wasn't sure I was ready for that. But the need for answers outweighed my fear.

I slipped out of the bar without saying goodbye to Hephaestus. Artie recognized I needed some space and let me out early.

The night air was cool, and a group of men stood outside smoking, their eyes tracking me as I walked by. They whistled and called out as I headed for the metal stairs leading to Artie's apartment. This place was crawling with outlaws, every one of them howling for my attention.

*"Aphrodite, where you going? Sexy, come here?"*

*"Ouranos's daughter looks like she gives good head."*

*"Maybe she's like her mother, I heard she was a fucking whore."*

I heard what they called me. *The Aetos' bastard.* It was a constant reminder that I was worth nothing in this world.

As I entered my bedroom, my fingers instinctively reached for the light switch. But before I could flick it on, a firm hand closed over mine. The door clicked shut behind us, plunging the room into darkness. The only source of light was the ethereal glow of the moon through the windows, casting a ghostly sheen across the room.

My breath caught in my throat as I took in the sight before me. Ares stood just inches away, his presence so overwhelming it seemed to drown out all else. The air between us crackled with a palpable tension, each second simmering with intensity.

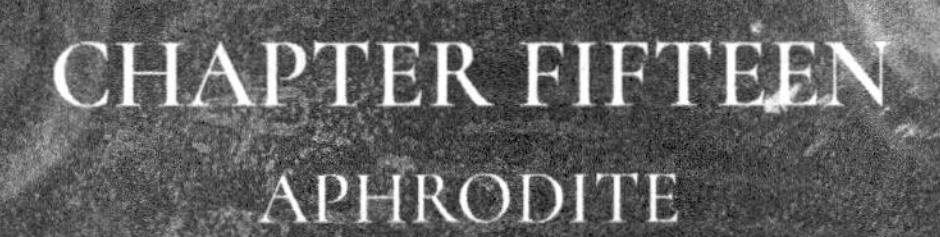

# CHAPTER FIFTEEN

## APHRODITE

I pressed my trembling body against the cool wooden door.

"What are you doing here?" I asked, my voice breaking. Ares approached me with menacing determination. The sensation of him pressing up against me was both exhilarating and euphoric, as if every nerve in my body had come alive.

His lips ravaged mine, and my heart thudded hard in my chest. The forbidden nature of our encounter drew me in, a dark allure I couldn't resist, pulling me deeper into a desire that consumed every thought and breath. I wrapped my arms around his neck, and he responded by grabbing hold of my waist. The air was dry and filled with the heat radiating from our bodies. I could taste whiskey and a lingering hint of smoke on his full lips.

"Stop," I said, my voice trembling. "You don't get to just show up here and act like nothing happened."

Ares looked at me with a hint of confusion. "What do you mean?"

"Don't play dumb with me," I snapped, my anger bubbling over. "You think you can just waltz back into my life after ignoring me since the fight? You think you can use me as your emotional backup when it suits you?"

Ares's eyes narrowed slightly. “What are you talking about?”

“Don’t act like you don’t know!” I continued, my voice rising. “I saw you with another woman. You’ve been distant, and then suddenly you show up here like you’re entitled to just pick up where we left off. Do you really think you can just use me like this, only to walk away when it’s convenient for you?”

“Tell me to go,” Ares growled, his voice a raw, primal edge as he inched away from my face, his gaze locked onto mine. The tension between us was a living thing, electric and wild. My body trembled uncontrollably, his proximity and the fierce intensity in his eyes igniting something deep within me.

His arms were still braced against the door on either side of me, trapping me in his embrace. I felt every bit of the strength and determination in his stance, his breath mingling with mine in the dim light. The storm of emotions he had stirred within me surged to the surface, overpowering my resolve.

Before I could fully process what was happening, our lips collided once again, fierce and desperate. The kiss was an eruption of all the unspoken words and unresolved tension between us. It was raw and hungry, a frantic expression of everything we’d both been holding back.

Gasping for air, I tried to pull away, but he held me in place, resting his forehead against mine. “I hated watching him touch you,” he whispered. I opened my eyes to see his dark gaze filled with a possessive gleam.

He trailed his lips along the curve of my neck as he whispered again, “You’re mine, Aphrodite, and I’ll destroy anyone who tries to take you away.”

I trembled as a moan escaped my lips, the sound barely audible over the racing pulse in my ears. Ares's lips traced a burning path along my jawline, each kiss sending shivers down my spine. His hand slid slowly to my neck, fingers grazing my skin with a tantalizing touch.

"I've craved you," he murmured, his voice a deep, husky whisper that vibrated against my skin.

Despite my desire, I whispered, "I can't do this."

Ares's presence made me shiver, every part of me responding to him with a fervor I couldn't ignore. His nearness made me feel exposed, stirring up emotions I'd never felt before. It was as if he had unlocked a new realm of sensation, one filled with lust and yearning that I had never dared to explore.

It was as if I was emerging from a long period of numbness, immersing myself in a torrent of desire and vulnerability. His touch ignited something deep within me, an urgent, raw craving that was both thrilling and disorienting. In his embrace, I was caught between the thrill of surrender and the fear of losing myself, drawn into a world where my sense of freedom felt both exhilarating and elusive.

"Tell me to leave, and I won't come back," he said, his voice sparking electricity in my veins, sending a pulsating energy straight to my core. He stirred something deep within me, coaxing me toward a place I was afraid to reach. "Go on," he urged, his voice dropping to a dark, throaty growl as his lips hovered just inches from mine. "Tell me what you want."

Every fiber of my being ached with longing. I wanted to cast aside all pretense, to bare myself completely before him—body, soul, and mind. In that moment, the pull of his proximity was irresistible, compelling me to surrender to the profound, seductive connection that seemed to draw me helplessly into his embrace.

"I will keep you safe," he whispered as his lips gently brushed against mine.

"What about that woman?" My voice quivered with jealousy.

"Eos? She's nothing but a distraction. Just a way to mislead others about what's really happening between us."

"She said that she was your girlfriend." I said as a matter of fact. Ares lifted his face, but I couldn't read his expression.

"Well, she isn't. The only person I want is you, Aphrodite." He groaned, laden with want.

"Prove it." I breathed, my voice trembling with longing.

Tension crackled in the air. I could feel his fingers, strong yet gentle, encircling my neck, their touch sending shivers down my spine. Still pressed against the door, he shielded me from the outside world, creating a haven just for us.

He caressed the small of my back with his other hand, building a fire within me that demanded attention. A tsunami of desire surged through my entire being and our lips collided once more. His grip on my neck tightened with a fierce possessiveness that matched the intensity of his kiss. I could feel my arousal begin to seep through my underwear. Oh gods, I wanted him.

Ares's hand slid across my breasts with urgency. I tugged at the bottom of his shirt, needing to feel his bare chest under my fingertips. Ares removed his shirt swiftly, revealing himself to me. The sight of him standing there bare chested ignited a primitive need within me. His scars crisscrossed his body like a battlefield, telling stories of past struggles and trauma. My breath hitched.

There was no holding back any longer. Ares tugged off my dress, leaving me in my just panties as he gripped my hips. His leg pressed between mine, and I could feel his excitement as clearly as he could feel my own, a thrilling connection that heightened our mutual desire. He released my hip, and his hand slid down to my panties. He toyed with the waistband of them, teasing me before his fingers slid further down and began to rub circles around my clit.

Another moan left my lips. His fingers were determined, working quickly as they rubbed with purpose. My thighs tightened around his leg. Ares let out a teasing chuckle that vibrated through his body.

"So wet for me, baby. I love how your body reacts when I touch you." He kissed my moan away. My sex pulsed for him, aching in a way it never had before.

As his lips parted from mine, I whispered, "Two can play at this game." I reached for him and skillfully unbuckled his jeans. I slipped my hand inside, feeling his cock hard for me. I couldn't help but wonder how many times he had fantasized about me while pleasuring himself.

I wrapped my hand tightly around him, my desire for him intensifying as I declared, "I want you to fuck me."

He removed his jeans, exposing his boxers beneath. He laid me down on the bed, and quickly pulled my panties off.

Anticipation coursed through me.

He placed tender kisses on my thighs that sent shivers down my spine, weakening me further. As his lips inched closer to my clit, my fingers entwined in his hair, feeling the gentle warmth of his breath against my skin.

The sensation of his tongue caressing my sex elicited a sharp intake of breath from me that echoed in the air. He firmly gripped my ass, and while looking up at me with his devilish grin, he licked his lips and said, "Be a good girl and spread those legs for me," I did as I was told, and I felt a ripple of pleasure scatter across my body.

Ares bit my inner thigh, as he rubbed circles around my clit. He eagerly delved back in with his tongue, provoking a passionate cry from me.

My thighs tightened, "Yes baby, you want more?" Ares teased as he thrust a second finger inside me. My back bowed off the bed, the bliss intensifying. I was aching with anticipation as his tongue worked its magic, exploring every inch of my being.

I could feel the pleasure building within me, like a storm about to unleash its fury. I screamed, my voice echoing to the heavens as he devoured me with an insatiable hunger.

The pleasure intensified, pushing me to the edge of pure ecstasy. I could no longer contain the sensations coursing through my veins. "Ares, don't stop," I cried out, my voice filled with a mixture of desperation and pleasure.

"You won't come until I tell you to," he growled dominantly against my clit, his words sending vibrations through my body.

I tried to resist the unstoppable urge that was washing over me, feeling such intense pleasure that it warped into pain, sending me gasping and pleading with him to let me come.

"Oh, please, Ares!" I shouted his name, grazing his hair, and his movements intensified.

"Come for me, Aphrodite. I want to feel you come." he rasped, propelling me deeper into the abyss of pleasure. Euphoria washed over me, causing my lips to release a cry that mirrored the intensity of the moment.

Blood rushed to my head, amplifying my orgasm as my body trembled and shook. In that moment, I surrendered to the blissful release that left me limp and fulfilled.

My legs relaxed and fell to the side gently. He leisurely ascended my stomach with tender kisses, igniting a trail of anticipation toward my breast. I could feel the rhythmic pulsation of his desire pressing firmly against my abdomen. The touch of his lips on my neck sent chills along my skin while the gentle caress of his thumb on my bottom lip brought me to focus on him.

"That's a good girl," he whispered, his voice filled with a mix of longing and dominance. With deliberate slowness, he continued his ascent of kisses that left a trail of fire. "We aren't done yet."

Never in my wildest dreams did I think someone could take hold of me the way he did. I didn't want to stop. I pushed him to the edge of the bed. He leaned up on his elbow as he stroked his shaft, watching me. I asked, "You like to think of me when you touch yourself?"

Ares stroked his cock. "I think about you all the fucking time."

I straddled him, and he sat up against the headboard. I grabbed hold of his thick cock and rubbed his dull head against my folds, soaking him in my pleasure. His hips rocked in response. I pressed him inside me, letting out a deep breath at the sudden fullness of him. Ares growled in the pure darkness that surrounded us. He gripped my waist tightly, and as I rode his cock, he guided me where he wanted me.

I craved the feeling of his body on mine, and I couldn't get enough. He kissed me deeply, and his hands pressed against my back, searching for a hold. I ground deeper. He kissed my breasts, and my head dropped back. He thrust harder, our breaths syncing to the rhythm we shared. Ares let out a moan, then squeezed my ass tighter. I kissed him harder.

"Make me come, baby," he moaned louder, his voice was filled with desire as his thrusts strengthened, gaining speed and force.

With each glorious pump, both of us inched closer to the edge. I could feel my thighs clutching around his waist, my body responding to his approaching climax. Ares leaned me backward, sending electrifying sensations throughout my body.

The intoxicating scent of our passion hung thick in the air. His thumb expertly found my clit as I rode him, every thrust and bounce eliciting desperate moans from my lips. His cock filled me perfectly, every movement sending jolts through my body.

With a final, powerful thrust, we were overtaken by a tidal wave of pleasure. Our bodies convulsed together, drowning in the overwhelming intensity of our climax. I felt the warmth of his release inside me, mixing with the slick, heady heat of our desire. As we rode out the aftershocks, our breaths came in ragged gasps, our limbs entangled in a fevered embrace, savoring the last shivers of our shared ecstasy.

Ares's strong, defined arms held me close as we lay intertwined on my satin sheets. Our breaths were heavy, our hearts pounding in sync as we basked in the aftermath of our fiery connection. His dark eyes locked onto mine, filled with a mix of adoration and an undying hunger. We could still feel the tremors of exhilaration coursing through us as if our souls had become one in that powerful moment of connection.

*How could something wrong feel so right?*

The room seemed to pulse with the energy of our passion, a sanctuary where time stood still, allowing us to revel in each other.

"My heart belongs to you," Ares confessed. There was vulnerability in his eyes as he revealed his true self to me. His words hung in the air, creating a delicate tension between us. Time seemed to freeze, giving me the chance to comprehend the gravity of his confession. Ares, stoic and impenetrable, guarded his emotions. But at this moment, his vulnerability shone through, captivating me like no other.

I couldn't help but study his face. The hard lines that usually defined him seemed to soften, revealing a side of him I had never seen. His eyes, normally filled with determination and strength, now held a mixture of fear and hope. It was at that moment that I realized the depth of his feelings.

The room swirled with uncertainty, anticipation, and an undeniable affection that grew stronger with each passing moment. The vulnerability he displayed had opened a door, inviting me to venture into a deeper connection with him.

My voice quivered as I spoke. "Ares, my heart belongs to you too." In that instant, I made a conscious decision to embrace the unknown, and to let my defenses down in the darkness that surrounded us.

# CHAPTER SIXTEEN

## ARES

As Aphrodite slept, I found a profound joy in watching her peaceful slumber. The gentle rise and fall of her breath a soothing rhythm to my restless soul.

It had been too long since I'd allowed myself such a luxury as sleeping in, but with her beside me, the world outside seemed to fade away. She had a way of making logic feel irrelevant, her presence unraveling the tight grip I kept on my emotions and drawing me into a whirlwind of emotions.

As I watched her, every gentle curve and subtle movement stirred a profound tenderness within me. Despite the storm of desire she stirred within me, I knew I had to stay composed. For her sake, I had to keep my turbulent emotions in check, savoring these quiet moments while she remained blissfully unaware of the effect she had on me.

Slipping on my boxer briefs, I moved over to her desk and opened the top drawer, finding a notepad and pencil inside. I sat against the wall, sketching her as she slept. When my thoughts refused to settle, drawing was my escape.

As I traced her silhouette on the paper, my mind wandered to the ghosts of those I'd killed. It was like sleep paralysis—the demons creeping in, trying to reclaim the lives I'd stolen. The men I'd taken down haunted me, their faces never far from my thoughts.

But with her, it was different. Somehow, she quieted the noise, silenced the demons. I didn't understand how or why she had that power over me, but I couldn't deny it.

The drapes were open and dim light from the November sky peeked in. She slept on her back, her bare body exposed. Her long, dark curls cascading against her olive skin.

I was focused on my sketch when I heard her waking up. I looked up and watched as Aphrodite stretched her arms above her head and took a deep breath.

Every day since we met, I tried to drown out the desire that simmered beneath the surface to distract myself from the intense longing I felt for her. But despite my efforts, it was clear I had been ensnared by my own heart.

As she caught me looking at her, her eyes fell on the sketchbook open in front of me. The drawings on the page were unmistakably intimate—every curve and line of her naked body rendered with a raw vulnerability that I could never fully admit to anyone.

My attempts to capture her essence were laid bare, and I could feel the weight of my own unspoken desires pressing down on me.

"Drawing me like one of your French girls?" she murmured sleepily, entangled in the sheets, causing me to bite my lip in anticipation of savoring her again.

"Just sketching this incredibly sexy woman lying right in front of me," I let out a chuckle, not hiding the fact I had a raging hard on as she laid naked in the bed.

The blood surged to my cock with such intensity that it was a struggle to keep my hand steady on the pencil. Every curve and line I drew made me ache to touch her again.

I yearned for the sensation of her goosebumps beneath my fingertips as they traced up her legs, reaching the curve of her breasts. My mind was consumed by the desire to feel her racing heartbeat as my lips tasted her in a kiss that would devour us both.

Aphrodite rose from the bed with a fluid grace that made my heart race. As she moved closer, her silhouette was a tantalizing blend of softness and allure; she was a vision.

I set the notepad aside, my gaze fixed on her as she approached. She straddled my lap with a confident ease that made my pulse quicken. My hands instinctively roamed to her waist, pulling her gently closer.

I buried my face in the curve of her neck, letting the warmth and softness of her skin overwhelm me. Every kiss I placed along her collarbone was a desperate attempt to savor the fleeting moments we had.

The intimacy of the touch, the scent of her skin, and the way her breath quickened under my lips all made it clear that I was lost in a world of pure, unfiltered desire.

She leaned in closer, her fingers lightly tracing the outline of a tattoo on my chest. The touch was electric, sending shivers across my skin. Her eyes, filled with curiosity and something deeper, settled on the ink.

"What's this tattoo about?" she asked softly, her voice barely more than a whisper as her fingers continued their gentle exploration.

"I remember seeing it when we were on the couch in your office," she added, her touch lingering, almost as if she was trying to decipher a secret etched into my skin.

"That is my armor," I whispered. "I was stabbed there, but miraculously, I didn't die. So, I decided to place my shield and sword there as a symbol of protection."

"And here?" Her dainty finger trailed down as she followed the lines of the artwork. "Memento mori?" she murmured.

"*Remember you must die*," I said.

Aphrodite looked back up at me, her lips parting, and said, "Ares, you are riddled with scars."

"I belong on a battlefield," I muttered, trying to mask the ache that crept into my chest. The haze of pain was familiar, but allowing her into my heart introduced a whole new level of risk—one that could cost us both our lives.

For as long as I could remember, I had kept the real me hidden from the world, fortified behind layers of cold indifference and well-practiced control. But with Aphrodite, those defenses started to crumble. She saw through the cracks, glimpsing the parts of me that I'd kept buried, parts I was afraid to even acknowledge myself. Yet, somehow, with her, I found the courage to let those walls down, to open my heart and let her in.

And that was the most terrifying battlefield of all.

We locked eyes, and a serene silence wrapped around us like a cocoon. Her fingers, delicate and warm, traced the line of my cheek with a feather-light touch.

"Your freckles are scattered like constellations," she murmured, her voice soft and affectionate. "I love them."

I couldn't help but smile, a warmth spreading across my cheeks. "Look at you, trying to be romantic," I teased, feeling an unexpected tenderness despite the ever-present shadow of my lingering darkness.

Our lips met in a kiss that was both tender and consuming. It was as though time itself had paused, allowing us to become one in that fleeting moment. Our kiss deepened, and I felt our hearts synchronize in rhythm. The world outside—filled with its threats and turmoil—faded into insignificance.

"FINE." SHE STOOD THERE IN HER SILK ROBE, POUTING WITH A DARKLY amused glint in her eye. "But you better be in my bed tonight. I'm not making any promises about what might happen if you don't."

I pulled her close and pressed a lingering kiss to her forehead, letting a wry smile creep onto my face. "Is this how the honeymoon phase goes? Because if so, I'm already questioning my sanity." Her playful prod at my ribs made me laugh.

"Better get going before someone finds me and decides I'm a prime candidate for an ass whooping." I said, only half-joking, the edge in my voice betraying a grim reality.

"Go," she purred. I kissed her one last time before slipping out the door, only to find Artie standing in the kitchen, her eyes narrowing as she caught sight of me.

Artie stood against the island and took a sip of her coffee. She said, "If you guys are going to be making this a thing, next time, let's try to relax on the moaning and growling. It sounded like there were a bunch of animals in there."

I glanced back and caught Aphrodite trying to conceal herself behind the door. I ran my hand down my face. "Please don't say anything to the guys," I begged her as I approached the island.

"I won't, but you guys really need to be careful," Artie cautioned. "Hephaestus has been searching for you, Ares. He asked me where you were, I lied and said you were at Pandora. I had to get Hades to hide your bike."

Artie set her cup down, running a hand through her hair before fixing her gaze on me. "I love you, Ares," she said, her voice soft yet firm. "I don't want to see you get lost in this. You don't let your guard down for just anyone, and that makes it even harder to watch you fall."

"I have genuine feelings for Aphrodite," I began, letting my words spill out to Artie, feeling the weight of them lift from my chest. "Since the moment she arrived at the compound, everything's changed. I've kept it all inside, but I need you to know—this is real. I'll do whatever it takes to protect her."

As I spoke, I noticed Aphrodite stepping out of her room and making her way toward me. My heart pounded with a mix of resolve and desire. When she reached me, I grabbed her hand, feeling the warmth of her touch grounding me.

"I want this, and she feels the same," I continued, my voice firm with determination. "And I will stop at nothing to deal with Hephaestus. I won't let him or anyone else tear us apart." "How? She has been chosen to marry our brother. You know it's dangerous to get between him and what he wants." Artie's voice quivered with fear.

The weight of everything I was feeling—the protectiveness, the desire, the sheer intensity of it all—was suffocating. I could barely breathe as the darkness inside me clawed its way up, threatening to consume everything in its path. My demons, the ones I thought I could control, were finally surfacing, and I knew that if I didn't get out of there, they would devour me whole.

"I need to go," I muttered, more to myself than to them, as I turned and headed for the exit. Each step I took felt like a desperate attempt to outrun the shadows that were closing in, but deep down, I knew I couldn't escape them forever. My feelings for Aphrodite were too powerful, too overwhelming, and they were dragging me into a darkness I wasn't sure I could survive.

TONIGHT, I WAS GOING TO VISIT ATLAS.

I arrived at the Nymph Hotel, an empire built by Atlas and Hermes in the heart of Aeolopolis City. Pulling up on my Sportster, I could feel eyes on me as soon as I got off my bike. To avoid unwanted attention, I decided not to wear my cut vest.

Having "Olympus Syndicate" plastered across my back wouldn't help matters in this situation. Being at the hotel was risky, but my priority was Aphrodite and helping her find the truth about her brother.

Following an employee, I crossed through the hotel casino. Crowds of gamblers gathered, drinking and smoking, betting their livelihoods away. I lowered my head, heart pounding, as I navigated the grounds of a property that had banned our club and all those affiliated with us.

We headed toward the elevator inside the hotel.

The elevator doors slid open to reveal the penthouse suite, where I was greeted by a deep, resonant voice echoing through the dimly lit room. "Well, if it isn't Zeus's war puppet," Atlas drawled, his words dripping with contempt. The city lights streamed in through the floor-to-ceiling windows, casting long shadows across the room, making the space feel both vast and suffocating.

I could feel the weight of his gaze as I stood there, the air heavy with tension. The room smelled of alcohol and cigars; bookshelves covered every inch of the walls, a reminder of Atlas's scholarly nature. We weren't here to be friends. We were here to discuss business.

"Atlas, let's cut the bullshit," I said, crossing my arms and locking eyes with him. I wasn't here to play games. After taking a bullet, my trust in him was hanging by a thread. "Did you put a hit on me?"

Atlas swirled his drink, his gaze distant as he scratched his chin. "If I did, do you really think we'd be having this conversation right now?"

"So that's a no, then?" I pressed, my voice laced with impatience.

"No, Ares. I might not be your biggest fan, but I respect you. Whether you want to believe it or not, that's the truth." Atlas's voice was calm, almost too calm, as if he was weighing each word carefully. "I had nothing to do with ordering that hit on you."

I studied his face, searching for any hint of deception. Atlas met my gaze without flinching, his expression unreadable.

After a tense silence, he leaned forward slightly, his voice low and cutting. "But I've heard some whispers, rumors that the hit might've come from within your own gang."

*That's bullshit,* I thought.

"No one in my family would harm each other. It goes against our code," I snapped, the words leaving a bitter taste in my mouth. The idea was absurd, impossible even. Loyalty ran deeper than blood within the Olympus Syndicate, and we all knew the consequences of betrayal.

But still, doubt flickered in the back of my mind as I stared at Atlas. I knew better than to take anything he said at face value, especially something as serious as this. "Well, I heard a rumor that it was the Four Horsemen," I shot back, my tone laced with disdain.

The Four Horsemen weren't a real threat—not in my eyes, anyway. They were a ragtag group of delinquents, wannabe thugs who thought they could play in the big leagues. They were young, reckless, and stupid enough to think they could stand toe-to-toe with a powerhouse like the Olympus Syndicate.

Atlas took a deliberate sip of his drink, the pause thickening the air with tension. He cleared his throat before finally responding, his voice low and measured.

"I can't say for certain, but from what I've gathered, the Four Horsemen took matters into their own hands. They torched the men responsible for the explosion at the Aetos' annual Halloween party. As for the ones who supposedly attacked you—they've vanished into thin air. Rumors, of course," he added, with a casual shrug that did nothing to ease the weight of his words.

His gaze drifted for a moment before he continued, "Hermes mentioned something about Titan and his... questionable activities. It's the kind of shit that could stir up trouble. If you ask me, it wouldn't be shocking if you had a bone to pick with him, given everything that's happened..."

Atlas's words hung in the air, a toxic mix of half-truths and insinuations. He was painting a picture—one that seemed designed to put me on edge. And it was working.

"Are you accusing *me* of killing him?" I seethed at his accusation.

Atlas shrugged, "I'm curious about everything, much like you."

"I had nothing to do with it his death." I stared at him with a blank expression as my anger surged through me like a pack of ravenous wolves.

"Listen, Ares," he lazily looked at me, seemingly uninterested in this conversation, "I'm just repeating what I've heard."

My nostrils flared as I locked eyes with him, my patience wearing thin. "And who informed you?" I demanded, my voice cutting through the tension like a blade.

Atlas leaned back, his grin widening, clearly enjoying the game he was playing. He let the silence stretch, feeding off my growing agitation. Then, with a deliberate pause, he uttered the name that sent a surge of fury through my veins, "Hephaestus."

My blood boiled as I sped through the streets. I sent a text to Hades, asking him to meet me at Pandora so we could talk without being seen or followed.

I parked my motorcycle outside the nightclub, avoiding eye contact with the crowd that eagerly waited to get in. My anger was simmering just below the surface, and I didn't trust myself to engage with anyone.

I moved quickly through the club, heading straight for my office. Before I could shut the door, Hades stepped inside, his presence a steadying force in the chaos I felt brewing.

He closed the door behind him, straightened his crisp suit jacket, and leaned against the wall. "So, what's the reason behind dragging me over here?" he asked, his tone casual but laced with curiosity.

I was pacing back and forth, trying to get a hold of my thoughts. Linking my hands behind my head, I turned to face him. "Hephaestus has been spreading rumors that I killed Titan," I confessed as I watched Hades process the words.

He pinched the bridge of his nose. "Where did you get that information?"

"Atlas." I needed a drink. I went straight for my whiskey collection in the bar cabinet. I took the nearest bottle and poured two glasses.

"Atlas? You know he's notorious for stirring up drama, Ares. And his kid isn't any different." Hades let out a groan of defeat as he walked toward me and grabbed the glass tumbler off the bar.

"What if he isn't lying?" I looked at Hades, my voice barely steady, the weight of uncertainty pressing down on me. "What if Hephaestus really has it out for me?"

My chest tightened as I confessed the truth. "I don't want Aphrodite to marry him. Something feels off about all of this." The words spilled out, raw and unfiltered. "It's only been a month since Titan's death, and now this wedding is being moved up. It feels too soon, too rushed, like a move in a game I haven't figured out yet."

I took a breath, the tension in my gut refusing to ease. "But it's more than that, Hades. There's something between me and Aphrodite. I feel it, but I'm walking a fine line here. Every step I take feels like I'm on thin ice, not knowing if the next one will break it."

After I finished spilling my heart out to Hades, he paused for an extended beat, long enough that a cold sweat began to bead on my forehead. I could see him weighing the gravity of what I'd just laid out. Finally, he broke the silence.

"Alright," he said, his voice low and resolute. "Let's investigate what Hephaestus is up to. No way we're going to Zeus with this yet. It'll only make matters worse if we bring him in on this now. Plus, the wedding is right around the corner. We need to stop it from happening before it's too late."

"We need a plan," I admitted, the words tasting bitter as they left my mouth. The weight of what lay ahead loomed over us like a shadow, and I couldn't ignore the gnawing dread building in my gut. I tossed my drink back, feeling the burn slide down my throat, and let out a low growl of frustration. The urge to act was almost unbearable, but the path forward was anything but clear.

Hades leaned back in his chair, studying me with those sharp, calculating eyes. "We'll start by figuring out who's really pulling the strings here. Hephaestus isn't acting alone. There's more at play, and we need to dig it all up before we make a move."

I nodded, my mind racing as I considered our options. Although I was eager to strike, the stakes were too high to rush in blind. "We'll need to be careful—one wrong step and it could all blow up in our faces."

Hades smirked, a hint of that familiar, dark humor creeping back into his expression. "Don't worry, Ares. If there's one thing I'm good at, it's navigating through hell."

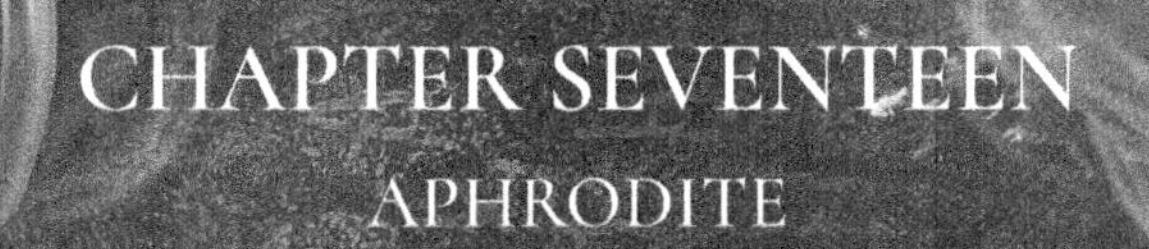

# CHAPTER SEVENTEEN
## APHRODITE

I had to admit, sleeping with my fiancé's brother complicated things.

The wedding was bearing down on me, just days away, and I felt torn between two forces. Ares, the one who held my heart with an unyielding grip, made me feel protected, while Hephaestus only saw this marriage as a way to gain access to the Aetos name and the power that came with it. I wasn't naive—I knew his true motives.

As I ascended the daunting trail that symbolized my life, my footing had slipped, and I tumbled down, momentarily losing sight of my purpose—Avenging my brother. The uncertainty of my future clouded my mind, but deep down, I knew which path truly called to me. It was dark, treacherous, but Ares was there, waiting in the shadows. My heart craved him, even as danger loomed over us.

I was on my way to the kitchen, ready for my daily dose of coffee, when a knock echoed throughout the apartment. Artie was at a hair appointment, so I was home alone.

A rush of excitement washed over me. I hoped it would be Ares standing on the other side. I had wished for this moment; certain he wouldn't leave me alone for long. Maybe Zeus had called him away for something urgent after he left. That would explain everything.

"It's about time..." I swung the door open but bit my bottom lip to stop from speaking when I realized that it wasn't the man I'd been waiting for.

Instead, my fiancé stood towering over me, wearing a heavy hoodie with his leather vest over top of it. His chestnut brown hair was unruly as he leaned against the door frame.

"Can I come in?" He brought his hand up to his mouth, and his fingers rubbed his bottom lip as he sized me up.

He caught me off guard, making me feel exposed despite being fully dressed in jean shorts and a racerback tank top. Gripping the door with one hand, I pushed it open wider, allowing Hephaestus to enter.

He walked in with his hands shoved into his pockets, his slight limp barely noticeable as he moved with purpose. His gaze swept across the apartment, taking in every detail as he slowly circled the island, the tension between us thick in the air.

I asked, "So, what brings you here today?" My voice carried a note of curiosity, but beneath it, I was wary. I couldn't afford to trust him.

"I have a wedding gift for you," he said, sitting on a barstool and resting his elbows on the stone countertop. I observed him closely as he rubbed his hands together.

I leaned against the cool granite as I crossed my arms. "Why?"

"Why not?"

*What was he playing at?* "What is it?"

"Go get changed," he said, flashing a devilish smile. I could see how he could be considered attractive. His icy-blue eyes lingered on me, drawing me in with their allure.

"Fine," I said. "But no peeking—you hear me?" I pointed at him.

Hephaestus pressed his hands on his heart. "I promise."

I walked into my room, shutting the door behind me with a heavy sigh. My mind was racing, trying to piece together why Hephaestus was here, what his true intentions were. Why was he so insistent on seeing me? His devilish smile and those icy-blue eyes lingered in my thoughts, unsettling me in ways I couldn't fully understand.

I leaned against the dresser, staring at my reflection in the mirror. The woman looking back at me seemed conflicted, torn between duty and desire, between the safety Ares represented and the enigmatic threat that was Hephaestus.

*What is he really after? Why now?*

I couldn't shake the feeling that there was something deeper at play, something sinister. He was too smooth, too calculated. The way he moved, the way he looked at me—it all felt like a game, one I wasn't sure I was ready to play.

But I had no choice. I had to face him, even if it meant diving into waters far darker than I ever imagined. With a deep breath, I began to change, the weight of uncertainty pressing down on me as I prepared to confront whatever lay ahead.

I walked out of my bedroom wearing dark black jeans, black boots, a matching sweater, and my brown aviator bomber jacket. Hephaestus stood and stared at me without breaking eye contact. "You, uh... You look beautiful," he said.

An unexpected blush spread across my cheeks as I responded, "Thank you. Should we go?" I asked as he nodded and headed toward the door.

We walked down the stairs in silence as he led me toward his bike. Hephaestus helped me with my helmet, and I put on some gloves he'd given me to keep warm.

"I've never ridden with you before," I confessed, my voice barely audible as I watched him secure my helmet with focused determination. When he looked up, our eyes met, and a sudden thrill surged through me. His lips curved into a small grin, and he reached out, gently brushing his finger against my cheek, sending a shiver down my spine.

“Let’s go before it’s too late.” He said as he straddled the motorcycle, reaching for my hand to help me on.

We sped through the night, the wind rushing past us as we slipped away from the compound. My arms tightened around his waist as he expertly wove through the streets, the powerful hum of the engine vibrating through us. Pressed against his back, I was surrounded by his scent—a mix of leather, musk, and smoky cologne. It was intoxicating, a dangerous allure that made my heart race.

I closed my eyes, letting the sensation consume me, and for a moment, I imagined Ares behind the handlebars instead. The memory of being on the back of his bike, his strong hand gripping my thigh as we came to a stop. It sent a shiver through me. Even though I wasn’t supposed to be with Ares, his presence lingered in my thoughts, refusing to be ignored.

We abruptly pulled into the hospital and parked, the sudden stop jarring my thoughts into a chaotic mess. Confusion washed over me—I had no idea why he would bring me here. Hephaestus killed the engine, the silence thick between us. Without a word, he extended his hand to help me off the bike, his expression unreadable, only adding to the uneasy tension swirling inside me.

"Why are we here?" I asked, running my fingers through my tangled curls, trying to steady myself. Hephaestus only responded with a wicked grin. His icy-blue eyes gleamed with a triumph that both unsettled and intrigued me, stirring something I didn’t want to acknowledge.

Despite the unease in my gut, I couldn’t deny the pull he had on me—a twisted attraction that made resisting him more difficult with each passing moment. He was dangerous, unpredictable, and that thrill both terrified and tempted me.

“Do you hate surprises?” He rubbed his bearded chin contemplatively.

"No, I just don't understand why we're here." My anxiety surged, but he grabbed my hand, guiding me toward the entrance with excited assurance. Navigating the hospital hallways with ease, he seemed to know precisely where we were going. Silently, we made our way toward the elevator. The suspense was palpable.

We stepped off on the fourth floor, the sterile scent of the hospital hanging thick in the air. A receptionist glanced our way, but Hephaestus barely acknowledged her, his grip firm around my hand as if he had done this a thousand times before.

Without hesitation, he led me down the long, dimly lit corridor, his pace steady, purposeful. My heart pounded in sync with each step until we reached a door at the far end. That's when he finally stopped, his hand still holding mine as the weight of the moment settled over us.

"For you." He raised his hand toward the room nearest to us, his voice carrying a sense of anticipation. With a hesitant breath, I swung the door open, unsure of what to expect.

Paris was lying in the bed, her eyes immediately locking with mine.

My heart surged, disbelief quickly giving way to joy. I let out a scream of excitement, the tension that had built up inside me shattering in an instant. "I can't believe it!" I dashed to her side, wrapping my arms around her in the tightest hug I could muster.

"I missed you so much," I whispered, my voice cracking with emotion. I pulled back just enough to look at her face, still in awe. "I haven't heard from you since the explosion. I tried calling, messaging... I thought I lost you for good."

"Oh, Aphrodite, I've missed you too!" Paris exclaimed as we embraced. I held her gently, not knowing the full extent of her injuries, but needing to feel her in my arms again. For a fleeting moment, it felt like a piece of my past life had come back to me.

"Why are you still in the hospital?" I asked softly, brushing my hand against her cheek.

Paris placed her hands on top of mine, her touch frail but full of warmth. “I was in a medically induced coma. I had a brain injury from the explosion. Waking up to that was terrifying, but they said I was lucky. They told me someone saved me. Thank you for that.”

“I failed you, Paris, look where you are. If it wasn’t for me, and my family, this would have never happened to you.”

“You’re the reason I’m alive. You saved me, Aphrodite,” she said, her voice soft, revealing the toll the trauma had taken on her. Her pale skin, the dark circles beneath her eyes—it was clear she wasn’t the vibrant girl she used to be. She was thinner, weaker, but alive.

I sighed, grasping her hand tighter, “I always will,” I whispered, pressing a kiss to her cheek. “You’re the only real family I have left.” Tears pricked my eyes, and I wiped them away before turning to the door. Hephaestus was gone, having left quietly, but I now understood that the gift he had given me was the most precious one—Paris.

“So,” Paris said, trying to lift the mood, “tell me, what have I missed?”

We caught up, talking about everything—Titan’s murder, the looming wedding, and my tangled feelings for Ares. It was clear the flood of information left her a little overwhelmed.

“Okay, wow, you’ve got two brothers after you?” she teased with a weak smile.

I shrugged, but the heaviness in my chest didn’t fade.

“Hephaestus... he has this temper, and he scares me. Something about him feels wrong, like I need to always be on guard. He’s cold, unpredictable. But then he brings me here, to you, and I don’t know what to think.”

“And Ares?” Paris asked, her gaze steady on me.

I sighed, rubbing my temple. “Ares is... everything. Fierce. Protective. He makes me feel alive in ways I didn’t know were possible, but he’s also terrifying. His intensity... I don’t know how to handle it.”

Paris squeezed my hand. “Then why not just be with Ares instead of Hephaestus?”

“It’s not that simple,” I sighed.

"Why not?" she pressed gently. "I can see it in you, Aphrodite. When you talk about Ares, you glow."

"I'm not supposed to be with Ares," I said, leaning against her. "I belong to Hephaestus. My father made sure of that when he traded me to the Olympus Syndicate. No matter what I feel, I can't just walk away from it."

Paris's expression softened as she listened. I continued, "And I haven't been able to focus on finding Titan's killer because... I've been so distracted by Ares."

"You can't blame yourself for feeling something, Aphrodite," Paris said softly. "You deserve love, even after everything you've been through. Especially after everything."

"You're right, I do," I admitted. "I just don't know how to handle this. I've never faced anything like this before."

Time seemed to slip away as I caught Paris up on everything that had transpired since Halloween. I tried to strike a balance between sharing the necessary details and overwhelming her, but the weight of the conversation was heavy. The doctor eventually came in, a gentle reminder that Paris needed rest. I hesitated, reluctant to leave her side, but I knew it was the right thing to do.

Before I left, I gave her my burner phone number, my fingers lingering on hers. "Make sure you call me," I said, my voice trembling with emotion. The connection we had, the bond forged through so much pain and loss, felt like a lifeline.

We embraced tightly, and as I pulled away, I saw the truth in her eyes. She was right—I did deserve happiness. Yet, even as her words comforted me, a storm brewed within. I was on the brink of a monumental decision, and the gravity of it weighed heavily on me.

Leaving the hospital room, I made my way toward the lobby, my thoughts consumed by Hephaestus. Today, he had done something unexpectedly kind, and I began to question my initial judgment of him. Perhaps there was more to him than I had been willing to see.

Outside, Hephaestus sat on his motorcycle, the engine purring softly. The sight of him—relaxed, confident—stirred something within me. His cocky smile, though infuriating, had a disarming effect on my heart.

"Thank you for today," I said, approaching him with a mixture of gratitude and confusion. Without thinking, I wrapped my arms around his neck. His touch was warm, his breath sending a shiver down my spine. The world seemed to narrow to just the two of us.

"I'll give you everything, Aphrodite, if you just let me in," he murmured, his blue eyes revealing a vulnerability I hadn't noticed before. Despite his rugged exterior, there **was** a tenderness in his gaze, a glimpse of a softer side that he rarely showed.

Hephaestus's touch was tender yet electrifying as he gently cradled my cheek, his fingers warm against my skin. He guided me closer, his gaze locking with mine in a moment of shared vulnerability. Our lips finally met in a kiss that began softly, hesitant and exploratory. It was as if we were both testing the waters, our breaths mingling as the kiss deepened with a mix of curiosity and longing.

The contrast between this kiss and the fiery passion I'd experienced with Ares was striking. Whereas Ares had always ignited a fierce, consuming flame within me, Hephaestus's kiss was more of a slow, deliberate burn. His lips moved against mine with a sensual rhythm, a gentle caress that felt both inviting and intoxicating. Each brush of his lips sent shivers down my spine, awakening a desire I hadn't fully recognized before.

As his embrace deepened, the kiss became more fervent. Hephaestus's hands slid from my cheek to the back of my neck, pulling me closer, his touch firm yet tender. The heat between us grew, and I could feel the intense pleasure he evoked with every lingering caress. My senses were overwhelmed, every nerve in my body attuned to the way his lips traced mine with an irresistible, almost desperate need.

In that moment, I was lost in him, the world outside fading away. The kiss was not just a physical connection but a revelation of a deeper, unspoken longing. I felt myself surrendering to the sensation, losing control as the intensity of his touch stirred desires I had tried to suppress. The kiss was a dance of passion and exploration, leaving me breathless and yearning for more.

When we finally parted, our lips lingering just a breath apart, Hephaestus rested his forehead against mine. Both of us were panting slightly, our breaths mingling in the charged air between us. The intimacy of the moment had shifted something profound within me, a recognition that this was no longer just a fleeting connection. The kiss had altered the landscape of our relationship, marking a point of no return.

"I could get used to that," I said softly, my cheeks flushed from the kiss and the emotions swirling inside me.

Hephaestus's smile grew, a genuine warmth in his eyes. "Stay with me tonight?"

I hesitated, crossing my arms as if to shield myself from the turmoil inside. "I'm not sure, Hephaestus," I said, struggling with my feelings. *What was I doing?*

He chuckled, the sound a mixture of charm and reassurance. "Don't worry, babe. We can take it slow. Or maybe I can take you on a proper date first?"

My mind drifted back to Ares, and the uncertainty of his whereabouts gnawed at me. I hadn't heard from him since our last encounter, and the silence only fueled my growing anger. I looked at Hephaestus, pushing a stray lock of hair from my face. "Well, considering I'm going to be your wife, I guess a date wouldn't be out of the question."

Hephaestus's eyes softened as he glanced at my hand. "Yes, you will be my wife," he said, his tone laced with a mix of seriousness and affection. "I should get you a ring." He traced his fingers over my ring finger, then lifted my hand to his lips, pressing a tender kiss to it.

I couldn't help but blurt out, "What happened to the grumpy Hephaestus I'm used to?"

A smile tugged at the corners of his mouth. "He realized he

doesn't need to fight this. He realized he shouldn't push you away but should embrace what's happening between us."

For once, I found myself speechless, unable to form a coherent response. The complexities of my feelings, the confusion, and the unexpected warmth Hephaestus had sparked in me left me at a loss for words.

We went to a local diner for our date. He barely touched his food, his gaze locked on me with a hunger that went beyond mere appetite.

"So, was it nice to see your friend?" He took a sip of his coffee that the waitress brought over. I watched him intently as his eyes followed the young woman as she walked away.

In the dim light of the diner, I saw Hephaestus more clearly than ever before. His beard partially concealed a deep red scar that extended up toward his eye. His deep blue eyes, like a stormy ocean on a rainy day, held an unsettling depth. When our gazes met, I swallowed hard, feeling the weight of his intense stare.

"Yes," I said warmly, as I gave him a small, genuine smile. "I missed her so much."

He nodded thoughtfully. "I figured you'd want to reconnect with someone from your past."

As the waitress delivered our plates, Hephaestus offered a nod of thanks.

"It's been a lot to handle lately," I admitted, glancing down at my food but not feeling hungry. "With Titan's death, the wedding, and the move to the compound, I've felt overwhelmed."

Hephaestus looked at me with a seriousness that made me uneasy. "I know I'm not the ideal choice for a husband, Aphrodite, but I promise I'll do everything in my power to protect you."

I met his gaze and offered a tentative smile. "I appreciate that,

Hephaestus. I know we've been distant, but I'm willing to give this a chance." I tried to convince myself, even though my thoughts kept drifting back to Ares. I would attempt to find peace and happiness with Hephaestus if it meant finding stability.

As I spoke about my life, Hephaestus listened intently, his eyes lighting up whenever I laughed or shared a happy memory. His smile, though faint, seemed to soften with every word, and I couldn't help but notice how his attention made me feel a little less alone.

Hephaestus was midway through taking a bite of his burger when I broached the subject of his mother. His piercing blue eyes shot up to meet mine, an unreadable expression crossing his face. Abruptly, he dabbed his mouth with a napkin and took a sip of his drink, as though to steady himself. I watched his every movement with a growing sense of unease.

As our gazes locked, he reached into his jacket and pulled out a small, black leather box. A knot tightened in my stomach as I recognized the significance of the gesture. "This was my mother's ring," he said quietly, lifting the lid with a solemn reverence.

Inside the box lay a gold band, exquisitely crafted with two delicate diamonds flanking a magnificent emerald that shimmered like a dewy forest after a rainstorm. Its beauty was breathtaking, evoking a sense of timeless elegance. I found myself momentarily lost in its allure.

"This is stunning, Hephaestus," I managed to say, my voice barely above a whisper.

Hephaestus carefully removed the ring from the box and held it out to me. As I took it in my hand, the weight of its significance pressed heavily on me. The ring was more than a piece of jewelry—it symbolized the path I was about to take. I looked up to meet his gaze, his intense stare conveying a depth of emotion that left me feeling vulnerable.

"Let me be your protector, Aphrodite," he said, his voice deepening with earnest gravity. "I'll stand by you, no matter what." His words carried a weight that cut through my defenses.

A tear escaped from the corner of my eye as the reality of his words settled over me.

This was my destiny unfolding before me, a fate I couldn't escape.

# CHAPTER EIGHTEEN
## APHRODITE

I never expected my engagement party to be filled with Olympus Syndicate members, but here I was, surrounded by the faces of those who would soon be my family by marriage. The ring Hephaestus had given me felt like a chain around my finger, a constant reminder of the cage I was trapped in.

Ares's absence was a gnawing ache in my chest. He had stopped his visits to my apartment, and every evening I would glance out the window, hoping for a glimpse of him. His place had become shrouded in darkness, its curtains perpetually drawn. The emptiness of his home mirrored the void he left in my heart.

*Why was he avoiding me?* Was he distancing himself because he couldn't bear to see me with Hephaestus? Or perhaps he was trying to protect me from the turmoil of our forbidden relationship, knowing that getting involved with him could bring even more danger into my life? It was equally possible that he was grappling with his own demons.

In the midst of this chaos, my focus had to shift. The days of shedding tears over unfulfilled romances were behind me. I needed to uncover the truth behind Titan's murder and navigate the treacherous waters of my impending marriage. The weight of it all was heavy, and with every passing day, the urgency to find answers grew stronger.

Patting some perfume on my neck, I felt a thrill of confidence.

I slipped into my red dress, the fabric clinging to my curves and the plunging neckline revealing just enough to be daring yet sophisticated. The slits on either side of the dress allowed for a glimpse of my legs with each step, adding an element of sensuality to my appearance.

As I looked in the mirror, I saw the woman they wanted me to be—beautiful, poised, and ready to play the part. But beneath the surface of glamour and grace, I harbored a burning resolve. I would not surrender my heart or my will to these men who sought to control me. They would regret ever crossing paths with me.

My father had arranged for the engagement party to be held at Aetos manor, with the intent to unite our families in a grand display of power and alliance. The opulent halls and shadowy corridors of the estate were about to host a gathering of dangerous men, each harboring their own dark intentions.

It felt as though the manor itself was bracing for an inevitable showdown, with tension thickening the air and secrets lurking in every corner. My aim tonight was to access my father's office covertly. After speaking with Hermes, I couldn't help but wonder if there was any relevant information in Titan's files regarding his so-called side businesses. All I had to do was ignore the noise in my head that somehow persisted and focus on my task at hand.

I left my bedroom and headed towards the kitchen. I saw Artie standing near the kitchen sink, wearing a sleek black dress with her hair pulled back. "Behold, the future bride!" she exclaimed. "I'm sorry I didn't make you a penis cake for your engagement party.

Maybe for the bachelorette?" Artie held her clutch to her side, her eyes settling on me and her lips turning into a wicked grin. "You look like you would eat up and spit out anyone that came near you."

"So, my outfit gives the right vibe?" I winked as I closed my diamond encrusted clutch.

"My brother is going to tear out every man's eyes tonight."

"Hephaestus will have to behave—"

"I wasn't referring to him," Artie said as a matter of fact, her expression devoid of emotion. Ares haunted my every thought, an intoxicating shadow that I couldn't shake. But I wouldn't let him distract me from what had to be done. No matter how his memory clawed at me, threatening to pull me under, I was determined. The ache he left behind, the desire that still burned within me—it would not control me. I couldn't afford to let him sway me. Not now. I had my path, and nothing, not even him, would tear me from it.

"Let's get going."

The cold night air wrapped around me as I descended the stairs, my heels clicking against the metal. I could feel eyes on me—hungry, captivated. The red dress clung to every curve, the plunging neckline daring them to look. With each step I took, the men around the compound turned their heads to watch, their gazes lingering. They were drawn to me like moths to a flame, but they didn't know they were about to get burned.

The sight of a black Range Rover parked up ahead caught my attention.

Hephaestus stood by the door of the vehicle, his eyes locking onto mine with a dark intensity that seemed to pierce straight through me. His rough hand rubbed at his bearded chin, and I found him more tempting than I had ever anticipated. His gaze alone flooded me with a wave of heat, but it was something deeper that sent goosebumps rippling across my skin—something dangerous in the air.

But then I saw him. A ghost lingering in the shadows. Ares, cigarette glowing between his fingers, watching me with that same unshaken indifference. He hadn't changed. My foolish heart still clung to the hope that he cared, even though I knew better.

Hephaestus reached for my hand, his touch refocusing me as he lifted it to his lips. His kiss lingered over my engagement ring, a silent reminder of the chains binding me to him. Yet, as he did, my eyes couldn't help but flicker back to Ares, as if he were the one holding the key to my freedom.

"You're my fucking goddess," Hephaestus whispered, his voice filled with desire. With a subtle tug, he tried to pull me closer, but I stopped just inches away, feeling the tension build. The intensity in his eyes told me that a simple kiss wouldn't satisfy him. He craved more, something far beyond what we'd already shared. And while I could feel that same heat pulsing through me, I wasn't quite ready to cross that line. Not yet.

"Ready?" I grinned. "It's time for our party."

His hand released my hand. "It would be my pleasure to take you to our party," he said, winking as he swung open the . Hephaestus helped me into the vehicle and closed the door behind me. Through the window, I saw Ares emerge from the shadows of the night, wearing a black helmet, a fitted suit, and a crisp white dress shirt.

The manor glowed. Even in the wake of his child's tragic death, my father expertly masked his grief behind an impeccable façade of opulence. Guests ascended the grand staircase while a line of luxury vehicles awaited the valet's attention. Gaia, ever the perfectionist, orchestrated every detail with ruthless precision, even for a daughter she never wanted.

The driver stopped and the valet opened my door to assist me in getting out. People watched us, but I remained focused on one thing —Titan. I wouldn't let anything stand in the way of uncovering the truth about his death.

As we walked through the manor's halls, memories unfolded before my eyes, replaying like a movie in my head. Titan used to chase me down the grand staircase while Gaia's voice echoed through the halls. Father would lock himself away in his office, a fortress of isolation.

I remembered the nights when Titan's face bore the marks of our father's fury, his cheek swollen and bruised, a painful reminder of the dark shadows that loomed over our family.

From a young age, it was clear that we were mere pawns in my father's elaborate game of power and influence. Our roles, our lives, were nothing more than pieces to be moved and sacrificed at his whim. The realization that my worth was dictated by his ambitions weighed heavily on me, shaping my every decision and fear.

But now, standing on the precipice of my own choices, I refused to be controlled or defined by his schemes any longer. I was determined to reclaim my autonomy and break free from the chains of his manipulation.

No one owned me.

Gaia's jaw tightened conspicuously at the sight of me. She regarded me with disdain.

"You should change." she sneered.

I wrapped my arms around Hephaestus, trying to step into the role of devoted fiancé. A faint blush crept over my skin as his rough hand settled at the small of my back. Instead of feeling uneasy, his touch brought an unexpected sense of comfort.

My thoughts swirled, knowing this seemingly small gesture carried weight. Hephaestus pressed a tender kiss to my temple, and I closed my eyes, feeling my heartbeat quicken with a mixture of tenderness and turmoil.

"I think she looks stunning," he said.

Gaia raised her champagne flute and drank the remainder of its contents. Her face was grief stricken. She seemed like she was fading away, mind and body. I couldn't imagine the extent of her despair.

While my affection for my brother was deep, it was nothing compared to a mother's love.

"There's my daughter," Ouranos's voice boomed through the grand hall as he appeared at the top of the stairs. He made his way down, extending his hand to Hephaestus. "And my future son-in-law. Welcome to the family."

"It's a pleasure," Hephaestus replied, his irritation barely masked behind a calm facade. They exchanged a brief, tense glance before Ouranos's attention turned to me. His smile was charming yet carried a predatory gleam, his eyes lingering on me with unsettling intensity.

"Daughter," Ouranos said, his voice carrying a mix of formality and disdain. He glanced past me, noting something—or someone—behind me. "Zeus, I'm pleased you could gather your crew for this." With that, he brushed past me, leaving a charged silence in his wake.

Zeus's voice cut through the stillness, laced with derision. "Is this what you call a party?" Hephaestus handed me a flute of champagne

The dimly lit hall, illuminated only by the flickering glow of a grand chandelier, exuded the eerie charm of a lavish haunted house. Blood-red flowers tumbled in a dramatic cascade down the ornate staircase, their dark hues adding a macabre elegance to the scene.

The room shimmered with golden light, the haunting strains of violins filling the air with a tense, gothic melody. As I stood there, it felt as though the room had transported me back in time, to the harrowing moment of my brother's execution.

My heart pounded with a desperate intensity as I struggled to maintain my composure. This wasn't a celebration; it was a masquerade of mourning, a funeral cloaked in the guise of a party. "I need some air." I murmured, struggling to breathe under the weight of the guests' piercing gazes.

The atmosphere grew even more charged when Atlas and his son, Hermes arrived. Rivals and allies mingled in this charged space. If there was an occasion to take someone out, this would be it.

"I'll come with you." Hephaestus rubbed my shoulder, "You're so tense."

"Give me a second, please."

I kissed his cheek and gently brushed his hair from his eyes. It was a small gesture, yet it stirred something deep within me. Subconsciously, I resisted the space he was carving in my heart, though I recognized its presence.

It offered a welcome diversion from the thoughts of Ares.

"Okay." His hooded eyes darkened with a slight smile, as he rubbed my engagement ring, "If you need me, I'll be here."

I nodded and said, "I'll be right back." Making my way past him, I headed towards a hallway that the staff utilized and exited on the other side of the manor.

Stepping onto the terrace, I caught sight of my father's fountain, the haunting silhouette a grim reminder of my place in this world. Taking a deep breath, I covered my face with my hands, letting out a shuddering exhale.

As I lifted my head, I caught sight of a flicker of movement near the edge of the forest. The shadows seem to part as he emerged from the darkness. The man who had taken me to the compound, the man I had once entrusted with my heart and soul, now stood at the forest's edge.

Ares strode toward me, his figure silhouetted against the low-hanging moon. The sharp, steady rhythm of his boots striking the stone pathway echoed through the still night, each step tightening the knot in my stomach. His eyes locked onto mine, piercing through the darkness with an intensity that made my skin prickle. The air around us thickened as his lips twisted into a devilish smirk, a predator closing in on its prey.

I could feel my heartbeat pounding in my ears, my palms slick with sweat. He was like a shadow, haunting and inevitable, and I could barely breathe under the weight of his gaze.

"What do you want, Ares?" My voice trembled despite my efforts to sound steady. The night air was chilled, yet his presence sent a warmth through me that I couldn't ignore. I took a step back, instinctively trying to create space between us, but it was futile. He ascended each step with a deliberate, almost predatory grace, closing the distance between us.

"I don't like seeing him touch you," Ares growled, his voice a low rumble that sent a shiver down my spine. In the dim light, his eyes glowed with a fierce intensity, a striking blend of gold and brown that seemed to pierce through the shadows.

He stood with an unshakable confidence, his sleeves rolled up as if prepared for a fight. As he slowly licked his bottom lip, my breath caught in my throat. "I'm losing control," he murmured, his voice dark and urgent. "I want all of you, Aphrodite. I can't stand seeing you with him." His words hung heavily in the air, charged with a dangerous desperation.

"Don't," I said, shaking my head in frustration. His presence grated on me, his anger unsettling. How dare he act like the scorned lover when he had vanished without a trace? I had bared my soul to him, trusted him with my deepest pain, and all he had given me was empty promises and false hope about finding Titan's murderer.

*Stupid girl*, I berated myself.

The anger that had been simmering inside me was boiling over. I felt a fierce heat rising in my chest, my frustration finally breaking free. How could he just disappear without a trace, leaving me to face everything alone? Each unanswered call, each ignored message was a cruel reminder of his absence, and it all fueled the fire burning within me.

"I'm done, Ares," I whispered, tears streaming down my face as my voice wavered with emotion. "I needed you," I cried out, my voice breaking the silence of the night. "After I bared my soul to you, you turned away. I gave you everything—my body, my very essence. I was terrified for you, but you didn't reach out, didn't even call." My words hung heavy, tinged with betrayal and frustration.

"I'm sorry, Aphrodite—Please, let me explain," Ares's voice suddenly cut through my thoughts, filled with frustration as he appeared in front of me. His hair was disheveled, his gaze intense. I saw the turmoil in his eyes—fear, regret, and an aching vulnerability. It chipped away at my resolve despite the hollow ache his unexplained absence had left in my heart. But this wasn't just about us anymore. It was a matter of life or death.

"I'm terrified, okay?" Ares continued, his voice rising, almost frantic. "I'm scared of what you make me feel, of how deep this could go. I don't know how to handle it—I don't know how to handle you. But I can't stay away, and it's driving me insane!" His confession hung in the air, raw and vulnerable, making the distance between us feel like an impossible chasm.

If Hephaestus were to discover our affair, his rage would go far beyond punishing his brother. He'd come for both of us, unleashing a storm that would drown us in its wake, turning our forbidden love into a dangerous game we might not survive.

I looked at Ares, my voice trembling with a mix of anger and sorrow.

"You're fortunate, Ares. You live freely while I'm trapped in a cage, treated like nothing but an object to barter with. I was auctioned off to the highest bidder. I've always been a pawn in my father's cruel game, and nothing has changed. My feelings, my very existence—they don't mean anything to anyone." The words spilled out, laden with the bitterness of being used and being disregarded. I felt as though I were nothing more than a pawn on a chessboard being played by forces beyond my control.

Ares crossed his arms tightly against his chest, his eyes narrowing at me as he spoke.

"Aphrodite, I'm the only one fighting for you," Ares said, his voice thick with a mix of frustration and desperation. "While I've been gone, I've been out there risking everything—my position, my life, my loyalty to the Syndicate—all to uncover the truth about Titan's death. No one else is doing that for you. Every time I leave, I'm putting a target on my back just by asking the wrong questions, by pushing people who don't want to be pushed. I've been trying to protect you, even from a distance."

His eyes, burning with a mix of fear and anger, bore into mine. "But you—going down this road with Hephaestus—you don't see what you're stepping into. And when you finally find out who killed Titan, what are you going to do? Are you ready to take a life?" His words hit like a knife, challenging and almost accusing, revealing more than just concern. "I don't believe you could lay a hand on anyone, and I don't think you realize the blood you'll spill if you try."

His tone softened, but the tension between us only thickened, his absence now filled with reasons I hadn't expected, yet still not enough to ease the anger and betrayal I felt. I didn't have to explain anything to him. Justice for Titan was the only thing that mattered, not his excuses or empty promises.

I turned sharply, ready to storm back toward the doorway, but before I could take another step, Ares's hand gripped my waist, pulling me back into him. His touch sent a shock through me, a cruel reminder of the connection I tried so hard to sever.

"I can't stand the thought of you facing those demons out there," Ares said, his voice rough with emotion. "You know what you mean to me, Aphrodite. You're my greatest weakness, the one thing that could destroy me." His hand lingered on my waist, the tension between us sparking like fire, his touch sending a wave of heat through me.

My lips quivered. "Ares," I whispered, barely able to keep my voice steady. I lifted my hand to his face, my fingers brushing against the stubble on his cheek, feeling the warmth of his breath as it mingled with mine. "In another world, another life... I would be yours, completely."

I paused, the truth of our situation sinking in like a dagger. "But we live in *this* world," I continued, my voice trembling with bitter resignation. "A world where I'm betrothed to your brother, where

I'm expected to marry him while pretending this—*us*—never happened." The weight of it pressed on my chest, suffocating me. "A world where we have to keep our feelings buried beneath lies and duty. And in this reality, what I need from you, Ares, is to help me avenge my brother's death."

The words tasted bitter on my tongue, each one a reminder of the chains that bound us to a life we didn't choose, where love was a dangerous luxury and loyalty to bloodlines came first.

I searched his eyes, filled with a sadness and desperation that mirrored my own. "I know you cared for Titan," I added softly, the weight of what I was asking hanging between us. "I can't do this without you."

I stepped away and he dropped his hands from my waist. I immediately felt cold and alone without the warmth of his touch.

"I'm going to search my father's office," I murmured, my voice edged with determination. "I need to know if Titan owed money, or if there's something deeper they've been keeping from us." The urgency in my tone betrayed the weight of the secrets lurking behind our family's polished exterior—secrets that, once uncovered, could bring everything crashing down.

Ares ran a hand through his hair, avoiding eye contact. "I'll come with you," he said.

I nodded. There were a lot of people here with prying eyes, and I needed someone to keep an eye on things while I looked around.

"When the first dinner course is served, I'll excuse myself," I said, my voice firm but low. "You should wait ten minutes before following me. Any sooner, and people might get suspicious."

Ares nodded, the resolve in his eyes matching my own before he turned to leave.

I took a deep breath, trying to steady the rapid drumming of my heart. The weight of the moment pressed down on me, and I felt my eyes begin to burn.

My father had made it clear that Hephaestus and I needed to present a united front. He encouraged us to engage with every guest as a couple, reinforcing the importance of our union.

This marriage wasn't just a personal matter—it was a strategic alliance that cemented the alliance between the Olympus Syndicate and the Aetos Family. The strength of our union would ensure that both families were not just allies but a formidable force, commanding respect and fear throughout the city.

"Overwhelmed?" I whispered to Hephaestus, his cologne—an intoxicating blend of musk and spice—enveloping me as it drifted on the air.

He intertwined his fingers with mine, his touch both warm and reassuring. "Not at all. You have a way of making me feel calm, even in the midst of this chaos."

"Really?" I chuckled softly, the sound hollow as I tried to mask my unease. "You don't know me well enough for that." I cast a fleeting glance around the room, doing my best to maintain a mask of composure. Yet, despite my efforts, a shiver ran down my spine as I felt the weight of two distinct sets of eyes upon me.

Hephaestus's gaze was intense and magnetic, radiating heat and searing into my skin. His charisma was almost tangible, a smoldering presence that demanded attention.

But it was the other gaze that tore at my insides. Ares, lurking in the shadows, watched me with a haunting intensity.

# CHAPTER NINETEEN
## ARES

I felt like I was being toyed with by the devil as I watched my angel slip further away from me. Because of potential gossip spreading, I had to keep my distance from Aphrodite.

Fear gnawed at me, the terror that she might discover my brother's accusations that I was somehow involved in Titan's death. She couldn't catch wind of what was being said. If she did, she might believe it. Although it wasn't true, any suspicion she had could destroy everything between us.

Despite my efforts to stay away, the thought of being close to her consumed me.

The temptation to taste her again was maddening; I craved the feel of her in my arms, her heartbeat syncing with mine. She was my temptress, my siren, luring me in even as she kept her distance. Seeing her with Hephaestus was agony. Watching her let him into her life, into her heart—it was like watching her slip further into a trap I could see so clearly. He was no good for her. His charm was nothing but a mask, a carefully laid snare.

Hephaestus's hunger for power was insatiable. He'd stop at nothing—lie, betray, twist the truth—to get what he wanted, and I knew he was using her to get it. The thought of her caught in his web, manipulated by his lies, made my blood boil. But getting close to her again was dangerous. I knew that. I felt it. Still, no matter the risk, I couldn't stop wanting her. I couldn't stop imagining what it would be like to hold her again, to make her mine like she should have been all along.

I was losing myself, teetering on the edge of obsession. But the need to be with her, to shield her from him, was stronger than my fear of what could happen if I gave in.

I grabbed a glass of whiskey from the bar, the burn of it sliding down my throat doing little to dull the ache inside. As I watched her effortlessly play the part of the perfect bride for my brother, something ignited within me—a burning anger that had nothing to do with her. It was me. I had failed her. Failed to say what needed to be said, failed to keep her from slipping through my fingers. And now, here she was, slipping further away, and it was my silence that had pushed her into this life.

Aphrodite's eyes flicked toward me, a brief glance that silently acknowledged the tension hanging between us. She leaned in, whispering something in Hephaestus's ear before standing.

My gaze trailed her every step as she moved gracefully through the room, past him and the guests, making her way toward the long table adorned with a lavish display of flowers—Gaia's handiwork, meticulously arranged to perfection.

Time dragged on, each second feeling like an eternity. When I finally glanced down at my watch, the ten minutes had passed. Careful not to draw any attention from my crew, I quietly slipped away from the table, all too aware that Hephaestus would soon sense something was off.

I slipped out of the grand hall and into the dimly lit hallway, my heart pounding as I quickly scanned my surroundings. The corridor was eerily empty, the silence unsettling. With a deep breath, I made my way toward Ouranos's office. But just as I turned a corner, a firm grip seized me, yanking me into a dark room before I could react.

Aphrodite squeezed my hand, her eyes locking with mine. "Ouranos is in his office," she whispered.

"I don't remember seeing him leave," I murmured, my mind scrambling to recall who had stayed behind at the table in the grand hall.

"That's because you were too busy staring at me." Her lips curled into a knowing smile, her eyes glimmering in the moonlight streaming through the window. The pull to touch her was almost unbearable.

"Is there anywhere we can listen in on what he's doing?" I asked, my curiosity heightened as I wondered if the manor held any hidden secrets.

"There's a closet next to his office with a vent. My brother and I used to eavesdrop through it when we were kids," she said, a faint smirk playing on her lips.

Moving silently, Aphrodite led the way down the hallway, our footsteps barely making a sound on the polished floor. We crept closer to the closet, and with a quiet twist of the handle, she pushed the door open, slipping inside. I followed, closing it softly behind us, the room instantly consumed by darkness.

I pulled out my phone and flicked on the flashlight, the soft glow illuminating her face for a moment. Her scent, that intoxicating blend of jasmine and warm vanilla, enveloped me, stirring a raw, primal need to pull her into my arms and feel her beneath my hands. But I forced myself to focus, the danger we were stepping into far more important than the temptation that clouded my mind.

The small, cramped space of the closet made everything feel unbearably intimate. I stood close to her, our bodies almost brushing, the heat between us palpable. The proximity, her scent, her warmth—it was enough to make my body react, a sharp reminder of the nights we'd spent together. My thoughts drifted back to the feel of her beneath me, the way she fit so perfectly.

The memory alone made me ache for her all over again. I could see the way she shifted, struggling to find space, but also affected by the tension between us.

It was undeniable, this pull—dangerous, consuming, inevitable.

My eyes began adjusting to the dark, and I instinctively reached for the light switch. She quickly stopped me, her hand wrapping around mine. "If we turn on the light, they'll know someone's in here," she whispered, her breath warm against my skin.

I licked my bottom lip, trying to steady myself, but the feel of her breath sent a pulse of heat straight through me; my dick hardening in response.

Being here with her felt like we were teenagers, sneaking moments in the dark, like a forbidden game of seven minutes in heaven. Every inch of me wanted to pull her close, feel her lips, run my hands along her thighs. I wanted her—more than anything.

I saw her eyes widen slightly. She gestured toward the vent, her voice soft but steady. "If you remove it, we'll be able to hear better."

My gaze lingered on her longer than it should have, my mind split between the task at hand and the unbearable desire simmering between us.

Reaching for the vent, I pulled it off the wall as quietly as possible. We listened closely, hearing Ouranos talking to someone on the other side.

"We still don't know who it could be." I recognized my father's voice.

"What?" Ouranos' voice boomed, followed by the sound of something crashing which echoed through the vent.

"We've got not leads," my father said, his frustration evident. "We've talked to everyone in the area, but there's nothing to go on after the explosion. Even the guy at the police station had no new information. The scene was cleared."

"How is that even possible?" Ouranos's voice was sharp with disbelief. "You're telling me you have absolutely no idea who did this? This isn't just some random act of violence. Titan's death isn't a small matter—it's a direct threat to the stability between our families."

He paused, his voice growing more intense. "You've got to understand, Zeus. Our alliance is fragile. There's a lot riding on the marriage between our families, and now this. I need to know if this is a message, a power play. If it turns out your people are behind this, it would mean a betrayal of the worst kind. Do you realize what that would mean for our relationship?"

Ouranos's voice dropped, filled with accusation and suspicion. "How can you be so sure it wasn't orchestrated by someone from your side? I need answers, Zeus. If it was your people who did this, it's more than just a threat—it's an act of war. And you can't expect me to sit idly by while my son's death goes unpunished."

"Come on, Ouranos," Zeus's voice was cold and dismissive. "What would we possibly gain from your son's death? The marriage to your daughter? You know as well as I do that she's not some prize to be won. Her value to us isn't measured by her family's wealth or influence."

Zeus's tone grew sharper as he continued, "Maybe you thought we had some grand scheme in mind, but you're wrong. This isn't about some twisted game or hidden agenda. We're dealing with a situation that's beyond our control, and there's no profit in Titan's death for us. The real question is why your son was targeted. If you're looking for answers, maybe you should be asking yourself why he was mixed up in something that got him killed."

There was a tense silence before Zeus's voice cut through again, more forceful this time. "We're already stretched thin dealing with the fallout. The wedding is days away, and that's where our focus needs to be. We've done everything we can to address this so-called crime. If you're looking for someone to blame, you'd better be ready to confront the harsh reality that Titan's death was a result of his own choices. It's a mess that neither of us wanted, but accusing us without evidence isn't going to solve anything."

Ouranos's frustration was evident. "Let me make one thing clear,

Zeus. If it turns out that your family had anything to do with Titan's death, you'll wish you'd never crossed us. You'll beg for mercy before I'm through with you."

As the heated exchange continued, Aphrodite rubbed her forehead, clearly distressed. I reached out, touching her cheek gently, trying to offer some comfort.

Despite the harsh words being exchanged, the underlying truth was that neither side had concrete answers. We were all left grappling with the uncertainty of Titan's murder and the strained relations between our families.

"We are going to find the person who killed your brother," I promised her, my voice firm despite the uncertainty hanging over us.

"There's nothing here!" she said, her voice cracking with frustration. "No one knows anything. Why even bother trying to uncover the truth? If we find out what really happened, what do we do then?" Her eyes brimmed with tears as one slipped down her cheek. I reached out and gently wiped it away.

"We would get what you wanted—justice for Titan," I reminded her, my gaze steady. "This wasn't a random act, Aphrodite. There's a reason behind it. We need to uncover that reason."

Her arms slipped around my waist, and I held her close, feeling the tremble in her body as she rested her head against my chest. "What if it was your family?" she asked quietly, her voice muffled by the fabric of my shirt.

I pulled back slightly to look into her eyes. She was trying to hide her tears, but the pain was evident. "It wasn't us," I said, my tone reassuring. "I know it wasn't us. We wouldn't have any reason to harm Titan. I promise you that."

She searched my face for the truth, her expression a mix of hope and doubt. "But if it wasn't your family, then who? Why would anyone want him dead?"

"I don't have all the answers yet," I admitted, "but I do know that we have to keep searching. There's more to this than we know, and we won't stop until we find out the truth. I'm not going to let this go. Not for you, and not for Titan."

Aphrodite nodded slowly, her resolve visibly strengthening despite the exhaustion in her eyes. "Okay," she said softly. "I'll keep going, but I need you with me. We need to do this together."

"We will," I promised, my voice resolute. "We'll get through this, and we'll find the answers. We owe it to Titan, and to ourselves."

I pressed a gentle kiss to her forehead, closing my eyes as I savored the warmth of her body against mine. I understood she was hesitant to get too close, to deepen the emotional connection between us. She needed her space, and as much as it hurt, I knew I had to respect that. The struggle of maintaining this distance was excruciating, but it was the only choice I had. I let her go and immediately felt empty in the absence of her touch. I turned toward the doorway and whispered over my shoulder, "Wait for five minutes before you come out."

I navigated the shadowy hallways, my heart thundering against my ribcage. The urgency in my steps quickened as I noticed the waiters slipping out of the grand hall, their departure a silent signal that time was slipping away. Just as I neared the door, Hephaestus appeared from the gloom, blocking my path.

"Where the hell have you been?" His voice was a harsh whisper, like a storm brewing. His grip on my forearm was unyielding, a vise of raw authority.

"None of your business," I retorted, yanking my arm from his grasp with a fierce pull. The force of the movement nearly spun me around, and I glared up at him, defiance blazing in my eyes. The air between us crackled with electric tension, every second charged with unspoken animosity.

"Where is Aphrodite? She always seems to be tagging along with you, like a lost puppy." he spat. "Where is my fiancé?" Hephaestus bellowed, his face red with rage. He crossed his arms, his gaze briefly meeting mine before shifting away. I followed his line of sight and saw Aphrodite approaching us.

"What's going on here?" Aphrodite asked, her voice a mix of curiosity and feigned innocence as she tilted her head slightly, trying to gauge the situation.

Hephaestus's eyes burned with frustration, his voice low but seething with anger. "Where the hell have you been?" His grip on my forearm tightened, a physical manifestation of his irritation.

"I told you, I just needed a moment," Aphrodite responded calmly.

I stepped in, trying to ease the escalating tension. "I went outside for a smoke, Hephaestus," I said, giving his chest a light pat. "No need to be paranoid. They've got meds for that." I nodded towards Aphrodite. "Come on, you two," I said with a smirk. "You've got an engagement to celebrate, remember? Try to enjoy it."

But as I turned to leave, Hephaestus moved in front of Aphrodite, blocking her path. His expression was intense, his anger barely contained. "You think you can just bounce between my brothers like you're some kind of plaything?" His voice was thunderous, and he gripped her chin, forcing her to meet his glare.

Aphrodite flinched, her eyes wide with a mixture of hurt and defiance. "Nothing happened!" she shouted, her voice cracking as she struggled to free herself from his hold.

*You mother fucker*, I thought as I clenched my fist.

"You get your fucking hands off her!" I snarled, my voice sharp as a blade.

I stepped toward him, my pulse quickening. Hephaestus turned to face me, his eyes narrowing in defiance. My heart thundered in my chest, a primal urge for violence surging through me. In one swift motion, I slammed Hephaestus against the rough wall, the impact reverberating through my bones.

His hands tried to pull my arms away from where they were tightly wrapped around his neck. "Don't you ever put your hands on Aphrodite!" He gasped as his neck tensed under the pressure of my grip, my hands desperate to squeeze the life out of him.

"Ares! Let him go!" Aphrodite pleaded, her voice desperate as she tugged at my shirt. Her fingers clutched the fabric, pulling me from my rage as I finally met her eyes.

I released him.

My hands trembled at my sides, fists clenched, barely holding back the fury that surged through me, each pulse of rage filling my heart to the brim. I stepped back from Hephaestus, who was hunched over, gasping for air.

Aphrodite, fear flickering in her wide eyes, scrambled to pull him away, her movements frantic as she shielded him from my wrath.

I had to get out of this place—before it swallowed me whole, before the darkness inside me did something I couldn't take back.

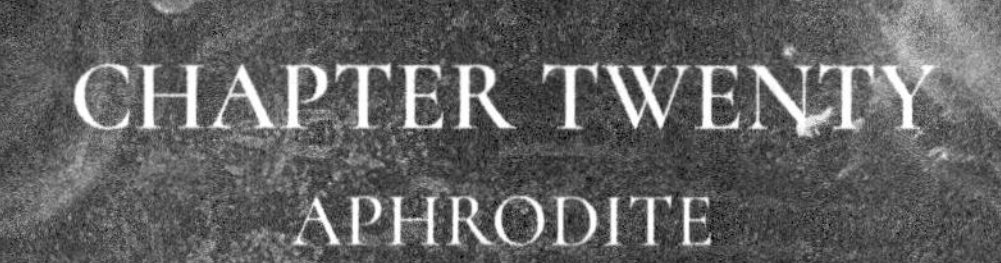

# CHAPTER TWENTY
## APHRODITE

I stood behind the bar, my hands trembling as I mixed another cocktail.

The neon lights of the club flickered and flashed, casting garish colors that only seemed to deepen the hollow ache in my chest.

Hephaestus had demanded that I bartend at his bachelor party, a clear message that he didn't trust me—not after what happened at the engagement party. Each drink I poured felt like a reminder of the control he held over me, a bitter taste of the power struggle that had left me trapped in this situation.

My mind flashed back to the manor, his eyes on me as he gripped my chin tight. There was a dark, menacing glint in his stare that sent a shiver down my spine. That was why he insisted on having me here tonight—so he could keep me within sight, where he believed I belonged.

As I poured drinks for his guests, my gaze drifted toward him, unable to resist. He was surrounded by half-naked women, their hands all over him, fawning and giggling like he was some kind of

God. Disgust twisted in my gut. Artie had wanted to punch him the second we walked in and saw the room full of his so-called "special guests."

Hephaestus appeared every bit the chivalrous gentleman at our engagement party, but his kindness and grace were a perfect mask. He expected me to endure this humiliation without a word, to silently accept it like I deserved some kind of punishment.

I had allowed myself to believe he was truly striving to be a decent man, only to have my hopes shattered. The realization of his deceit left me feeling not just foolish, but betrayed, as though a dark shadow had crept into my heart, tainting the trust I had so naively offered.

His jealousy of Ares wasn't unwarranted, but the truth was Ares and I would only be working together to find my brother's killer. That's all our relationship could be. No matter the tension that crackled in the air whenever we were alone, no matter the way his eyes lingered on mine, or how my pulse quickened at the thought of him, it couldn't go beyond that. It *shouldn't*. I couldn't let it. There were too many risks.

"Why are you dressed like a nun?" Artie said, breaking me out of my reverie.

Glancing down at my outfit, I realized I was dressed in far less revealing clothing than the other women here. I wore a long leather skirt and black satin blouse, with my hair in a loose, messy bun. "I didn't need to dress any differently than usual. I'm here to work." The truth was, I had no interest in pleasing Hephaestus.

Artie snatched a pair of scissors from behind the bar and hollered, "Get over here, girl. Apollo, handle the bar!" She grasped my hand firmly and guided me down a narrow hallway. We entered an office where Athena was meticulously organizing a stack of paperwork.

Athena's eyes flicked up from her work, taking in my attire before her gaze narrowed at Artie and the scissors. "You'd think by now you'd have figured out how to dress appropriately around here," she said, her voice dripping with disdain as she leaned against the back of her chair, arms crossed tightly over her chest.

"Stop being a bitch, Athena. She's hardly got any leather to work with," Artie snapped, pulling me closer and flashing a grin that was both comforting and defiant.

"They didn't give me the memo about what to wear," I replied, shrugging nonchalantly. "I'm stuck with what was provided. Hephaestus has me confined to the compound." I met her gaze squarely, refusing to let her criticism unsettle me.

Athena pointed at my clothing with a critical eye. "Cut the skirt and get rid of the top," she instructed sharply.

"What?" I exclaimed, taken aback.

Artie leaned in, dropping to her knees with scissors in hand. "I'm with the boss on this one." I hesitated for a moment before removing my shirt, leaving me in just my bra. Athena handed me a black leather corset.

"This will do," she said, her tone leaving no room for argument. "Lose the bra."

"Now everyone will see that you're officially one of us," Artie whispered with a hint of mischief. She deftly cut my skirt, transforming it into a miniskirt that barely covered anything.

Athena then cinched the corset tightly, the leather wrapping around me so firmly that it felt as though I was encased in it. I struggled to adjust my posture, trying to breathe and move in ways that felt foreign and restrictive.

"Now we're talking!" Artie was pleased. I shook my head in disapproval.

Athena spun around to face me, her eyes blazing. "Listen up, girl, you need to show these assholes that you're not here to play games. They're idiots, driven by one thing, and it sure as hell isn't their brains. Make them see your worth—show them you're more than just a piece of eye candy. You're not just some object they can toss around. Make them respect you or make them regret it."

"Dressing like this--," I pointed to the outfit, "Makes me look like an object."

"Do you know how spies use sex as a weapon?" Athena asked, her tone a matter of fact, as if she were discussing something as ordinary as the weather.

"What?" I replied, my voice tinged with confusion, trying to grasp the sudden shift in the conversation.

"Spies use their seductive abilities to manipulate their targets," Athena explained, her voice unwavering and authoritative, as though she were detailing a well-known strategy rather than offering advice. "They exploit allure and desire to control and deceive."

She paused, her gaze piercing as if measuring the weight of her words. "So, my best advice? Use what you've got and get even," Athena spoke with the poise of someone who had mastered the art of turning weakness into strength, of navigating treacherous waters without flinching. Her confidence was palpable, rooted in a wealth of experience and an unyielding determination to stand her ground against those who sought to undermine her.

Understanding her intention, I nodded, the weight of her words sinking in. Before exiting, Athena shared a meaningful glance with her sister, their silent exchange carrying a weight of unspoken understanding.

Artie, rising from the floor and brushing off her clothes, met my gaze with a reassuring smile. "Athena is a woman of few words, but she makes a whole lot of impact," she said. "You're ready."

Every man in the room seemed eager for my attention as I poured their drinks.

Except for one.

Hephaestus was surrounded by a group of unfamiliar men, a

woman casually perched on his lap, unaware that his future wife was mixing their drinks behind the bar. I tried to brush it off, faking my laughter while chatting with another guest.

The music pulsed so loudly that my head throbbed with each beat, the rhythm mirroring the tension tightening in my chest.

Behind the polished wood of the bar, I mixed drinks with mechanical precision, each motion automatic as I struggled to conceal the turmoil seething beneath the surface. I was lost in the repetitive motions—shaking cocktails, pouring shots—when I felt a sharp, unsettling gaze.

Glancing up, I caught Ares's eyes from across the room. He stood amid the group of men, his intense gaze locked onto me.

"He hasn't been able to look away from you," Artie's voice pulled me back to reality as I served shots over the bar.

Ares sat down in the corner, bathed in the soft glow of the neon sign above him.

Despite the busy bar, I couldn't help but look at him. Every time our eyes met; a shiver ran down my spine. The air between us crackled with that familiar electricity, just like we felt back in that closet.

Whether it was a fleeting glance or an attempt to appear disinterested, his hazel eyes sent waves of longing through me, making my body tremble with an unmistakable desire.

Swallowing hard, I knew he was watching, his gaze sending prickles scattering across my skin. "I don't think so," I muttered.

"Listen," Artie said, turning to face me, her expression serious.

"Ares is in love with you."

The moment she said "love," my mouth went dry. The music in the background faded to a distant hum, and all I could hear was the pounding of my heart against my ribs. I shook my head vigorously, trying to reject the idea.

"You're in denial, girl. You're straddling the fence," Artie continued, pouring shots for an older man who clearly should've been cut off long ago.

"I need to focus on finding—"

"Yes! I get that. But you can't ignore what's happening between you and Ares. You have feelings for him, too. What is going to happen when you marry Hephaestus?" Leaning her head to the side, she gripped the counter's edge and gave me a scrutinizing look.

I felt a wave of frustration rise within me. "You don't think I know that?" I snapped, my voice edged with desperation. My heart pounded as I struggled to keep my composure. The emptiness that had settled inside me since Ares started distancing himself felt like a gaping chasm. I rolled my eyes, trying to mask the turmoil, but my hands trembled slightly as I refocused on the drinks, desperate to avoid facing the raw truth of my feelings.

When I glanced back to where he was sitting, he was already gone, leaving behind a void that seemed to echo with his absence.

"I need to take five," I said, giving Artie's shoulder a gentle squeeze. She nodded, understanding that I needed a moment to catch my breath.

I left the towel on the counter and made my way down the dimly lit hallway. Suddenly, out of the darkness, a hand shot out, grabbing me by the waist and yanking me aside. A small cry escaped my lips as Ares pulled me into an empty room, slamming the door shut behind us.

He lifted me effortlessly onto a table, the movement both possessive and tender. Our lips met in a searing kiss, and I was immediately enveloped by the rich, whiskey-flavored warmth of his tongue. It ignited a fire within me, one that spread through my entire being with a fervor that left me breathless.

In that moment, I knew, without a shadow of a doubt, that I belonged to him, and all I yearned for was to feel cherished by him once again.

As our kiss deepened, I wrapped my arms around his neck, pulling him closer. His hands roamed with a heated intensity, squeezing my ass possessively as I pressed my thighs firmly against his waist.

Every touch, every caress from Ares made me feel like I was worthy of love, like I could mean everything to someone who truly cared. His presence was a powerful affirmation of my own worth, a stark contrast to the emptiness I had felt before.

I craved more than just physical connection. I longed for a man who desired to consume me entirely—body and soul—a man who would not only make me feel desired but also treasured. Ares had become the embodiment of that yearning, igniting a deep and insatiable desire within me for a love that was all-encompassing.

I leaned in, pressing my body against the warmth of his solid chest, aching to close the distance between us even more. Every inch of me craved to be closer, but I reluctantly pulled away, my lips lingering in a silent plea for more. His eyes snapped open and locked onto mine, causing my breath to hitch in my throat. The intensity in his gaze spoke volumes, conveying a thousand unspoken words that wrapped around my heart with an electric charge.

I reached up, my fingers tracing the contours of his face. As I caressed his skin, I felt the tension in his muscles gradually dissolve beneath my touch.

"Leave with me tonight." he said, his voice a low, urgent whisper that left me speechless. His hands mirrored mine, and I felt the roughness of his palm as he caressed my cheek. "Be with me, Aphrodite. Forget everything that's happening around us. We can start our own lives somewhere far—"

"I—" My mind struggled to grasp his words. The idea of leaving with him was thrilling, a chance to escape our suffocating reality. But the harsh truth was that if we fled, we'd become targets, and Ares's life would be at risk. "Ares," I said, a wave of sorrow crashing over me. "We can't. It's too dangerous. They'd never stop hunting us. They'd kill you."

"Yes, we can!" he insisted, his voice a fervent murmur that cut through the despair. "We'll change our names, reinvent ourselves. We can be whoever we want to be."

"They will never stop searching for us." I ran my hand through his hair, and he leaned his forehead onto mine in response.

"I can't watch you marry Hephaestus." Ares nestled his head into my shoulder and kissed my collarbone gently. My arms found their way around his neck, and he moved his lips up to my jaw. "I am in love with you, Aphrodite. And I don't know how not to be."

Lifting his head, he met my gaze with eyes that were reddened and full of raw emotion. "Look at me when you say that," I urged, needing to see the sincerity in his eyes.

Ares gazed into my eyes, "I love you, Aphrodite, in so many ways that I can't even begin to express."

I kissed him deeply, the intensity of our passion overwhelming, but I pulled away once more, the reality of our situation crashing down on me. "We can't do this, Ares."

"Why?" He pleaded, holding my chin gently. "Tell me why? Because we can't keep ignoring this."

"I'm scared," I confessed, feeling my heart take over. Our passion was intense, our desire undeniable. "I'm terrified of loving you."

I clung to his shirt and pulled him closer. Without hesitation, Ares lips crashed into mine. I felt as though the rest of the world faded into insignificance.

The flame that burned in my heart was his and his alone, an all-consuming fire that made everything else seem trivial in comparison. Our kiss transcended mere physical space; it was as if we were reaching beyond our bodies, touching the very essence of each other's being.

Pulling apart, we stood close, our breaths mingling. The intensity in Ares's eyes mirrored the desperation in my own.

He understood the restraints of my loveless marriage and the heavy chains that bound me to Hephaestus, making it impossible to break free. My impending doom overshadowed any possibility of happiness we could have shared.

"I'll make sure this marriage becomes nothing more than a

distant memory," Ares vowed, his hands cradling my face as our bodies pressed together. "No matter what it takes."

"How?" I asked, my voice tinged with despair.

Ares stepped back and dug into his pocket. He pulled out a small plastic bag, filled with small white pills. "Tomorrow, after the wedding, Hephaestus will be expecting you to come to his bed. I'll handle getting him sufficiently intoxicated, but it'll be up to you to slip him one of these when the time is right."

Fear widened my eyes as I whispered, "I'm not going to drug him."

"It will only make him fall asleep for a few hours," Ares explained, his tone firm yet soothing. "He won't be harmed."

"What if he wakes up?" I asked, anxiety gripping me. "What then?"

Ares rubbed his face, a mix of frustration and sorrow etched into his features. "We'll deal with it if it happens. I have a plan to ensure he stays out of the way long enough for us to find a solution."

I tugged his face toward mine, feeling the weight of his anguish seep into me. Our eyes locked, and in his gaze, I saw the reflection of my own torment and desperation.

Being with Hephaestus would crush me just as much as it would crush him. I knew that accepting this arrangement was a bitter pill to swallow, but I had to push through my pride and summon every ounce of courage I had left.

"We must face reality, Ares," I said softly, my voice trembling with resolve. "I need to marry him so that I can stay with you."

Ares's brow furrowed in determination. "We'll keep our affair secret. No one needs to know the truth. We'll find moments to be together in private, away from prying eyes. I'll make sure you're safe, and we'll navigate this dangerous path together."

I clung to him, my heart aching with the weight of our forbidden love. "How can we possibly manage this?"

Ares's gaze was unwavering as he spoke. "We'll be careful. We'll communicate through coded messages, meet in hidden locations. It won't be easy, but we can make it work. We have to. I refuse to lose you."

With a deep breath, I nodded, steeling myself for the challenges ahead. "Then let's do it. Let's fight for what we have, even if it means living in shadows."

# CHAPTER TWENTY-ONE

## APHRODITE

The sun taunted me as it hid behind the dark December clouds.

After the events of last night, I was taken to stay at my father's place. It was the eve of the wedding, after all. My wedding. And I would not be marrying the man I desired.

Standing in my childhood bedroom now, it seems like ages ago that I was sitting here feeling trapped, like a caged animal waiting to be sold off by my father to the highest bidder.

Ares had pleaded with me for us to escape. But deep down, I knew the Olympus Syndicate and my father's henchmen would hunt us down.

No matter where we tried to hide, they'd never stop. Ouranos's network reached far and wide, like an invisible web binding me to him no matter how far I ran. Freedom seemed like an impossible idea for me.

My stomach twisted into painful knots, haunted by the fact that everything—the chaos of the wedding, the ongoing struggle—was a cruel distraction from Titan's death. The search for the truth seemed to pull me further into an abyss, a consuming darkness that felt endless and impenetrable. It was as if every effort to uncover the truth only deepened the shadows around me, leaving me to wonder if the light would ever break through. In the past weeks, that looming darkness had become an all-encompassing presence, overshadowing every aspect of my life.

I slipped on my silk robe, the fabric cold and heavy against my skin, and pressed my hands to my face, trying to stifle the mounting frustration. A sigh escaped my lips, a release of the tension I couldn't fully express. Tears were no longer an option.

THE ALLIANCE OF THIS MARRIAGE WAS AN OBLIGATION, AND THAT'S ALL IT would ever be.

I'd be married to Hephaestus on paper, but he would not be the one who occupied my heart. The only man that could hold that place was Ares.

I looked in the mirror as the hairdresser finished the final touches, a vacant expression displayed on my face. I didn't understand why we needed such an extravagant wedding when all we technically needed was a piece of paper to be married legally. I would sign and be done with it. No need for an elaborate event.

But this wedding wasn't merely about forging an alliance. It was a stage for my father's grand display. To him, it was all a twisted game—a spectacle to flaunt his power. He understood that by showcasing the union of the two most notorious crime families, he would cement his dominance and ensure no one would ever challenge him.

Gaia walked in behind me, holding my dress in her hand. She laid it on the bed, and I watched her walk like a zombie, distaste for me clearly displayed on her face. Not surprising, seeing as she never wanted me in this family to begin with.

"Are you done? Because we need you on your way out—Now." Gaia crossed her arms, her gaze sharp and seething with such intensity that it felt like a physical assault. I swallowed hard, trying to steady myself, and shifted my gaze to the hairdresser, seeking a brief reprieve from Gaia's penetrating stare.

"She's ready."

Getting up from the chair, my movements were devoid of emotion. I shed my robe, exposing my white lace corset and matching underwear. Gaia helped me into my dress, which was a halter style gown with a flowing tulle cape attached to the back. The silk fabric was pristine white and hugged my figure perfectly. The neckline dropped down, revealing my ample cleavage. It was sensuous and stunning, and it highlighted my body in every good way possible.

The astonishing gown would have been ideal for a wedding with someone I genuinely loved and cared for, rather than the man that I was set to marry.

Gaia then handed me two enormous diamond drop earrings, leaving me baffled at this seemingly kind gesture. They had been a gift from her mother. I only knew because Titan would show them to me when we snuck into their bedroom as children. I looked into her eyes and saw that she was void of emotion.

"Thank you." I whispered, feeling a unique sense of honor.

"We never saw things the same way, but I pray for salvation for you. Because without it, you will end up just like me." She held my gaze for a moment, and then she walked away.

I had just closed the door to my bedroom for peace and quiet, when I heard the jiggle of a doorknob. Turning to look over my shoulder, I saw the doors to the Juliet balcony swing open as Ares dashed inside. He quickly closed the doors behind him, standing before me in a dark hoodie and black pants, his presence a mix of danger and desire.

I rushed to his side, my heart pounding as I threw my arms

around him, desperate for his touch. His lips met mine with a fierce intensity, and the world seemed to blur around us.

Our kiss was a mixture of passion and urgency, leaving me breathless and gasping for air when we finally pulled apart. The tension between us hung heavy, a tangible force.

"Ares, what are you thinking?" I exclaimed, my voice filled with concern. "You could be risking everything just by being here." But despite my words, I clung to him like he was my lifeline, unable to let go.

"Listen to me," his voice was barely a whisper. Outside, the sound of distant laughter and music filtered through the closed windows, a reminder of what was waiting for us beyond these four walls. "Do what needs to be done today," he urged, his words laced with a mix of determination and vulnerability.

I knew what he meant, the sacrifice we both had to make for the sake of our love.

He continued, "I'll endure every moment of this, even as I watch you marry him. My love for you will remain, through it all." he said, and his grip on me tightened ever so slightly. We were two souls bound by a love that defied the odds, vowing to endure whatever trials lay ahead.

"When I'm up at that altar, I will be imagining you standing before me instead of him," I confessed as I watched his eyes deepen with heartbreak. Despite not being able to prevent the wedding from happening, we were determined that our love would continue to thrive in secret.

"You're so beautiful, Aphrodite," Ares stated as he took in my appearance. "When you're marrying Hephaestus, I'll be thinking of us and all the time we'll have together. We will figure out a way to end this marriage one day. I will do everything in my power to make it happen."

Ares held me close. Our fates were sealed, but that didn't mean we would back down. Outside forces controlled this marriage, but I knew our love was greater than the game that was being played.

"You need to go," I said, regretting the words instantly. He looked exhausted, the dark stubble along his jawline giving him a rugged edge. I pressed a gentle kiss to his cheek, which naturally flowed into a deeper kiss on his soft, full lips. To the world, Ares was a warrior—a force to be reckoned with—but to me, he was my sanctuary, my refuge in the world.

"I need to go," he repeated.

I nodded even though I wanted nothing more than to escape with him.

"I love you, Ares," I whispered, my voice trembling as I averted my gaze, terrified of how he might react to what felt like my final confession before marrying another man. For a moment, the silence stretched between us, heavy with uncertainty. But then, to my surprise, a slow, heart-stopping smile spread across his face, his eyes softening with unspoken emotion.

"I LOVE YOU," HE MURMURED, HIS VOICE LOW AND INTENSE, LIKE A PROMISE. His hand brushed my cheek, sending a shiver down my spine as he pulled me closer. It wasn't just an admission—it was a vow, one that made my heart race with longing and fear all at once.

We were interrupted by a brief knock at my door, and we quickly let go of each other.

"Just a minute," I called. Ares snuck onto the balcony and jumped over the railing to scale the terrace down. I opened the door to my bedroom and Artie was standing in the hall.

"Are you ready?" she asked softly as she slipped into the room, her sleek black dress clinging to every curve with an effortless elegance that commanded attention.

It was time.

WILDFLOWERS FLOWED DOWN THE RAILING OF THE GRAND STAIRCASE INTO A display reminiscent of a vibrant forest. My father stood at the base of the stairs, scrutinizing me as I walked toward my inescapable destiny.

His eyes, usually as icy and unyielding as the statues around our house, now carried a touch of sadness—a rare glimpse of vulnerability. I couldn't tell if it was for me or my dead brother. The thoughts hidden behind his gaze remained a mystery, just like always.

My gown trailed behind me. I reached out for my father's hand, and he reciprocated the gesture. Hidden beneath a veil, my despair consumed me. I had stepped into a den of predators, and knowing my father had orchestrated this entire exchange felt like the cruelest betrayal.

As we entered the grand hall, I felt the weight of the guests' stares following me like unsettling shadows that refused to dissipate.

Tonight, they would observe the eternal binding of an alliance between two powerful families. With this alliance, the Aetos' connection to Olympus Syndicate would show everyone in Aeolopolis City that we were unbeatable.

Every step I took felt like I was walking towards hell on earth. Flowers surrounded the candlelight; red roses filled the room. Gaia must've chosen my favorite flowers, but as I approached the walkway, it felt like I was heading to my own funeral.

Hephaestus had his back to me as I gazed down aisle. He was dressed in a black tuxedo, exuding dominance as the future ruler of my destiny.

My love's flame flickered like a ghost in the shadows as I descended the aisle.

Ares had completely captivated my soul, enticing me to tear down my walls and let the flame of our love glow brightly. Our passion was concealed, much like the veil that masked the truth of my purpose. Ouranos held my hand tightly as we walked towards Hephaestus.

When we got to the platform, he spun around and gazed down at me and my father. With his hand outstretched, he walked towards us, and my father placed my hand in his. Hephaestus lifted the veil from my face. I felt intense sadness and anxiety, knowing that this was my inevitable fate.

The priest began the ceremony. "We are gathered here today to join Hephaestus Olympios and Aphrodite Aetos in holy matrimony."

I swallowed hard. A pang of unease enveloped me as Hephaestus watched me out of the corner of his eye.

I wasn't paying attention to the priest. A piercing siren was screaming in my head and made everything unbearable, just like the night of the explosion. The knots in my stomach felt like snakes coiling tighter and tighter, their suffocating grip making it hard to breathe.

Facing Hephaestus, he took hold of my hand and repeated each word the priest had recited, "I, Hephaestus Olympios, take you, Aphrodite Aetos, to be my wife."

As his lips formed the vow, "Till death do us part," my gaze flickered to the crowd.

There, amidst the faceless masses, was Ares, watching me from the shadows, his presence an anchor in this sea of chaos.

But as Hephaestus's words echoed in my ears, a chilling realization crept over me—this was never about love. To him, I was a possession, a means to an end. Hephaestus would stop at nothing to seize control of Aeolopolis City. Even if it meant crushing me under the weight of his ambition, even if it meant risking my very life, he would pursue power until it consumed us both.

Power and unity filled the reception space, a grand display masking the chains that bound me. Every smile, every toast felt like a mocking reminder of the control Hephaestus now had over me. I longed for freedom, but it was just out of reach, with Hephaestus dictating every step I took. He demanded a submissive wife, someone who would silently stand by his side while he basked in his new alliance with Ouranos.

"I'll be right back," I said softly, patting my husband on the shoulder. He leaned in, kissing my temple with a chilling affection. He was like Jekyll and Hyde, and the unpredictability of which version of him I'd get terrified me the most.

I hurried through the crowd, offering polite smiles and nods as I excused myself, my heart racing as I pushed open the French doors to the terrace. The frosty night air hit my skin like daggers, but the cold paled in comparison to the weight pressing down on my soul.

Gripping the railing, I glanced down at the golden band on my finger, feeling its heat like a brand against my skin. I stood there, waiting, my mind swirling with fear and uncertainty, until a familiar warmth enveloped me.

Strong arms wrapped around me, pulling me from the darkness as Ares pressed his chest to mine—his presence, my sanctuary. His hands cradled my face gently. "You need to slip the pills into his drink, Aphrodite," he whispered, urgency lacing his words. "It's the only way to make sure he doesn't come for you tonight."

My heart raced, and fear gripped me.

"He'll know, Ares," I stammered, eyes wide with panic. The storm inside me threatened to break free. "He'll know it was us, and he'll punish us both."

"No," Ares growled, his voice edged with desperation. "I won't let that happen."

His eyes blazed with a madness that reflected the torment we shared.

The thought of what I had to do sickened me. To keep the facade intact, I'd have to fulfill my wifely duties, including the unthinkable. Sleeping with Hephaestus felt like a betrayal that I couldn't escape, but it was necessary for survival—for both of us.

I looked up at Ares, my voice breaking as I whispered, "Tonight, when I'm with him... I'll close my eyes and imagine it's you."

His fists clenched at my words, his jaw tight with barely contained fury. "You don't have to do this," he said, his voice raw with pain.

"I do," I breathed, tears stinging my eyes. "But know that in my heart, it's you I want. It's always been you."

Ares's gaze softened, the rage tempered by the same helplessness I felt. He kissed me fiercely, as if trying to imprint every bit of his love onto my soul. We both knew the torment wasn't over—it had only just begun.

# CHAPTER TWENTY-TWO

## APHRODITE

The air was thick with the warmth from our bodies, and I covered my nakedness with silk sheets, an arm draped over my stomach. I had laid awake all night as the scent of the forest that surrounded the manor wafted in through the open window.

Once I left Ares's side last night, I returned to a nightmare.

Hephaestus had spiraled into a reckless frenzy, the alcohol dulling his senses but not his desires. His eyes were glazed, his breath heavy with the stench of liquor, yet none of it stopped him from asserting his so-called marital rights.

My heart had raced as he cornered me, his touch clumsy and unfeeling, a stark contrast to the tender warmth I had shared with Ares. I closed my eyes, desperately trying to escape into the sanctuary of my mind, recalling every stolen moment with Ares—his hands, his lips, the way he made me feel alive.

But no matter how hard I tried to hold onto those memories, Hephaestus's hands on me shattered every illusion. His body was on mine, heavy and cold, and all I felt was a hollow disgust as he claimed me like a possession, a prize he had won.

Each movement felt mechanical, devoid of intimacy. He was oblivious to my despair, too lost in his own intoxicated haze. The seconds dragged on, feeling like an eternity of humiliation.

He didn't last long before collapsing beside me, his breathing slow and labored as he succumbed to the alcohol, passing out without a word.

When I was sure he was asleep, I had bolted from the bed, my skin crawling with the remnants of his touch. I rushed to the ensuite, trembling as I turned on the faucet, scrubbing my skin raw in a futile attempt to wash away the shame that clung to me.

The weight of everything—the wedding, the betrayal, the lies—pressed down on me like a vice, tightening around my chest until I could hardly breathe.

I stood there, staring at my reflection in the mirror, feeling utterly broken. My eyes were red, my body numb, and the profound sadness threatened to swallow me whole.

As I returned to the room after my shower, Hephaestus let out a small groan. The light peaking through the curtains illuminated his olive skin.

He was undeniably beautiful, but his charm ended at his looks—beneath that striking exterior, his personality was utterly repulsive. I understood why women admired him, but they were unaware of his darker side beneath his charming facade. His eyes flashed open, revealing his deep blue irises.

"Good morning," he greeted, his lips curving into that familiar crooked smile, one that never quite reached his eyes.

"Good morning," I echoed, mirroring his expression despite the tightness in my chest. Our gazes locked, and for a moment, the silence between us felt like a battlefield. What was he thinking? Was he aware of the turmoil beneath my calm facade?

Hephaestus pushed back the covers and approached me, the movement deliberate, calculated. Standing before me, he reached out and gently tucked a curl behind my ear. His touch was soft, but it felt like a chain tightening around me. I swallowed hard, willing myself not to cry. The weight of everything that had happened, everything that I'd been forced to endure, pressed down on me like a suffocating fog.

"You're so beautiful, Aphrodite," he whispered, his voice low and possessive, laced with a strange mixture of reverence and control. His fingers lingered on my skin, sending a cold shiver down my spine. "I'm so lucky to have you."

His words were meant to sound tender, but all I heard was ownership.

The possessiveness in his tone was unmistakable, and the tension in the room thickened, suffocating. His gaze lingered on me, as if he was admiring his prize, the woman he had won. I felt like a possession, something to be kept and controlled, rather than loved. And the worst part was that he believed it—that I belonged to him now.

"What's on the agenda for today?" I asked, my words were more a distraction than a genuine inquiry. I clutched the towel around me, seeking a shield against his gaze.

"I've got some business with Zeus," he replied casually, though the lack of honeymoon plans struck me as peculiar. I nodded, silently welcoming his departure. I was grateful for the respite from my wifely duties.

"Don't worry, I won't be gone long. Get ready, I'll drop you off at the clubhouse," he said, turning to head towards the ensuite without another word.

Later that evening, as I descended the grand staircase, I observed the manor's servants, busy and efficient as they stripped away the remnants of last night's revelry. The sound of their work echoed through the opulent halls. My eyes trailed over the glittering decorations they carried, now nothing more than hollow symbols of the life I was forced to play a part in.

At the base of the stairs, Ouranos stood in his usual commanding stance, talking animatedly with one of the staff members. His presence was impossible to ignore, but I made a conscious effort not to meet his gaze. I didn't owe him my attention—or my respect. Not after everything.

He noticed me lingering on the landing, his sharp eyes cutting through the distance, but I refused to acknowledge him. A real father wouldn't manipulate his daughter into becoming a pawn for his own gain. A real father would stand by her side, protect her from the ugliness of the world, and shield her from the cruelty that came with it. But that wasn't the reality I was given.

"Congratulations, Aphrodite." Ouranos's voice dripped with smugness as he spoke, his eyes gleaming with cold satisfaction. The smugness in his tone sent a wave of fury through me, as if every syllable was designed to mock my misery. He stood there, tall and unbothered, the architect of this twisted fate he'd thrust upon me.

I took a breath, my heart pounding as the anger bubbled up, threatening to consume me.

"You are dead to me." My voice was low but full of venom, every word laced with a deep, simmering rage. I could see his lips curl into an almost amused smirk, as if my defiance was just another piece of entertainment for him.

"Oh, my dear," he said, unfazed. "Don't be so dramatic. This is your future. You should be grateful for what I've given you."

I clenched my fists at my sides, fighting the urge to scream.

"Grateful?" I hissed, my chest heaving with the force of my anger. "For what? For selling me off like some object? For forcing me to marry a man who only sees me as a tool? Is that what you think I should be thankful for?"

Ouranos narrowed his eyes, stepping closer, his expression hardening. "You think you're the only one who has to make sacrifices? This is how the world works, Aphrodite. Power doesn't come without a price. You've done your part. Now, live with it."

I stood my ground, my gaze unwavering. "You may have chained me to Hephaestus, but you'll never break me, Ouranos. You'll never have the power to control me completely." I glanced away for a moment, swallowing down the sadness that crept into my throat. "Titan would be proud of me if he were here," I whispered, though my voice cracked slightly.

Ouranos's expression darkened at the mention of my brother's name. His smugness faltered for a split second, a flicker of something unreadable passing through his eyes.

"You think Titan would approve of your defiance?" His voice turned cold. "He's gone. Dead. And no amount of rebellion will bring him back."

The pain of Titan's loss stabbed through my chest. "His death happened over a month ago, and I still don't know what really happened that night," I said, my voice trembling with both grief and rage. "But I will find out, Ouranos. And when I do, I swear you'll regret every moment you've tried to manipulate me."

Ouranos's face twisted into a sneer. "You're digging in dangerous territory, Aphrodite."

I stepped closer to him, standing tall and unflinching. "I don't fear the truth. And I don't fear you."

I turned to leave, only to see Hephaestus stalking down the hallway towards us.

"There you are." he said to me as he exchanged a glance with Ouranos. "Are you ready?" He reached for my hand.

"Yes, I'm ready." I replied, not looking back in Ouranos's direction.

As we made our way towards the exit, I told myself that this would be the last time I ever stepped foot in this place.

Marrying into the Olympus Syndicate was a dark twist of fate, one that thrust me into the arms of those I once considered adversaries. I struggled to accept their world, caught between loyalty and survival. I hadn't fully embraced their way of life, but I was attempting to accept that this was my reality for now. At least until I find a way to escape this marriage.

The sound of the motorcycle's engine reverberated through the night as we pulled up to the main building of the compound. Without a word, he turned off the engine and headed into the clubhouse.

I slipped in quietly behind Hephaestus, my eyes scanning the room as I spotted Artie making her way down the stairs. Off to the side, Hades and Apollo were deep in conversation, their low voices blending into the background.

Out of nowhere, Hephaestus smacked my ass. The sound of it echoed in my ears, and a wave of nausea rolled through me, a sickening reminder of the power he wielded.

"Come along, wife," he ordered, his voice laced with smug authority. He gripped my wrist, yanking me toward the cold metal staircase that spiraled upward.

We walked along the catwalk and towards a door at the end of the walkway—a heavy, imposing metal frame that seemed like a boundary between two worlds.

With a swift motion, Hephaestus swung it open, revealing a secret sanctuary within. My breath caught as I stepped inside, realizing this room had been created specifically for me.

Books lined the walls, their spines nestled between cascading vines that softened the otherwise industrial environment of the compound. Expansive windows bathed the space in natural light, creating an unexpected tranquility.

Hephaestus slid open a pair of glass-paneled doors, revealing our bedroom beyond—a canopy bed draped in rich fabrics that matched my tastes perfectly. My wardrobe was already filled, my personal items meticulously placed in the ensuite.

I turned and saw him leaning casually against the brick wall, watching me closely with those icy-blue eyes, his hands tucked behind his back, his expression unreadable.

"How did you...?" I trailed off, still processing the effort behind this space.

"It's just a small gift," Hephaestus said, his voice low and measured. There was something disarming in the way he spoke, a vulnerability I didn't expect. "I wanted to make this place feel like yours."

I frowned, glancing at the room again, unsettled. "How did you know my favorite colors... the books I love?" I wasn't sure if I should be grateful or unnerved. It felt too personal for a man who kept himself so distant.

He straightened, his eyes softening as he approached me. "I watch. I notice things." There was a pause, and then he added, his voice quieter, almost pained, "I know I don't show it, but I've tried to understand you."

His confession hung in the air, and for a moment, I wasn't sure how to respond. I didn't trust his intentions, yet I could feel the weight of his words. Hephaestus was like a puzzle—pieces of him revealing themselves slowly, yet none of them fitting together.

"I don't understand you," I whispered, shaking my head slightly, more confused than before.

"I don't expect you to," he said, stepping closer, his presence both commanding and oddly intimate. "I'm not easy to figure out. But I've always thought you were out of my league, Aphrodite."

His admission startled me, stirring something I hadn't anticipated. For reasons I couldn't quite explain, I felt a pang of sympathy. Maybe it was the fact we were tied together now, or that we had been intimate with each other, but something in his expression made me soften.

"Don't say that," I murmured. Without thinking, I reached up, gently pushing the hair back from his face. His tension eased under my touch, and for a brief second, I saw a glimpse of the man beneath the armor.

"Let's have dinner tonight," he said, his tone shifting into something warmer. He leaned in, brushing a kiss against my cheek—so unexpected, it sent a shock through my body.

"I can cook," I replied, forcing a smile as I played the role I was now expected to fill. The perfect wife.

Hephaestus smiled faintly, but it didn't reach his eyes. "I look forward to it, Aphrodite."

As I smiled back, a hollow feeling settled in my chest. No matter how much effort he put into building this space, I still felt like a stranger here. And despite the facade of warmth between us, the truth was much colder.

As I was adjusting to my new surroundings, Hephaestus had to head out for a meeting with Zeus. He gave me a quick, lingering kiss goodbye, and for a moment, I felt a flicker of warmth amid the chaos.

After he left, I decided to explore a bit more and get myself ready for the evening. I made my way downstairs, hoping to find some semblance of normalcy and, ideally, some company.

In the kitchen, Artie was busy preparing a drink, her movements practiced and smooth.

"Hello, newlywed," she greeted with a knowing grin, sliding a glass towards me.

I took a seat on one of the stools, feeling a bit more at ease with her presence. "Hey, sister-in-law," I replied with a smile. Artie was the one good thing in this whole situation, and I was glad to have her around.

She leaned against the counter, using her hand as a headrest, and passed me a drink.

"I like the sound of that. You saw the apartment?" she asked.

I nodded, "I can't believe he went through the trouble of all of that for me." I said, squeezing my lime and stirring the straw in the liquor.

"He asked me to help him. He was very insistent. It seems like he's trying to make this work between the two of you," She gave me a serious look and whispered, "What about Ares?" Artie's eyes searched mine.

I sighed, pressing my hands to my forehead. "I haven't forgotten him, Artie. It's just... everything's been a mess lately. I don't know how to handle it all."

"Well, what are you going to do?" Artie asked, her gaze steady.

"I honestly don't know, Artie. This is all too much," I admitted.

"Well..." Artie hesitated, waiting for me to meet her eyes. "I suppose it might be worth giving Hephaestus a chance. You're married now, after all." She studied my face and continued, "But it's probably best if you keep whatever's happened between you and Ares under wraps. If Hephaestus finds out, it won't end well."

I swallowed my pride, acknowledging the truth in Artie's words. A tear slipped down my cheek as I confessed, "I love Ares, Artie. I tried to keep my distance, but I couldn't help falling for him."

Artie placed her hands over mine, her touch a small comfort amid the storm of my emotions. I struggled to find my voice, the weight of my feelings making it hard to speak.

"I know it feels like you're lost at sea right now," Artie said quietly. "But you need to remember why you're here and hold onto that purpose. It might help you get through this."

"Thank you for being a refuge in all this chaos," I said, dabbing at the tears on my face.

Artie's expression softened as she placed a comforting hand on my shoulder. "I'm here for you, Aphrodite," she said gently. "You're not alone in this."

I took a shaky breath, grateful for her presence. "I don't know what I would do without you," I admitted, my voice quivering.

Artie gave me a reassuring smile. "Oh, and just so you know, Ares isn't coming to the clubhouse today. He's staying at Pandora. He doesn't want—"

I folded my arms, feeling a pang of understanding. Ares didn't want to witness the reality of my marriage to Hephaestus. I knew seeing us together would be too painful for him.

"He doesn't want to see this," Artie continued, her voice tinged with sadness. "It's too difficult for him, given how much he still cares for you."

# CHAPTER TWENTY-THREE

## ARES

The agony was unbearable, like a thousand knives twisting in my chest.

To stand by, helpless, as the person I loved was bound to a man I despised with every fiber of my being—it was an unbearable torment beyond words. Every glance, every word exchanged at that cursed ceremony felt like a dagger to my soul. In that moment, I vowed this would not stand. The fire of my wrath would shake even the gods.

*Hephaestus.* Just his name left a bitter taste in my mouth.

He was a venomous serpent, slithering his way into the highest echelons of power, tightening his grip on authority with every deceitful move.

I knew Zeus had orchestrated this vile union, but deep down, I sensed Hephaestus' insidious influence, pulling the strings to fulfill his twisted desires.

By marrying the daughter of the most powerful mafia boss in Aeolopolis City, he had cunningly embedded himself into the heart of the Aetos family's empire. It was a calculated move that sent shockwaves through the underworld. Suddenly, he had a seat at the table, rubbing shoulders with the most feared men in the city.

I had to wonder how he planned to juggle his role as vice-president of the Syndicate while managing these volatile ties with the Aetos clan? The question gnawed at me, but I knew the answer in my gut. He wasn't just ambitious—he was dangerous.

I saw right through his facade.

Beneath his charm and carefully crafted smiles, he was a wolf in sheep's clothing, and when his true nature was revealed, blood would spill.

Every evening when I returned to the clubhouse, Hephaestus's bike was conspicuously absent. Hades had mentioned that he suspected Hephaestus was seeing another woman. The thought of my brother being with someone else while he was still married to Aphrodite struck me with a twisted sense of satisfaction. It felt almost like poetic justice to think of him being unfaithful, as if his actions were a reflection of the emotional turmoil I was forced to endure.

*Oh, Aphrodite.*

When she first arrived, she was a fragile flower trembling under the harsh winds of our world, her delicate petals battered by the relentless storm.

Titan had told me about his sister—a gentle soul who had been neglected and rejected by those who should have cared for her. And now, she was married to a man who treated her just like everyone else, her suffering echoing the same pain and neglect she had known before.

A week had passed since the wedding, and the atmosphere in the clubhouse had shifted noticeably. Today, we were heading to the Aetos-designated drop-off points, navigating Ouranos's exclusive network of private roads and bridges, built for the sole purpose of facilitating his business transactions.

This was no ordinary delivery; it was our largest and most critical deal yet—transporting a substantial shipment of drugs into his turf. The stakes were higher than ever, and everything had to proceed flawlessly. Any misstep, any sign of negligence, could unravel our business relationship and threaten to dismantle everything we had built.

The winter night breeze cut through the air, making the ocean chill bitter and sharp.

I couldn't help but feel a pang of envy as Hades lounged comfortably in his sleek Boss Mustang, insulated from the cold that stung my skin.

Apollo, Prometheus, and Athena were crammed in the cargo truck, where the shipment of drugs was securely stowed. Zeus, Hephaestus, and I rode alongside them on our motorcycles, engines roaring against the frigid night.

Our mission was clear and uncompromising: *protect the truck at all costs.*

I revved the engine, slipped on my gloves, and rubbed my hands together, trying to ward off the cold.

We were just about to head out when I noticed Aphrodite step out of the clubhouse with Artie. I pulled up my mask to shield myself from the chill, but my eyes stayed locked on her.

They stood on the clubhouse porch, watching us. Hephaestus blew Aphrodite a kiss, and I felt my jaw clench as I fought to keep my anger in check. Hades caught my eye, his expression clear; *Chill the fuck out.*

Zeus scanned the group with a sharp, unwavering intensity, underscoring the importance of a flawless operation. Our safety and success hinged on our precision tonight. With a curt nod, he mounted his bike and roared off into the night, Hephaestus on his heels. The stakes were high, and every move had to be perfect.

I stole one last look at Aphrodite before we rolled out of the compound. Her lips moved slowly, forming a silent message: I love you. The sight tightened my chest, a painful reminder of the distance between us. I inhaled deeply, forcing the thought of her to the back of my mind.

The Olympus Syndicate roared through the city streets, our thunderous presence breathing life into the night. The darkness around us was a canvas for our unleashed warrior spirits. I took my place at the front of the group, fully aware that every risk we took carried its own set of consequences.

My restless mind thrived in the chaos we willingly embraced.

THE AETHERION BRIDGE, STRETCHING ACROSS NEPTUNE'S ABYSS, OFFERED an alternative route into the next city which bypassed the main highway.

It was the perfect place to dispose of a body—Neptune's powerful currents would carry anything far into the ocean, making recovery impossible. I knew this all too well, having delivered more than a few bodies to those unforgiving depths.

Hephaestus and Zeus led the way, with Hades driving the Mustang. I rode alongside him, while the cargo truck followed close behind. The bridge, spanning about a third of a mile, loomed ahead. We came to a stop, the dim city lights fading in comparison to the radiant silver moon that guided our path.

"Where are they?" Hades shouted over the roar of the engine as I pulled up beside him and removed my mask.

"Not here," Zeus growled, his voice tinged with frustration.

The plan was to meet Zeus's brother, my uncle Poseidon, on the bridge. He had significant power and served as leader of our group out in Arcadia.

Ironically, Zeus and Poseidon could never get along. Hades often had to step in and mediate between them. This sibling rivalry had been a longstanding issue, causing tension and conflict within our groups. That said, we had been collaborating with them recently, thanks to Hephaestus. He had been working behind the scenes, establishing a connection that seemed to hold promise for our collective goals.

Even with these developments, I couldn't shake the nagging suspicion that something was being concealed. The true nature of our mission felt shrouded in secrecy, and I was left with a growing sense of being intentionally kept in the dark. The shadow of unresolved conflict and hidden agendas loomed over our collaboration, leaving me with a gnawing unease.

"Poseidon is always late," Hades muttered through clenched teeth, his fingers pressing into his temples in frustration.

"It's only been five minutes," Apollo's voice was steady, but it did little to ease the mounting tension.

I killed the engine and dismounted my motorcycle, a sense of dread prickling my skin. My heart beat heavily in my chest, a warning that something was amiss. I felt like I needed to be cautious as I stood next to Zeus.

"Where are they?" I demanded, my voice taut with frustration.

"He'll be here. You know how he is," Zeus replied, leaning against his chopper with an air of forced calm, his arms folded tightly.

My gaze flickered to Hephaestus, who stood apart, his hands trembling slightly.

"What's wrong with you?" I asked sharply, and he shot me a look that sent a chill down my spine. His pupils were unnervingly dilated, his eyes dark and hollow, as if some dark force had taken hold of him.

"It's cold," he said, his voice low and jagged, his jaw clenched tightly.

In the blink of an eye, bullets began raining down upon us from the far end of the bridge. Instinctively, we crouched low, adrenaline surging as the sharp crack of gunfire echoed through the night. My heart pounded in my chest, each beat drowned out by the relentless echoes of violence that surrounded us.

Through the blur, my eyes locked onto a black car speeding toward us, windows down, gunmen leaning out and unloading a storm of bullets our way.

Zeus was sprawled on the ground, motionless.

Without hesitation, Hephaestus retaliated by returning fire. I rushed to Zeus's side, summoned every ounce of strength I could, and dragged him toward the waiting cargo truck. Once we came into their sightline, Athena and Prometheus hopped out to help me.

"Where is he hit?" Athena roared, the sound of bullets and the current mayhem drowning out all other sound.

"I don't know, just get him to the fucking hospital!" I growled as rage engulfed me, but for once, the rage didn't own me—I owned it.

I yanked out my gun and fired, emptying round after round into the night.

The car screeched away, but I kept shooting, desperate for just one hit. Every second dragged, each pull of the trigger feeling slower than the last. But nothing. The bullets missed their mark, and rage boiled inside me.

Hades yanked at my arm, but I barely registered it.

The wail of sirens blurred with everything else, their screeching overwhelming his voice. My eyes were still locked on the tail lights disappearing into the distance. They got lucky this time. Next time, though, there would be no escape. No mercy.

Suddenly, Hades grabbed my face, pulling me from my haze. "Ares, we need to go! Now!" His voice cut through, snapping me back to reality.

My father's condition weighed heavily on me, his presence a stark reminder of the betrayal and danger surrounding us.

My thoughts were a chaotic swirl of fear and anger as I raced through the frosty night, the reality of his critical state sinking in with every beat of my pounding heart. I pulled up to the hospital and parked in the emergency bay. A paramedic shouted at me as I dismounted my motorcycle and raced towards the hospital doors.

"Sir! Please stop! You're bleeding!" They exclaimed, rushing towards me.

Ignoring her plea, I said, "I need to find my father. They brought him here. He was shot." I side-stepped the paramedic and entered the hospital through the automatic doors.

"Athena!" My voice roared down the hallway, people turned their heads toward me. "Athena!" I repeated, frantically searching for her.

"Sir! You're bleeding—you need to see a doctor." An older nurse hurried over to me.

"I'm not the one who's been shot!" I protested, but all of a sudden, I felt a sharp pain in my chest. My sides throbbed with an intensity that stole my breath.

I looked down and saw blood spreading across my shirt. Time slowed, as I came to a startling realization; I was hit.

The nurse called for assistance, while the others placed me on a gurney. Panic rushed through my veins, a cold paralyzing fear that gripped my heart.

With each breath, the pain intensified, a relentless pressure crushing my chest and making it feel like my lungs were failing to keep up. My vision swayed and darkened at the edges, blurring the world around me.

Just as I felt myself losing grip on reality, Aphrodite emerged from the haze. Her curls draped over her shoulder; her hazel eyes illuminated by a soft, ethereal light framing her face.

This wasn't the end, it couldn't be.

A SHARP PAIN IN MY RIBS JOLTED ME AWAKE. I RUBBED THE SLEEP FROM MY eyes and looked around the sterile hospital room. Aphrodite sat on the edge of my bed. I attempted to get my bearings, but everything was blurry. I pressed my hands to my head. "What happened?"

Aphrodite gently touched my chest and gave me a small smile, her eyes swollen. Her skin was pale, and her lips were deep red.

*Was I in heaven?* My fingers grazed her cheek, yearning to kiss her.

"You were shot in the ribs. You're lucky they were able to remove the bullet and stabilize you in time."

"You have nine lives, kid." Hades leaned on the door frame with his arms crossed against his chest, a slight smirk on his lips. Aphrodite let out a forced laugh, but tears quickly took over.

"You were out for two days," she confessed.

"Dad?" I asked, glancing at Hades, but Aphrodite placed her hands on my chest.

"You need to keep calm, Ares," she said, reaching for my face and diverting my attention with those enormous eyes.

Hades sighed. "Zeus is in a coma." He explained how Zeus had suffered a cerebral contusion. The bullet grazed his head, causing internal bleeding within the brain, making it swell. "They were uncertain at first, but it's likely he'll wake up."

I felt my heart squeeze painfully in my chest. I had never experienced this kind of sensation because of my dad before. When my mom passed away, my grief had spiraled into a furious, reckless anger that drove me to lash out in ways I hadn't anticipated. It was a storm of emotions that consumed me. But this, this was different.

The depth of my feelings for my father, the fear and helplessness, was a new kind of anguish I hadn't expected. It was as if the grief and worry were tangling together, creating a raw, intense ache that was both bewildering and overwhelming.

I pulled Aphrodite into an embrace, burying my face in her neck, overwhelmed by the pain shooting through my ribs and the flood of emotions that came with it. As her fingers traced gentle lines through my hair, I tilted my face upward, feeling the warmth of her breath as her lips moved closer to mine.

"I have to leave before Hephaestus catches us together," she whispered.

Hades attempted to avert his gaze. "I'll keep watch." I couldn't wait any longer, the urge to kiss her lips was overwhelming. The taste of her was intoxicating, a blend of sweetness and fire that ignited every part of me.

# CHAPTER TWENTY-FOUR
## ARES

I made it clear to everyone that I'd be leaving the hospital the next day. The police didn't bother investigating, even though the nurses had raised questions about the incident.

Cold hard cash always has a way of silencing these types of things.

I stepped into the shower, wincing from the pain of my injury. The hot water did little to wash away the unease gnawing at my gut.

We were in deep trouble, and I knew it.

After Aphrodite left, I laid out my plan to Hades. We had to get out of here. The Olympus Syndicate had been hit hard, and I couldn't bear the thought of anything happening to Aphrodite. I'd risked my life for my family more times than I could count, but after what went down last night, a persistent sense of dread told me I was now a marked man.

I had to leave before things got any worse, but escaping the Olympus Syndicate came with its own set of consequences. The only way someone gave up their leather cut was when they were six feet under. It wasn't just about my own safety; it was about hers too. I'd rather face death than put Aphrodite's life at risk.

I put on the clothes Hades brought for me and held onto my leather cut vest with the Olympus Syndicate crest. I had wrapped my identity up in what that crest meant as the thunderous roar of motorcycles had drowned out my heartbeat, day after day.

I APPROACHED THE ICU WITH A HEAVY HEART, THE WEIGHT OF THE NIGHT pressing down on me. Prometheus was stationed by the door, but he was slumped against the wall, clearly exhausted. His breathing was slow, and his head nodded forward in an uneasy sleep. I made a deliberate effort to jostle him awake, my hand meeting his arm with a sharp nudge.

"Ugh!" he startled, blinking rapidly as he came to. "Ares! I'm sorry, I must've dozed off. Didn't expect you so soon."

"It's fine. Just go get yourself some coffee or something. I need to be alone with my dad," I said, my voice steady but laced with urgency as I pushed the door open for him.

"Right, right. I'll be quick." Prometheus rubbed the back of his neck, the fatigue evident in his movements as he slowly rose and stretched. With a final glance, he headed down the corridor, leaving me standing at the threshold in the sterile, dim light of the ICU.

My father lay in the hospital bed, ensnared by a maze of tubes and wires that crisscrossed his body like a cruel reminder of his vulnerability. The rhythmic beeping of the heart monitor punctuated the silence of the ICU room, each beep a reminder of the fragile thread connecting him to life. I pulled the chair close and sank into it, the cold metal biting into my skin as I watched him.

Life had seemed to unravel for Zeus following my mother's death. In his grief, he had sought solace in fleeting relationships and immersed himself in the club's identity, leaving little room for his children. My knee jittered, a reflexive response to the mounting tension as I waited for Prometheus's return.

The door swung open with a sudden jolt, catching me off guard. But instead of Prometheus, the last person I expected slithered into the room: Ouranos. His presence was unsettling, his eyes darting around as if he carried some dark secret. He moved with an unsettling air of deception, each step calculated and cautious as he came and sat down beside me.

"Seems to me that you guys had a bit of a situation." He looked smug.

"Seems like it." I replied, attempting to remain composed. I didn't want to stir up hostility before we had a chance to escape.

We sat in silence, our eyes locked. The coldness radiating from him felt like pure evil.

Finally, unable to endure the silence any longer, I asked, "What are you doing here?"

"Paying my respects." His voice was melodic with a subtle hint of sarcasm.

"He isn't dead." My voice was a growl.

Ouranos gave me a mischievous grin and asked, "How is my daughter?" When he muttered the word *daughter*, I clenched my knuckles in revulsion.

"She's fine." I said through clenched teeth.

"I see everything. Remember," he looked at my father, "The darkness holds the most secrets, but sometimes they come into the light."

He got up and began whistling a slow, haunting tune as he walked out of the ICU room. His deliberate, casual gait only heightened the menace of the scene. The sound of his whistling echoed down the sterile corridor, casting a chilling shadow over the beeping of the life-support machines.

His departure left a chilling silence in its wake, and the weight of his words—spoken or unspoken—hung heavily in the air. I could feel the urgency clawing at me, a relentless reminder that we needed to escape as quickly as possible. The threat wasn't just looming; it was imminent, and every second counted.

As always, a crowd of people waited outside Pandora, eagerly waiting to enter.

I parked at the rear of the building, avoiding the busy scene. My intention was to slip in and out unnoticed. I had to gather my cash and weapons and leave this town behind for good.

I swung the door of my office open, house music blasting in the background. I made my way toward the safe I kept hidden behind a piece of artwork.

"What are you doing, Ares?" Hades asked, his arms crossed tightly, his voice tinged with frustration. "You can't just run away from this. You need to face it."

"I'm not here to argue my decision," I snapped back, my voice harsh with urgency. "The hit on us wasn't random—it was a calculated move, meant to eliminate Zeus and me."

"Why are you so sure of that?" Hades challenged, his skepticism clear. "We don't have solid proof. It's possible someone else was involved, maybe someone who knew about the drugs."

"Think about it, Hades," I said, turning to face him with a hard glare. "Who stands to gain the most from our downfall?"

Hades's eyes narrowed. "Everyone," he said with a humorless chuckle, as if dismissing my concerns as paranoia.

I rolled my eyes. "Hephaestus." He had always wanted nothing more than to reign as the supreme authority in and outside of the club.

It all clicked into place. The club meeting a few weeks ago, where Zeus informed us that Hephaestus set up our meeting with Poseidon's crew. My brother's disdain for me was obvious, but I never thought he would stoop so low as to try to ruin this club. But it was him all along. He was the one that organized the drop, and it had gone south.

"You're being ridiculous," Hades said, running a frustrated hand down his face. "Hephaestus knows he'd end up dead if he went against his own family."

"Then why the hell don't we have any details about Titan's murder?" I demanded, my frustration boiling over. "Hephaestus was in charge of the investigation. We're talking about someone who's renowned for his ability to unearth the most hidden secrets. If anyone could get us answers, it would be him. Yet here we are, still in the dark. How is that possible?"

Hades made his way over to the bar cart and poured himself a drink.

"Did you get shot in the head?" he asked, a hint of disbelief in his voice.

"He could never pull off something like that," he said, shaking his head. "Titan was probably mixed up in some shady deal that got him killed. Maybe they meant to take out Ouranos too, but they settled for the only target they could reach. We don't have all the details, Ares. We've tried everything to get to the bottom of it, but no one will—"

"That's just it," I cut in. "No one wants to spill any details. It's weird, right? At the engagement party, everyone, even his family, got super uncomfortable whenever Titan was brought up. It's like they were hiding something or just didn't want to talk about him. If there's nothing to hide, why are they all acting so shady?"

There was a prolonged silence as Hades weighed my words carefully, the reality of the situation settling over him. He took a sip of his liquor and let out a deep sigh.

"I don't think you should leave, Ares. Not now, especially with Hephaestus's wife. You know it's only going to escalate things."

"He wants nothing to do with her." I spat.

"I've always had your back, kid," he said, his gaze steady as I stared down at my hands, my rage barely contained. "But this is your riskiest move yet. You're not thinking straight," he pleaded. I refused to dwell on his opinion.

Brushing off his words, I tried to push aside his doubts. I felt a knot grow in my stomach, my palms grew clammy, and my mind raced with anticipation.

This conversation had infuriated me enough. I reached for my bag in the safe with the money I had put aside for my own security. "Pandora's yours for now. You love it more than I do, and Titan would be proud to hand it over to you."

Hades stared at me, eyes wide. "Ares, what—no, this place is yours. It belongs to you."

I shook my head, pressing the keys into his hands. "Aphrodite is my chance at freedom. Even if it means living a quiet life in the suburbs, as long as she's with me, I'm fine with that."

Hades chuckled, "Didn't think you'd become the suburban, khaki-wearing type."

"That would absolutely destroy me." My smile mirrored his, but quickly dissipated. "My lives are running out, Hades. I'm covered in scars. It would be tempting fate by staying, and since they already tried to end my life, I know it can only get worse. I can't be the warrior anymore. I need to focus on living a life that isn't constantly on the edge."

Hades nodded, rubbing his chin as he seemed to weigh his words carefully. "Then there's something you need to know," he said, finally meeting my gaze with a solemn expression.

"What?" I narrowed my glance, bracing myself for what he was about to say.

"Zeus named Hephaestus as the next President of the Olympus Syndicate if anything were to happen to him," Hades said, his tone heavy with concern. "He mentioned it to me just before the attack. It wasn't a casual remark; it was something he was seriously planning. Zeus always had a sense of foreboding, and he clearly anticipated that his position might be under threat." Hades paused, letting the weight of his words sink in.

THE NIGHT SKY SWALLOWED THE LAST TRACES OF SUNLIGHT AS DARKNESS took hold.

I knew I had to move—I needed to get to my woman. The Odyssey was packed with desperate men, all vying for a chance to get lucky, but I had only one thing on my mind.

I caught a glimpse of Aphrodite working behind the bar, trying her best to give a shit about the man she was serving, but I knew she didn't care.

She broke away from the drunk patron and looked up at me. In the dim light of the bar, I saw her expression shift from distaste to anxiety, her eyes brimming with worry.

I nodded toward the back room. She dropped her apron and followed in my direction, keeping a safe distance between us.

My heartbeat thudded steadily against my ribcage as I pushed through the door to my office, trying to steady myself. Moments later, Aphrodite slipped in behind me.

I rushed to her, grabbing her face gently, and pressed my lips to hers, the tension of the night melting away in that brief moment of connection.

*There was no turning back.*

Aphrodite broke away. "What's wrong, Ares?" Countless worries were written all over her face, but somehow, she still looked effortlessly beautiful.

I gently touched her curls and looked into her eyes. "We've gotta go," I said.

"Why? What's happening?"

"Aphrodite..." I took a deep breath, struggling to keep my voice steady. "Hephaestus tried to have me killed. I can't trust anyone here anymore; it's getting too dangerous. If anyone discovers what we're hiding, he'll come after you with everything he's got." Her eyes widened as the harsh reality of my words hit her.

"Oh my god, Ares," she exclaimed, the situation sinking in. "Do you think Athena will say something about us?"

"I know so." I nodded, there was no doubt in my mind that Athena would side with Hephaestus.

Aphrodite trembled in my arms. "Where will we go?" Her voice was barely a whisper, quivering with fear.

"I know a place," I whispered, holding her closer, her head resting on my chest. "Don't worry, I've got you. Pack your stuff now —we're getting out of here tonight. I don't know where the hell Hephaestus is or what he's up to, but we need to be gone before he even catches a whiff of this."

Aphrodite glanced at me, tears in her eyes, as her fingers gently brushed my scruffy face.

"I'll go wherever you go." she said.

Relief washed over me, mixed with an overwhelming sense of uncertainty. I just needed her by my side, no matter the risk. The idea of our escape seemed both a lifeline and a leap into the unknown, but as long as she was with me, I was ready to face whatever came next.

# CHAPTER TWENTY-FIVE
## APHRODITE

Ares locked eyes with me, and reality finally sank in. I tried to shake the fear creeping into my bones, knowing we would soon risk our lives.

Hephaestus and I argued intensely after my visit to Ares in the hospital, and the tension between us had become thick and suffocating. His anger was a force, and his eyes burned with fury. No matter how hard I denied it, he sensed the forbidden connection that lingered between Ares and me.

"Should I tell Artie?" I asked, placing my hands on his chest and looking deeply into his eyes. Fear and determination waged a fierce battle inside me.

"I'll talk to her," Ares assured me, his brows furrowing as if darkness was creeping in, draining the world of its colors. Adrenaline surged through my veins.

He gently lifted my chin, and our eyes locked once more. In that moment, it was like a revelation—he was the one I'd needed all along. Our lips met, and it felt like a breath of freedom.

The kiss was slow and searing, a dance of passion that spoke of unspoken desires and dark promises. It swept away the chaos and desperation, replacing them with a profound, consuming connection. I held him tightly, feeling the heat of his body against mine, his hands exploring my curves with a tenderness that only heightened the intensity of our embrace.

The kiss deepened, igniting the flame that had been kindling since we first met. Our hearts beat in sync, an intimate rhythm that bound us together. In that moment, every touch and caress whispered of the future we could build—a future where nothing could stand between us.

"Go get ready." Ares murmured against my lips, "I will meet you downstairs in an hour." he said, planting a kiss on my forehead. I nodded, giving his hand a squeeze before slipping out of the office. I made my way back into the bar, pretending everything was normal.

I smoothed my hair and dress. I knew my lips were raw from his rough beard. I was unsure of what time Hephaestus would be back, but I needed to act swiftly.

Approaching Artie, I said quietly, "Artie, I need to go."

"What's happening? Are you okay?" Her voice was filled with concern as she tilted her head to see past me. I followed her eyes, looking over my shoulder to see Ares nod at her before slipping through the crowd.

"I can't say," I confessed, then bit my bottom lip. "Ares will tell you more when he can."

Artie tugged me toward the side of the room where it was quieter. "What is going on, Aphrodite? You need to tell me," She whispered as she surveyed our surroundings.

I swallowed hard, knowing I wasn't supposed to tell her, but she was the only real friend that I had made throughout my time here at the compound.

"We're running," I said, my voice heavy with urgency.

"Running? Where to?" she asked, her eyes wide with confusion.

"I don't know exactly," I admitted, shrugging as anxiety clawed at me. "But we have to leave now. Ares has picked up on something serious—there's danger brewing, and I can't stand the thought of him getting hurt anymore. I love him."

Artie took a deep breath, her expression a mix of concern and frustration. "Hephaestus won't stop until he finds you both. He's ruthless—he'll use every resource at his disposal to destroy you." Her voice carried an edge, a mix of irritation and something deeper, more troubling. I could sense her anxiety; if my own brother were involved, I'd feel the same. No one leaves Olympus Syndicate; They die first.

"I know. Ares is set on this. We're leaving in an hour. I need your help. If you see Hephaestus, please cover for us." I pleaded with her, desperation in my eyes.

She rubbed her face. "Fine. Go ahead, and hurry." Artie pulled me into a hug. "Please be safe, Aphrodite, and contact me when you're able to talk."

"Of course." I rested my head on her shoulder and gave her a squeeze. With that, I turned and walked away. Time was not my friend.

I rushed toward the exit at the back of the building which led straight to the clubhouse.

Grabbing my jacket, I slipped into the alley's darkness, trying to make myself inconspicuous as people lingered about.

The cold night air hit my body like icy daggers.

The silver light of the moon broke free from the night clouds and illuminated the clubhouse stairs. I kept glancing over my shoulder, my heart racing with every step, making sure no one was watching where I was going. The shadows played tricks on my mind, and every distant noise sounded like footsteps approaching. My hands trembled slightly, and I clenched them into fists, trying to calm my nerves.

I glanced to my right, and through the dim light of the street, I noticed the soft glow of lights in Ares's apartment. Relief washed over me. He was there, just as planned. I knew he must have been preparing for our escape—gathering the few things we needed, making sure everything was ready.

Every movement was deliberate as I hurried up the metal stairs, my footsteps echoing as I crossed the catwalk that led to the apartment I shared with Hephaestus.

The clubhouse felt heavy and devoid of Zeus's presence. The usual energy and lively atmosphere had vanished, replaced by an eerie stillness that settled over everything like a thick blanket.

Darting inside the apartment, I rushed toward the closet and pulled out a backpack. I grabbed practical clothing and every single pair of underwear I owned. Since I didn't know where we were going, I wasn't sure what weather to pack for.

In the bathroom, I snatched my toiletries and wedged them into the opening of my bag, camouflaging them as best I could. I switched into black jeans, a matching hoodie, and a pair of Converse.

Zipping the bag closed felt final.

I looked down at my wedding band, the cold weight of it suddenly unbearable. I didn't need it anymore. I didn't want it. Slowly, I slipped the ring off my finger, feeling a sense of bitter satisfaction as I placed it on Hephaestus's bedside table.

I was never truly his wife.

The gods had turned a blind eye when he trapped me in this life, but now I begged them, whispered my prayers to the shadows—keep me far from his path, no matter what he becomes. Let him burn in his own fires. I would be free.

The buzz of my phone made me jump.

Slipping it out of my pocket, I saw that Artie had texted me.

ARTIE

Hephaestus is here at the compound.

My stomach dropped. I rushed to grab my backpack off the bed and headed for the door, my heart pounding like a war drum in my chest. The hanging pendant lights cast eerie spotlights along the catwalk, creating unsettling pools of light in the darkness.

I moved as silently as possible, knowing Hephaestus was on his way. The mere thought of facing his wrath sent a chill down my spine. If he didn't find me at the bar, he'd come straight to our apartment. There was another way out, but it was risky—desperate, even. The fire escape stairway clung to the building's exterior like a metal skeleton hidden in the shadows.

A cacophony of noise made me hurry toward the back exit.

"Where the fuck is she?" Hephaestus's voice roared through the building as I concealed myself against the wall.

"Listen," Artie said, her voice strained with concern, "Can you calm down? She's probably just sleeping. She mentioned she wasn't feeling well."

I approached the fire escape window, my breath shallow as I gripped the edge of the frame. With a steadying exhale, I slid open the heavy pane of glass, the groan of the metal faint but sharp in the stillness. Cold air rushed in, biting against my skin, but I welcomed it—it felt like a step toward freedom.

With caution, I placed the backpack on the windowsill, making sure it was secure. Swinging my leg up and over, I straddled the ledge, feeling the bitter cold bite into my skin.

The fire escape platform outside was unstable, and a single set of rickety stairs led down. Half of them were missing, making the descent even more treacherous. Each step I took sent a rattling sound through the metal structure, amplifying the tension in the air. I clenched the railing, my hands growing numb from the chill.

Time was of the essence. I needed to move faster, but I knew I couldn't be too loud. Hephaestus, always vigilant, would notice the open window. My heart pounded as I forced myself to quicken my pace, despite the fear clawing at my gut.

Reaching the last rung, I glanced down. It was an eight-foot drop to the ground below. I kneeled on the last step, feeling the rough texture of the metal beneath my knees. I summoned all my courage and leaped into the darkness.

*Bad idea.*

I gasped as a sharp, searing pain shot through my back. The

backpack had done its job to cushion the fall, but the jolt still rattled me, leaving me breathless and disoriented.

I could feel the sting of a bruise beginning to form, the kind of ache that would linger and throb. But I pushed the pain aside, forcing myself to focus on the bigger picture. A bruised back was a small price to pay for what I was gaining. Pain might linger, but freedom—true, lasting freedom—was worth far more.

Taking a deep breath, I rolled onto my side, pushing through the lingering pain to get up. As I moved, a rush of blood to my head made me momentarily dizzy, but I steadied myself and sprinted down the narrow alley behind the building. My phone buzzed with a new message, and I quickly checked it, my heart racing even faster.

ARES

Meet on the far side of the bar. I'm there.

Ares was finally offering me the freedom I had been yearning for. Love was calling me with an urgency that I could feel in every corner of my being. I was answering that call with every ounce of strength and hope I had left. Our souls were intertwined, bound together in a connection so deep and unbreakable that nothing, no obstacle or no force, could sever it.

A pair of headlights flashed in my direction. I recognized the vehicle; it was Hades's Mustang. It pulled up beside me, and Ares leaned over to open the door to the passenger's side.

"Get in! Hephaestus is here." he shouted over the roaring engine.

"I know, hurry!" I slipped onto the leather seat and slammed the door shut as Ares peeled out of the lot and barreled down the street. The nerves in my body tingled with a mix of anticipation and relief as I leaned into Ares, pressing a soft kiss to his cheek.

Ares's eyes darted to me with sharp concern, his gaze quickly scanning my face as his hand instinctively tightened on my thigh.

"Are you hurt?" he asked, his voice a blend of worry and urgency.

I met his gaze with a reassuring smile, trying to dispel his worry.

"I'm fine," I said softly, my voice steady despite the adrenaline coursing through me. "I just took the emergency steps."

"You did what?" Ares' voice was a mixture of shock and awe as we sped down the main street, picking up speed. "There is a reason we blocked it, you know. It's basically being held up by a thread." He shook his head in annoyance, but a flicker of approval in his eyes betrayed his underlying admiration.

"Maybe someone helped me become a bit of a warrior myself." I teased as I intertwined our fingers together. He lifted my hand to place a kiss on my knuckles.

With a tender smile, he uttered, "You were already a warrior."

# CHAPTER TWENTY-SIX
## ARES

I can pinpoint the exact moment I fell in love with Aphrodite. It wasn't some grand, dramatic event; it was in the way she looked at me with those intense, vulnerable hazel eyes. There was a raw edge to her gaze, a steely resolve that told me she was determined to avenge her brother's death, no matter the cost. She wasn't asking for a handout; she was ready to throw herself into the fire to uncover the truth about Titan.

Her resilience was undeniable. She took on every challenge with a fearless determination that made me fall for her harder than I ever thought possible.

I saw our future laid out before me—a future that I was hell-bent on securing. I knew then that I would do whatever it took to protect her, to protect us. Giving up my family, my old life—it was a sacrifice I was willing to make. My love for her wasn't just some fleeting emotion; it was a force that drove me to stand by her side, no matter the cost.

We arrived at the drop-off point where Hades had left another vehicle for us. I kept clear of the city's main roads and drove onto the overpass, blending into the shadows as we made our escape.

Serenity enveloped us as we traveled together, her head finding solace on my shoulder while my hand rested gently on her thigh.

Snow fell, looking like stars escaping from the sky as I turned into the parking lot of the Aegean Shores Motel. I felt guilty for bringing her here. She deserved a motel that wasn't a cesspool of grime and neglect, somewhere clean and inviting, not a place that looked like it hadn't been touched by a broom in years.

Turning the engine off, I leaned back and gripped the steering wheel, turning to face her.

"Ares," Her voice was like a soft caress. "It's our first trip together."

We both let out a laugh, easing some of the tension. Aphrodite pressed her hand gently against my cheek. The flickering glow of the vacancy sign cast a soft light into the vehicle, highlighting the shimmer in her eyes. She drew me close, and our lips met, the world outside dissolving into a haze of tension and fear. In that fleeting moment, there was only us.

As she pulled away, her gaze lingered on mine, her voice a sultry whisper.

"Let's go inside."

I ran my fingers through her curls as I flashed her a cocky smile. "To be continued?" She rolled her eyes as she turned away and swung the door open.

I walked into the motel and approached the old wooden desk. The receptionist, a foreboding man, checked us in for the night.

From the corner of my eye, I saw Aphrodite standing with her arms crossed. Even in this bleak, desolate setting, she seemed to shine like a vibrant flower in full bloom. I slid some money across the front desk, quickly grabbing the key and avoiding any unnecessary conversation.

I took Aphrodite's hand and led her to a room in a distant part of the motel. I unlocked the door and swung it open. The smell of smoke and mothballs hit hard as we entered.

I locked the door behind us while Aphrodite turned on the lights.

The walls boasted dated vine wallpaper with tan furniture that had been patched so many times, I was surprised it was still holding it together. It looked like they hadn't swapped out the comforter on the bed since the eighties, and the bathroom still had those pink tiles from the fifties. The bar had a broken fridge, a flycatcher, and there were dirty ashtrays all over.

"Well," Aphrodite placed her hands on her hips and let out a laugh, "Are you up to date with your tetanus shot?"

I sat on the edge of the bed, covering my face with my hands, letting out a frustrated sigh. This wasn't how I pictured things. I knew danger was part of the deal when we planned to escape, but it gnawed at me that our only refuge was this dingy motel.

She walked over to me and took my hands in hers. With a seductive gaze fixed upon me, she placed one knee on the bed, followed by the other, and settled onto my lap. Leaning in, she pressed her lips against mine, taking hold of the back of my neck as I pulled her waist closer. The intensity of our kiss was overwhelming, like a wave crashing against me repeatedly.

With a trembling hand, I cupped her cheek, savoring the sight of her before me as I caressed her soft skin. She moaned in response to my touch, making my dick throb painfully in my jeans, begging to be let free. As our kiss heightened, I gave into the impulse to explore every inch of her body. I traced the curves of her breasts. Her moan broke our kiss, giving us a chance to catch our breath.

She removed her top, revealing her stunning figure adorned in a black lace bra. Then, she pulled my shirt over my head and tossed it aside. Her fingers brushed over the bandage that covered my wound. She traced delicate lines over my abs and chest, and I tightened my grip on her ass. "I love you, Aphrodite."

Her eyes, brimming with a deep, aching longing, locked onto mine. Her lips parted slowly, "I want you to reveal your darkest desires to me," she breathed, her voice a seductive caress that sent shivers down my spine.

The weight of her words held a daring challenge that ignited a fire within me. She gazed at me with a tantalizing mix of anticipation and surrender, as if she was daring me to uncover the depths of our shared darkness.

Standing before me, I couldn't tear my eyes away as she unhooked her bra with a slow, deliberate movement. Her breasts were a vision of supple perfection, flawlessly rounded and impossibly inviting. Aphrodite's fingers tangled in my hair, pulling my chin up so that I was completely at her mercy. Her gaze was a hot, insistent flame, holding me captive.

With maddening slowness, she slid her hand to the button of her pants. My pulse raced, a desperate urge to rip her clothes off surging through me. I fought the impulse, letting her take control as she continued her slow striptease. She dragged her pants down her hips with a sensual grace, letting them fall to the floor in a whisper of fabric.

Her skin glowed under the moonlight streaming through the window, making her look almost otherworldly. The sight of her, illuminated and exposed, stoked the flames of my desire until I could barely hold back. My restraint was slipping away fast, the need to possess her overwhelming and impossible to ignore.

I stood, my eyes locking onto hers as she watched me unbuckle my belt with one hand and lower my jeans and boxers. Her eyes widened at the sight of me standing naked before her, fully exposed, my cock already hard for her. I lifted her off the ground with ease, and she wrapped her legs around my waist as I carried her to the bed. Placing her down, I positioned myself above her, ready to devour this woman entirely. I watched as the moonlight danced on her bare body. I couldn't wait any longer.

She was finally mine.

I kissed her intensely, trailing along her collarbone and down to her breasts. I squeezed her hips, and her body arched into me. An electrifying sensation coursed through my veins. I slid my fingers along her folds, feeling her wetness, and she moaned in response to my touch. Without warning, she pushed me onto my back and straddled me.

In one swift, commanding motion, she lowered herself onto my dick until I was sunk to the hilt. It felt miraculous to be inside of her again. Her hips moved tantalizingly, grinding against me as her breasts bounced, perfect nipples pebbled and hard.

Gods, she was beautiful. I wanted to feel her body erupt against me. I needed her closer. I sat up and pressed our bodies together.

"Ares," she breathed as I drank in her embrace.

"I surrender to you, Aphrodite." I said between ragged breaths.

Our hungry gazes locked. I growled, bound by her hold. Our bodies moved together as if we were one. Our connection transcended the physical boundaries of intimacy.

Rapture consumed me as her head tilted back with a cry that resonated to the heavens. Kissing her neck, I savored the sight of her flushed skin, and with each kiss, I could feel the quickened rhythm of her heart.

"I surrender to you, Ares." she said, moaning my name.

I pressed my lips against hers with the fervent need to taste her. I turned us around, pinning her down beneath me. Aphrodite let out a small whimper as I raised her hands above her head. Thrusting harder into her, I watched her eyes widen as she cried out.

I could feel her heart pounding as I released her hands and placed mine around her neck. My fingers stroked her skin, feeling the vibration of her moans.

I wanted to feel her body unravel completely as I took her fully, filling her with every part of me, leaving her trembling and consumed.

"I'm fucking coming, baby," I growled, my voice rough and desperate as I pressed my lips against her neck. The sensation of my climax was crashing over me like a tidal wave, and I could feel her body responding with mine, her cries of pleasure rising.

"Ares!" she screamed, her voice raw and fragmented as she reached her peak. Her body clenched and trembled around me, the explosive pleasure of our simultaneous orgasms sending shockwaves through both of us.

As my climax hit, a guttural growl escaped my lips, my face buried against the slope of her shoulder. The intoxicating scent of sweat mixed with her floral perfume filled my senses.

Every nerve was on fire, and I felt an overwhelming need to possess and dominate her completely. "I want to fuck you every chance I get," I whispered fiercely against her ear, feeling her shudder and convulse with the aftershocks of our intense release.

Lying in bed, Aphrodite rested her head on my chest as I gently twirled a strand of her hair. With a light laugh, I said, "I want to have babies with you."

"Is that so?" She lifted her head, her eyes locking with mine for a moment.

"You make me feel like I deserve to be happy, to have a family," I confessed. "Even after all the shitty things I've done in my life." The confession hit me like a ton of bricks. I never thought I was worthy of redemption, but with her, it felt possible

She gently caressed my cheek, her hair falling into her face. "Ares, nothing could ever make my love for you fade, no matter what your past is."

"Tomorrow," I said, "Let's go wherever you want. We can leave our old lives behind and become completely different people." I smiled at her, imagining the possibilities.

"I like the sound of that," she replied, biting her bottom lip.

Despite the sacrifices of the day, my heart swelled with emotion.

"Ares?" she whispered, pulling my face close to hers.

"Everything has changed," I said with a shrug. "I'm ready to leave it all behind."

“We don’t have to leave,” she replied softly. “We can figure out a way to stay and make it work. I can get a divorce—”

“Aphrodite, you’re worth it,” I interrupted, turning to lie on my side as I held her hands in mine. “You’re worth everything.”

She pulled the covers over us, and we snuggled underneath, finding comfort in this fleeting moment of normalcy. It gave me solace to know that even in our cruel world, we could find happiness together.

My demons were mine to battle, but I knew Aphrodite would be by my side.

We fell asleep holding onto each other, finding peace in each other's embrace. A while later, I was awoken by the feeling of something cold pushing against my temple.

Opening my eyes, I saw Ouranos’ face, his gaze piercing through me as he stood above us, a gun pressed against my head in the darkness.

“Get the fuck away from my daughter,” Ouranos growled, the sound of his voice reverberating off the motel room walls.

Aphrodite’s eyes snapped open as she was jolted from her peaceful slumber.

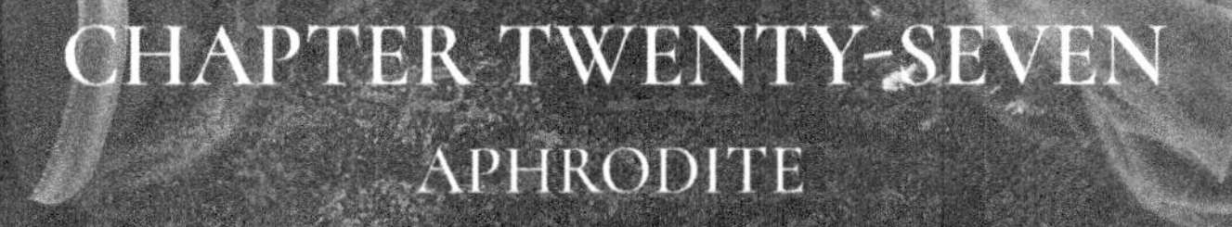

# CHAPTER TWENTY-SEVEN

## APHRODITE

"I'm not surprised that you would spread your legs for this man." Ouranos seethed, towering over us, his gun against Ares's temple as I hid my body underneath the sheets.

"Don't fucking talk to her like that." Ares's anger was evident in his voice as he pushed into the gun with his forehead as he sat up, seeming unfazed by the weapon. I scanned the room, noticing that my father had come alone, none of his ghouls present.

"I can talk to her anyway I want!" Ouranos voice was a menacing force, "Get dressed, both of you. Now!" he commanded.

Ares and I moved to get dressed, picking our clothes up off the floor piece by piece. Ouranos had his gun trained on Ares, intently watching his every move.

From outside the motel room door, a voice rang out, "Are they ready to go?" The second I recognized it, my blood ran cold.

*Hephaestus.*

I hastily threw my shirt back on, heart racing as my eyes flicked to the door. Ares stood, his bare chest gleaming in the dim light that spilled in from the open doorway.

The air crackled with tension as Hephaestus entered the room.

My eyes shot a furious glare toward Ares's brother, but he ignored me completely, dismissing my presence as if I were invisible. A deep sense of shame flooded through me, helpless as I watched the scene spiral into chaos. The three men stood locked in a brutal standoff, their expressions cold, their bodies coiled with lethal tension, each refusing to back down. No mercy was to be found here.

Ouranos stepped closer, his face mere inches from Ares, their eyes locked in a vicious stare. With deliberate malice, Ouranos pressed the barrel of the gun back against Ares's temple, his fingers twitching ever so slightly, as if daring him to flinch.

"Please! Leave him alone!" I cried out, trying to get my father's attention, but he wouldn't look at me.

"Why the hell would I leave him alone when he's the one who murdered my son?" Ouranos spat, his voice a venomous hiss dripping with rage and accusation. The intensity of his gaze bore into Ares, a raw, unfiltered hatred that seemed to ignite the very air around them.

The accusation sliced through me like a guillotine, severing any pretense of normalcy. My world seemed to shatter in an instant, leaving me grappling with the fragments of my reality.

My gaze locked onto the man I loved.

"He wouldn't have killed him," I pleaded, desperately searching for something to hold onto, a shred of hope. Ares turned to me, his vibrant eyes were filled with desperation, mirroring the turmoil raging within me. My heart pounded against my ribs, its rhythm becoming erratic as panic coursed through my veins. I struggled to breathe.

Ares's face was etched with anguish. His hands trembled, revealing the inner chaos he was struggling to contain. We were both being consumed by the same whirlwind of emotions.

"No, he wouldn't kill him," I repeated, my voice a mix of determination and vulnerability. I was pleading not only to those around us, but to the universe, seeking reassurance that the man I loved was not capable of such an unthinkable act.

Ares reached out his trembling hand and brushed mine. It was a simple gesture, but in that touch, I felt that glimmer of hope, a lifeline. Our connection, once so solid and unbreakable, now felt fragile, as if hanging by a thread. But I knew we had to confront these accusations head-on, to fight against the mounting suspicion and prove the depth of our love.

Ares held my gaze, sincerity brimming in his eyes as he said, "I didn't kill Titan." He whirled toward Ouranos, his voice a fierce, guttural roar. "You bastard! That's a fucking

lie—Titan was my friend!"

"A friend? Is that so?" Ouranos's voice erupted like a storm, filling the cramped room with chilling authority. "We have the proof." His words struck with an icy certainty, each syllable heavy with the promise of damning evidence.

"He wouldn't hurt him! Father, please!" I screamed, my voice cracking with desperation as I lunged toward my father. But Hephaestus's grip was unyielding, his arms like iron bands clamped around my waist, pinning me in place.

"Let me go!" I begged, my tears spilling over and blurring my vision. The anguish of the moment was almost unbearable as I watched the man I loved being accused of murdering my brother. Ares was a killer, a man forged in darkness and trained to be a relentless force, a nightmare for anyone who crossed him. Yet, despite the horrors he was capable of, I clung to the deep belief that he would never betray me.

Ouranos's gaze hardened, his voice cold and unwavering. "We have irrefutable evidence," he said, his tone brimming with accusation. "An informant from the police force gave us the details. Your DNA was found all over Titan the night of the explosion, and on the bomb that was meant to wipe out my entire family."

Ares's eyes blazed with a mix of fury and disbelief. "That is a fucking lie, and you know it!" he roared, attempting to lunge at Hephaestus with a sudden, desperate surge of aggression. But before he could reach his target, Ouranos swung the butt of his gun with brutal precision, slamming it against Ares's head. The impact sent Ares crashing to the ground, his body crumpling with a sickening thud.

"You son of a fucking bitch!" Ouranos roared, his face was a mask of pure rage as he spat the words.

"Stop it!" I cried out, my voice cracking with desperation and fear. "Stop! Ares didn't do this!"

"You're a damn fool if you think he's innocent, Aphrodite!" Ouranos's voice was laced with scorn, each word dripping with contempt. "You think he's different? They're all the same—ruthless, power-hungry monsters!" His gaze flicked to Ares with unrestrained venom. "He wanted to control you, to own you, and you fell for it! You're nothing more than a pawn to him, a mere tool in his twisted game. Just like your worthless mother. You're so fucking blind!"

His words hit me like a tidal wave, crashing over me with a force so overwhelming that it left me gasping for air. I barely had a moment to process the weight of his words before his hand flew toward me.

The slap came down with brutal, unforgiving force, the sharp crack of it echoing through the room like a thunderclap. My face stung fiercely, the burn of his hand searing into my skin.

The slap wasn't just a physical assault—it was a violent assault on my very soul.

It felt like every bitter, hateful word he'd thrown at me was now imprinted on my skin, each accusation a fresh wound. My cheek throbbed with a fiery pain, but it was the emotional onslaught that nearly crippled me. His words, slicing through me with surgical precision, cut into my heart like daggers, leaving me breathless and trembling.

I stumbled back, the room spinning around me, a whirl of chaotic anger and despair. The intensity of his fury was like a storm, lashing out and tearing through the fragile barriers of my resolve. I stood there, stunned and broken, overwhelmed by the crushing weight of his rage and the brutal, unrelenting torment of his words.

Ouranos placed his foot on Ares's chest, digging the heel of his boot into his bullet wound. The stitches tore open, and his blood began to seep through the fabric of his shirt, staining it dark and crimson.

"Don't...hit... her..you piece..of shit!" Ares struggled and tried to push Ouranos's leg off him, but it was no use. He'd been hit hard.

Ouranos drove his heel deeper into Ares's wound, eliciting even more guttural, anguished screams that echoed through the room.

"I am not a fool," I declared, pushing through the searing pain in my head, my voice rising with a fiery intensity that surprised even me. The words erupted from deep within, driven by a force I hadn't fully realized I possessed until that moment.

Raw power surged through my veins, igniting my resolve and sharpening my focus. The sight of Ouranos's doubting eyes only fueled the fire within me, spurring me on with an unyielding determination.

I knew Ares, and I refused to accept the twisted image Ouranos tried to impose on me. The scent of defiance hung thick in the air, mingling with the faint aroma of my fear, but I refused to let it overpower me.

I could still hear my father's accusations branding me as a whore echoing in the recesses of my mind, each word like a lash against my spirit. I was a force to be reckoned with, and nothing he said could take that away from me.

"Take her," Ouranos said to Hephaestus, his gun trained on me, "before I put a bullet in her skull." The silence that followed was drawn out, amplifying my father's anger.

Without hesitation, Hephaestus picked me up and threw me over his shoulder. I thrashed around, desperately trying to grab onto something to make him stop and put me down. But there was no point. He was stronger and his hold on me was firm, making it hard to breathe.

There was no way out.

Hephaestus stopped abruptly. Shifting my weight to get a better view, I watched him hand a wad of cash to the scummy motel manager. He must have recognized Ares and tipped them off about our location, which is how they managed to track us down.

In the distance, Ares's screams of agony pierced through the night, each cry a jagged edge of torment. Tears streamed uncontrollably down my cheeks, the feeling of helplessness encompassing me.

We approached the vehicle, and Hephaestus moved with unsettling efficiency. In one swift, practiced motion, he yanked open the trunk and tossed me inside, the cold metal slamming shut behind me with a final, resounding thud. The dark surrounded me as I kicked against the lid of the trunk.

Suddenly, the sound of the engine roared through the vehicle.

I kicked and screamed, desperate to break free, my voice lost in the blaring heavy metal music that erupted, drowning out my cries. Adrenaline surged through me, a frenzied pulse of fear and confusion. I had no idea where we were headed or what was happening.

The air was thick with the stench of rusted metal and musty fabric, an oppressive odor that seemed to close in on me. Anxiety clawed at my thoughts, making my body tremble uncontrollably in the dark confines of the trunk.

I forced myself to calm down, my mind racing to devise a plan. My hands searched frantically along the inside of the trunk lid, feeling for the release lever. After what felt like an eternity, I finally found it and yanked with all my might. But the lid remained stubbornly shut, and my fleeting hope evaporated into the suffocating darkness. Despair began to settle in, but I refused to surrender.

Using all my strength, I kicked at the taillights as hard as I could, trying to shatter them and get a signal out to anyone who might be driving behind us.

Hephaestus drove with reckless aggression, the vehicle lurching violently as he took sharp turns. I was thrown sideways, slamming my head against the hard trunk walls.

A searing pain shot through me, and I tasted the sharp, metallic tang of blood, realizing I had split my lip open. The car stopped abruptly, and my body flew forward, slamming into the metal with a bone-jarring impact. The violence of the stop left me gasping. The engine cut and I heard a door open and then slam shut.

I had no option but to fight, even if he was much stronger than me.

The trunk opened and the light of the streetlamp above flooded in, silhouetting an imposing figure before me. Hephaestus yanked me out of the trunk with ruthless force, and I fought back with everything I had. My nails raked across his skin in a desperate attempt to break free, but his grip only tightened. I thrashed about unrelentingly, but Hephaestus' hold on me was ironclad, offering no freedom.

He slung me over his shoulder like I weighed nothing, the force knocking the wind out of me. I struggled to get a glimpse of my surroundings, but all I could see were dark, towering trees looming like silent witnesses to my fate.

The ground crunched beneath his heavy boots as he trudged through the snow, each step taking us closer to a dilapidated barn that rose from the shadows like something out of a nightmare. I realized he wasn't taking me back to the compound. The most unnerving thoughts ran through my mind.

*I was going to die.*

"Hephaestus, let me go!" My voice was sharp, cutting through the cold air. "You're making a mistake—this won't end the way you think it will!" I held onto that defiance, even as his grip bruised my arms.

I couldn't show him my fear, couldn't let him see how desperate I truly was.

He dragged me into the barn, and the smell of damp wood and rust filled the air, making it harder to breathe. The walls, splintered and aged, seemed to press in, shrinking my space, choking the life from me. My chest tightened, panic rising as his hands yanked me toward a pulley system hanging from the ceiling.

"No!" I screamed, thrashing with every ounce of strength I had left. My legs kicked wildly, but Hephaestus was relentless. His fingers dug into my skin, refusing to let go. I twisted in his grasp, teeth bared, trying to bite him, but he only tightened his grip. Pain shot through my limbs, but I refused to give in.

My throat burned from the effort of screaming, yet I kept fighting. Hephaestus's silence was more terrifying than anything he could have said. His determination was like a wall of ice, cold and unmovable, and I felt it sinking deeper into my bones.

With a savage tug, he grabbed my wrists, binding them tightly before moving on to secure my ankles. With one lift, he strung me up from a hook. My arms stretched painfully above my head as I dangled a foot above the ground. I bit down a scream as I lashed out, my foot connecting with his ribs in a sharp, desperate kick.

The force sent Hephaestus stumbling backward, his body crashing into the old barn wall with a heavy thud. He groaned in pain, his shout echoing in the cold barn.

I gritted my teeth, trying desperately to hoist myself up, muscles trembling as I strained against the ropes digging into my wrists. My arms screamed in protest, my fingers numbing from the effort. I felt the rough fibers tear into my skin, but no matter how hard I pulled, I couldn't break free.

Panic surged through me, thickening my throat. I thrashed, trying to find any leverage, any hope of escape, but it was useless. The ropes wouldn't budge. I was trapped, suspended, as Hephaestus recovered from the blow.

He stormed towards me. "You fucking bitch." He sneered as he delivered a punch to my stomach. Air whooshed from my lungs. I wheezed from the sudden pain in my gut as my weakened body dangled from the hook. A chilling realization crept into my mind.

This would be my judgment day.

"Why are you doing this?" I gasped, my voice raw with fear and anger as I lifted my head to meet his cold, unfeeling eyes. Sharp pain radiated through my stomach, each breath sending waves of agony through my body. The pressure in my skull built with every heartbeat, blood pounding in my ears as I fought to keep focus.

"You were just a pawn, Aphrodite," he hissed, his hands gripping my chin, lifting my head so that I had no choice but to meet his merciless stare. "I could never love the bastard daughter of Ouranos," Hephaestus said coldly, his voice devoid of any emotion. "I knew all along you were in love with my brother. You were the perfect distraction, really, keeping him occupied while I executed my plans."

"I...I don't understand." I said with a raspy voice as I tried to catch my breath.

Hephaestus's lips curled into a wicked smile, his eyes glinting with dark satisfaction.

"I always knew I was meant to lead the Olympus Syndicate," Hephaestus continued, his tone sharp with arrogance. "My father was too distracted, always chasing after a new wife, looking for his next conquest, instead of focusing on what really mattered. He was blind to the empire crumbling under his feet. But I saw it. I've always seen it." He circled around me, his gaze predatory and calculating. "And Ares? He's nothing but a thorn in my side – more trouble than he's worth. I was tired of taking care of everything. I was tired of being the leader when no one paid attention," He stepped closer, the shadows deepened around him as he continued. "So, when I saw an opportunity, I took it."

I struggled to process his words, my mind racing as he reached into his back pocket and pulled out a syringe. The world around me seemed to blur, nothing making sense anymore. He methodically twisted off the cap, the sharp metal gleaming under the dim light, and I felt a surge of dread tighten in my chest.

"What are you doing?" I snapped, trying to swing my body away from him, but it was no use. He gripped my waist tight.

"Hold still," he said, his voice chillingly calm. "This will give you some short-lived relief. Get some rest, Aphrodite," his gaze boring into mine with a menacing intensity. "Because the real show is about to begin." He grabbed my chin tightly as he sank the needle into my neck.

I tried to scream, to fight back, but his hand covered my mouth, muffling any sound I could make. The effect was almost immediate.

A wave of numbness surged through my body, as if icy tendrils were wrapping around my nerves, erasing all sensation. My vision blurred and darkened at the edges, flickering briefly before succumbing to the overwhelming darkness. As consciousness slipped away, the last thing I managed to utter was, "Ares will kill you."

# CHAPTER TWENTY-EIGHT
## ARES

I couldn't save her.

I watched from the ground as Hephaestus tossed Aphrodite over his shoulder. Ouranos had me pinned down, his boot pressing mercilessly into my wound. Every shift of his foot felt like a fresh, brutal assault. My screams of agony echoed throughout the room as I desperately clawed at his leg. Through the haze of torment, I couldn't look away from Ouranos's sinister smile—a twisted expression that seemed to savor every moment of my agony, reinforcing this brutal reality.

I tilted my head, trying to get a clearer view as a group of determined henchmen stormed into the room. Ouranos finally lifted his boot from my wound, and a fleeting wave of relief washed over me, but it was short-lived. One of the men yanked me roughly forward, my back scraping painfully along the rough stained carpet.

I roared in defiance, trying to summon every ounce of strength I had left.

Even as they tackled me, I fought back with raw, unyielding power. My fists swung wildly, catching one of the henchmen across the jaw. He snarled, eyes blazing with fury, struggling against their hold. "You think you can just take me down?" I roared, my voice filled with a guttural rage. "I'll make you fucking regret this!"

I wasn't going down without a fight. They swarmed me, one bastard pinning my shoulders to the ground while I roared and thrashed. "Get the hell off me!" I bellowed, my voice a snarl of defiance. My kicks and wild flailing couldn't break their grip; they just kept piling on, holding me down like I was a sack of cement.

Through the mess of it all, I caught a glimpse of Aphrodite. She was trying to rise, her voice cracking with desperation. "Ares, don't give up!" The raw edge in her shout hit me hard. Seeing her like that, helpless but fierce, only stoked the fire in my gut. I fought harder, feeling the crushing weight of their bodies, but I wasn't about to give in.

Just then, I noticed one of the men on top of me was holding a syringe. My heart rate accelerated. "We use this to tame the beast," he said.

I thrashed violently, every muscle in my body fighting against my restraints. "You touch me with that, and I'll rip your fucking throat out!" I roared, my voice cracking with a mix of rage and desperation.

He ignored my threat, his eyes gleaming with cruel amusement as he moved closer. The syringe glinted menacingly in the dim light, and I could feel the icy grip of terror tightening around my chest. I tried to wrench myself free, but their weight pressed me into the ground, my struggles growing weaker.

He jabbed the needle into my neck. Within seconds, I could feel the drug enter my system, and my breath caught in my throat.

"This will allow you to experience every sensation as if you were awake, but you won't be able to scream." The henchman laughed with delight.

"You brought this on yourself, Ares." Ouranos stood looming above me, radiating invincibility. I felt like I was being submerged in the icy depths of the ocean, and I observed him from beneath the surface.

My muscles were beginning to stop working, and thick fog engulfed my mind.

Ouranos's henchman bound my hands behind my back. The next thing I knew, I was being thrown into the back of a cold white van. The heavy door slammed shut with a resounding thud. I lay there completely dazed; senses dulled.

Desperate to escape, I attempted to fight against my restraints, but my limbs were unresponsive. An acrid stench filled the air as metallic blood dripped from my nose to my lips.

I summoned every ounce of strength I had left, trying to create friction on the rope in a desperate attempt to fray it. My muscles, numb and sluggish from the sedative, barely responded. Blinking against the dim light, I struggled to focus. My gaze locked onto a sharp blade glinting in the corner of the floor.

The truck's movements became more aggressive with each turn. Despite my weakened state, I forced my body to lurch forward, eyes locked on the blade I had spotted. Every jolt and bump felt like a brutal assault on my already battered body. Summoning every last ounce of strength, I maneuvered myself closer, my movements fueled by raw determination.

Pain flared through my muscles as I slammed into the metal wall, but I managed to snatch the knife from the floor, its cold steel biting into my palm as I gripped it tightly.

Drowsiness from the drugs began to kick in.

I started cutting into the rope with everything I had left, my hands clumsy from the muscle relaxer. Each slice was a battle, my movements sluggish and awkward. I fought through the numbness, the blade biting through the fibers until the rope finally snapped. I let the knife drop with a clatter that echoed in the cramped space

My hands, slick with blood and trembling from exhaustion, moved clumsily up to my face. The rough surface of the rope had left deep, angry lines across my wrists, and the blood seeped freely from them, streaking down my arm in thick, crimson lines.

The engine cut out with a jarring thud, my heartbeat pounding like a jackhammer in my ears. I could feel the blood trickling down my arm, and the urge to stop the bleeding was growing more desperate by the second.

The drug's haze made my movements sluggish, but I wasn't about to let that slow me down. My hand fumbled for the blade, my only shot at turning this around. I had no intention of letting Ouranos take me down like this.

I gripped the knife tightly, fighting through the fog in my head.

Yanking my bandana from my back pocket, I wrapped it tightly around the blade, using it to absorb any blood and keep my grip steady. I could barely make out the contours of the weapon, but it was all I had between me and whatever was about to come through that door.

The moment the door swung open, a blinding blast of headlights cut through the dim haze, momentarily throwing me off balance. As my vision cleared, I saw the early morning sky giving way to a dull gray light, the first hint of dawn breaking through. The harsh glare was almost unbearable, but I forced myself to focus.

A menacing figure emerged from the darkness beyond the door. It was Ouranos, his silhouette a dark, imposing shadow against the blinding headlights. He moved with a predatory grace, his men flanking him like a pack of wolves.

"I've got to give you credit, Ares, you are a warrior. You never give up, do you?" he growled, his words dripping with contempt. "Put the fucking blade down. You're outnumbered."

I locked eyes with him, my glare burning with a seething hatred that felt like it could ignite the very air between us. My entire being roared for the chance to tear him apart, the rage in my veins screaming for vengeance. "What the hell do you want from me?" I growled, my voice low and edged with a fury that barely contained itself.

Ouranos signaled with a nod, and his men advanced toward me. I was determined to defend myself, but the drug in my system was making everything blurry.

Someone grabbed my arm, and I responded by delivering a blind punch. It connected to his nose, which cracked under the force. He brought his hands to his face, cradling his injury, just as another man stepped forward and landed a hard punch to my stomach, leaving me winded and gasping for breath. I fell to the ground, and my head hit the dirt, pain spreading throughout my body, the drug making it worse. My world spun uncontrollably.

Ouranos's face twisted into a malevolent grin, his eyes cold and pitiless. Leaning in close, his breath hot and rank against my skin, he hissed, "You're just as weak as my son. That's why I had to eliminate him. Weakness like yours has no place in my world."

My eyes widened in shock at his confession.

The ground felt like it had slipped out from under me. "You're the one who did it? You killed your own son?"

"He wasn't my son," Ouranos boomed, his eyes turning black. "My wife is a whore. She deceived me, Titan was never mine. I had planned to entrust everything to him, but I learned the truth. Gaia's web of lies came undone, and I realized the necessity of taking him out."

I tried to lift myself, but it was useless, the muscle relaxant was in full effect.

"Don't get up," he continued, then delivered a kick to my ribs. I cried out from the pain.

*You need to get up,* I thought. *You need to find Aphrodite.*

"Was it Hephaestus?" I could hardly speak as my face pressed into the cold dirt.

"Oh, you clever boy," he taunted, his voice dripping with malice. "You see, I struck a deal with him in exchange for marrying my daughter. We had mutual interests—he wanted to eliminate your father and seize his place as the head of the OS, and I wanted Titan dead. It was the perfect exchange."

He leaned in closer, the cruelty evident in his gaze. "We met in secret before we discussed the trade with Zeus and the others," His hand flexed, rubbing his knuckles as if relishing the memory of the treachery.

Ouranos's breath surrounded his face in an icy cloud as he leaned down next to me. "Hephaestus had to get rid of you too. You made a mockery of yourself, chasing after some pretty piece of ass while pretending you were anything more than a pathetic, weak little shit. You thought you could play with the big boys, but you were just another dumb fuck who got chewed up and spit out. And now, look where you are."

He reached for my hair and yanked my head back, forcing me to meet his eyes. "What Hephaestus doesn't realize is that I will kill him too. I'm going to wipe out every last one of you.

I'll own this city, and there won't be a shred of Olympus Syndicate left. Your filthy presence will be erased, and as we speak, my men are heading to the hospital to finish off your pathetic old man. This is just the beginning." Ouranos threw my head down, and disorientation washed over me. My body was stiff, battered, and weak. I lay on my back, defeated, feeling the information haze through my mind.

It was all a lie. Titan's murder, the supposed betrayal—every bit of it was orchestrated to manipulate me, to turn me into a pawn in their game of power. The realization hit me like a cold wave, freezing my blood. "You fucking bastard," I growled through gritted teeth, my voice low and dangerous. "You're not just killing us. You're tearing apart everything we ever stood for."

His smile widened, devoid of any trace of remorse. "You see, it's not just about killing you or your father. It's about erasing everything you've ever believed in, everything that made you think you were worth something. By the time I'm done, there won't be a single soul left who remembers your name."

Ouranos was giddy at the sight of my bettered body splayed out on the floor, defeated.

My brother's greed had torn everything apart. His hunger for control drove him to try and take down our father. He'd always been desperate for approval, striving to be the son our old man could be proud of. But this? This was beyond betrayal. It was a gutless, weak move. Taking it to murder? That's not ambition—that's cowardice at its worst.

"I am going to burn the Olympus Syndicate clubhouse to the ground with your entire family inside. Maybe, while I'm at it, I'll even have some fun with your sisters." Ouranos winked at me, his laughter booming obnoxiously in my face, spit flying from his open mouth.

"I'd love to see you try," I growled, my voice laced with fury as I glared at him, rage thrumming through every muscle in my body. His words lit a fire deep inside me, igniting the part of me that refused to surrender, even when my body begged me to. He thought he had the upper hand, but I wasn't about to let him destroy everything my family had built.

The Olympus Syndicate was more than just a name. It was blood, grit, and legacy. And no one—especially not this smug bastard—was going to burn it down without a fight.

Pain radiated through me, but I pushed it aside. I was built for this. The blood, the struggle—this was what I lived for. He could throw everything at me, but I wasn't backing down. Not now. Not ever.

That's who I was.

"I will kill you with my bare hands." I uttered through the cold, the thought of my family fueling the little hope I had. Perseverance hit my body like lightning, my will to fight unrelenting. I raised myself up onto my knees. "You will not win, Ouranos. I will make damn sure of it."

Ouranos cackled maniacally as his hands came to rest on his hips, "You son of a bitch," he said, rubbing his chin before nodding toward his men, "Dispose of this worthless scum."

Scanning the area, I realized that we were on the Aetherion Bridge. The rough waters below filled with sharp rocks; Ripped body parts from past disposals were strewn all over, leaving behind only remnants of their demise. There was a low chance for anyone to survive if they went over. I didn't know how the hell I was getting out of this, but I knew I had to dig deep and find the strength to survive.

Two of Ouranos's henchmen gripped my arms tightly and dragged me across the rough terrain. I fought the haze from the drugs, trying to break free. There was so much at stake—Aphrodite, my father's life, and my family's legacy, all teetering on the edge, waiting to be swallowed by the wrath of Ouranos.

I couldn't let that happen. Not while I still drew breath.

Gripping one of the henchmen's arms, I slithered my hand around his hold, twisting his wrist in an unnatural motion. He released me as he gasped in pain.

"You motherfucker!" He lashed out, trying to punch me, but I dodged sideways and punched the other man in the crotch, causing him to topple over, groaning in pain.

Ignoring my badly battered body, I ran for my life.

Bullets went off, the deafening pops ringing out behind me, and my heart pounded violently against my chest. I pushed my way through dense forest, every branch seeming to whip against me along the way.

Exhausted and bloody, I reached the water's edge beneath the bridge. Glancing back, I saw a calvary of men gaining on me. There was no chance to hide and I knew I couldn't outrun them. I took a deep breath. The water roared around me. I had reached the end of the road.

So, I jumped in.

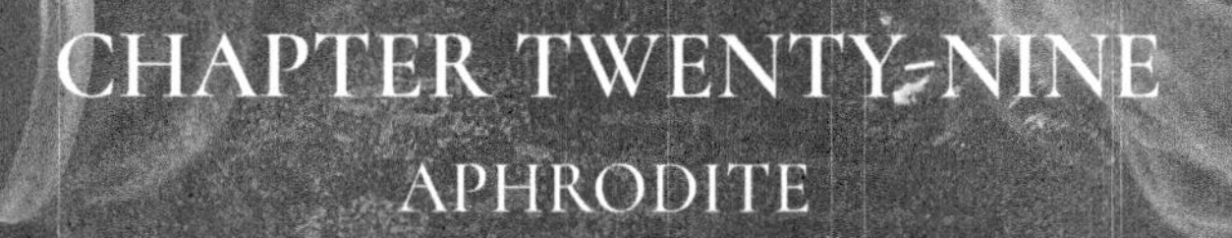

# CHAPTER TWENTY-NINE
## APHRODITE

I could feel the hook's cruel bite as it held me suspended, the ropes around my wrists like chains of torture, tightening with every desperate twitch. I widened my eyes, trying to see in the darkness, and took a deep breath. The drugs had worn off, and my head throbbed with pain.

My worst nightmares had become real.

Hephaestus was a disgusting, evil demon who thought he could take advantage of me when I was at my weakest. He was a coward. He didn't just want to hurt me—he wanted to destroy me. Torture me until I begged for mercy, or kill me outright. Maybe both.

Either way, his intentions were clear: he wanted to see me shattered, but he'd have to do more than that to take me down. I was aching all over, and when I looked down at my body, I saw fresh cuts glistening with my blood. There was a numbness in my limbs, and I couldn't feel much of anything when I attempted to wiggle them.

I screamed to the heavens, and tears streamed down my face. The pain faded as adrenaline surged through my body. Panic enveloped me as I considered the seriousness of my situation. I was determined not to be defeated. Hephaestus wasn't the only person who had darkness raging inside of him.

I concentrated on wiggling my fingers, trying to regain their feeling. They tingled, but responded, moving stiffly as pain shot through my hands. Swallowing hard, I summoned all my remaining strength. Gritting my teeth, I swung. My body moved through the air, aching with every injury I had sustained.

I didn't care. I had to break free.

No one was going to come for me. No one knew where I was. I swung faster and faster, the grinding metal emitting a high-pitched shriek as I dangled precariously above the rotted wooden floorboards; My wrists getting torn to shreds on my unrelenting binds. I curled my legs into my chest, using every ounce of energy I could summon and propelled myself upwards.

The rope lifted, slipping off the hook.

I fell to the ground with a thud. The impact sent a sharp pain through me, and I screamed in agony. I watched for a moment, dazed, as the hook above me swung back and forth.

I rolled onto my stomach and pushed myself up from the gritty dirt and hay beneath me. With a determined effort, I managed to get to my knees, lifting one foot, then the other, despite my trembling limbs. My head spun, blood rushing to my head and making everything feel hazy.

My body was streaked with blood and covered in cuts, each one a searing reminder of the ordeal I'd just survived. I took a deep breath, trying to steady myself, focusing on finding my footing again.

*I was going to kill Hephaestus.* The thought raced through my mind in a repetitive loop.

With each cautious step, I surveyed the barn, my eyes adjusting to the dim light. The air was thick and musty, saturated with the scent of dust and hay that clung to everything. The silence was suffocating, pressing down on me as I moved.

I slid the heavy barn door open, and the sudden flood of morning light stung my eyes, forcing me to squint as I stepped out into the day. The contrast between the dark, musty barn and the bright, open world outside was jarring, yet it propelled me forward, urging me to face what awaited. I knew I needed to get back to the Olympus Syndicate compound, but something kept me lingering about, a nagging sense of unfinished business.

Squinting, I tried to adjust to the brightness. An empty field stood before me, a vast stretch of barren land surrounded by dense trees. It had a dirt path which ran straight down the middle, leading to nowhere in particular. The cold air nipped at my skin, sending a shiver through me as I stepped into the brisk landscape.

The emptiness of the scene struck me—there was no sign of life, no hint of anything remotely nearby. The only sound was the crunch of gravel under my bare feet as I moved forward, watching my breath turn into a foggy mist that hung in the air before dissipating. The solitude was overwhelming, but there was no turning back now.

I ran with urgency, my heart pounding in my chest as my feet propelled me forward.

Heat surged through me, my body breaking out in a cold sweat. It was an odd, uncomfortable feeling—sweat dampening my skin even as I shivered.

Fear lingered, but I wouldn't allow it to slow me down. I sensed Titan's presence beside me, and for a moment it felt like he was here, cheering me on. It was as if his spirit had the power to make me run faster.

My feet were raw from the rocks and debris slicing into my skin, but I didn't care. I pushed through the relentless pain and the tears that blurred my vision, each step a battle against the agony coursing through me. My body felt like it was on fire, every movement a reminder of the hurt. But no matter how hard it was, I had to reach Ares. The thought of him kept me going, fueling my determination. With each staggered step, I focused on the urgency of getting to him, fighting through the haze of pain and emotion that threatened to overwhelm me.

My chest squeezed, working to catch my breath. I spotted a pair of headlights making their way toward me. A vehicle came into view, a small blue sedan. It wasn't just a car—it felt like a sign from Titan, a symbolic gesture of his love and support even after death. The sight of it gave me a surge of hope, a reminder that I wasn't alone. I waved as hard as I could, trying to get their attention. They zoomed past me.

My head tilted up to the sky as the snow fell, despair gripping me. I closed my eyes and inhaled, feeling the crisp air enter my body. Exhaustion was seeping into my muscles.

Suddenly, there was a honk.

My eyes widened, and I turned my head to see that the car had stopped down the hill. I sent a silent thank-you up to the heavens. Despite my crumbling body, I managed to push my legs to pick up speed and I headed toward the blue car.

I gripped the window and leaned down to face an older lady. She seemed dressed to go to church, and her eyes widened upon seeing the horror my body had endured. It was a mangled mess. I took a deep breath and said, "I need your help."

"I'll take you to the hospital, honey. Get inside," she said as she reached for the door handle to open.

"No!" I protested, shaking rapidly. "I need to get to the Olympus Syndicate compound."

The old woman's face dropped. No one went there without a reason.

"Oh, I will not go there." She said, a stern look on her face as she shook her head, "I'll drop you off at the hospital. That's as far as I'm willing to go."

My head hung low as I took a deep breath. "Okay, that's fine, take me to the hospital. Do you mind if I use your phone?" I bargained. She handed her phone over to me. "Thank you. I'll just be a second."

"Okay, honey. Don't take too long now, your injuries look serious." She observed, turning off her car. I straightened and walked to the back of the vehicle, dialing the person I knew could help.

Hades.

He had made me memorize his number in case I ever found myself in a situation I couldn't get out of. A situation like this.

It took three rings before I heard the phone line click.

"Hades, I need help!" I exclaimed into the phone, the panic in my voice was evident.

"Aphrodite? Where are you? What happened?" His voice was deep with worry.

Bringing my hand up to my forehead in exasperation, I said, "They found us, Hades." The weight of the night's events suddenly crashed over me, and I felt my eyes well up with tears. I continued, "Hephaestus took me to a barn and tortured me. Ouranos took Ares. I can feel it, something's happening. War isn't just coming. It's already here, and we're right in the middle of it." Tears streamed down my face, emotional turmoil writhing inside of me. As I looked to the driver of the vehicle in front of me, I said to Hades, "I found a lady who will drop me off at the hospital. Can you pick me up?"

Without hesitation, he said, "Of course. I'll be there soon."

I ended the call, and a sick feeling settled in my stomach. It was as if I already knew who would die today. I wished I could bargain with the gods, to trade my life for his.

My heart ached with the weight of it all, but right now, I had to put on my mental armor and control my emotions. There were lives on the line, and my love for Ares fueled my strength to face whatever came next.

Carme, the older lady who saved me, gave me some fresh clothing before dropping me off at the hospital. She said, "Stay safe, Aphrodite, and take this." She handed me some homemade bread. Eating was the furthest thing from my mind, but my stomach growled too loudly to ignore.

I nodded to her once. "Thank you."

She gave me a small smile before driving away. I stood in the cold, wearing a flannel shirt and shoes that were a little big. As I waited for Hades to arrive in the parking lot, I took a bite of the bread. I knew I had to keep my energy levels up for what was to come.

The black Mustang purred as Hades drove toward me with purpose. Prometheus was in the passenger side. The vehicle came to a stop, and he hopped out. "I'm going to check on Zeus. Make sure nobody has done anything to him," Prometheus said. "Be careful." He nodded to me.

"I will." I watched him slip through the doors as I sat down in the passenger seat and swung the door shut. Hades accelerated before I could buckle my seatbelt.

"Tell me everything," Hades roared. His anger aligned with mine.

"Hephaestus told me I was just a pawn," I said to Hades, trying to keep my voice steady. "He never cared about me—just used me to keep Ares busy while he set his plans in motion. He's always wanted to take over the Olympus Syndicate, blamed his father for screwing things up. He was sick of being ignored and jumped at his chance." I took a shaky breath, "I can't shake the feeling that he's struck a deal with Ouranos—everything seems too planned, too precise."

My mind wouldn't stop racing, trying to piece together fragments of conversations and actions that hadn't made sense before but now seemed part of a larger, twisted plot.

Could Hephaestus really be involved in Titan's death? It seems almost impossible, but what other explanation is there for his actions? What could he possibly gain from all this?

I continued, "Ouranos has Ares." Tears streamed down my face, and my voice cracked with desperation. "I don't know what's happening to him. We have to find them—now." I clenched my fists tightly, my determination cutting through the storm of emotions that threatened to overwhelm me.

Hades turned to face me, his eyes burning with fierce resolve. His nostrils flared as he gripped the steering wheel so hard his knuckles turned white. "Hephaestus and Ouranos are dead men," he growled, his voice low and seething with anger. "I won't rest until they're brought to justice. If it means dragging them to hell myself, so be it." His gaze was unyielding, filled with a cold, fiery resolve. "We're going to the manor. We'll find out what's happening, and we'll put an end to this madness."

THE MANOR GATES STOOD WIDE OPEN, AN UNSETTLING SIGHT. OURANOS WAS notoriously strict about security, never letting anyone in without a thorough search. A sense of unease settled over me as I glanced at Hades, who was slowly approaching the front entrance. We sat in silence as he cut the engine, the quiet amplifying my growing anxiety. The door to the manor was ajar, and a cold wave of fear washed over me. Turning to Hades, I found him watching me with a serious expression. "Do you know how to use a gun?" he asked.

I paused for a second, remembering when Titan had taken me to the shooting range to teach me. I nodded at Hades. "Titan had insisted I needed to learn for my safety," I said.

Hades reached into the glove compartment and pulled out a small handgun, its black metal gleaming ominously in the dim light. He handed it to me, the weight of the weapon heavy in my trembling hands. As I wrapped my fingers around the cool, solid grip, a steely resolve settled over me. The heft of the gun felt like a promise of protection, a tangible source of strength. With the weapon now in my grasp, I felt ready to confront whatever dangers lay ahead.

Stepping out of the vehicle, we cautiously approached the front of the manor, Hades leading the way with a measured, deliberate pace. My heartbeat quickened with each step, the tension mounting as we drew closer.

Hades moved towards the door with the precision of a soldier preparing for action. I forced myself to keep fear at bay, focusing instead on the task at hand. I tapped his shoulder to signal him to proceed. With a steady hand, he pushed the door open, and it creaked wide, revealing the dimly lit entryway. We stepped inside, emerging into the subdued glow of the manor's interior, ready for whatever awaited us.

Bloody handprints lined the floor, and made it look like someone had been dragged through the manor. I swallowed hard, feeling the sudden sickness of knowing someone was probably dead. A chill ran down my spine. Hades followed the bloody markings on the floor toward the ballroom. I removed the safety from my gun, preparing myself for battle.

Hades strode through the darkness. Light from the windows highlighted dark puddles of blood on the floor. The trail led to the open doorway of the ballroom. Hades signaled for me to stop. My heart pounded in my chest.

Hades slammed the door open, gun at the ready, and stepped inside. The gray light from the open drapes cut through the darkness, revealing Gaia sprawled out in the middle of the ballroom floor. Her lifeless body and wide, terrified eyes painted a gruesome picture. I staggered back, my breath hitching as I took in the horrifying scene. Hades moved swiftly towards her, his anger barely contained.

"I finally did the job right. Pay me," Hades read the words as he turned to face me.

Tears welled up in my eyes as I took in Gaia's lifeless body, her eyes staring blankly at the ceiling. Despite her cruelty and manipulative ways, seeing her like this was a brutal shock. It felt wrong—inhuman.

My chest tightened with grief, the kind that makes your breath catch and your heart ache. But as the horror of the scene sunk in, that grief rapidly twisted into something fiercer.

"This was Hephaestus' doing." Hades rubbed his face. "Fuck!" He roared, his voice booming throughout the room as I stared at Gaia's dead body.

Suddenly, something clicked.

If Hephaestus was hired to kill Titan, it stands to reason he was also behind Gaia's murder and the attempts on my life. The connection was undeniable—each act of violence seemed part of a coordinated effort, a twisted strategy that tied back to him. But why? What could he possibly gain from this trail of bloodshed?

Hades's phone rang, slicing through the tense silence. He glanced at the screen, his eyebrows furrowing in confusion and concern. "Hello?" he answered, his voice tight with a sense of impending dread. As he listened, his expression shifted from confusion to sheer terror, his eyes widening in horror.

# CHAPTER THIRTY

## ARES

The water's current revealed its true power. Each strike of the tumultuous waves against me felt sharp and forceful as I fought against it. Desperate for air, I took a long gasping breath, trying to fill my lungs before I was dragged back under by the water. It seized me with a vise-like grip, rendering me powerless, I was as limp as a ragdoll. The unseen boulders beneath the murky depths hammered against my body, targeting me without mercy. My muscles burned with exertion. The water crashed around me, its force threatening to consume me. Every breath was a battle. Lightning streaked across the sky, illuminating the treacherous waves.

I pushed against the violent tide, the deafening roar of thunder fueling my determination. I felt the weight of the abyss, pulling me deeper, but I refused to surrender. Aphrodite's name echoed in my mind, her divine presence giving me strength as I kicked and thrashed, desperate to break free from the current's clutch.

The water was a relentless adversary intent on dragging me down. My lungs screamed for air. I could taste the murky water as it burned its way down my throat. My vision blurred, but I refused to let go.

With one last burst of energy, I propelled myself up toward the surface. The water fought against me, but I swam with all my might. The world blurred, a whirlwind of chaos around me.

And then, like a phoenix rising from the ashes, I emerged from the bitter depths. Gasping for air, I clung to the edge of survival with every ounce of my strength. The unruly sea roared around me, but I was determined to overcome it. I would rise from this struggle, transformed into a warrior reborn, ready to face whatever came next.

I noticed a branch looming up ahead. Harnessing the flow of the current to my advantage, I navigated toward the shoreline.

*Save her*, the voice in my head repeated. This was not how I would die.

I reached out, desperately grasping for the sturdy branch, my only lifeline. The roar of the water slamming into me was deafening, a relentless assault that pounded in my ears.

Determination surged through me, fueling my drive to push harder. My muscles protested with every movement, straining against the crushing force of the waves, each second a battle against the overwhelming pressure.

Pushing. Pulling. Pushing.

Once I reached the edge of the shore, I climbed up the rocks onto a deserted beach and collapsed, exhausted. My cuts stung from the saltwater, and my jeans clung to my skin. If I didn't seek help soon, I would likely get hypothermia.

My lungs burned as I stared up at the sky. The saltwater had dried out my lips, and I felt like every ounce of energy had been drained from me. But deep down, I knew I couldn't give up—I had to keep pushing forward.

Sitting up, I looked around, wiping the blood from my forehead. My chest ached, and I struggled to breathe. I pulled myself up from the ground, my drenched skin covered in dirt, coughing and shivering from the cold. My body throbbed with pain, a sharp, relentless ache radiating from my left leg where it had slammed into a rock beneath the water.

Staggering to my feet, I took in my surroundings. The dense forest around me was eerily silent, the usual sounds of wildlife drowned out by the crashing waves of the violent waters.

I had no idea how far I had been swept from the bridge, but I knew I needed to figure out a way to get to a phone and call Hades. Every step I took was agony as I limped through the underbrush, my injured leg protesting with every movement. I pressed on, driven by the primal instinct to survive. The forest floor was a treacherous mix of mud and slick leaves, making my progress slow and painful. My vision blurred from the blood running into my eyes, and I wiped it away with a trembling hand.

Bursting through the undergrowth, I found myself at the edge of a road. There weren't any vehicles around. I fought through the pain as I started to run down the road, picking up speed. After a couple of miles, I noticed a sign on the side of a road up ahead.

As I approached, a building came into view, fluorescent lights blaring through the night fog. It was a diner. With resolute strides, I walked into the restaurant, bloodied and bruised, my clothes soaked from the brutal fight I'd just survived. The stench of death and the sea clung to my tattered clothing.

Everyone in the diner froze as they watched me. I sat on a stool and collapsed my head in the palm of my hands as I took a deep breath, feeling the aches take over my body and my soul.

"Oh my..." The lady's voice was soothing, but I looked up to see her eyes in fear, "Someone call 911!" she shouted, but I shook my head.

"No." I could barely speak. "No! I need food, extra clothes, and a phone." My voice was edged with desperation. After a moment of stunned silence, she nodded quickly, her face pale, and darted toward the kitchen.

"Hey, mister!" a gruff voice called out from the back of the diner. I turned and headed toward him. The man's skin was weathered, his hair wild and white beneath a worn baseball cap. "I've got some clothes in my truck," he said, his voice rough but steady, as he handed me a phone. I stared at it for a moment, feeling the weight of everything hitting me at once, then quickly dialed Hades's number, my fingers trembling as I pressed the buttons.

He answered after one ring. "Hello?"

"Hephaestus has Aphrodite. Ouranos is going to kill her and everyone we ever cared about," I whispered frantically, the words spilling out in a desperate rush.

My voice trembled as I spoke, and the rhythm of my heart echoed in my ears. Tears streamed down my face, carrying the weight of my anguish, each droplet an expression of the love and despair that consumed me. With every tear that fell, a surge of vulnerability coursed through my veins, breaking down the barriers that had kept me safe. The invisible armor I wore to shield myself from the world had shattered, leaving me exposed and defenseless.

The world came to a halt in that sliver of time. Aphrodite was a beacon of hope. She ignited a flame within me, allowing me to experience the depths of love in all its forms. I dared to believe that I was worthy of being loved by her. The thought of losing her, of losing the possibility of her pure love, was unbearable. My existence hinged on her presence in my life.

"Ares," He cut me off, pausing for a moment that felt like a lifetime. Hades continued, "She's with me. She's safe."

I buried my head in my hands, relief washing over me. My voice broke, "Can I talk to her?" I said, wiping away my tears. I squeezed my eyes shut.

She was alive. I loved her. I loved every part of her being. She was my reason to fight, and I was ready to go into battle knowing she was alive.

"Ares!" Her voice was panicked as she spoke into the receiver.

"Yeah, baby, it's me." I let out a small laugh, "Nothing can kill me."

"Where are you? We will come to you." She sounded relieved, but there was a frantic edge to her voice, echoing the urgency I felt to get back to her.

"I'm at the diner near the bridge. Hades knows. I love you," I said, my voice shaky but urgent, hoping the words would reach through the chaos of everything going on around us. I needed them to land, to ground us both in something real.

There was a brief pause, then, "I love you too." Her voice was soft but strained, carrying the weight of everything we had endured.

I stood out in front of the diner, freshly cleaned after washing up, wearing the clothes the old man had provided. The scent of soap still clung to my skin, and the new clothes, though comfortable, made me look like a fisherman. I waited for them to arrive, feeling the weight of anticipation as I readied myself for whatever was coming next.

Headlights flashed, and Hades skillfully steered the sleek vehicle into an empty parking space in front of the diner. Aphrodite flung the door open and hurried toward me.

Standing there in the worn-out attire of an old man, I eagerly embraced the love of my life, wrapping her in a secure hold. I lifted her delicate form in my arms, relishing the sensation of her against my chest.

Our lips collided with intense passion, unleashing a torrent of desire. As I caressed her face, a symphony of tears mingled with our pleasurable moans. We clung to each other, unwilling to let go, cherishing every precious moment. We leaned our heads together, sharing a moment of solace and unity.

I looked at her face and saw bruises and cuts marring her skin.

"What did he do to you?" I reached out to touch her face, but she pulled away. I tenderly reached out again, fingers grazing lightly along her jaw. She crumpled in my arms. Anger surged within me as the harsh reality sank in—I hadn't kept her safe when it mattered most.

"I'm sorry," I murmured, the words escaping in a ragged sigh as I leaned into her shoulder, the weight of my failure pressing heavily on me.

"No!" she shot back, her voice firm and resolute. "It wasn't your fault, Ares. We have to stop them. Look at me." Her gaze was fierce and unwavering. "I need you to be strong. Be the Ares you were trained to be."

I took her hand and pressed a gentle kiss to her palm, my voice low and heavy with concern. "If I go down that path, there's no turning back. I'll become the demon they say I am, and it won't be easy to claw my way out." I looked up at her, my eyes reflecting a deep, unspoken fear. "I'll need you, Aphrodite. There are times when my rage takes over, dragging me into a darkness I can't escape on my own. Without you, I don't know if I can break free."

"I will be here." Aphrodite whispered, pressing her hand to my heart.

Hades cleared his throat with a deliberate cough, cutting through the moment. "Sorry to break up the reunion," he called out from the car, his voice tinged with urgency. "But we're on the brink of total chaos, and we need to get ourselves ready."

I pressed my forehead gently against hers, savoring the fleeting connection, and took a deep breath, trying to steady the pounding of my heart. With that, we began to move toward the Mustang. Aphrodite sat in the backseat, and I climbed into the passenger side. Hades revved the engine as he peeled out of the parking lot.

"So, you going to tell me what's happening?" Hades looked at me with determination.

"Ouranos' plan is to kill every single OS member." I started, a grim expression on my face. "He manipulated Hephaestus into killing Titan to solidify their alliance." I paused, watching Aphrodite's eyes widen with shock. "But Hephaestus was deceived. He thought he would be spared if he cooperated. Ouranos plans to eliminate him too, ensuring the destruction of our family." My voice came out harsh, a growl of barely contained anger.

I tightened my grip into fists, feeling the knuckles press into my palms. The thought of confronting my brother and Ouranos was like a fire burning within me, fueling my readiness to inflict pain and exact vengeance.

"Wait," Aphrodite said, her voice barely a whisper. I turned my head to face her. A tear streaked down her dirty cheek. She blinked and looked up at me. "Hephaestus killed Titan?"

A vivid memory of Aphrodite at Titan's funeral suddenly flashed through my mind. She had loved her brother. I reached for her hand, grasping it tightly. She blinked a couple of times, letting the tears fall.

"Ouranos wanted him dead because he wasn't his son," I replied, my voice strained and tired. "He didn't want Gaia or Titan to see a single cent of his legacy. That's why he had Titan killed."

"And Gaia too." Aphrodite added.

My eyes narrowed, taken back by her comment, "What do you mean?"

"Gaia's dead. Hephaestus finished the job." she said, releasing a deep breath, her lips trembling. "I will kill them. I will kill them both." Her voice was a fierce whisper.

Her eyes darkened, a fierce determination etched into her features. It was clear nothing mattered more to her than avenging her brother's death. Anger blazed in her eyes. "Was he trying to kill them the night of the Halloween party?"

I nodded slowly, the gravity of the truth settling heavily on my shoulders. Aphrodite's eyes filled with tears as I reached for her hand, my voice a low murmur almost lost in the suffocating silence. "You deserve to know the truth."

From the corner of my eye, I noticed Hades' grip on the steering wheel tightening, his knuckles white against the dark leather. His jaw twitched, a telltale sign of the storm brewing inside him.

This was the war we had been bracing ourselves for, the culmination of years of tension and unease. Hades had always been wary of the dark forces gathering strength, convinced that they would ultimately seek to bring about our downfall and unleash chaos upon us all. Now, as the tension in the air thickened, the grim reality of his fears was closing in on us.

# CHAPTER THIRTY-ONE

## ARES

The sky darkened, a sudden thunderstorm looming overhead, making the air feel gritty.

Even the gods had foretold this day.

The fated moment when two titans would collide, causing bloodshed and despair. While Ouranos ruled as the tyrannical king, shadows crept over Aeolopolis City, and we lingered in their dark embrace. His reign wouldn't last.

I had every intention of sending him to the pits of hell, where my brother would join him in eternal torment.

Heavy rainfall pattered on the roof of the Mustang, as Hades steered towards the gates of the Olympus compound. We were parked a good distance from the lot, but close enough to see everything unfold. We could see some of Ouranos's henchmen lining the area around the buildings. They were destroying everything in their paths, their faces hard and merciless.

Screams began echoing through the air, chilling me to the bone.

Condensation rolled down the windows in the car, and I watched Aphrodite as she wiped some away to get a better look. My knuckles turned white with tension, the urge to squeeze the life out of these wretched bastards burning through me.

"What are we going to do? It's just the two of us," Hades confessed.

"Three," Aphrodite corrected.

The sound of shattering glass pierced the air, grabbing our attention. Molotov cocktails had been thrown through windows, and we watched as a furious blaze ignited from the Odyssey.

People fled from the building as thick, choking smoke filled the air.

Ouranos loomed above Olympus, his towering presence casting a dark, imposing shadow over the compound as he watched the impending carnage below with cold indifference. The sky above seemed to darken in his wake, a reflection of the power he wielded.

From his vantage point at the foot of the grand doors to the main building, he stood motionless, a figure of menace. His gaze swept over the chaos beneath him, the destruction playing out like a twisted symphony of violence, but there was no flicker of emotion in his eyes.

Only the deep, quiet certainty that more ruin was inevitable.

"Drive!" I commanded, my voice ringing out in the confined space. Hades floored it towards the back of the buildings. We reached the dark alleyway, finding it completely deserted.

I hurried out of the vehicle and rushed to the locked metal gates at the back of the compound, quickly entering the four-digit code. Nothing happened. As the rain began to pour, I turned and ran back to the car.

"Looks like they cut the power." I said, slipping inside the vehicle and slamming the door shut behind me.

Hades let loose a sigh. "My poor Mustang." He rubbed the dashboard, then revved his engine.

"What are you doing?" Aphrodite exclaimed, panic rising in her voice.

Suddenly, Hades slammed his foot on the gas, plastering me to the back of my seat.

"You're paying for the damages!" he yelled in my direction. The car roared forward, and before I could fully grasp what was happening, we were airborne, hurtling toward the gates at full speed. "Hold on!" he screamed as the vehicle soared.

I gripped the seat tight, bracing myself as the Mustang slammed into the metal gates with a bone-jarring impact. Sparks flew like fireflies, dancing in the air as the metal groaned and twisted under the force. The gates were ripped from their hinges, flung into the distance like discarded toys. The car screeched to a sudden stop, jerking me forward, but before I could slam into the dashboard, Hades's hand shot out, pressing firmly against my chest, pulling me back into my seat just in time.

Aphrodite, thrown sideways in the backseat, was already pushing herself up, a mix of determination and fear in her eyes. Hades wore his familiar devilish grin as he turned off the vehicle. "Let the show begin," he said with a cold edge to his voice

We all climbed out of the car, the smell of burnt rubber hanging in the air. Hades popped open the trunk and pulled out a stash of guns, handing them out like candy at a party. He grabbed his dagger, slipping it into the clip on his boot with practiced ease.

Aphrodite approached me, flashing the gun she had tucked into the back of her pants. My chest tightened, feeling the weight of her pain as if it were my own. I wished, more than anything, that this wasn't her world, that I could shield her from the darkness closing in around us. But here we were, caught in the chaos. All I could do now was stand by her, protect her in the only way I knew how—by never letting go.

"Do you know how to use it?" I asked, my voice low, though the question felt heavy with the weight of the moment.

"Titan taught me how," she replied, her gaze steady and resolute. "This is for him."

"This is for Olympus," Hades added, his voice cold and unwavering. He handed me my gun, the familiar weight of it grounding me in the chaos.

We moved forward, a silent understanding passing between us. The air grew colder as we approached the OS clubhouse. Each step felt like a descent into something darker, like we were walking toward the very gates of the underworld itself.

The shadows stretched long, and with every heartbeat, I could feel the gravity of what was coming. There would be no turning back now.

I glanced at Aphrodite, her face set in grim determination.

For Titan. For Olympus. For us.

THE DISTANT SOUND OF FOOTSTEPS ECHOED THROUGH THE DARKENED BACK of the main building; Henchmen that moved cautiously, their eyes scanning the shadows for any hint of intrusion.

Hades slithered beneath us through the shadows, his movements like a wisp of smoke. Silence was his weapon, his presence melding seamlessly with the backdrop of abandoned machinery and rusted pipes. I watched from above, my heart pounding. We needed to move.

Aphrodite and I slowly crossed the catwalk, trying to stay as silent as possible. I watched as Hades executed stealth takedowns on two men while we made our way to the opposite side.

We descended the stairs, my boots landing gently on the cold metal grating. I focused on maintaining control, inhaling deeply and exhaling slowly.

I tightened my grip on the gun, the weight was reassuring in my hands. I had trained for this, honing my skills to perfection over countless hours. I reached the bottom of the stairs, blending in with the darkness, my body one with the night. The tension in the air was suffocating.

My senses grew heightened, every nerve on edge. There were more henchmen within reach, their figures illuminated by a dim, flickering light. Without hesitation, I struck. The first henchman fell, as my bullet found its mark. The others turned in confusion, their eyes wide with disbelief.

Chaos erupted, bullets flew, and echoes of gunfire reverberated through the factory.

Hades emerged from the shadows, his knives glinting in the dim light.

He was a force to be reckoned with, his movements a dance of death. Together, we fought as one, a symphony of violence. The air was filled with the metallic scent of blood, mingling with the stale odor of the abandoned factory. The henchmen fell one by one, crumbling beneath our onslaught of vicious attacks. They didn't stand a chance.

We stood among the fallen, our breaths ragged and bodies smeared with sweat and blood, when our eyes fell upon a shadowy figure inching toward us through the darkness. As the figure emerged, it was Athena, her eyes gleaming with cold triumph.

We shared a look, both of us knowing that our fates were waiting around the next corner, and with them, the secrets we were about to uncover.

As we pushed through the chaos, the factory echoed with the ghosts of its past. The place seemed to hum of old battles, the walls scarred from every fight that had raged here. The air was heavy with the remnants of past violence, and each step we took stirred up the ghosts of conflicts long gone, making the factory feel like a silent witness to all that had happened within its battered walls.

Aphrodite's finger cut through the dim light, pointing toward the front of the building. There, Artie was bound tightly against a pole, her figure barely visible in the shadows. The sight of her, restrained and vulnerable, fueled a surge of urgency. Hades, his expression set with grim determination, was already gearing up to take out the lone henchman standing guard.

Just as he was about to make his move, I grabbed his shoulder, halting him in his tracks. My grip was firm, pulling him back with a mix of force and urgency. "Look!" I exclaimed, pointing to the far side of the room where a couple more men had just entered.

Artie's cries of pain reached our ears.

"I'll take care of them," Hades said, his voice filled with determination.

"Wait," I whispered as we kneeled hiding in the shadows. I looked over at Aphrodite who shook with fear, "You need to get out of here."

"I'm not leaving," she said with steely determination. "I need to be the one to end my father's life, and I need to watch Hephaestus fall with my own eyes." she argued fiercely, but I cut her off, pressing my hand against her mouth with a firm grip.

"Do this for me—please," I pleaded, desperation edging my voice.

Her eyes flashed with defiance as she struggled against my hand. "No, Ares," she said, her voice muffled but resolute. "I will go with you into the pits of hell if I have to. I'm with you. Now, let's go!" Aphrodite's voice quivered with a mix of fury and fear, her hands pushing against mine as if to assert her determination.

"Enough of this fucking sappy shit," Athena announced as she stood up cocked her gun. "Let's kill these assholes."

As the tension in the air reached its peak, I took one more look at Aphrodite before glancing at Hades and Athena who awaited my signal.

Beads of sweat dripped down my brow as I took a deep breath, bracing myself to unleash the chaos of war. The targets were in my sights, and I knew this was the start of something massive.

The tension in the air was thick, and every breath felt heavy with the weight of the coming conflict. This wasn't just a battle; it was the beginning of an all-consuming storm, one that would reshape everything in its path.

I cocked my gun and pointed it at the guard next to Artie.

Taking a deep breath, I started to countdown.

"Three."

"Two."

"One."

Our reign of bullets echoed throughout the factory as the guard fell. Hades and Aphrodite hurried to Artie's side. Two more men approached them, but Athena swiftly shot them in their heads, not missing her target. Meanwhile, Aphrodite untied Artie and helped her stand while Hades kept watch.

"Go!" I screamed as they rushed back toward the path we came from.

Hades waved at me to signal the coast was clear. I continued to cross over the main area of the clubhouse, trying not to get shot. There were other members of our club being beaten by Ouranos and his men in the distance.

Despite being outnumbered, I was determined to fight. I hurried forward, exposing myself as the henchmen were closing in from above. As one of them was coming down the stairs, the air erupted with gunfire.

"Ares is here!" The man shouted. I shot him in the chest before another word could leave his mouth. The impact pushed him back, and he fell off the stairs and landed with a loud thud against the hard cement floor.

Hades yelled, "Good shot!" while I rushed downstairs. "Let's get them on the inside," Hades instructed, but just as I was going to speak, Aphrodite ran back inside.

"What the fuck are you doing?" I snapped at her. "Go with Artie!"

"No, Ares! This is my battle too!" Aphrodite pressed her finger to my heart, "Your brother hurt me in ways you can't comprehend, and I will be part of killing him and my father. I want to take the final shot."

My nostrils flared at her request, and I rubbed my eyes, my frustration evident.

"Ares, there's no time for logistics. We need all the hands we have. Now let's fucking go." Hades said. He didn't wait for a response as he disappeared into the darkness.

"Stay next to me, you hear?" I demanded.

She nodded, and we headed down the dark hallway.

The exit sign illuminated us in the blackness. I signaled for Aphrodite to stop when I heard voices coming from the kitchen door. They were muffled, but I could make out Ouranos speaking. Taking a quick glance inside, I saw two men guarding a door—the door that led to the Odyssey. I leaned my head against the wall and turned to face Aphrodite.

"Hold my gun." She took it, and I reached for the knife in my pocket. "Wait here."

I slipped around the corner and pressed my back against the wall, moving closer to my target. A man opened the door, lighting up the hallway, giving me the perfect opportunity to strike. I covered his mouth with my hand and slid my knife across his throat. His body went limp, and I gently lowered him to the ground.

Aphrodite peeked around the corner, and I signaled for her to come over. But then a sharp, unsettling scent hit me, stopping me in my tracks.

Gas.

That was when I heard the cries. "Fire!"

"What are we going to do? We need to get to Ouranos!" Aphrodite yelled.

I wiped my hands on the dead man's jacket. Quickly, Aphrodite slipped past me into the doorway and crawled behind the bar. I tried to catch up to her, to stop her. But it was too late. A henchman grabbed her, and she screeched. I didn't hesitate—I lunged forward ready to take him down before he could hurt her.

"Take your hands off my woman!" My booming voice was threatening. I didn't allow the man the chance to react, as I charged toward him. He wouldn't attack my girl. No fucking way. I squeezed his neck with both hands. My fingers felt his pulse as I tightened my grip. Out of nowhere, something slammed into my head. I fell backward, and the man jumped on top of me. He punched me in my face, and Aphrodite screamed.

A bullet saved me.

The gunshot echoed in the darkness as I watched the man's soul depart his body, and he fell forward onto me. His blood and mine mingled together as I pushed him off.

"Ares! Are you okay?" Aphrodite cried out as she took my face in her hands. I nodded once, before shifting my gaze to look in the distance.

Hades one the one who had pulled the trigger.

Just as I pulled her into a tight embrace, I saw Apollo bound and lying next to the very person I was itching to strangle—Hephaestus.

"Well, well, well. If it isn't our hero." Ouranos slunk out from behind the shadows. He looked at Aphrodite, then me. "Hephaestus, you didn't do your job. She's still alive." Ouranos glanced back at my brother.

"I am going to kill you, Ouranos." Aphrodite uttered her words with intensity. Her eyes widened and her nostrils flared as she stiffened. "Why did you do this?"

He walked toward us, his voice booming through the clubhouse as he explained, "My wife deceived me!" he roared, his presence like a dark storm. "She thought she could hide the fact that Titan was not my son. I always had my suspicions, and I don't ignore suspicions. You see, there were whispers—little signs that didn't add up. So, I took matters into my own hands and conducted a DNA test in secret. The results confirmed it. Gaia knew all along that I was not the father, and she hid it from me. She wanted all my money and power to be given to Titan. But nobody steals from me, her deception had to be punished." he hissed, his eyes burning with a cold, unyielding rage.

He continued, "I had sensed something was amiss with the Olympus Syndicate after Hephaestus paid me a visit. I had invited him over to gain intel about Titan's business dealings, but it didn't take long for our conversation to turn to darker matters. We discovered that we could help each other. I wanted my family dead, and he wanted his dead in return."

Ouranos pulled a matchbox from his pocket, flames already flickering in his eyes.

"Hephaestus didn't hesitate to jump at the job, and I agreed to offer my help."

He lit the match.

"And now I'll burn this place to the ground."

Without a pause, he threw the match against the wooden bar. A flame ignited along the sides, following a trail of liquid.

"You're fucking dead!" I snapped as I grabbed at him, but one of his henchmen held me back. I watched as flames overtook the clubhouse walls. The fire surged with no restraint.

Ouranos' wicked grin distorted his already terrifying appearance as he turned and headed for the exit, flanked by two of his men.

Just as I was about to tear the man restraining me limb from limb, I saw Hades storming down the stairs, unleashing a storm of bullets that ripped through the room.

The crack of his pistol echoed through the room as he gunned down the man holding me. I reached for my gun. The flames released thick black smoke into the air. I turned and rushed after Ouranos, but a wall of men blocked me, stopping me dead in my tracks. I tried to break through their defense line, but they held strong as Ouranos was getting away.

Hades moved with the precision of a vengeful god, picking off henchmen one by one. His gun roared with the fury of the underworld, each shot a relentless judgment. The henchmen, stunned and scrambling, fell before his wrath. As he advanced with the calm of one who commands shadows, his gaze was as unyielding as the gates of Hell.

"I need to get Ouranos!" I snapped, turning to face my family. The air was heavy around us. The flickering amber light of the fire illuminated the space.

Rushing back toward our group, bullets whizzed through the air as Hades and Ouranos' men exchanged fire. Apollo, injured and limping, made his way over with Athena by his side, supporting him as they struggled toward us.

Aphrodite's screams echoed behind me, pleading for me to wait, but I didn't listen. My bloodlust was insatiable—I needed to kill. Ouranos was nearly at the door when Hades charged forward like the reaper himself, his presence a dark omen. His firearm spat death, mowing down the advancing men with cold precision.

I noticed Hephaestus slumped against a wall, his face pale and contorted with pain—he must have been shot.

"Where is Artie?" Apollo yelled over the chaos, his voice raw with desperation. He was covered in bruises and blood, barely able to stand, but Aphrodite and Athena supported him, each taking an arm to lift him up.

"She's outside! Go! Now!" I ordered, my voice leaving no room for argument.

Athena made a move toward Hephaestus, but I grabbed her, pulling her back. "No!" I growled, my teeth clenched as I held her firmly. She narrowed her eyes at me, fury flashing in her gaze, but I tightened my grip on her forearm.

"Let go of me, Ares!" she demanded, her voice trembling with frustration and anger.

I looked into her eyes, pleading. "He did this. He wanted to kill our father. He has to face the consequences."

"Not like this." She pulled away from me and rushed to Hephaestus' side.

Hades was charging toward us when a Molotov cocktail shattered through the window, erupting in a wall of flames. The fire quickly consumed the room, black smoke swirling thick and suffocating. I gasped for air, the smoke clawing at my lungs, as our world turned to a raging inferno before my eyes.

"We need to get out of here!" Hades yelled, yanking me toward the exit. I glanced over and saw Aphrodite choking on the thick smoke.

"I'm not leaving until I know he's dead," I insisted.

Hades glanced at me, then back at Apollo, who was struggling to stay on his feet. Without hesitation, Hades moved to support Apollo, guiding him toward the exit. Apollo needed medical attention, and Hades knew they had to get him out of the burning building before it was too late.

Before I could stop her, Aphrodite bolted through the fire, deeper into the building toward Ouranos. The scent of sweat and gunpowder filled the air. My legs burned from exhaustion with every step, but I forced myself forward, chasing after my love as she ran straight into the flames of hell. Finally catching up to her, I reached the clubhouse porch and saw her standing there, weapon steady in her hands, aimed straight at her father.

He was alone.

His men were trapped in the burning building, their screams echoing through the night, but Ouranos stood by. He was convinced he could still manipulate Aphrodite into submission. But her eyes were filled with defiance.

The sight of her standing strong against the odds, unbowed and resolute, made it clear that that my love for her burned as fiercely as my wrath.

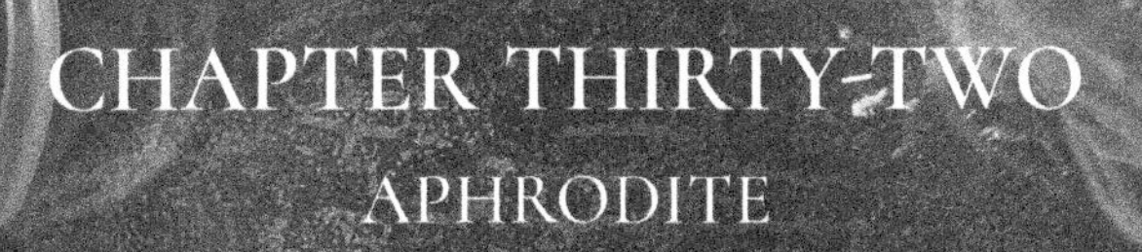

# CHAPTER THIRTY-TWO
## APHRODITE

Long shadows flickered and danced ominously on the porch as sweat trickled down my forehead. My father stood before me, his eyes wide with terror, pleading for his life, but his words fell on deaf ears. Hatred burned within me, a fire fueled by years of pain and betrayal.

Every fiber of my being screamed for retribution, for justice to be served. My finger tightened on the trigger, the weight of anger and vengeance pressing down on me hard. The lines between right and wrong had blurred, lost in the fury that consumed me.

The glass windowpanes behind me shattered from the heat of the flames, but it didn't break my focus. The power I had summoned from deep within held firm, a dark thrill coursing through me as I faced the man who had caused so much suffering. He was supposed to be my father, but he was nothing more than an enemy.

His gaze hardened into a venomous sneer as he taunted, "You won't do it, Aphrodite. You're weak, just like your mother." But his words only fueled my resolve.

The crackling flames and the screams echoing around us seemed to mock me, much like the man standing before me.

Ares shouted at my side, "Let me do it, Aphrodite—You can come back from this!"

But my eyes stayed glued to my father.

Ouranos raised his hands with a derisive grin, positioning them on either side of his chest. I recalled the countless horrors he had inflicted on both me and my brother over the years.

His tyranny had tainted the whole city, leaving it in ruins. He always found new ways to bring destruction, slithering through like a serpent seeking its prey.

As I stared at him, I felt the last shreds of any lingering kindness or mercy drain away. I was done being a victim. It was time to face him, to put an end to his reign of terror, and to reclaim the strength that he had tried so hard to crush

I was no longer a pawn on his chessboard.

I was a queen.

Checkmate.

"Ready to face your end, old man?" I snarled, my voice cold and dripping with malice. My finger steadied on the trigger, aimed straight at his heart.

Ouranos stepped closer, his gaze piercing. "Look at you," He paused with his hands still raised on either side of his chest in mock surrender. "You truly *are* my daughter. That darkness lurking within you—that's me. You may have tried to keep it hidden all these years, but I see it hiding just beneath the surface, waiting for its moment to emerge." A smirk of arrogance twisted his lips as he spoke.

"Don't listen to him, Aphrodite," Ares pleaded. But my gaze remained fixated on my father, refusing to let him slip away again.

The air was heavy with my own regret and anguish.

Ouranos's presence was like a noose tightening around my neck. Every word he uttered left a permanent mark on my soul, tattoos of torment etched into my very being. Deep within, I knew that if he drew breath, I could never be free.

I squeezed the trigger.

The evil grin on my father's face disintegrated as the bullet sliced through the air.

My heart pounded as the bullet hit its target.

I tried to hold onto the gun, but it slipped from my hands. Ares rushed toward me, but amidst the surrounding chaos, my gaze remained locked on my father. His bullet wound bled profusely as he sank to his knees, and I watched as his soul seemed to drift away like smoke rising from the flames. Time itself seemed to stand still as his eyes glazed over, and he keeled over, his face looking up toward the heavens.

Ouranos was dead. I had shot him straight through his heart.

I killed my father.

Loud, piercing screams attacked me from within as my body trembled.

Ares tried to hold onto my face; He spoke, but all I heard was sirens in the distance. Pushing out of Ares's hold, I went to kneel next to my father, my hands shaking. I spoke with authority, "I will never be your victim again. May you rot in hell."

As I stood and turned to face Ares, flames engulfed the clubhouse behind me. My eyes burned. Tears welled in my vision. I knew we had to move quickly, but in that moment, I finally felt like a part of my soul had a semblance of release. I reached for Ares, seeking solace in his presence as the inferno raged on around us.

"I'm sorry, Aphrodite" Ares whispered as he pulled me into a comforting embrace, planting a kiss on my forehead. He'd risked it all, embracing the darkness, to be the ruthless protector I knew he could be.

"You did everything you could, Ares," I said against his chest, his warmth soothing the sorrows that clung to me.

Over Ares' shoulder, a figure emerged from the darkness. Tall and imposing, with a presence that sent shivers down my spine. His icy blue eyes pierced the darkness with an eerie luminescence. Shadows clung to his form, merging with the night. As he walked into the light, his face revealed itself, and a wave of dread washed over me.

*Hephaestus.*

He charged toward us, his limp prominent, covered in blood and debris. Each step he took seemed to echo with the weight of his malevolent plans. He had orchestrated the very nightmare we were living in. His eyes locked on Ares, a chilling focus that spoke of unresolved vendettas and a darkness that refused to die.

"This is my fight," Ares growled, his voice harsh and unyielding. He spun on Hephaestus, fire in his eyes. "You did this!" he roared at his brother.

Hephaestus sneered back; his face twisted with rage.

"This club has always been a joke!" He roared, his voice echoing with raw, bitter anger. His eyes blazed with a fire that matched the inferno consuming the clubhouse behind him. "You all know damn well I was the one who deserved to be president. Zeus screwed up, didn't see the real threat coming. While he was busy chasing after his own glory, Ouranos was plotting our downfall." Hephaestus's gaze swept over the chaos, his face twisted with rage and vindication.

"I had to step up because no one else had the balls to see the danger for what it was. Ouranos was gunning for us from the shadows, and I took charge to protect what was left. He made me do this," he said, gesturing towards the burning wreckage of the clubhouse.

His voice dropped to a menacing growl, each word dripping with dark satisfaction. "After our wedding, I planned to finish what I started. I was going to kill Aphrodite, make her pay for every single thing Ouranos took from us. I was going to make sure that her death was a fitting tribute to the chaos and ruin that Ouranos has wrought upon our lives."

I was stunned by his words, unable to grasp the depth of his depravity. My eyes shifted to Ares, whose face was a mask of shock and revulsion as the horrifying truth was laid bare.

Hephaestus continued, his rage almost palpable, "He has forced us into the darkest corner of the city, a place so grim it's as if we were buried alive. He wanted to keep us hidden, silenced, and forgotten, terrified of the power we could unleash. Keeping us in the shadows was his way of maintaining control, of ensuring we'd never rise against him. And I'm fucking done with it! He shattered everything we built—left us to rot and suffer in the muck! It was time to settle the score, to drag him into the light and make him pay for every ounce of suffering he's inflicted!" Anger seethed from Hephaestus as he revealed his plans.

"No, Hephaestus—You are addicted to power. Being second best was never good enough for you. You are no different than Ouranos." Ares snapped back, his anger piercing through the crackle of flames and the roar of exploding motorcycles. We were going to be swallowed up if we didn't get out soon.

"We have to go, Ares!" I cried out as I reached for his hand, but he pulled away, facing his brother.

"I will not let you destroy what is left of us!" Ares's voice cut through the chaos, firm and unwavering. His eyes blazed with fierce determination as he confronted Hephaestus, the weight of his words hanging heavily in the air. "I've always been the warrior of this family—the one who stands against the darkness that threatens us. This isn't just about revenge; it's about justice for everything Olympus has lost."

He took a step forward, his form radiating a potent mix of defiance and resolve. "You think you can unravel everything we've built, that you can burn our legacy to the ground? I will not stand by while you trample on our honor. No matter the cost, no matter the bloodshed, I will see those who've wronged us brought to their knees. This ends now."

Ares's movements were swift and decisive. He aimed the gun at Hephaestus before his opponent had a chance to react. With a cold, deliberate pull of the trigger, the shot shattered through Hephaestus's skull, execution style, and he collapsed to the ground.

Ares stood over him, his hand lowering slowly as he stared down at his brother's lifeless body. "You were better than this, brother," he said, his voice heavy with disappointment.

The smoke filled my lungs and my heartbeat faster from the fear of us being burned alive.

"Ares, we need to go!" I begged him, and he finally turned toward me. Grabbing my hand, we ran as hard as we could with whatever strength we had left in our body. I would not allow the darkness to win.

As we exited the building, we saw everyone standing at the edge of the compound while fire rescue and police created barricades for the public. Ares ran to Artie and embraced her, as Apollo and Hades watched on in disbelief. Athena was notably missing.

We searched for her, but she was nowhere to be found. "I need to go back," Ares said as he let go of my hand. "I have to save my sister."

"Wait, Ares, let the rescue team handle it! It's too dangerous!" I screamed, my voice trembling with desperation. "Don't go, please!"

"I have to save her," he replied, his voice firm, his resolve unshakable.

Ares pressed his lips to mine in a brief, fierce kiss, then turned and bolted back into the burning clubhouse. Panic surged through me, and I tried to chase after him, but Hades grabbed me by the waist, holding me back. I struggled against his grip, my heart pounding in my chest as I watched Ares disappear into the roaring inferno. The flames swallowed him whole, and my heart sank, a crushing weight of fear and helplessness pressing down on me.

The seconds turned into minutes. I collapsed into Hades's arms and cried, believing there was no way that Ares was going to make it through the fire and come out alive. The flames devoured the buildings that I had called home these past months. Hades and I stood together, watching the firefighters' attempt to control the flames.

Two of them charged into the burning building. The flames roared, and smoke billowed.

Paramedics, equipped with oxygen masks hurried toward the building as well, ready to provide immediate medical help.

The police formed a human barricade, pushing us back to keep order and ensure safety. Frustrated by the distance, I strained my eyes to get a better look at the unfolding scene. From where I stood, I watched as firefighters pulled Ares from the building and laid him on a sturdy board. They quickly began administering oxygen.

Meanwhile, Athena stood nearby wrapped in a silver blanket, distressed, and watching the medical team work on her brother.

The paramedics gingerly lifted Ares onto a gurney and made their way toward the waiting ambulance. Athena trailed behind.

I was overwhelmed with helplessness. All I could do was brace myself for the moment I'd be able to hold his hand inside that ambulance, clinging to a desperate hope that this time, the chaos wouldn't be enough to take him from me.

The police kept pushing us back, but I wasn't about to be stopped. I shoved my way through the crowd, driven by a frantic need to reach Ares as they loaded him into the ambulance. Nothing was going to keep me from being by his side.

THE AMBULANCE ROCKED SLIGHTLY AS IT SPED THROUGH THE CITY STREETS, its sirens piercing the night. I sat next to Ares, holding his hand, my heart pounding in my chest. He lay on the stretcher, eyes closed. His tattooed skin was pale, and his clothes were torn up and singed from the flames. The paramedics worked around us, their voices calm and efficient, but all I could focus on was his shallow breathing and the faint rise and fall of his chest.

I squeezed his hand, whispering words of encouragement and love, desperate to keep him tethered to the present, to me. "Come back to me, Ares." I whispered as tears fell down my hot skin. The harsh fluorescent lights above us flickered, casting a surreal glow over the scene. I felt helpless, terrified, but I refused to let go. We were racing against time, and all I could do was hope and pray that we'd make it to the hospital in time to save him.

The drive felt like an eternity as I watched his heartrate drop. I squeezed his hand tight, kissing it fervently as I prayed to whomever was listening to me. Ares was all I had left in this world, and I couldn't lose him.

"Come back to me," I begged, my chest tightened with longing and desperation.

The ambulance stopped abruptly as we arrived at the hospital. They swung the door of the vehicle open, and two men came rushing for the stretcher.

I watched it all unfold as they proceeded to take my Ares away from me. Running behind them, I watched as they swept him away to the emergency room, leaving me standing alone, feeling my world crumble around me.

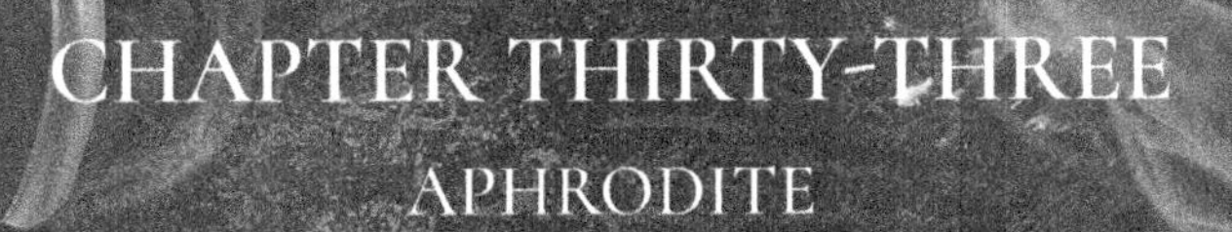

# CHAPTER THIRTY-THREE
## APHRODITE

The violence that unfolded had left the apartments, the club, and the surrounding buildings with shattered windows and charred walls. Everything was in ruins. The echoes of sirens and distant cries reverberated in my ears, a haunting reminder of the terror we had just experienced.

As I stood among the wreckage, I couldn't help but feel a profound sense of loss and despair. The Olympus family, once vibrant and united, now lay shattered. Loved ones were gone, taken away by the merciless hands of fate. The pain of their absence burdened my heart, a weight that seemed insurmountable.

The destruction had left behind a haunting distortion, twisting the familiar sights and sounds into a place that was unrecognizable. The streets were now cluttered with debris, and an eerie silence permeated the air.

Broken dreams lay scattered among the ruins, a stark reminder of what once was. It felt as though the battle had not only shattered lives but also fractured the very essence of our existence, leaving behind a palpable sense of emptiness and anguish.

But amid the devastation, a flicker of hope emerged. The

strength and resilience of the surviving members of the Olympus family shone through. We would rebuild what had been lost, together. Faced with tragedy, we found solace in each other's presence, offering support and love as we navigated through the devastation.

The days had turned into weeks, and a semblance of normalcy returned. The shattered pieces of our lives came together, like a jigsaw puzzle.

It was a slow and arduous process, but with each passing day, our wounds healed, and the scars became a testament to our resilience. Though the battle had left us battered and broken, it also reminded us of the strength that is hidden within us.

Now, we would create a future that would honor the memories of those we had lost. The Olympus Syndicate had become my family, a new and unbreakable bond forged through shared struggles and loyalty. I was no longer an outsider but an integral part of this circle, united by blood and battle.

The night of the fire, I waited at the hospital for any news of Ares. I underwent a check-up for minor injuries, such as cuts and bruises on my body. After, I learned that Ares had been put into a medically induced coma due to smoke inhalation. The excessive fumes had affected his respiratory system. Hades mentioned that his brain was not receiving enough oxygen due to the toxic smoke.

Each day since, I sat by his side, holding his hand in the sterile chill of the pale blue hospital room. Today, the gray skies cast a gentle glow through the windows, while the winter snow fluttered in the air.

I watched the rhythmic heart rate monitor as Ares's chest expanded and relaxed. Tubes covered his mouth and his beard had grown, a reminder of the time passing by.

I reached for his hand and traced the lines of his fingers with mine.

I didn't want him to die. He was all I had left.

He was fighting for me again, clinging to life despite everything. The thought alone made my heart ache. I couldn't bring myself to leave his side, terrified that even the smallest distance might be fatal.

The Olympus Syndicate was staying at the local motel for the time being, but I couldn't bring myself to leave Ares's side. Each night, I barely slept on the hard chair beside his hospital bed, my exhaustion pushed aside by my need to be there for him.

Hades, ever the voice of reason, finally intervened.

"Aphrodite, you need to take a break," he said firmly as he stepped through the door, his voice cutting through my fatigue. "You can't help him if you're running on empty."

I looked up at him, my eyes red and weary. "I can't just walk away, Hades. What if he wakes up and I'm not here? I need to be here for him."

"He's not going anywhere," Hades replied, his tone softening. "But you will burn out if you don't take care of yourself. He's fought through worse. He's strong, and he'll need you in better shape than this."

Reluctantly, I nodded and stepped outside.

The chill of the night air hit me like a wave, and memories of that horrific day rushed back, each one sharper than the last. On my way to the motel, I drove past the compound, hoping to catch a glimpse of a new beginning taking shape amidst the ruins

My heart clung to the hope that Ares would return to me.

TODAY, THERE WAS A GLIMMER OF HOPE. THE TUBES HAD BEEN REMOVED, leaving only an oxygen mask on Ares's face. The doctor had

mentioned signs of improvement, and my heart was tethered to the hope that he would soon wake up.

His siblings visited the hospital one by one, and the tension in the room was tangible. Athena, with tears in her eyes, approached me first, and her voice trembled as she apologized for what had happened. She explained she had wanted to save Hephaestus. Seeing her burdened with guilt broke my heart. Hephaestus had turned on her in the end, attacking her. In the chaos, a heavy beam had fallen on her, trapping her in the burning wreckage.

"Ares stormed into the building like a charging horse." Apollo teased as he crossed his arms against this chest, leaning against the wall.

"Ares managed to free me. I'm forever indebted to him," Athena whispered solemnly as she rubbed Ares's hand. "The effort it took to free me took a toll on him. He was gasping for breath, and I tried to carry him to safety, but my body was weak." Athena said, her voice barely above a whisper, eyes downcast and shoulders slumped under the weight of her unspoken guilt.

I looked into Athena's eyes as I held her trembling hands and assured her that none of it was her fault. I reminded her we were facing a danger that none of us could have anticipated. She had acted with the best intentions, trying to save someone she loved.

The blame rested on Hephaestus, whose betrayal set everything in motion. Together, we would get through this by supporting each other, knowing that sometimes things happen that are beyond our control, but we can heal as a family.

As the hours ticked by, I stayed by Ares's bedside, my thoughts fixated on the hope that he'd wake up soon. I rested my head against his side, trying to feel close to him, wishing he was dreaming of me. Suddenly, a gentle warmth brushed against my cheek, pulling me from my reverie. I opened my eyes to find myself gazing into the deep, familiar chocolate brown eyes I adored. His fingers, tender and deliberate, traced the contours of my jawline.

"Ares?" I whispered, lifting my head in disbelief.

He blinked, then raised his hand and removed his oxygen mask from his face.

"We've got to stop meeting like this." He coughed, attempting to release a laugh. I pressed my lips to his forehead, and my tears fell onto his skin.

I called out, "Nurse! He's awake! He's awake." I sobbed as I intertwined my hands with his, and his eyes softened.

"You can't get..." He took a deep breath and exhaled, "...rid of me."

DESPITE ZEUS STILL BEING IN THE PROCESS OF RECOVERY, HIS PRESENCE after Ares's awakening surprised everyone. It was a testament that beneath his anger toward his father, there was still a bond between them—a deep, unwavering support for each other.

Zeus was deeply affected by Hephaestus's death.

I learned that he was desperate to reclaim his son's body, driven by grief and a sense of loss. Artie shared with me one night, as she stayed by my side, that her father had been profoundly shaken by the loss. The void left by a loved one's death casts a long shadow, leaving the world feeling like a hollow echo of what it once was.

Hades mentioned he'd talk to Zeus about the situation. Zeus felt like everything he'd built was crumbling, like it didn't stand a chance anymore. But Hades pushed him to face the truth—that the tension between the members couldn't be ignored any longer. If the Olympus Syndicate was going to rise again, we had to stand together, united.

"So, what did I miss?" Zeus joked as he sat in the chair next to Ares's bed.

"Well, for one, we have a new badass family member," Hades said as he crossed his arms, looking at me with his devilish grin.

"She knows how to shoot—which is scary, if you think about it,"

Ares teased, watching me with his deep brown eyes. His scruff had thickened into a beard, and I'd told him I liked the new look.

"Careful," I shot back with a grin, "I might end up being the one saving your ass." The room erupted in laughter, and Ares raised an eyebrow, clearly amused.

"Oh, Ares, I have something for you," Zeus said, reaching into his backpack. He pulled out a leather vest. "Listen, son, I want you to be my vice president. You saved us. Your perseverance is the reason we're all still together."

Ares took the vest from Zeus's hands. He stared at it, his eyes following the intricate stitches of the new label underneath his name. I watched as he gripped it tightly, a fresh sense of determination burning in his eyes.

He looked up at me, and I let out a soft gasp, my heart swelling with pride.

Our shared excitement filled the room. The scent of new leather wafted through the air. I flashed him the biggest smile I could muster, feeling the warmth spread across my face.

ARES COULDN'T CONTAIN HIS EXCITEMENT AS HE WALKED OUT OF THE hospital.

The time spent confined to a bed had been torturous for him, and now, finally free, he was ready to embrace the new year. Ares was worn down, but he knew he could rely on me to keep him steady, drawing strength from our connection.

We walked hand-in-hand, and the streets seemed livelier than ever, bustling with people preparing for the upcoming festivities. Ahead, leaning against the sleek frame of his black Mustang, was Hades.

As we approached, he held the back door open for me, and I slid into the leather interior, while he adjusted the passenger seat for Ares.

"Where the hell are we going to stay?" Ares asked as Hades closed the door, and I watched him round the vehicle to the driver's side.

"I don't know," I lied.

Fortunately for us, my father's arrogance kept him from ever changing his will, certain he'd outlast us all. That made me the rightful heir to everything—his businesses, his estate, his money, and his power. I was now the head of the Aetos empire, and the irony wasn't lost on me.

Here I was, the unexpected recipient of everything. My father, always so meticulous, always so in control, never anticipated this twist. He must be rolling in his grave, knowing that the Aetos family was now in the hands of the daughter he desperately tried to keep from inheriting his empire.

Karma is a bitch, Father.

Privately, I had met with Zeus to discuss what Ouranos had unknowingly given me. With the help of the lawyer, I gifted the manor to the MC, deemed as the new Olympus Syndicate compound. We were selling off everything inside, stripping it of the past, and making it a place that felt right for us.

The only thing I wanted was to shatter the statue my father had cherished above all else.

Driving down the road, Ares was unaware of what the future held for us. But I knew that everything was coming together, and I wanted to surprise him.

We pulled into the driveway of the manor, and Ares turned his head toward me, confused and on alert. He looked at Hades as well. "Why are we here?" he said, his voice panicked.

Pulling up front, Hades cut the engine. The rest of the family, including Zeus, who was now using a cane, stood at the entrance of the manor that I once harbored so much hatred for. But it felt different now. It felt free of the demons that used to inhabit it.

"What is going on?" Ares stepped out of the vehicle as I slipped out of the backseat. Holding his hand, we walked past everyone and entered the foyer.

On the wall hung the charred metal sign that once guarded the gates of the Olympus Syndicate compound. It was displayed prominently, visible to all.

Ares's eyes widened, and he turned to face me. "What the hell did you do?"

I smirked, leaning in slightly. "Ouranos must've never thought I'd be the last one standing. Everything he had? It's mine now."

"Everything?" he said as a flash of disbelief crossed his face.

"She has everything!" Apollo cheered, and the rest of the family let out a small laugh.

Ares rubbed his hands down his face. "I don't know what to say." He looked around. Everyone started to scatter, giving us privacy while we stood at the front entrance.

"We can finally start our lives together," I confessed, wrapping my arms around his neck. Ares grinned, then he pushed a strand of my hair away from my face. "Thank you for being my rock," he whispered before he kissed my lips gently.

This was all I wanted. He was my future.

"So where are we staying?" he asked, breaking the kiss as he held my chin, his eyes lifting to meet mine. I watched as his molten chocolate irises deepened with desire.

"I'll show you to our bedroom." I said, taking his hand in mine.

"That sounds perfect," he murmured, his voice low and laden with promise. "I'm eager to see where I'm going to make love to you next." He bit his bottom lip, and he flashed me his cocky smile. I knew without a doubt that he was the love of my life, and I couldn't wait to spend forever with him.

"Follow me." I kissed his cheek, and we headed up the stairs.

Ares trailed behind me as we ascended the steps leading to my old bedroom. I hadn't been here since before I was sent to live at the OS compound. Memories flooded my mind; Titan and I riding down the stair banisters, Gaia yelling at us to keep it down when we would spend all night staying up and talking. My heart ached for him.

We approached the door to my bedroom—our bedroom, and I swung it open.

Ares didn't hesitate before closing the door behind us and sweeping me up into his arms. I laughed, surprised, and wrapped my arms around his warm shoulders. He placed me down on the bed and hovered above me, my heart pounding in my chest. His eyes darkened with intensity, and I felt a familiar magnetic pull towards him. I swallowed hard as my hand caressed his cheek, and he turned his lips to kiss my palm.

"Aphrodite," He whispered, his voice a husky and low growl, as I felt the heat from his body awaken my soul.

My breath hitched as he inched away from my face, his lips brushing mine just barely, igniting a spark that seemed to dance between us.

"I will love you in this lifetime and will find you in the next so I can love you once more." He pressed his lips to mine and electricity ignited every nerve in my body.

My hand found the back of his head as our bodies pressed desperately against each other, as if making up for lost time.

Ares's hand slid to my breast as I moaned against his lips, feeling his control over me. I slipped my fingers to the hem of his shirt, my hands craving the feel of his bare body beneath my fingertips. We broke our kiss, as I tugged it up and over his head and discarded it onto the floor.

I slipped off my shirt, bearing myself to him wearing a black lace bra.

"I want to rip that bra off of you," Ares growled, biting his bottom lip as he started to unbuckle his jeans. I could see how hard he was by the bulge in his jeans.

"Maybe you should?" I arched my back as I raised my hands over my head, teasing the beast as I watched his eyes darken with pleasure.

Without warning, Ares's hands tugged on the fabric and with his strength, he ripped it with one pull, exposing my breasts like a present on display for him. He kissed his way down to my nipples, lightly biting one as he teased the other.

The euphoric feeling of this sexual thrill sent the blood coursing to my most tender areas, causing my core to pulsate with desire. Ares' lips trailed down my body. He unbuttoned my jeans, eyeing me up like a predator as he ripped them off.

I lay there in my black lace panties, waiting for him to strike again.

He pushed his jeans down, exposing his thick cock as he gripped my hips closer. I pulled my legs up to wrap around him.

Ares licked his finger as he hovered over me, watching me intensely as he began stroking my clit outside of my panties, the feeling of his glorious tease sending my head spinning with desire. He gingerly moved my panties aside, and his finger drove into me with purpose. My breath caught, feeling my heart pound as he pumped his finger faster and harder inside of me. He dipped his head to the nape of my neck, "I want to fill you up with my cock."

"I want you too," I cried as I wrapped my arms around his neck, squeezing his back, feeling my desires swirl with the intoxicating scent of Ares.

"You want me baby?" He growled as he lightly bit my neck, and I dug my fingernails into his skin.

"I want every inch of you." I begged him as I watched his devilish eyes glint with excitement. He slowed his pace, pulling his fingers in and out, circling my clit and covering me in my own arousal. He grabbed my panties by the crotch and ripped them apart with ease. I let out a gasp and our eyes met.

"Then take all of me." He said, his voice was rough with desire.

There was no waiting any longer, he drove his cock into me, thrusting hard as he seated himself fully inside of my pussy. My body trembled, as I let out a resonant moan.

I pulled him closer, my hands caressing his back as his lips found mine. We connected again, and for a moment it felt as if we were one. We moved in sync, picking up the pace, as we moved faster and faster.

I wanted to savor every inch of him, to make him a part of me forever.

Our eyes locked as we panted, our erratic breaths a harmonious rhythm. Feeling the orgasm lingering close, the raw intensity of everything we'd endured ignited, the wrath of his soul coming alive with the wrath of my love.

"Oh, Ares, I'm so close," I breathed, panting, as my eyes rolled back. He thrusted faster into me as he panted against my ear. "Don't stop," I urged, my pussy clenching against his cock as he growled with pleasure.

"I love you, Aphrodite."

With one final passionate thrust, we both climaxed. Crashing through waves of ecstasy and euphoria as we both trembled, our bodies slick with sweat.

In that moment, nothing else mattered but the intense, undeniable need we felt for each other. The world outside ceased to exist, and with a fierce passion, we embraced the love that had forged us in fire.

As the stars blazed above, we vowed to conquer every storm, every battle, knowing that together, we were unstoppable. Our love was the flame that would never die, an eternal force that would burn brightly against the darkest night.

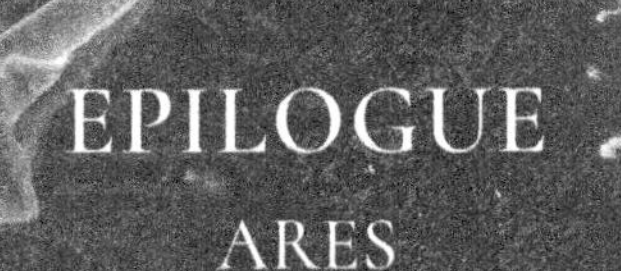

# EPILOGUE

## ARES

*FOUR MONTHS LATER...*

Aeolopolis City fell under the watch of my old lady.

Aphrodite not only inherited Aetos' power after Ouranos' demise, but she revolutionized the entire establishment.

She transformed the Aetos mafia into a force to be reckoned with. Gone were the days of brute force and mindless violence. Aphrodite introduced a new era of strategic planning and calculated moves.

I couldn't help but feel a surge of pride for her. She stood on a pillar of control, fierce and unyielding, her words cutting through the smoky air like a blade as she commanded the new era of the Aetos mafia.

She was a true leader, destined to reshape the family.

I watched her in her office, seeing the men standing before her begin to nod in agreement, made me realize just how powerful she really was. And she was all mine.

Aphrodite used her charm to forge connections with other influential families in the underworld. Under her leadership, the Aetos mafia expanded its reach and solidified its control over expanded illicit activities in the city.

Aphrodite's vision for the future of the Aetos family wasn't just about survival; it was about expansion. Her plans went beyond the traditional rackets of gambling, extortion, and smuggling. She saw potential in areas that had previously been dismissed as too risky or unworthy of their time.

As her right hand, I witnessed firsthand the transformation of the mafia into a sophisticated organization fueled by Aphrodite's vision. Her reign inspired loyalty and devotion, as members of the mafia rallied behind her, eager to follow her lead. Together, we were united, proud to be part of a new era of beauty, intellect, and cunning.

Aphrodite and the rest of the Aetos mafia joined forces with Olympus Syndicate. I never expected to be so eager for a business partnership, but here we were.

Zeus, with a victorious gleam in his eyes, forged an agreement with Aphrodite. The rest of the gang embraced every aspect of the changes. The city had been a battleground for Olympus Syndicate, a relentless fight for protection and recognition. But now, with this newfound alliance, the air was humming with possibilities.

Aphrodite wasn't attached to Aetos Manor, so Apollo stepped up and transformed the space into our clubhouse. It was a rugged haven, with heavy leather furniture, dark wood, and walls adorned with motorcycle memorabilia.

"What are you doing?" Aphrodite came down from the second floor as I stood in the foyer, staring at the walls that once held the Aetos portraits. Those had vanished, replaced by OS members. Excitement coursed through my body, knowing the future was changing.

Crossing my arms against my chest, I watched my girl stroll over to me in her black floral dress, her curls bouncing as she watched me with curiosity. Nothing else mattered when I was with her. She was all I lived for. She was my purpose.

Aphrodite embraced me with her arms around my neck, and my hands found their place on her hips. Despite the things I had done in my life, I still couldn't believe I deserved her.

"I can't help but admire how incredibly beautiful you are, Aphrodite" I said, flashing a confident smile. She was stunning, and I knew she belonged to me in every way.

I craved her, and I was fortunate enough to have her every night. Every opportunity I had to be with her, I took full advantage, exploring every inch of her body. I think we'd tainted every inch of this manor with our passion. Athena was appalled when she caught us in the atrium. We were disheveled, trying to catch our breaths and our clothes were in disarray. "

I don't go for corny, Ares," she purred, her voice dripping with seduction. "Where's my rugged bad boy?" she teased.

I rolled my eyes with a smirk, then lifted her effortlessly. Her legs instinctively wrapped around my waist as she let out a playful squeal. I captured her lips with a deep, passionate kiss.

As our lips met, the world faded away. The softness of her against me sent a rush of warmth through my body. Her delicate fingers traced the contours of my face, igniting a tingle of anticipation that coursed through my body. The sound of our breaths mingling created a symphony of desire. Every touch, every kiss, fueled the fire within, leaving us hungry for more.

"You horny bastards," Hades interrupted as he walked in on our passionate embrace.

We let out an embarrassed laugh as she slipped her legs down my body, my dick twitching as her breasts pressed against me. I would fuck her right here, but I knew tonight was important, and once we started, we wouldn't stop until sunrise.

We were having a grand opening party to celebrate our new headquarters. We had announced to the world that Aeolopolis City's biggest star would be performing a private show just for us, though we kept their identity a secret.

"Sorry, Hades." Aphrodite said, leaning against my chest as I flashed him an annoyed glance. “Is everything coming along for tonight?”

“Yeah, Apollo has been getting everything ready with Prometheus. Zeus wrangled Poseidon into coming tonight too,” Hades replied, sliding his hands into his pockets.

Everyone knew the three brothers never got along. Poseidon always craved power, constantly striving to take control. Zeus, however, believed that because he was the beloved firstborn, he should be granted full authority. Hades was the only one that never felt the need to intrude. He was fierce and firm, yet never felt he needed control.

“Can I at least know who the hell is coming to perform tonight? Or at least tell me if she’s hot?” Hades sighed. I was keeping this all a secret.

“You can wait for tonight,” I said. “But right now, I need to take my girl somewhere.” Without warning, I picked up Aphrodite and threw her over my shoulder. I headed up the stairs to our apartment.

“Ares!” she squealed, her hands pounding playfully against my back.

I laughed, enjoying the thrill of the moment, and continued up the stairs with her, savoring the way her laughter mingled with my own.

Night fell as the guests arrived at the entrance of the Olympus Syndicate's new establishment. There we were in our vests, showing the world that what happened to us would not destroy our reputation. We asserted our authority and knew that every person was looking at us differently, aware that we were representing two armies tonight.

Dressed in a snug black halter dress, Aphrodite exuded power as she stood alongside her guards, embracing guests with a welcoming smile. From my vantage point across the room, I sensed the aura of dominance she commanded. Yet, despite her poised exterior, she was facing constant threats.

The chilling realization washed over me that some individuals greeting her likely harbored murderous intentions. Unbeknownst to them, I, a fierce warrior, would unleash a torrent of fury upon anyone who dared to cast a malevolent gaze in her direction.

The ballroom that once held events for the Aetos mafia, was now the official new Odyssey, improved with a stage, bold neon lights, and tables with booths along the side for patrons to sit and enjoy their time. With the help of Pandora's staff, it looked good. The space exuded sophisticated allure, blending the grandeur of its past with a fresh, dynamic energy.

"Take a seat. The show is about to begin." I said as we slid into the booth with the rest of the Syndicate. The place was packed, and everyone, including Aphrodite, rippled with anticipation.

Aphrodite had hired Paris as the entertainment manager for this place. After getting the approval by her doctors for her to return to her life, she was ready to join us at Olympus Syndicate. When she mentioned her connections to some of the biggest artists in the music industry, I jumped at the chance to have her here. Aphrodite vouched for her, knowing that we needed someone who was going to help us with this business venture.

The black velvet drapes pulled away from the stage, and Paris walked out in a sequined black dress. The crowd cheered. Aphrodite leaned against me as I rested my arm on the ledge of the booth, waiting with anticipation.

"Hello, beautiful people! I'm Paris, your hostess for tonight's event, and the event manager of the new and improved Odyssey!" Everyone, including us, cheered and whistled. Hades turned to face me and gave a subtle nod of approval.

Paris continued, "I have the absolute pleasure of introducing the main event for tonight. This artist was truly excited to partake in tonight's affair, and we are so happy to have her here. So, let's give a round of applause for the beautiful and talented award-winning singer, Persephone!"

Emerging from behind the luxurious drapes, Persephone glided forward in a bewitching lace gown. Its ornate fabric hugged her slender frame, accentuating a daring slit that revealed her toned legs. Her expressive eyes sparkled, framed by high cheekbones and full lips. Warm brown skin emitted a gentle glow as she elegantly swept her long black braids away from her face.

She approached the microphone, and the stage lights cast an enchanting glow, causing her eyes to darken with intensity.

From my peripheral vision, I glimpsed Hades, who appeared agitated.

"What the hell is she doing here?" Hades spit with anger.

"What is your problem?" I snapped. He stood abruptly.

I glanced up at Persephone and caught sight of her gaze following Hades as he turned to leave, her normally vibrant eyes tinged with melancholy.

Aphrodite turned her attention to me, her expression filled with concern.

"What is going on, Ares?" she asked, her hazel eyes boring into me.

I glanced at her, my gaze lingering, before shifting my eyes back to the empty spot at the booth, a heavy emptiness settling in my chest. "I have no fucking clue."

TO BE CONTINUED

HADES & PERSEPHONE

# ACKNOWLEDGMENTS

I started this journey sitting on a balcony in Alvor, watching the sunset paint the sky in hues of orange and pink, and contemplating the idea of creating a story about a romance entwined with Greek mythology. The idea blossomed as I imagined a tale where gods and mortals, love and betrayal, destiny and free will, all collided in a narrative as timeless as the myths themselves.

Little did I know it would open the doors to the Olympus Syndicate. This project was going to be big. I was taking a chance on a subject that made me so nervous. I have always loved Greek mythology, and I desperately wanted to write a story that somehow intertwined with that world. I still remember sitting in front of my tablet, telling myself, "Let's do it."

Now, as I write this thank-you note at the end of the book, I'm completely blown away that I managed to bring this story to life. But I must tell you—it took a village to create this. I couldn't have done it without these special people in my life.

Michele, my best friend, my shoulder to cry on, my Alpha—the person who kept me strong throughout this entire writing process—you! I don't know how to express just how grateful I am for our friendship. I'm literally teary-eyed as I write this because you believed in me when I didn't believe in myself. Thank you for always listening to me, for guiding me through the darkness, and for encouraging me to take chances. You are forever in my heart, soul sister. I am indebted to you, and I promise we will make that Salem trip happen! I can't wait for us to continue our adventures together and have more Abba moments.

Paige, you were the first person to randomly message me about my first book, and you've since become such a close friend. My official P.A.! You don't give yourself enough credit for how amazing you are. Thank you for always listening to me and offering the best advice, both during the writing process and in my personal life. If I have to shout it from the rooftops: "You deserve to be happy!" Because it's the truth!

Brittney, working with you has been a pleasure, as always. You've done an amazing job of keeping my voice intact throughout the story. Thank you for your hard work and dedication in helping bring this writer's vision to life!

Reacher! Yes, you know who you are. Thank you for helping a friend out and making this book come together. I guess it's time to start the next one at the cottage, right? Your support and encouragement throughout this process have meant the world to me. Thank you!

Shay at Disturbed Valkyrie Designs, I can't express how much I LOVE MY COVER! Thank you for taking on this project at the last minute and helping me conquer my fears. You captured exactly what I envisioned for my book—the look, the ideas, everything. You're incredibly talented, and I can't wait to see what we create next!

To Ink & Velvet Designs for my map and Bella.Artt for the character art, you both absolutely killed it! I know I had a hard time explaining my vision, but you took it and showcased your incredible talents. I'm so happy with everything you've done. I can't wait to work with you on future books!

To my betas—thank you for helping me shape this story. I entrusted you with this project, hoping you would believe in me, and you did. I never imagined I would write a story that anyone would enjoy, but your support has brought a smile to my face. Your messages and encouragement have made me realize just how thankful I am to have you all by my side.

Melissa – Holy smokes! You totally saved my butt with the blurb! I must've rewritten it a hundred times, and nothing even came close to what you helped me craft. Ready to dive into the next project?

To my fans – it still feels surreal to say that because I never thought I would write another book. After the first one, I seriously considered giving up, but it was the encouragement and messages from all of you that made me believe I was a worthy author. You don't know how much that means to me. I never imagined I could do something like this, but you believed in me. I hope you enjoy this story, and I can't wait for you all to meet the rest of the Olympus Syndicate!

To my family—thank you from the bottom of my heart for being my number one fans. You have always been there through it all—the late-night writing sessions, the endless hours spent on this journey, and all the ups and downs along the way. Your unwavering support means everything to me. I can't thank you enough for believing in me and encouraging me to take chances when I was too afraid to jump. I'm truly blessed to have people who love me and support my dreams.

*Oh—Dad! Happy Birthday (It's on Halloween).*

To my daughter, I know you can't read this yet, but one day you will—I want you to know that you can follow your dreams, no matter how big they seem. Never let go of the possibility that something magical can happen. I love you, Evie.

So, this is just a little "see you later," because I've got to get back to writing the next one. Hades and Persephone are waiting, and trust me, it's going to be a wild ride! I'm already stocking up on coffee and plot twists.

# ABOUT THE AUTHOR

Vanessa is a passionate weaver of romantic tales, crafting worlds where love knows no bounds and the power of connection transcends all obstacles. With each stroke of her keyboard, she brings to life the magic of a chance encounter and the depth of lifelong bonds. Her stories take readers on an emotional journey through the heart's most profound experiences, inviting them to explore the limitless possibilities of love alongside her.

As the author of Right Where You Left Me, Vanessa resides just north of Toronto with her husband, daughter, and their playful puppy, Maverick. When she's not writing, you can find her designing beautiful spaces or binge-watching the latest crime dramas.

For those eager to get an exclusive first look at upcoming projects and participate in special giveaways, Vanessa warmly invites you to join her readers' group. Come along for the adventure and explore the world of love together!

Follow Vanessa at:
Instagram, TikTok, & Facebook: @authorvanessastock
https://www.vanessastock.ca/

Made in the USA
Las Vegas, NV
01 November 2024